# I KNOW YOU ARE, BUT WHAT AM I?

*The Artemis Necklace Series, Book 4*

## J.J. RUSSELL

By J.J. Russell


**The Artemis Necklace Series**

Suck It

Bite Me

Go Magic Yourself

I Know You Are, but What Am I?

# Chapter One

*Focus, Vânători. You'll never learn to channel our powers if you keep jumping at every noise in the woods.*

I bristled at Artemis's rebuke, though I was the only one who could hear her. It was a cold morning in the backwoods of Maine, and a bracing wind only made it colder. We'd been out here for almost two hours while I worked on learning to harness Artemis's powers and use them as a more tangible weapon. I was supposed to be channeling energy from my core, out through my arms until it formed a ball of energy that I could throw at my enemies (which was currently a fallen tree branch I'd stuck into the ground vertically).

So far, I'd only managed to produce a ping-pong sized ball of energy that fizzled out about a foot after it left my hands. It didn't help that my hands were numb despite my thick gloves and my face felt frozen. Not for the first time, I wished I'd found a warmer place to take up residence while hiding from vampires.

Since she lived in my mind when I wore the necklace, Artemis sensed my negative thoughts.

*Stop wishing you were elsewhere. Be here in both mind and soul,*

*Vânători. You cannot master the use of my powers if you are not fully present.*

"I also can't master these powers if my hands freeze off," I fought to say through frozen lips. "I think we should call it a day, Artemis. We can try again tomorrow. Maybe the wind won't be so bad." I didn't need to speak out loud since the goddess could hear my thoughts just as easily, but it had become a force of habit so Ramble would know what we were talking about.

At the moment, my fire breathing hellhound sidekick had wisely chosen to stay inside next to the warm wood stove.

I envied him. It was difficult not to turn around and glare at the cabin windows since I was sure he was watching my unsuccessful attempts at throwing energy balls while he was all curled up and warm inside.

*If you continue to procrastinate in your training, you won't survive when the time comes to defend yourself. Now, focus and try again.*

"Artemis, I've been out here for forever this morning. I wouldn't exactly call that procrastinating!"

Our relationship had been a little rocky ever since Artemis had tried to take over my body. She'd promised not to do it again, but I didn't believe that for a minute. She wanted to be free of the necklace's confines in order to go on a suicide mission to kill the uber-vampire, Morvalden.

I shivered, but not from the cold. The father of all vampires had haunted my dreams for some time. It was hard to shake my fear of him, but Artemis was the more present threat right now.

The thing was, Artemis would have to have my permission to take over my body, so there was nothing to worry about. I could just say no, right?

Then again, Artemis had existed for a long, long time and was much sneakier than I was. She'd plot and scheme her way into getting me to say yes again at some point. I just hoped the less I wore the necklace, the longer I would stay myself before she convinced me to give in and give her control again.

I'd begun limiting how often I wore the necklace, mostly keeping it to when we did these training sessions in the morning. She'd protested, but I had the good excuse that training burned through a lot of power. We didn't want to use her magic up too quickly and have to ask Louis for more of his vampire blood.

*Try at least once more, Vânători.*

I bit back a snarky retort and tried to refocus. Hands at chest level pretending to hold a ball of energy: check. *Now, find the well of energy within*, I told myself and closed my eyes to mentally look inward.

The magic inside me was like the faint glow of a steady beacon in the distance. When we'd started the training earlier, it had been more like a bright flashlight. Because I was only part Vânători, I required something a little extra to power the necklace: vampire blood. Unfortunately, the power I gained from drinking vampire blood didn't last forever. This short practice session had drained quite a bit of power.

I mentally reached for that beacon of power and let it course through me. I breathed in, imagining the power filling me like the air filled my lungs. Power sang in my veins, giving me a heady rush.

*Good. Now, focus the energy into your hands.*

This was where things usually went wrong.

I imagined the magic gradually moving from my chest, out through my arms, and down to my hands to form a ball between my palms. The magic slowly complied. As it moved, it seemed to take any residual warmth with it. By the time the magic coalesced in my hands, the rest of me was shivering from the cold.

*Excellent,* Artemis said with what sounded like checked excitement. *Now open your eyes to find your target.*

I followed her command and glanced down to see a spinning sphere-like energy ball between my hands. The moment my eyes fell on it, it wobbled and started to shrink.

*Focus on the target!* Artemis snapped. *Focus, aim, and release!*

I tried to follow her instructions, I really did, but I could feel the energy slipping away now. It was like trying to carry water, and it slipped easily through my fingers. Before the ball completely lost all its energy, I chucked it at the branch.

As the energy ball sailed through the air, it shrank as it got further away from me. By the time it hit the branch, it was no bigger than a dime, but it did leave a small burn on the branch.

"Ha!" I cried in triumph. "Look at that!"

*What an accomplishment. You can now defend yourself by burning cigarette-sized holes into your enemies. Of course, they'll have to stand very, very still and also wait for you to slowly rebuild your energy ball every time—*

"How about a 'good job, you hit the branch,'" I fumed. "You know, positive reinforcement is a thing nowadays. Not many people are motivated by toxic negativity."

*I do not know what toxic negativity means, Vânători, but you do not have the luxury of being coddled while you learn. What you learn here could very well be your only weapon on the battlefield.*

I started to tell her there *were* no real battlefields anymore, but saved my breath. Instead, I walked forward and knocked the target practice branch down. "We're done for the day."

*Once more, Vânători. You almost had it that time.*

"Nope. That *was* just one more. We're done for the day."

*Vânători—*

I cut her off by pulling the necklace up over my head and shoving it in my jeans pocket before heading inside. I felt a little guilty for essentially locking her away in the necklace again, but told myself it was the best way to conserve energy.

Inside, I kicked my boots off at the front door and walked down the hall to stick my head in the living room. Sure enough, Ramble was sprawled out in front of the woodstove, soaking in the warmth.

I stood in the doorway long enough that he finally cracked open one eye.

"Having a nice nap?"

He snorted.

"Uh huh. I'm glad one of us gets to stay inside where it's warm," I grumbled under my breath and headed to the kitchen for breakfast. Artemis had barely let me get a cup of coffee into me before bullying me outside to train. I wasn't sure why she insisted on training at the ass-crack of dawn. It wasn't like we had plans for the day.

As if to prove me wrong, my phone rang when I was halfway through a bowl of cereal.

"Vianne," Sheriff Allen said, "I think I've got a job for you."

After helping the sheriff sort out the accidental drowning death of a pixy caused by an out-of-state tourist, I'd agreed to act as a consultant to the local law enforcement (consisting mainly of the sheriff). Now I got paid hourly as a consultant when the sheriff called me in on anything that had to do with the not-so-human residents of Ricketts.

He laid out the new gig he had in mind.

"You've got to be shitting me," I said through a mouthful of cereal. I quickly finished chewing and swallowed before continuing. "Gremlins? Seriously? Come on."

"I'm *not* shitting you," the sheriff responded and, though I'm sure he was doing his best to stay serious, he only barely managed to tamp down his amusement. "Father Patrick swears there are gremlins in the church attic."

"Belfry." I pushed the bowl of cereal away from me and sat back in the chair.

My kitchen was sparsely furnished with a wood table and a few matching chairs. If you didn't know me, you might think I was a poor graduate student trying to scrape by while I finished my studies and not the descendent of a kick-ass monster hunter with a magical talking necklace that was supposed to help me be more badass but mostly just ended up being untrustworthy and annoying.

"What?"

Suddenly not hungry, I stood and took my half-finished cereal to the sink. As if sensing that food was about to be wasted in his presence, Ramble trotted into the kitchen and lifted a brow at me.

I set the bowl on the floor. "Go for it," I murmured to the hellhound. At least I wouldn't be wasting it. I turned my attention back to the sheriff. "If the section of the church Father Patrick is referring to is the one that has the bell, then it's a belfry. And," I perched on the edge of the table, "it's probably bats, not gremlins."

"So...you're saying Father Patrick has bats in his belfry?" Now I really could hear the smile in his voice.

I rolled my eyes and couldn't help but smile at the dad joke. "Maybe." In the long silence that followed, I sighed. "I guess you want me to go take a look, huh?"

"I mean, if you'd like an easy paycheck, it might be worthwhile."

I knew I should be grateful for his call—and I was, honestly...but I was not looking forward to driving the Maine roads after the six inches of fresh snow that Mother Nature had just dropped.

Especially in a car that had no heater.

"Well?" The sheriff shook me from bleak thoughts about my cold car.

"Alright. When do they want me to check it out?"

"Father Patrick said the sooner the better. The church has its Thanksgiving Supper coming up, and he doesn't want any hijinks for that."

"Can't have that," I drawled, then got Father Patrick's contact information and the church address.

Before I could hang up, the sheriff said, "Whatever you do, don't blow up the church."

"The shed was *not* my fault!" I squawked.

"Right, right. It was the mountain god, Pamola's fault."

"Better not piss him off," I warned, only half-serious. It had been over a week since I'd gone into Pamola's mountain to retrieve Ramble. I'd only been allowed to leave because the pixy, Summerstorm, thought it would be fun to trade her hand in marriage for my and Ramble's freedom.

"I'll do my best to stay on his good side."

This time he was only half joking. I couldn't blame him. He'd seen how the shed outside my rented cabin had been obliterated by the angry mountain god. I was *still* picking up wood splinters around the yard. Or at least, I had been before the latest snowfall hit.

I hung up and tried unsuccessfully to stifle a groan. Ramble, long finished with my cereal, watched me expectantly. He raised a brow in question.

"Yup. Looks like we got another job. Wanna come?"

Ramble looked pointedly back to the living room where the wood stove warmed the whole house. It was Ramble's favorite spot. In fact, the other night I'd woken to find him missing from bed, only to discover he'd found a new sleeping space *on top* of the scorching hot wood stove.

Apparently, hellhounds didn't mind a little heat. Then again, he did breathe fire.

"C'mon," I coaxed. "If you come with me, maybe we can

finish the job sooner and get something better for lunch than cereal. Like, maybe something with meat in it?"

Ramble eyeballed me for a second as if deciding whether I was pulling his leg, then he gave a gruff, "Whuff," for yes.

If there was one thing I knew about Ramble, it was that the way to his heart was through his stomach. Metaphorically, of course. I honestly had no idea where a hellhound's heart was located. I hadn't even known Ramble once had three heads until recently, and I still hadn't gotten the story about that. It wasn't like he could talk to tell me.

"Awesome. I'll get my coat."

Twenty minutes of granny-slow driving over slippery back roads later, I finally parked in front of the church. Father Patrick waved to us from the open doorway. Well, he waved to me, anyway, since Ramble was invisible to most people.

I'd called Father Patrick before we left, and he'd only agreed to have me come out on the condition that I take my time on the icy roads. I had no problem agreeing to that.

I got out and held the door open for Ramble, who made a low noise in his throat and lay down with his paws across the center console.

"What the hell?" I whispered, leaning in and pretending I was getting something out of the car so as not to stress out the priest watching us. "You said you were coming with me," I whispered.

Ramble snorted, jerked his head once at the church, then put his head on his paws.

I stared at him, trying not to get angry, before I realized what he was trying to tell me.

"You can't go into a church?"

He shrugged. Which either meant he could and just didn't want to right now or that he couldn't go into a church and that I shouldn't make such a big deal out of it.

Honestly, it would've been great to have a companion who

could communicate with me. Hard to complain, though, when Ramble had saved my skin more than once.

"Alright." I hand-cranked the window all the way down. "I'll leave this down just in case the gremlins—which I still think are just bats—get the better of me." Amusement danced in Ramble's eyes as I shut the door. I turned away and added under my breath, "But I'd rather have you at my back than Artemis."

Pasting on a smile, I approached the priest and held out a hand. "Hi, Father Patrick, I'm Vi. Nice to meet you in person."

His hand closed over mine, warming it. "Wonderful to finally meet you, Vi. I've heard many wonderful things about you from the people here in town. Let's go inside where it's warm before we get started, shall we?"

He dropped my hand, and I followed him in, wondering if he realized that most of the "people" in town who knew me were a little more than human.

Then again, he *had* called about gremlins.

After walking through a small vestibule, we entered the larger space where he held worship services. The ceiling soared overhead, held up by old wooden beams that had probably been cut from the very woods around the church. (I wondered how Pamola would feel about *that.*) There were ornate stained-glass windows along the side walls, each showing a different stage of Jesus' life, and one large stained-glass mural at the front of the church depicting the Crucifixion.

I followed the priest up a red carpeted aisle that was lined by old wooden pews. They faced a slightly raised dais on which was a podium where Father Patrick held his services. Behind the podium was an altar covered with a white cloth which held candles and...was that incense? It didn't smell like any incense I was familiar with.

I almost made a comment about how both witches and Catholics used altars, but the serious expression on Father Patrick's face made me squelch the urge to share. I hadn't exactly been raised in a religious household and had little faith in organized religion. Which was actually too bad, since faith was one weapon I could've had against Morvalden and his vampire minions. Ah well.

"It's not much," Father Patrick said, lifting a hand to indicate the church, "but I kind of like the simplicity of it."

I wasn't so sure I'd describe a church with so many stained-glass windows as "simple," but who was I to judge?

"We would love to have you join us for a service sometime."

Oh boy.

I forced a smile. "I'm usually busy on Sundays."

Father Patrick gave me an almost knowing smile. "I hold a smaller mass every other weekday, but no pressure."

"I appreciate the offer." I cleared my throat and covered up my awkwardness by getting down to business. "So, I understand you may have some, ah, unwanted guests?"

This earned me a smile that seemed somehow...off. "Something like that." He beckoned me to follow him toward a door at the back left of the church and continued talking as I followed. "I thought they were mice or rats at first, honestly," he turned as he walked, catching my eyes briefly, "but then I caught sight of one of them this morning." He shook his head once and turned back to open the door. "And they are definitely something more than that."

"You told the sheriff you thought they were gremlins. What made you think that?"

"You mean, how do I know I didn't just see a racoon or a possum?"

I made a sort of yes shrug in answer as we passed a confessional booth.

There was that weird smile again. It was like he was shooting for a soft, patient smile and landing on awkward.

"I'm not one of the tourists, Vi. I've lived in this town for many years. I understand that the world holds more than just the darkness found in the hearts of men. Remember, the Gospel of Mark recounts how Jesus frequently confronted and cast out demons. It's a reminder that there are forces beyond our ordinary understanding at work in the world."

Alrighty then. I wasn't so sure about literal demons, but I'd met a few vampires who were close enough.

"Got it," I said.

He hesitated. "Have you ever dealt with a gremlin before?"

Shit. What could I say to that? Technically, I was supposed to be the supernatural professional here, but I felt like an imposter. Without my faithful hellhound or my magical goddess trapped in a necklace, I was just a recovering alcoholic and parole violator with a famous family name in the monster-hunting world.

This was the only gig where I could legally make money. I didn't want to blow it. Ousting a gremlin from a church should be simple, right?

"I haven't specifically worked with gremlins," I hedged, "but I've had my fair share of run-ins with the less friendly members of the supernatural community."

A grin flitted across the Father's lips and was gone before I was even sure I'd seen it. "Come on. I trapped it up in the belfry tower." He turned and led me to a door at the back of the church.

I could have sworn he mumbled "supernatural community" under his breath, but I graciously ignored it.

On the other side of the door were stairs leading up to a trapdoor in the ceiling. The Father took a deep breath, steeling his nerves, before reaching an arm up and shoving the trapdoor open.

The moment he threw open the trapdoor, the environment changed. I instantly regretted my laissez-faire attitude about the gremlin.

Cold air rushed in through the trapdoor, but I was too busy staring at a growling ball of claws, fur, and—were those bells? Before my brain could register what it saw, the creature flashed through the air toward my face.

I instinctually ducked and threw my hands up. The gremlin slammed into them, then latched on to my arm. If I had not still been wearing my thick jacket, its sharp teeth would certainly have shredded my forearm. Panicking, I whipped my arm down, trying to dislodge the yowling ball of destructive energy. The move flung the gremlin into the floor, headfirst.

It paused for a moment, shook its head once as if dazed, then after one stumbling footstep, the gremlin zoomed down the stairs.

"It's getting away!" The Father shouted and started after it.

I won't lie. It took me a moment to collect myself. I'm not sure what I'd been expecting, but it hadn't been a raging ball of teeth and claws.

"Vi!"

Father Patrick's shout broke me from my daze. I thundered down the stairs, catching up with him. When he halted in the doorway to the church, I almost plowed right into him. This earned me a look he probably reserved for naughty children.

"Why did you let it out of the belfry?" He hissed.

"Me?" I had to choke back a tart retort before I settled on, "I'm not the one who opened the trapdoor, Father."

We stood in the safety of the doorway, looking out at the plain wooden pews that made up the seating for the parishioners. The church was eerily quiet as we stood stock still, listening hard for the scrape of a clawed paw or a quiet peal from one of the tiny bells that the gremlin had around it.

After about two minutes of that, I risked a glance at Father Patrick.

"Maybe it left?"

Oh boy. The glare I received made me wonder if I should just leave him to it. I was pretty sure he could just lock eyes with the gremlin and it would wither away to nothing on the spot out of sheer mortification.

"Gremlins don't just *leave* of their own free will once they choose a space to call home."

"Huh," I took a few steps forward, still scanning the room, then knelt down to look under the first row of wooden pews before doing a quick visual scan under the others from where I knelt.

I didn't see any sign of the gremlin, but he could have been tucked up into the corner underneath one of the pews, and I wouldn't have been able to see him. Something told me that wasn't where he was, though. I turned to the slightly raised dais at the front of the church where an altar-like table had been draped with a green silk cloth. Beside it was a run-of-the-mill podium backlit by the large stained-glass window of Mary and Jesus.

Other than that, the space was pretty empty.

My eyes stayed on the altar with its long tablecloth that brushed the floor.

Great place to hide if you're a small gremlin.

I met the Father's eyes to get his attention and jerked my head at the altar. His brows rose in surprise, then his mouth creased into a line of grim determination. He started toward the dais, but I held up a hand. He stopped.

Swallowing, I took a step toward the dais. The thing was pretty fast. I had the Artemis necklace in my jeans pocket, but I didn't want to use her powers if I didn't have to. I'd used up most of my supernatural abilities from training that morning, which meant Artemis could only help me by telling me what I was doing wrong and how a real Vânători wouldn't do it that way.

The thing was, my job wasn't just to capture or kill things that weren't human. I was a liaison between the supernatural community and the human community. Which meant I had to at least *try* to reason with the gremlin. After all, what if this was just some misunderstanding?

"Hey buddy," I said, and almost died of embarrassment when my voice cracked with nerves. "Listen," I tried again. "There's not really anywhere for you to go, so why don't you come out? I promise not to hurt you as long as you don't attack me or anyone else here."

Nothing moved.

The Father stared open-mouthed at me. "You can't *reason* with a gremlin." His voice dripped with disdain. "You root them out and kill them. It's the only way to be rid of the vermin."

I suddenly wasn't so sure that I liked him anymore.

"Maybe you don't know, but my job isn't to murder everything that isn't human. I'm a *liaison,* not an *executioner.* You called me here to do my job, so let me do it."

...even if I have no idea what I'm doing, I silently added.

Reluctantly, I stepped closer to the dais, keeping a close eye on the folds of the tablecloth in case the gremlin took another leap at me. The old church floorboards creaked under my weight as I moved, but other than that, the room was silent.

I cleared my throat, which sounded like an avalanche breaking the quiet stillness.

"Ah, hey buddy. Listen, the Father doesn't want you to stay here, so you're gonna have to leave." I knew it sounded stupid, and I flashed back to every old *Gremlins* movie ever made where some idiot side character tried to reason with the creatures who were interested only in mayhem. It had never ended well for any of them.

But that was a movie, and this was real life. I couldn't automatically assume that the gremlin was in the wrong here. I needed to see if I could communicate with it or get it to leave peacefully.

When nothing happened, I took a quiet breath and moved another two steps closer to the dais. I was only a foot or so away from the tablecloth which, on the raised dais, put it at face level. Not great.

"I'm really just here to help you, I promise."

Behind me, Father Patrick grumbled something I didn't quite catch. I ignored it, choosing to instead focus my whole being on what was hiding beneath that tablecloth. I licked my lips and said, "I can help you find somewhere else to live."

Then I dredged up the nerve to lean forward, reach out, and grasp the hem of the tablecloth. Since I didn't want to scare the gremlin unnecessarily, I moved slowly. I lifted the tablecloth up and up, waiting the whole time for the gremlin to shoot out at me—only to find the space empty.

I'd been talking to myself the whole time.

God, I was an idiot.

"Where did it go?" Father Patrick demanded. His patient demeanor had vanished.

I couldn't blame him. It wasn't every day that he had to deal with a gremlin tearing around his church and causing a mess he'd have to clean up.

"I don't know," I said at the exact same second the damn gremlin dropped from a light fixture right on top of Father Patrick.

"Ah!" The priest automatically jerked back, but the gremlin's claws punctured the man's thin shirt enough to dig into his skin and hang on tight.

Father Patrick grabbed at the gremlin while spinning in a circle, trying to yank the creature off himself.

"Get it off! Get it off!"

I ran over and grabbed the Father's shoulder to stop him from spinning, then I got one hand on the creature's neck and another on its abdomen. It screeched and clawed, leaving small gashes on my hands as I dragged it from the Father. It bit the webbing between my finger and thumb, and sudden pain forced me to drop it.

Of course, the moment I did, it ran for a door that was on the right side of the dais. It clawed at the wood of the door, leaving marks at the bottom. Then it leapt up and gripped the handle in its tiny hands, pulling backward with all its might to open the door. The entire time, it was making desperate chittering noises. If it hadn't bitten my hand, I probably would have felt a lot sorrier for it.

I walked around the dais, trying to decide how best to approach the gremlin.

There was a short set of stairs on the right of the dais. The moment I set my foot on the bottom step, the gremlin looked over and, seeing me approaching, it fled. It catapulted itself off the door handle to land in the middle of the dais, took three jingling steps, then leapt off the raised platform and onto the floor.

It easily avoided the priest's attempt to grab it, then made a beeline for the front door.

"Get it!" Father Patrick shouted at me.

"What? Why? It's leaving. Just let it leave!" I shouted back, but the Father had already run after it. I shook my head and followed, not knowing what else to do.

The gremlin wasted no time. He scampered over to the front door and leapt for the handle, leaving a cacophony of clashing music notes from the many bells wrapped around him. There was a moment when I feared the priest was going to catch the gremlin again, and it maniacally jerked the door handle back and forth. Just as the priest reached out, the door snicked open, the gremlin dropped to the floor and reached his tiny paw into the doorway, opening it just far enough to slip outside.

I stopped.

"Looks like the problem solved itself...hey!" I said in surprise as the priest yanked the door open and attempted to chase the gremlin. Annoyance simmered in my gut. The gremlin had left the church. There was no reason to chase it down.

I started to run after the Priest again, this time to stop him, and almost plowed into him for the second time that day. He'd stopped just outside the church's front door.

A low warning growl greeted us.

Stepping around the priest, I saw the reason he'd stopped.

Ramble stood at the bottom of the small front stoop, glaring at us. The gremlin peered around the hellhound's legs from his safe space beneath Ramble. Seeing us, the gremlin gave a fierce grin, showing us all his sharp teeth and letting out a growl that seemed a little puny next to Ramble's.

I wasn't sure what Father Patrick could see since, to most people, Ramble was invisible, but clearly he knew *something* terrifying was on his front stoop protecting the gremlin.

"Hey, Ramble," I said evenly. "This a friend of yours?"

The hellhound stopped growling and seemed to pause in thought for a moment before giving me a noncommittal shrug.

Alright, then. Sometimes I thought I should be grateful I was the only one who could see Ramble.

"Um," I said, not sure exactly what the plan was here. "Are we taking him home?"

Ramble huffed, turned, and ambled back toward the car. The gremlin, still hellbent on intimidating us, almost didn't notice that his savior had left. He did a comical double-take between us and Ramble, then skedaddled after the hellhound. Ramble walked up to the car, looked pointedly at the gremlin, then up at the car window.

Without skipping a beat, the gremlin leapt onto Ramble's back and used it as a springboard to leap through the open window.

Shit. Did I just collect another sidekick?

I felt more than saw that Father Patrick was going to say something, so I beat him to it.

"Well, looks like we've solved your gremlin problem."

"*We?*" His shocked tone gave me a bad feeling about where this was going. "*We* didn't do anything. *You* stood around and did nothing, even though you had a perfectly good opportunity to catch that thing and exterminate it."

I shrugged (which, oddly enough, is something that winds men up when done by a woman who's not interested in his opinion). "Like I said, I'm not here as an exterminator. I'm a liaison. I'm here to help people communicate with the super-natural community."

"Communi–" the priest sputtered. "You're kidding, right? That thing doesn't understand us. It's just a creature. It's barely smarter than the average animal."

"Honestly, I'm pretty sure you just described like half the human population, Father." I started to leave. I hadn't been sure coming to the church would be a good idea, and now I was thinking I'd been right.

"Wait."

I stopped, hoping maybe he'd want to pay me, or at the very least, thank me for helping him remove the gremlin from his church even if it hadn't left the building in a plastic trash bag.

Instead, he asked, "What was that thing on the porch with it? I couldn't see anything there...but there was definitely something there, right?"

I didn't bother to suppress my smile. "Oh, there was something there alright. That was my partner in crime." I shrugged. "I guess he decided not to wait in the car after all."

There was a brief second when I considered telling this man of the cloth just exactly what Ramble was, but it seemed like that would just create more of a headache than anything else.

"You have a good day, Father. I'm glad we could help you with your *vermin* problem."

Walking toward the car, I glanced down and noticed the new rips in the sleeve of my jacket.

I guess he was my vermin problem now. Shit.

# Chapter Two

❧❦❧

"I hope you're proud of yourself," I told Ramble in the rearview mirror, carefully navigating the last slippery turn before we would reach our cabin in the middle of nowhere. "We've just made a potential enemy of that priest by taking in this little guy."

Since the gremlin gave off some decidedly male energy, I'd decided on the drive home that those were the pronouns I'd go with until someone told me otherwise.

Ramble grunted in response. The "little guy" in question was currently perched on top of the passenger seat headrest, watching wide-eyed as the world whipped by outside. I could only guess that this was his first car ride.

Unfortunately, my loaner car's headrest was going to be the worse for wear after his tiny claws were done with it.

I caught Ramble's pointed look in the mirror before I put my own eyes back on the road.

"I know," I sighed, "We couldn't exactly just leave him there. I'm just not sure what to do with him. You know he's going to destroy everything in the cabin, right?" I glanced up in the mirror just in time to see Ramble look quickly away.

Oh yeah. He knew alright.

I made the final turn into the driveway at a snail's pace, snow crunching under the tires.

"Dang it. I *just* shoveled this."

There wasn't much snow this time, but the night before, we'd gotten several inches. It had been kind of beautiful to look at from the warmth of the wood-fire heated cabin—a perfect blanket of snow muffling all of winter's ugliness...and then I'd gotten the call from the Sheriff to head out to the church.

Suddenly, all that perfect snow became a back-breaking chore.

It had taken the better part of an hour to make a path for the car to get from the driveway to the road. I guess I could have chanced it and driven the car over the damn snow, but I was pretty sure it was a puny front-wheel drive that would get stuck the second its tires touched the slippery stuff.

Of course, most of that time had been spent figuring out a snow shovel. Once upon a time, before the great and powerful Pamola had blown it up, there had been a perfectly fine, raggedy shed next to the cabin where those kinds of yard tools were stored.

While the shed had been replaced with a slightly smaller, though nicer version, the tools inside were another story. Whoever had dropped off the shed (I hadn't been there when they did) had taken all the broken tools and dumped them on the floor inside for me to deal with. Occasionally, I would find that a tool had suddenly been mended by duct tape. I wasn't 100% sure, but I had a feeling that a grateful gnome was to thank for those repairs.

Unfortunately, the only snow shovel in the shed had been one of those tools that had been "repaired." Someone had taken the broken end of some other tool and taped it to the splintered two inches of wood left sticking out of the snow shovel's plastic scoop.

Seemed great until I got too much snow on the shovel and the two pieces of wood came apart.

It had felt like a long morning of shoveling.

At least the main road was frequently plowed, so I didn't have to worry about snow there.

As the tires came to a stop on the fresh snow that had fallen while we were gone, the gremlin grunted. I looked over and found him glaring at me. He stuck his small clawed paw out at the front window and grunted again. It took me a moment to understand what he was trying to tell me.

"No. The ride's over. We're here." I waved at the cabin, then unbuckled my seatbelt.

The gremlin let out a high-pitched screech and jerked his arm at the front window so hard that his little bells let out a peal as if in accompaniment to his anger.

"No," I said more firmly. "The ride is over." I pointed at the cabin, then gave a come on gesture. "Let's go inside."

The gremlin slammed his hands on top of the headrest and sucked in a big breath as if readying himself for a major tantrum.

A rumbling growl rolled through the car. Ramble had apparently had enough. He made a huffing noise at the creature. The gremlin immediately deflated like a balloon, slunk down off the passenger seat, and jumped over to stand next to Ramble. They looked at each other for a moment as some silent communication passed between them, then they looked expectantly up at me.

"Oh, that's right. I'm the chauffeur. Just one moment, and I'll get the door for you, dear sirs."

I got out and opened the back door. Ramble got down first, then looked back at the gremlin and gave a tiny nod. I tried not to let my jaw hit the floor when the gremlin leapt onto Ramble's back and the hellhound *let* him ride him like a horse.

Ramble shot me a look that suggested if I ever told anyone about this, that he would fry me to a crisp. I held up my hands. "Hey, you do your thing, buddy."

With an annoyed huff, Ramble headed up the front steps.

Of course, he didn't have hands, so he had to wait for me to unlock and open the door for them. I did my best not to notice that there was a gremlin riding a hellhound standing beside me.

It was distracting.

Once the door was open, Ramble stepped inside, stopped, and twisted around to glare at the gremlin on his back. The little guy immediately dropped to the floor of the cabin, bells jingling. Then, realizing he was in a new space, he began zipping around to inspect everything.

Super.

"Is he going to destroy our house, Ramble?"

The hellhound shrugged, clearly unconcerned that we might have to pay for the destruction of property.

"What do you think Rosalyn would think of having a gremlin in the cabin she rented to us?"

This earned me a slightly open-mouthed grin.

I saw his point. After Rosalyn had put us in harm's way by omitting the fact that the cabin was at the edge of a mountain god's region, Ramble and I weren't too keen on the leader of the local witch coven. Maybe I would get over it one day, but that day was not today.

I grinned back. "How about you make a fire, and I'll figure something out for lunch while I check in with Artemis?"

Ramble grunted in agreement and started toward the wood stove while I headed for the kitchen. I pulled the necklace from my pocket and, trying not to cringe, put it on. I immediately felt the goddess's presence at the back of my mind. I wish I could say it was reassuring, but I'd be lying. Instead, I felt radiating waves of annoyance from Artemis.

*It is about time, Vânători.* Artemis's voice sounded in my mind the moment the cool metal of the necklace touched my skin.

"Sorry. We had a bit of an adventure at the church today." I nodded at the gremlin who had slunk to the entrance of the kitchen and was watching me intently. He reminded me of a puppy who was sure he was about to get in trouble at any second.

*Vânători, is that...is that a gremlin? In our home? You must eradicate it this instant!*

Jeeze. I was kind of starting to feel bad for the little guy.

"We're liaisons, remember? Not executioners." I stopped next to the window and pulled aside the curtain to look out on the backyard, which really just consisted of a short run of snow that ended in thick woods made up of mostly pine trees. I'm not sure why, but I'd fully expected to see someone standing out there, looking back at me. Weird. Maybe Pamola, the mountain god, was out wandering around, trying to give me the heebie jeebies?

*You do not allow vermin in your home, Vânători! It will tear this whole place apart!*

I let the curtain fall back into place and began gathering what I needed for boxed macaroni and cheese with hotdogs. Apparently, my non-response was unacceptable to the goddess. She let out a small noise of outrage in my mind.

*Where is the hellhound? Surely he would not allow this vermin in his home!*

The vermin in question scoped out the table and chairs, sniffing their legs, then walked slowly under and around them like they were foreign objects.

"You've got to chill out, Artemis. Ramble is the one who invited him home."

There was a moment of stunned silence. When she spoke again, her tone was unsettlingly calm.

*Please explain.*

While I boiled water for the macaroni, I described our morning and the call for assistance from the church. How I'd tried to help Father Patrick capture the gremlin. Then how Ramble had swooped in at the end and rescued the gremlin from his tormentors.

By the time I finished, the macaroni was ready. I drained it and returned it to the pot to add milk and the powdered cheese. We couldn't quite afford the luxury of adding butter, but we'd get there. I also didn't have a grill (and it was the middle of winter), so I threw the hotdogs in a bowl, added water, and nuked them in the microwave.

This was one of my go-to meals for saving money. Well, this and ramen. After spending a year in jail for driving under the influence one too many times, I'd been forced to get help for my alcoholism. I'd been clean for some time before vampires, hellhounds, fairies, and gremlins had shown up in my life. But it hadn't been until I embraced the whole monster hunter thing that I actually started to make a living and even some friends.

Well, friends who thought it was a-okay to put me in danger from a mountain god so that they could test my fit with the town by seeing if Pamola ripped me apart or not.

Maybe "friend" was too strong a word.

Artemis was silent while I recounted our morning. When I finished, she held the silence for another moment or two, to the point where I wondered if I'd lost my connection to her again. It hadn't been that long since I'd last had vampire blood to power our connection and my Vânători abilities, but Artemis's voice was already getting a little quieter.

*I thought our agreement was that you would include me in any consultations for the supernatural community.* Her voice was even and she didn't even try to make fun of my term for the non-human folks in town.

That was bad.

I hesitated. "Our agreement was that I would check in with you once a day to let you know what was going on."

*Yes. And...?*

"...and that I would let you know if I thought I needed your help." I pointed at the gremlin, who was staring out the kitchen window, watching as snow filled the air again. I ignored the fact that I'd have to shovel again. "And look! I didn't end up needing your help."

*Then why is there a GREMLIN in your HOME?!*

Okay. Apparently, she was a little angry. But then again, when was Artemis *not* angry?

Of course, the gremlin chose that moment to leap up, catch the bottom of the curtain, and claw his way upwards like a cat. Halfway to the top of the curtain, the fabric gave way beneath his sharp claws.

RIP!

His claws shredded the fabric as gravity took over, and he slid back down to the floor. He chittered maniacally to himself, a big grin on his tiny face. Apparently, that had been a lot of fun. When he leapt back up to repeat the process, I decided I'd better step in.

"Whoa, hey!" I turned the stove off and hurried over to the window. "Let's not rip up the curtains, man. You're a guest here."

*Are you trying to reason with a gremlin, Vânători?*

*Not helping,* I thought back at her as the gremlin completely ignored me. His eyes lit up as he suddenly realized there was an untouched curtain panel on the other window. When he leapt for it, I tried to stop him.

Not a good choice.

He immediately turned and snapped his teeth at me.

"Hey!" I shouted, "This is my house, buddy! You will *not* bite me."

The gremlin turned back to his task of completely annihilating my window curtains. Now, I'm not a materialistic kind of gal, but I've had a very limited amount of nice things in my life, and those curtains were one of them.

Hands on hips, I turned to the open doorway. "Ramble! Your little pal here is ripping apart my curtains!"

I heard a belabored groan from the other room and could only imagine Ramble heaving himself up from his spot beside the wood stove. Seconds later, he sauntered into the room just in time to see the gremlin swinging from the curtain rod between the shredded curtain.

He looked from the gremlin to me, then raised his eyebrow.

"Oh no, you don't! That guy is *not* my problem. You are the one who invited him into our home."

There was a loud POP from the microwave.

"Shit!"

I rushed over and hit the button to turn it off, noting that I'd set the time for way longer than the package's instructions recommended. Had I not been paying enough attention, or —

The gremlin had stopped swinging from the curtain rod and was looking right at me with a shit-eating grin on his tiny mouth.

"Did you change the time on the microwave? What the hell!"

*Vânători, gremlins are notorious for causing mayhem and mischief in a home. It is what they do. It is their very nature. What did you think he would do? Sit at your table and break bread with you?*

"I dunno," I said out loud for Ramble's benefit. "I thought

maybe he would take a damn chill pill and relax until I could figure out a better living situation for him!"

*I do not know what this 'chill pill' is, but it is unlikely your modern science has developed a medication that can —*

"It's just a phrase, Artemis. I'm saying I didn't think he'd wreck the house like this. I can't afford to replace all my stuff, let alone the stuff that came with the cabin rental!"

I closed my eyes for a moment, then got my wits together and opened the microwave. One hotdog had exploded, leaving pink chunks all over the microwave. Super. I pulled the bowl out and set it on the counter before grabbing a rag from the sink and pointing at Ramble.

"This is your doing, bud, so you better get your little friend here under control." I turned back to the mess and internally asked Artemis, *Okay, so what else do I need to know about gremlins?*

*Now you seek my assistance? Had you allowed me to accompany you from the outset, Vânători, we would not be having this conversation.*

"I don't really need you to read me the riot act, Artemis. You want me to apologize?" I asked as I mucked out the exploded hot dog. "Fine. I'm sorry I didn't take you to the church with me. I'm trying to use you sparingly so we can go a little longer without having to ask for more blood."

*Since you are not a full-blooded Vânători, drinking the vampire's blood is simply a part of what you must do to access your full powers. That is the way of it.*

Her words sounded an awful lot like, "It is what it is." That was my least favorite phrase.

"Super," I said, grinding my teeth to keep from lashing out at the goddess. "So...what else do you know about gremlins? What do I need to do to calm this guy down?"

Ramble answered that one with a rumble that reverberated around the room. The gremlin immediately dropped to the floor, head hung low, but I knew that trick now.

I eyed him as Ramble led him out of the kitchen and into the living room.

"Don't let him tear up the living room!" I yelled after the hellhound as I dragged the trash can over and threw away pieces of exploded hotdog. At least I'd caught it before they'd all exploded. I would have been seriously pissed at losing an entire meal like that. I had to pay for this food, and money didn't grow on trees.

Actually, was I even going to get paid for helping the priest out at the church? I'd better. I made a mental note to connect with Sheriff Allen later to make sure I claimed the short time I was there, so I would get paid.

My mood, previously bolstered by the idea of a simple but good meal, somehow soured.

"Well?" I prompted Artemis again when she didn't immediately start dishing on gremlins. When she still didn't answer, I could tell that she was thinking about continuing to give me a hard time for not initially requesting her help to catch the gremlin.

Whatever. I could play the silent game, too.

She must have decided that this was not the hill to die on, because a few minutes later, she finally began to share.

*While they may look, as you would say "cute", Gremlins are creatures with an eye for havoc and destruction.*

"Okay. You've kind of said that already," I grumbled while cutting the salvaged hotdogs into bite-sized pieces and dropping them into the bowl of macaroni and cheese.

*Do you want me to tell you or not, Vânători?*

I rolled my eyes and spun the knife in the air in a "keep-going" gesture. "By all means."

*Thank you.* She paused to collect her thoughts. *Gremlins are like rats. Individually, they are more of a nuisance than anything else.*

*But when they amass in a group, they become bent on the destruction of anything in their path.*

"Okay," I slowly said, spooning out the mac and hot dogs into two bowls. After a moment of indecision, I got out a third, smaller bowl and dished some food into it, too. "So, if they're not a problem alone, why are you so stressed out about the one we brought home?"

*I am not finished, Vânători. Allowing even one gremlin to live can have astronomical consequences. It only takes one gremlin to create hundreds of offspring.*

"They reproduce asexually?" I sat down at the table with my bowl of macaroni and set the other two bowls down on the floor. "Ramble! Dinner!"

*If they get wet, their bodies will create copies of themselves.*

"Wait, no way! Are you saying that a movie made in the eighties actually got it right?"

*I do not understand.*

"Someone made a movie about gremlins, and in that movie, if they get wet, they reproduce. Is it also bad to feed gremlins after midnight? And are they not supposed to be exposed to sunlight?"

*I do not think that sunlight bothers them, though they are typically nocturnal creatures because of their natural inclination to stay out of human sight. And you are not supposed to feed gremlins because it will encourage them to stay near you.*

"Okay, got it." Ramble and the gremlin came trotting into the dining area, the gremlin's bells jingling, all attention focused on the bowls of food. Realization hit me as they began scarfing down the macaroni and hot dogs.

"So, they're not supposed to get wet. Is that why you helped him get from the car to the house earlier? So he wouldn't get wet in the snow?" I asked Ramble.

The hellhound gave me a look that clearly said, "Yes, dummy."

"Got it. Don't get him wet. What's with the bells, though?"

*Gremlins are drawn to the sound of some bells. It makes them easier to trap and hunters previously used bells to lure them out from their hiding places.*

*To kill them,* I mentally responded, not wanting to stress out the little creature now licking his empty bowl. I scooped up more mac from my bowl and clicked at the gremlin to get his attention. He looked up and, seeing the spoonful of food, held up his bowl for it.

All I could think as I deposited the food into his bowl was Oliver Twist saying, "Please sir, can I have some more?"

*Yes. To exterminate them before they can reproduce and cause massive damage to whatever building they've sheltered in.*

"Huh." I thought about our morning. "Father Patrick seemed to think he'd trapped the gremlin in the belfry, but it sounds more like that's exactly where he wanted to go because of the bell there."

*Yes. That is the likely explanation.*

*So, now what do we do with him?* I silently asked Artemis while I ate.

*You know what I am going to tell you, Vânători. Why ask?*

Because you know I'm not going to kill this gremlin. Not when he hasn't done anything more than snap at me and destroy my curtains. He has a right to life like any other creature.

I could almost feel her shake her head in my mind. *You may have a different perspective in the next few hours.*

"What's the worst that could happen?" I asked.

Why? Why would I say that? So, so dumb.

Of course, right then my phone rang. I immediately got a bad feeling in the pit of my stomach when I saw it was Sheriff Allen.

"Hey, Sheriff," I said when I answered, trying to keep a

neutral tone while the gremlin, realizing his bowl was empty, held it up to be filled again. "Surely you don't have another job for me that quick? I only left the church about an hour ago." I waved at the gremlin with one hand to show him that the food was gone, and he wouldn't be getting any more.

In response, the little ass chucked the bowl at the floor. I was lucky I'd thought to give him a plastic bowl and not something breakable.

"An hour, huh?" The sheriff said. "Listen, Vianne, did you and Father Patrick have a fight?"

"A fight? No. I mean, he wasn't thrilled that I didn't want to kill the gremlin hiding in his church, but I wouldn't call that a fight. Why? Is he mad?"

"No," the Sheriff sighed. "He's dead."

# Chapter Three

"Dead! Wha—How? I was just there!"

"That's why I'm going to need you to come by so we can ask you some questions, Vi."

Oh shit. Was I a suspect?

*Do not go, Vânători. It could be a trap,* Artemis cautioned.

*I'm pretty sure it's not a trap,* I mentally responded while out loud to the sheriff, I said, "Of course. I just have to clear the snow off the car, and I'll be right over." I couldn't help but hesitate. "Am I...am I a suspect?"

He sighed again, and I got the distinct feeling that whatever came out of his mouth next was for the benefit of whoever was there within earshot on his end. "Well, not officially. I'm not arresting you, but you were the last person known to be seen with him before he was found." He hesitated, then quickly added, "But to be honest, it's *odd* the way he died. Definitely *unnatural*. Like everything was squeezed out of him, yet there wasn't much of his blood left at the scene."

What did that even mean? I opened my mouth to ask, then closed it again. Maybe he was hinting that the Father had been sucked dry by a vampire? The only vampire that I knew in town wouldn't have killed Father Patrick. At least, I didn't think he would. Louis seemed to do his best to blend in with the humans as the friendly motel owner.

Okay, maybe not *friendly,* but I didn't think he would kill Father Patrick. And it seemed even less likely that he'd leave a body behind to be discovered by the police.

*It's a trap, Vânători. A vampire killed the priest after you left, and now it's trying to bait you into town to capture you and take you to Morvalden.*

*You think they would go to all that trouble to kidnap me from a sheriff's office? Seems like it would be a lot easier to just come out to the cabin and take me from here. Or, hell, if that was the goal, why not just attack me when I was at the church?*

During my pause, the sheriff added, "You or Preston wouldn't know anything about that, would you?"

This was really bad. I only knew one Preston, though I'm not sure how the sheriff knew about my run-in with the lawyer. I'd only spoken to him twice, and the second time he'd pulled a gun on me when I was helping a gnome recover dirt from his backyard. (It was a long story.) I didn't exactly consider us friends.

It took me a moment to process that the sheriff was dropping a veiled hint that I should bring a lawyer with me. The fact that he was being so subtle also meant that someone he didn't trust was listening to this conversation, and he didn't want them to know that he'd just suggested I bring a lawyer with me. Great.

To the sheriff—and for the benefit of whoever was apparently listening in—I quickly said, "That *is* odd. I'll be down as soon as I can dig out my car." I hung up.

"Shit," I said out loud, then started clearing up from our meal, placing the bowls in the sink. I could wash them later, assuming I didn't get arrested for a murder I didn't commit.

*What does this mean, Vânători?*

"It means I might be a prime murder suspect, and we can't rely on the sheriff to keep me out of jail."

Ramble stared up at me, glanced over at the gremlin, then back to me again.

"Yeah. you're going to have to stay here and watch him. Otherwise, I don't think we'd have a cabin to come back to." I headed back to the foyer, and Ramble followed, watching me shove my boots on before throwing on my coat. The poor shredded sleeve would have to wait to be patched until after I got back. I remembered to grab my hat and gloves at the last second, which was good because my sad loaner car didn't have any heat.

An inquisitive whine escaped the hellhound.

"I know you don't want to stay here, but if I need help, I'll call on you to pop in and break me out of jail." There were definitely perks to having a hellhound as a friend, and magically appearing where I directed him was one of those perks. I gave Ramble a half-smile then turned to leave before reminding him over my shoulder, "Don't let the gremlin get wet!" I shut the door behind me and hoped I wouldn't need Ramble's help.

*Alright Artemis, you said you wanted to go do something. Here we go,* I mentally told the goddess as I headed down the short set of stairs to the car. That feeling I'd been having of being watched increased as I stepped out into the open space between the cabin and car. I paused and looked around. Nothing stirred, and there were no footprints or any other telltale signs that someone was hanging around our cabin. Maybe I was just being paranoid after learning of Father Patrick's death?

*You should flee,* Artemis urged, snapping me back to the present. *You cannot risk being trapped in a cell. It would be too easy for Morvalden to capture you then.*

I pulled my head back into the game and cleared the light dusting of snow off the car as I answered. "We can't just run away every time something gets difficult, Artemis." As I spoke, I also decided not to bother trying to shovel the driveway again. It hadn't snowed enough for me to bother shoveling a path from the car to the road yet, but if it kept snowing all day, I'd probably have to park on the side of the road and shovel out the driveway before I could park again. "Besides, don't forget that our only source of keeping you powered up lives in this town. If we run, we'll lose that."

I got in and started the car, wishing again for a heater as I huddled in my sad jacket and traversed the slightly slippery driveway in reverse

Why do people live in places like this again?

*Louis could also be the murderer.*

I wasn't sure I believed that. I mean, yes, Louis was an old vampire, so I was pretty sure he'd probably murdered someone at some point, but I didn't think it made sense for him to kill the priest.

On the way to the sheriff's, I made a phone call.

"Preston Powers speaking." The lawyer's tone was crisp and professional without coming off as cold.

"Um, hi Preston. I'm not sure you remember me. My name's Vi, and I—"

"I remember you." The professionalism was suddenly gone. "I *knew* there was a reason I've been having such bad luck. You and your gnome friend just won't stop, will you!"

His vehemence threw me off. "Whoa, hey, I'm not sure what you're talking about."

"Bullshit." He bit out the word with a hard "t" but at least he wasn't yelling anymore. "I've lost multiple court cases that should have been open and shut. My pipes froze and burst last week. I was rear-ended *twice in one day* at the same time that my car insurance somehow stopped getting auto-paid so

I, *a lawyer*, looked like I didn't have insurance. *And* all the things I planted outside *died*."

"I mean...it is winter..."

"No!" He made a sputtering noise as he struggled to keep control of his anger. "You *know* that's not why. You and *your friend* did something. I want you to fix it, or else...or else..." He trailed off clearly at a loss for what actual threat he could make when he knew his claim of me giving him bad luck sounded ridiculous.

*Sounds like he has been cursed*, Artemis silently offered.

*Do you think Hyssop could do something like that?* I asked.

I felt the mental equivalent of a shrug. *Maybe...but unlikely. Their magic is usually earth related. If he has been cursed with bad luck, it is more likely a witch.*

That was something to think about since Hyssop currently lived in the library where a witch worked.

I let Preston sit in silence for a moment before gently saying, "I'm sorry if you've been having bad luck lately. I honestly don't know anything about it."

He made an indignant grunt of disbelief.

"I really don't. I can ask Hyssop—the gnome—to see if he knows anything. You know there are *other* beings in this town who can do things like curses. I'm not super knowledgeable about what gnomes can do, but I'm pretty sure that's not really their area of magic." The silence on the other end of the line suggested that Preston was listening. "You haven't made someone else in town mad lately, have you?"

"Not to my knowledge," he quickly said, then added, "But then again, who knows? I didn't know I was pissing off a *gnome* by moving here and changing *my* backyard to suit me."

"I mean... it was Hyssop's garden and home for longer than either of us have been alive. He just doesn't own it on paper."

"He should have sued me for squatter's rights, then."

My eyebrows shot up though he couldn't see me. "I don't think that would have worked out too well seeing as how most people don't know he exists." I'd been driving during our conversation and pulled into a parking spot outside the Sheriff's Department. Seeing the building was a reminder that I hadn't been calling Preston to start a fight, but actually to ask a favor.

"Look, I really don't know anything about why you're having an unnatural streak of bad luck, *but* I'm willing to help you figure out what's going on. The thing is, I'll need a favor in return."

"What kind of favor? Or is this one of those, 'I'll need a favor for the future' kind of deals?" He paused for a millisecond, but before I could respond, his professional tone was back and somewhat clipped. "And I'll remind you that I'm a lawyer. I can't go around breaking laws for you."

"Actually, I'm calling you specifically *because* you're a lawyer. And the time that I need your services is in about five minutes." I gave him a brief rundown of the situation. He didn't seem phased that gremlins exist, but then again, I guess it wasn't too difficult to believe in gremlins if you'd already met a gnome.

Thankfully, Artemis stayed mostly silent during our exchange. Sometimes I wondered if she was using these opportunities to get a better grip on what modern life was like and how people spoke and interacted. I hoped that was a good thing and wouldn't bite me in the ass in the future.

Preston asked me some lawyer questions (Was I under arrest? I didn't think so. Did I do it? No, absolutely not.). Then there was a long pause while he thought it over.

"How do I know you didn't cause my bad luck just so you can come 'solve' my problem as a favor for clearing your name?"

*Tell him you're too stupid to think that far ahead.* Artemis was apparently done being silent. I started to reproach her then realized it wasn't a bad answer.

"Honestly?" I told Preston, "I don't really think that far ahead. I mean, I'm sitting outside the Sheriff's Department right now. Plus," I added as I had a thought, "It would be kind of dumb to cause you bad luck and then ask you to be my lawyer. Wouldn't your bad luck hurt me?"

Shit. Maybe I shouldn't be asking him for help if he really was cursed with bad luck right now. What if it got me arrested?

"Both fair points." He sighed. "I'll be there. Don't tell them anything they don't already know until I get there." Then he hung up.

*Hopefully, he gets here sooner rather than later.*

I looked over at the official looking concrete building of the Sheriff's Department. A little shiver slipped down my spine at the memory of my last visit. I'd been dragged inside by a deputy who could turn into a monster and was hellbent on annihilating the people in town who belonged to the supernatural community.

I'd almost died in one of the cells. It had not been a fun visit.

Just looking at the building brought back sharp memories: Surprise as a knife slid into my flesh...the heavy weight of sinking into a final darkness...

I took a deep, shuddering breath and tried to ground myself in the present by noting the cold Maine winter and leaning into a distant hunger pang for vampire blood. I hadn't realized being back here would affect me so much.

I took another moment to send out a silent prayer to the Universe that Preston would arrive soon, then forced myself out of the car, down the short, snow-dusted sidewalk and into the building.

It looked exactly the same as before. Except this time, I wasn't handcuffed...yet.

The sheriff met me inside the front door. His crisp brown uniform almost matched his hair and fit snugly over his belly. When not dancing with amusement, his eyes tended toward kindness or sympathy which was why I didn't mind working with him.

Plus he paid me.

"Thanks for coming down so quickly," he said with a half-smile. He turned to a woman beside him with blue eyes that were as cold as ice chips.

"Vi, this is Harriet Englewood. She's my new deputy and is assisting me on this *unusual* case."

The woman was maybe mid to late thirties. She stood a foot taller than me and easily filled out her deputy uniform with what looked like pure muscle. She smiled as we shook hands, but the smile didn't quite reach her eyes.

Based on Sheriff Allen's wording, I got the feeling Harriet wasn't wise to the existence of the supernatural community yet. Was she new in town? And was she the one who had been listening when the sheriff called me?

I could tell she was assessing me while I was doing the same thing to her. Ironically, while I'm sure she saw me as a suspect in Father Patrick's death, I saw her as a suspect, too. Not because I knew anything about her, but because the last deputy had been a hateful, murderous bigot. It was kind of hard not to automatically associate her with him when they'd held the same position.

*Is she human, Artemis?* I silently asked.

*It seems so.* She paused, as if still sizing up the situation. *...I have a bad feeling about this.*

*That makes two of us.* I suddenly wished Ramble were here. I felt totally exposed and vulnerable without my fire-breathing hellhound sidekick.

"Great to meet you," I said as the woman crushed my hand in a death grip.

"Likewise." Her reply was cool as a cucumber.

When she released my hand, the sheriff ushered us further into the building and back to his office. I'd never been in this part of the building before. Last time, I'd been taken straight to the jail cells, something I wanted to avoid this time around.

Seeing the sheriff's personal office was like getting a little glimpse into his brain. Though there were neat stacks of files and paperwork on the periphery of his desk, the middle was a flurry of haphazard documents and crime scene photos which partially covered the computer's keyboard and mouse.

In the corner was an extra chair with a filing box on it. As we entered the office, he hastily put the box on the floor, pulled the chair out a little, and waved me to sit there before shuffling some of the messier stacks of paper into a pile. He quickly gave up on that endeavor and spun his own chair away from the desk to take a seat. That left Deputy Englewood standing in the doorway.

Was she blocking the doorway so I couldn't leave? Surely not.

"Don't clean up on my account," I murmured with a smile to the sheriff as I sat.

He started to grin back then caught himself as if he shouldn't be joking when someone had been murdered. Or maybe it's because he didn't think he should joke with a murder suspect.

"Thanks for coming in, Vi. I know you just finished a consultation job that I sent your way."

I nodded, not sure what he was looking for here.

"Like I mentioned on the phone, Father Patrick was found dead not long after you left."

*He has already told you this. Why is he repeating himself, Vânători?*

*Good question,* I thought back at Artemis. Then it struck me: this was all a show for the deputy. Which was...odd. Didn't the deputy work for the sheriff? So why would he need to put on a show like this?

I did my best to play along with the sheriff.

"Do you know what happened? He seemed fine when I left."

The sheriff opened his mouth, but the deputy cut him off before he could say anything. Interesting.

"Actually, we were wondering if you could tell us that, Ms. Mason."

It took me a minute to remember that Mason was the fake name I'd given when I first came to Ricketts. I'd gotten too used to most people in town knowing my true name.

"Well, I—"

"Hold on. Stop right there, Vi," said a man from the doorway. "Not another word." It was Preston Powers, my lawyer for the day. His tall frame towered behind the deputy.

With her back to the door, the deputy hadn't seen him coming. She jumped about a mile when he spoke then turned with an angry look on her face, clearly ready to ream him out. He cut her off before she could get started.

"I'm Preston Powers, Vi—Ms. Mason's lawyer, and she will not be speaking with you outside of my presence." His smooth use of my fake name was pretty impressive, especially since I hadn't remembered to share that detail with him. He must have heard the deputy use it.

He glanced down at me. "I see that my client is not in handcuffs. Am I right in assuming that she is not currently under arrest?"

"Of course not," the sheriff quickly confirmed.

"Good." Preston looked around the office, taking in its

slightly haphazard state which was in complete juxtaposition to his own crisp gray suit and blue tie.

Oh man. If I can't solve his luck problem, I'm gonna end up in SO much debt to him if his suit is any indication as to how much he costs.

*We could drop him into Between once he has cleared your name,* Vânători.

I fought to keep a straight face since I was the only one who could hear her and mentally replied, *I don't think abandoning our allies to be lost forever in Between is the best idea.*

Preston spoke again, regaining my attention. "Perhaps we could move this conversation to somewhere a little roomier." He addressed the sheriff directly. "I'm sure you have an interrogation room that would do nicely."

The sheriff stood, but it was the deputy who answered. "Of course we do. We simply wanted to provide a more friendly environment for Ms. Mason. We didn't want her to feel that she was a suspect being interrogated." She gave Preston a not-so-friendly smile that suggested she ate lawyers like him for breakfast.

"Right, I understand. Except that it appears that she *is* a suspect, yes?" He nodded in answer to his own question. "I wouldn't want her saying something in this *friendly environment* that might somehow implicate her in a crime she had nothing to do with."

I saw a slight look of surprise flit across the sheriff's face. So, it had been the deputy's idea to speak with me in his office. Damn. The sheriff was clearly in over his head with his new deputy if she was already manipulating him like that. Preston was right. I totally would have told them everything that happened between the Father and me since I felt like I was friends with the sheriff. Plus, I knew I was innocent.

But being innocent didn't necessarily mean you wouldn't be found guilty of a crime.

The sheriff grabbed a folder from his desk, then led us to an interrogation room. It was just like I'd seen in the movies and honestly wasn't that much bigger than his office had been, but at least it had four chairs. I went in first, followed by Preston who stopped in the doorway and turned to face the sheriff and deputy.

"I'd like a moment alone with my client." Without waiting for a response, he closed the door in their faces.

Damn. I wanted to be like Preston when I grew up.

# Chapter Four

Preston set his briefcase down on the table and ushered me to take a seat beside him. Next, he conjured a legal pad and a fancy pen from this briefcase, then waved at me to begin.

"Alright, I know what happened, but let's go over it in more detail. Perhaps you can enlighten me as to why they're calling you Mason instead of Vânători."

I explained the fake name first, which meant having to spill everything. I walked us through my alcoholism and eventual drunk driving, which landed me in jail, then how I'd been doing okay after getting out on parole, right up until I'd been jumped by a vampire.

Preston seemed to take it in stride that vampires existed and let me continue, uninterrupted. I omitted the part about burning down a vampire's house and jumped straight to fleeing the state since that was the more important issue here. I wasn't sure if Preston had some kind of legal duty to report something like that or not. And honestly, though I'd been the one to spread gasoline around that hell house,

Ramble had technically been the one to set it on fire. All around, it just seemed best not to mention it.

After I'd basically word-vomited my past on him, Preston paused to take it all in.

"So...not only are there gnomes, hellhounds, and gremlins, but vampires as well?"

"Yes, but not everyone knows about the vampires. It's better if we try to keep it that way and let people from the supernatural community choose who they share their real nature with."

"But if whatever did this is a vampire, you'll need to share that with the sheriff."

"If it's a vampire that killed Father Patrick, I won't keep it from him," I promised.

*Vânători, we do think it is vampires...*

*We suspect it might be vampires, but we don't know for sure. Let's get more information before we share too much with the sheriff.*

"Vampires," Preston said, tilting his head in thought. "I can think of a few youthful colleagues that I've always wondered about..." He trailed off before giving a definitive nod, as if filing that info away for further review later, then got back to business. "So, I know the sheriff called you and set up a meeting between you and Father Patrick, but what exactly happened at the church if you got the gremlin out?"

I threw up my hands. "Nothing. Father Patrick had trapped him in the belfry. When I got there, we went up, let him out, and chased him around the church a little." I held up my shredded jacket sleeve. "The little guy fought back when I tried to catch him. And honestly, who could blame him since Father Patrick was yelling to exterminate him?" I felt a pang of sympathy for the gremlin as I suddenly saw the scenario from his point of view. I'd have fought back too if I was being chased around by people five times larger than me.

"Then what?" Preston asked, reminding me that I wasn't finished yet.

"The gremlin ran for the front door and ended up hiding behind Ramble—he's the hellhound you met before. He's like my business partner." I shrugged. "I guess Ramble decided the gremlin needed his protection. The three of us loaded into the car, and Father Patrick watched us leave from the doorway."

Preston scratched some notes on his legal pad. "And it was just the four of you in the church? You, Father Patrick, your... partner, and the gremlin?"

"Actually, Ramble mostly stayed in the car until the gremlin ran out the front door. Not that anyone would have seen him if he'd decided to go inside."

The reminder of Ramble's invisibility had the lawyer looking around the room. "Is he...is he here now?"

"Ramble? No. He had to stay back at the house and watch the gremlin so he doesn't do anything...destructive." I remembered the shredded curtains. "Well, anything *more* destructive."

Preston looked down at his notes, sighed, then met my eyes again. "You'll definitely be a suspect. You were the last to see Father Patrick...but I don't see how they can directly tie you to his death."

I let out a sigh of relief.

"Don't relax just yet," he cautioned. "I'm going to let them in here now, and they're going to ask you a ton of questions to see if they can poke holes in your story."

"You think the sheriff would do that?"

"I think it's his job to gather evidence and find out what happened before charging someone."

"That's a very neutral response. I honestly think we have more to worry about from the deputy than from the sheriff. She seems to have it in for me."

"Let's just see how this goes. I rarely work cases in Ricketts since it's so small and where I call home. Once we see how they interact with you, I'll have a clearer picture of what the Sheriff is like." He stood, but before he opened the door, he paused and said, "Keep your answers short and sweet. Only your lawyer needs all the details. They get the bare-bones version. You're not here to paint them a picture."

With that, he opened the door.

The sheriff was propped against the wall in the hallway just outside, holding a manila folder against his chest with crossed arms. He shot a look over to the right, and the deputy suddenly appeared in the doorway from that direction. She followed Preston in first with the sheriff right on her heels.

"Most innocent people don't need a lawyer, Ms. Mason. Just thought you should know that."

Preston rolled his eyes at the woman, clearly more than ready to handle a small-town deputy's pissy party. "One should always bring in a lawyer when being officially questioned by law enforcement. And if you're advising otherwise and refusing people their right to a lawyer, that would be illegal."

"Good thing that didn't happen," she drily responded.

"Alright, settle down folks," the sheriff said. "Let's get this over with so Vi can head back home."

"On a first name basis, are we?" The deputy asked with a quirked eyebrow.

"Since the sheriff's department has used her consultation services more than once, yes. I am on a first name basis with her. I'm the one who called her in the first place to respond to the Father's complaint. I would also have accompanied her, but as you know, we were busy elsewhere at the time." His eyes found mine for a moment before they flicked away again.

It felt like he was trying to lend weight to what he'd just said. So...what had *they* been so busy with?

The deputy ignored the sheriff's logic. "We have a few questions to ask you, Ms. Mason. If that is...it's okay with your lawyer."

I looked at Preston and, at his brief nod, said, "Sure. Ask away."

"You were called out by the Sheriff here to investigate a disturbance at the church, is that right?"

"Yes."

See? I could totally do short and sweet.

She waited for me to say more and when she realized that was all she was going to get, she prompted, "And? What happened? Did you go out to the church?"

"As requested, I went to the church where Father Patrick greeted me outside. He told me he had a gremlin problem and—"

The deputy cut me off with a snort. "A gremlin problem? You're joking, right?"

I glared at the deputy. "What kind of consultant do you think I am, Deputy Englewood?"

"I have no idea, Ms. Mason," she said, suddenly serious. "Why don't you tell me?"

The necklace bristled. *I do not care for this woman.*

*You and me both*, I thought back.

I hesitated to explain what I did. What had the sheriff been writing on my checks again? Oh yeah.

"I'm a preternatural consultant. When something seems a little out of the ordinary, I go in and investigate to see if there's actually something supernatural occurring or if it's just something odd that has a more mundane explanation."

Yeah, that was not at all what I did. I was more of a liaison between the supernatural community and the human police. However, something told me that Deputy Englewood wouldn't be too keen on treating me like fellow law enforcement.

"Uh huh," she said, tilting her head forward in disbelief. "And did you help the Father find a gremlin in his church before or after you murdered him?"

"Excuse me?" I said at the same time that Preston reached out a hand and said, "Don't answer that, Vianne."

Preston glared at the deputy, then gave a questioning look to the sheriff. "Is this the kind of clown show investigation you're allowing to go on behind these walls, Sheriff? Because I do not appreciate the accusatory nature of that question, and if that line of questioning continues, then my client and I will leave unless you decide to place her under arrest."

My head jerked toward Preston. Under arrest! What the hell was he doing?

"Now, hold on," the sheriff said. He shot a quick warning look at his deputy before refocusing on Preston and me. "No one is under arrest. I'm just looking for an official statement from Vi about what happened today. That's it. Deputy Englewood, I think I can handle it from here. Why don't you go start that run-down of the Father's parishioners."

The deputy opened her mouth to protest, but the sheriff cut her off. "I don't think this is something that requires both of us."

Clearly knowing that she'd been dismissed, Englewood's jaw clenched. "Sure, *Sheriff.* No problem."

When she was finally out of the room and the door closed behind her, I couldn't help but ask, "What's up with her?"

The sheriff shook his head. "She came to us straight out of the Portland police department. Seemed smart to hire someone with actual law enforcement experience after my last deputy, but she's not used to the relationships we have to maintain in such a small town."

"Huh," I grunted. "How's she gonna take it when she finds out about all the nonhuman citizens?"

"I don't know." The sheriff glanced at Preston and raised a brow.

"Preston has had some run-ins with a few of the *locals*," I explained, with an obvious emphasis on the last word. The sheriff nodded. He looked tired as he rubbed his chin and sighed. "She's going to have to loosen up a little just to fit in with the humans. I'm not sure how she'll take the rest."

Preston cleared his throat. "Uh, how many other types of nonhuman—"

"People from the supernatural community," I corrected.

"Ah, yes. Thank you. How many people are there in the supernatural community here?"

I shrugged. "I'm honestly not sure. I seem to meet someone new every day. And unfortunately, many of them are a secret even to each other." I thought of the trolls who owned and operated the Flying Pie restaurant at the edge of town. You'd never in a million years guess they were anything but hard-working restaurant owners. Seeing Preston's slight look of worry, I quickly added, "But most of them blend in because they want to just live their lives like us and be a part of society."

The sheriff put the folder he'd been holding on the table and opened it before sliding it in front of me. "I know you didn't do this, Vi. But I wanted to make sure it wasn't some-thing that your...partner could do." His eyes slid to Preston, then back to me.

"Preston knows about Ramble and what he is," I said, then suddenly stopped talking as my eyes landed on the picture in the file. My mouth went dry. From the way the sheriff had spoken, I'd expected to see the priest's body with obvious claw marks or bites and drained of blood.

This was something very different. I'm not sure how else

to describe what was left of Father Patrick's body. It looked like a pile of ripped-apart flesh or like someone had taken the priest's body and run it through a meat grinder, then left it in a pile on the floor of the church.

"I'm sorry to show you that," the sheriff said, and he really did look sorry. "I wanted to see if you noticed anything out of place from when you were there." He moved the top picture aside to show several other photos of the murder scene.

I swallowed and forced myself to take a closer look at the other pictures. Whoever killed him had left him in a small closet but had rolled up a towel or something and placed it in front of the closet door to keep the pool of blood from seeping out.

Another picture was of the raised dais, except it was a mess. Someone had flipped the little altar table and shoved the podium off the platform.

The last picture was taken from the dais and looked out on a scene of destruction. Several of the pews were splintered and broken, while others were thrown on top of each other or shoved to the side.

My eyebrows rose. "My partner wouldn't have left a mess like that—not of Father Patrick's body, nor of the church itself. Look how those pews are smashed up. That's not really how he operates."

"What about the person who blew up your shed?"

"Someone blew up your shed?" Preston asked, then seemed to remember that he was working. "I mean, I'm not sure it's Vi's job to find you another suspect if she's not working this case, Sheriff."

I waved the lawyer off, then looked back at the sheriff. "No, it's fine. I don't think he would have any kind of beef with Father Patrick. And if he did, I've never heard of him leaving something like *that* behind." I jerked my head at the Father's remains, then had a thought.

"How could what's left of his body look like that, but there isn't any blood anywhere else in the room?"

"We're not sure. I thought you might have some suggestions on what could do something like this."

*Thoughts?* I asked Artemis. Maybe she could shed some light on this.

*In all my years working with your ancestors, I have never encountered a being who leaves a body in that state. A vampire drains the body of blood, but this is not the work of a vampire. At least not a sane one, at any rate.*

Super helpful. So, it was either an unknown being or a crazy vampire.

"I'm sorry, Sheriff. I'm not sure what would—or could—do something like that." I forced myself to look at the grisly picture again. "Do we even know those *are* Father Patrick's remains?" I swallowed. "It seems like it would be hard to tell."

"We have a perfect match on his DNA," the sheriff said. At my surprised look, he added, "Years ago, when we first got the technology, I asked him to come by and help me test it out." He sighed. "I knew he wouldn't have any kind of record, so he wouldn't mind having his DNA in our system." His voice roughened with suppressed emotion. "I never imagined I'd be using it to identify him after he'd been *murdered* in his own church."

"I'm really sorry, Sheriff. You must have known him for a long time."

The sheriff nodded, then seemed to put his game face back on. "Is there anything else you can tell me that would help us, Vi? What happened while you were at the church with him?"

"When I last saw him, he was watching me drive out of the parking lot." I looked at Preston, then decided I wasn't in any danger revealing more. "He wasn't very happy that I didn't kill the gremlin. He knew exactly what it was and had trapped it in the belfry before I got there. We let it out, and then he was pissed that I didn't share his view that the gremlin was vermin."

"The gremlin couldn't have gone back and done this, right?"

I shook my head at the sheriff's question. "No. Trust me, he was within my sight the entire time from when we left the church right up until you called me to come here." As I said it, I couldn't help but wonder how much mayhem the gremlin was getting into at the cabin while I was away.

"And could there have been more than one gremlin in the church?"

*Gremlins did* not *do that*, Artemis stated matter-of-factly.

I shook my head. "I'm pretty sure gremlins don't leave bodies like that. And, though they can apparently be pretty destructive, they're not really strong enough to demolish the pews either."

"It would have been nice to have an easy case for once." He sighed. "We've requested an autopsy but had to send Father Patrick's...remains to a larger town since we don't have a coroner with that kind of forensic experience. But, if I had to guess without an official report? It looked to me like something drained him of blood..." he grimaced at the memory so fresh in his mind but was able to finish, "...and then turned him inside out."

Preston's eyes snapped up to mine at the mention of drained blood.

I shook my head for both Preston and the sheriff's benefit, though for different reasons. "I don't know of anything that would drain a person of blood *and* leave a body like that."

Unless...

*Maybe a vampire purposely made this mess to mislead us?* I asked Artemis.

I could feel a wave of doubt coming from the goddess, which was ironic since she'd been the one to initially assume this was vampires out to get us. *Why bother to mislead us?* She asked. *As you said, why go to all this trouble? You would not be difficult to track to the cabin. The only reason to kill the priest and leave his body so desecrated would be to get our attention. What now? What would they gain from this?*

I started to verbally respond, then remembered that this conversation was occurring entirely in my mind. Also, Preston and the sheriff were staring at me. Apparently, I was getting too used to carrying on conversations in my mind. Hopefully, I hadn't made a face or something during my conversation with Artemis.

"I'm sorry about your friend, Sheriff. I'm honestly not sure what killed Father Patrick."

"We've had too many bodies in this town lately, Vi. If the supernatural community doesn't step up to stop their own, then they're going to get exposed by incidents like this if they keep happening."

I couldn't help my look of surprise, followed by annoyance. "In case you forgot, Sheriff, it was your own deputy who murdered all those people from the supernatural community. Not the other way around. If anything, maybe *your* people should step up to stop their own from killing people in the supernatural community who just want to live their lives in peace."

I know I probably should have kept my mouth shut, especially since the sheriff was providing my only paying gig. That and he knew I had skipped out on my parole in another state. He could easily make a phone call and have me dragged back to Indiana and thrown in jail for that.

The sheriff opened his mouth to answer, then paused and reflected on what he'd said. "You're right, Vi. I didn't mean it like that."

He had, but I let it go. I didn't want to alienate all my allies. "It's fine. Are we done here?"

He nodded. "I'll file a report with your official statement about what occurred. I don't view you as a suspect, Vi, but it would be good if you could find out more information about who or what might have done this."

"Does that mean I'm officially on the case as a consultant?"

He hesitated, and Preston stepped in. "My guess is that having you investigate this case would be a conflict of interest, since you might still be considered a suspect."

My mouth dropped open. "But he just said—"

"He said *he* didn't consider you a suspect. Not that you weren't still officially considered one. Right, Sheriff?"

The sheriff nodded and didn't meet my eyes.

"That is some bullshit." I shook my head. "I better at least get paid for removing the gremlin." I turned to Preston. "Can we go now?"

"Unless the Sheriff has any other questions, you should be free to go."

The sheriff nodded and stood. "Of course." He walked us out of the interrogation room and all the way back to the front door. "But Vi, make sure you don't leave town. And maybe try not to be the last person to interact with anyone else before they turn up dead."

He shut the door before I could think of a witty comeback.

Preston saved me by taking me gently by the arm and guiding us to the parking lot. "Come on, Vianne. Let's get a coffee and talk."

# Chapter Five

"Just a cup of coffee for me, please," I told the server.

"Are you sure you don't want something else?" Preston asked. "This is on me."

Though my stomach was still in nervous knots from meeting with the sheriff, and I hadn't eaten that long ago, I figured I should take free food anywhere I could get it. Plus, Ramble would eat any leftovers I brought him.

"In that case, how about the club sandwich?" I asked the server, who nodded and walked away, leaving Preston and me sitting in our corner booth a few tables away from the other customers.

Though the cafe was in the middle of town, making it the most convenient spot for Preston and me to talk, I hadn't been sure it would be a great meeting spot. After all, I'd inadvertently killed one of their servers. Of course, the server, Cheri, had been helping the deputy in his murder spree. I hadn't meant for her to die, but that didn't make me feel any less guilty. I'd been avoiding the cafe ever since.

It was in between mealtime rush hours, so the place was mostly empty with just an older couple at a table near the back of the room. I didn't recognize the new server either, and I was pretty sure she didn't know me. So at least I had that going for me.

"I'm sorry for earlier—blaming you for my streak of bad luck," Preston said out of nowhere.

"Oh." I was a little surprised. "You more than made up for it by saving my ass from the deputy back there."

"She certainly has it out for you."

I sighed. "I'm not sure why."

We sat in a moment of awkward silence before I thought of something to ask.

"So, tell me more about what's going on with your luck. You mentioned a few things that have happened, but I'm wondering why you're convinced that it's not just coincidental bad luck."

The lawyer grimaced. "It's probably just my imagination. Saying out loud that I think I'm cursed just makes me sound..."

"...like you believe in the supernatural?" I finished for him when he trailed off.

He choked out a laugh and adjusted his tie, clearly feeling uncomfortable about the conversation. "It's one thing to listen to others discuss it, but it's harder to truly admit to myself that something exists outside the realm of what science says is possible.

I waited to see if he'd say more. When it was clear he was stuck, I prompted him. "You've met several beings from the supernatural community already. Kind of hard to go back now and say it was just your imagination."

"True. How *is* Hyssop doing?" Preston suddenly asked, shifting our conversation.

"He seems to be doing okay. I guess he's been managing some potted plants inside the library. He says he moved his own dirt into some potted plants to let him stay inside during the winter. Seems to be working."

"That's good. Good." Preston seemed a little sheepish about asking after the gnome, which was totally unlike the badass lawyer I'd just seen in the sheriff's department. Then again, he *had* destroyed Hyssop's home when he bought the house where the gnome's garden was. By the time I came along, the lawyer had already remodeled the entire backyard, tearing up Hyssop's home in the process. Hyssop would have had to start his garden from scratch again, anyway. He might as well start in a space where he wouldn't be kicked out again, so we moved him across town to liven up the library's garden.

We hit another silence just as a man entered the café. He glanced our direction then away again before the server greeted him and sat him at a table against the front window. I cleared my throat to push past our awkward silence and determined to hold up my end of our bargain. "This bad luck, you make it sound like it started after Hyssop left?"

Preston nodded. "A few days after. That's why I thought it might be linked to him."

"And you mentioned that all your plants died?"

"Every single one. Even the indoor potted plants."

*A gnome would not harm plants, Vânători.*

*I mean, Hyssop harmed his own plants to get back at Preston before I convinced him to move.* I told the necklace. To Preston I said, "I can see how you'd draw the conclusion that your bad luck came from something Hyssop was doing, but last time I spoke with him, Hyssop seemed pretty at peace with the situation."

I stopped talking when the server dropped off our drinks. She left again without a word, but not before I caught a look of disgust from her.

Uh oh. Had someone told her about Cheri?

*You worry too much, Vânători.*

That was rich coming from a being in a necklace who didn't have to worry about dying or being put in jail. Then again, I suppose the necklace was sort of like her own jail.

"Maybe I'm just jumping at shadows," Preston said with a sigh as he ripped open two packets of sweetener together in a well-practiced move and dumped them into his steaming coffee.

"Maybe, but maybe not."

*Ask him if he's noticed anything unusual around his home—inside or out—that does not belong there,* Artemis suggested. *If it is a witch's curse, they may have left something at his home to help target the curse on him. Small bags or bundles of herbs, a curse written on small parchment paper, dead animals, or, in some cases, a sigil written above an outer door.*

When I relayed the question, Preston thought it over, then shook his head. "Not that I've noticed."

*Any other ideas?* I asked the necklace, and we went through a bevy of possibilities, including cursed objects, ghosts, and even demons. The conversation let my stomach unclench a little, but unfortunately (or maybe fortunately since who would want to deal with a demon?), Preston hadn't seen or experienced anything that would indicate any of these were the root of his bad luck.

Artemis was stumped, which didn't happen very often.

*Perhaps the barrister is truly 'jumping at shadows' as he suggested earlier.*

*Maybe, but we promised we'd try to help.*

"I'm sorry, Preston, I'm not sure what's causing your bad luck, but I'll keep trying to figure it out."

He nodded, then cleared his throat and straightened his back. "Perhaps it will clear up. Let's refocus on your case."

The knot in my stomach reappeared. "Do you think I should be worried about getting the blame for Father Patrick's death?"

"I think if they don't find evidence that points to someone else, then you're their best suspect." He drank the last of his coffee and hit me with an intense look. "You don't think it was vampires that did that to the priest?"

I leaned in, not wanting the other diners to overhear our gruesome conversation. "I mean, his blood was drained, but I've never seen a vampire leave a body the way Father Patrick's was. No, I'm pretty sure something else did that."

"What if you're wrong?"

I opened my mouth to respond but was cut off when to-go bags were suddenly dropped unceremoniously onto our table. I hadn't noticed the server return, and when I looked up, I found myself looking up and up into the face of an irritated man.

"I thought you understood that you're not welcome in my cafe, Vânători." The man slammed two paper to-go cups on the table as he spoke, then took the coffee from my hand and poured it into one of the to-go cups. "I will not have a murderer in my cafe."

Preston recovered more quickly than me. His face scrunched down in anger. "My client is not a murderer, sir."

The man looked pointedly at Preston, then gestured for the lawyer to hand over his cup of coffee. Preston obliged, but since his cup was already empty, the man just set it and the empty paper cup on the table. Apparently, Preston would not be receiving a coffee to go.

*How* dare *he!* Artemis barked. Her outrage helped me find my voice.

"I don't even know you, *and* I haven't even set foot in this cafe since that happened."

"Exactly. I thought by staying away that you understood you weren't wanted here."

I opened my mouth to retort with something that surely would have been witty if I could figure out what to say, but the man completely ignored me and returned his attention to Preston.

"You are, of course, welcome to come back any time." He pointed a finger at me. "But *she* murdered one of my staff. I know she did. And the cops won't do anything about it."

He slapped the bill on the table, causing the other people in the café to look our way, then walked away before I muttered, "The police don't care because *your server* was murdering people in town." My statement didn't matter though since he'd already disappeared into the back of the restaurant.

The looks we got made me want to disappear into the ground. My brain conjured an image of Ramble setting the cafe on fire in revenge, but it was unlikely that he would want to burn down one of the few places in town that served a decent burger.

When I returned my attention to the table, I found Preston staring at me with a raised eyebrow.

I sighed and answered his unspoken question. "Long story short, all those deaths the sheriff mentioned earlier? The server here was helping the deputy kill people."

"People from the supernatural community?"

"Yes. Does that matter? She still helped murder them."

"No, I don't mean it like that, but maybe *he* does." Preston jerked his head toward where the man had disappeared.

"Oh."

Artemis's bitter voice filled my head. *He is probably right, Vânători. Humans have always looked the other way when nonhuman beings are slaughtered.*

*You don't seem to mind too much yourself if they're what you consider lower beings,* I dryly countered.

*That's different.*

I didn't bother arguing with her. Preston paid, and I collected the to-go bag. I was hungrier than I'd realized because I was practically drooling at the aroma wafting from the bag. Did I dare eat what I'd ordered? Or would the man have spit in it or done something worse to the food?

When we stepped outside, I caught a shimmer of something in the sky and paused mid-step. I had that distinct feeling of paranoia again. Other than the usual downtown traffic, though, there was no one else around.

*Did you see that?* I mentally asked Artemis.

*See what, Vânători?*

I guess that was a no.

"You okay?" Preston asked, looking at the same spot where I'd seen the brief glimmer.

"Yeah, sorry." I pulled my attention back to the lawyer and gave him a sheepish grin. "I guess it's just been a long day."

We headed toward our cars. My puke-green loaner looked pretty sad next to Preston's rented SUV. I guess his car was in the shop from the accidents he'd mentioned.

"I hear you." Preston said and checked his watch. "Actually, I have to get going. I have an appointment I need to get to." He leaned in and took his wrapped sandwich from the bag.

"Busy, busy," I joked, then noticed the bag was still fairly full. "You don't want your fries?"

"No." He gave me a smile. "Give them to your partner, and tell him they're from me."

I couldn't help but grin. "Trying to get in good with the hellhound, huh? He likes fries, but he really loves greasy burgers. Just so you know, for next time."

"Duly noted." He flipped back into his lawyer tone to add, "Let me know if the sheriff brings you back in for anything or if you think of anything that might help your case."

"I thought there *wasn't* a case?" I asked, worry making my voice tight.

"Vianne, you're the last person to speak to a local priest who was brutally murdered, and you're from out of town. Of *course* there's a case."

"Shit."

"Do me a favor and stop being around people who wind up dead," he said, echoing the sheriff. He walked around the driver's side of his car and halted.

"God damnit." His expression shifted to anger first, then resignation. His shoulders drooped.

"What's wrong?" I walked around the side of this car to see what was wrong. The front tire on the driver's side of his car was completely flat, and we didn't have to guess what caused it because a large nail stuck out from the side wall.

"Fucking flat tire." He gestured to the tire and looked up at me. "See? This is what I've been talking about."

"I hate to ask it, but are you sure it's bad luck and not someone who's deliberately sabotaging you?" I crouched down in front of the tire. "I'm no car expert, but I feel like picking up a nail in the *side* of your tire is pretty rare." I stood back up. "Someone could have done this while we ate."

"You think I'm crazy."

I put up my hands. "No, no. I just think we should rule out all possibilities here."

His expression became pinched, and he seemed to shut down. I moved out of the way as he opened his car door to put his sandwich and bag inside.

*Oh!* It felt like Artemis jerked in surprise in my mind. *Vânători, get closer to the vehicle, please.*

What is it?

*Something inside is emitting magic. Can you sense it?*

I tried to concentrate on Preston's car. *I don't feel anything.*

*Hmm.* In that one sound, Artemis conveyed her disappointment in me. *Something is there, Vânători. Please seek it.*

That was the second time she'd said please. Was Artemis

trying to make amends by being more polite? It honestly just made me more suspicious of her.

"Uh, Preston." He turned to look at me, his phone in hand. "Do you mind if I take a look inside your car? I think there might be something inside that's causing this."

"Wait, now you believe me?"

I shrugged, not wanting to lie to the lawyer since he'd probably be able to tell. "When you opened the door, I thought I might have felt something."

He waved at the car. "Go crazy. I need to call the tow truck."

I started to tell him we could just change the tire ourselves and put on the spare if he had one, but he'd already put the phone up to his ear. Plus, Artemis was urging me again to look inside.

*Alright, alright. I'm doing it,* I told the goddess. Apparently, her politeness had just been in passing.

We went through Preston's vehicle section by section. I started at the rear hatch since I thought that was the most likely place for someone to have hidden something magic. Being a rental, the process was made that much easier since it was practically empty. We examined the rear hatch area, the back seats, and the front passenger side before Artemis felt a tingle of magic from the driver's side area again.

*Put your hand out, Vânători.*

I looked around. Preston had long since finished his phone call and now leaned against the car, staring down at something on his phone.

*Do not worry about the barrister. You must learn to feel for magic, Vânători.*

*I mean, I kind of thought that was your area,* I mentally mumbled.

*We must learn to work as a team. That is what will make us the strongest.*

Kind of sounded a little too after-school-special to me. Next, she'd tell me that it wasn't about winning against Morvalden, but about the friends we made along the way. Still, I wasn't going to argue with her. So, feeling stupid and hoping that Preston didn't look my way, I put out my hand and tried to feel for any magic.

*Now, try and open your mind. You may find it easier if you close your eyes.*

Though I could sense Preston now paying attention to what I was doing, I did what I was told. Standing in front of the open driver's door, I closed my eyes and tried to empty my mind. Since clearing my mind was part of our morning training sessions, it wasn't too difficult to achieve, even with Preston looking on.

I took a deep, calming breath and tried to *feel* what Artemis sensed inside the SUV. Initially, I didn't sense anything, then it felt like warmth filled my body. Was Artemis lending me more energy? I didn't want to break my concentration to ask.

*Follow any sensations you have.*

I imagined myself like a metal detector for magic. I didn't sense anything where my hands were currently, so I slowly moved them to follow, but never touch, the contours of the driver's seat. A frown of concentration creased my face as I reached the floor of the SUV.

*I don't sense anyth—whoa.*

A spark zapped the tip of my pinky that was closest to the floor. It was like static electricity. I moved my hand back to that spot. The spark came again, then calmed to more of a pins and needles sensation after that first zap.

*Yes! You felt it. Now hone in on the source of that magic, Vânători.*

A little thrill of excitement bubbled up at having done something right. I followed that spark of energy down to hover over the floor, then slowly panned my hands to the left, toward the gas and brake pedals. The rest of my left hand and then gradually my right had that pins and needles feeling like they'd fallen asleep. I moved a little further to the left, and the sensation of magic began to disappear. I stopped and moved back so that my hands were centered over whatever was emitting the magic.

*Well done, Vânători,* Artemis said. Her rare praise made me flush a little with pride.

I opened my eyes to find that my hands hovered above the corner of a rubber floor mat. Interesting. I reached to lift it.

*Proceed slowly, Vânători. We do not yet know the extent of this magic. It could be a curse that is designed to backfire on the one who discovers its source.*

Super. I took a breath, turning my body a little to mitigate how much of me would be hit if the thing exploded, then took the edge of the mat between my thumb and forefinger like a smelly sock. Though I was no longer actively feeling for it, the hand holding the mat tingled with magic. Slowly, I lifted the durable rubber mat—

—only to reveal some crushed greenery.

My confusion and disappointment that I obviously hadn't found anything clashed with the sharp inhalation from Artemis.

*What is it?* I asked.

*Strong magic, indeed, Vânători. These are four-leaf clovers.*

I sat with that for a moment. Nope. Still confused.

"I thought four-leaf clovers were supposed to bring *good* luck?"

My question brought Preston over. He peered at me at the clovers. "Um, I thought so, too."

"Did you put those there?" I asked him.

"No, of course not. I know I've been having a streak of

bad luck, but I'm not *that* superstitious. Plus, I've never found a four-leaf clover...wait." He stopped and gave me a puzzled look. "Actually, that's not true as of this last week. I found several in the garden boxes out back."

I wisely held my tongue against asking why he hadn't mentioned that oddity earlier. Instead, I turned my focus inward. *Do you know what the four-leaf clovers mean or what they do, Artemis?*

*I think it is quite obvious by now, Vânători. One clover brings you luck, but more than that causes the opposite.*

"Apparently, having more than one four-leaf clover can cause bad luck," I explained.

*But the clovers must be close by in order to work. Or a concentrated amount could cause luck to someone nearby.*

"How many four-leaf clovers have you found in your garden boxes?"

"I stopped counting at fifteen."

*If he continues to spend time around them, he will eventually be struck down by bad luck.*

I relayed this to Preston, who looked like he wasn't sure he quite believed me.

"What am I supposed to do with them all? Can I just pull them up?"

Artemis gave instructions in my mind that I shared with Preston. "I'll come out to your house with Ramble and burn them. Just pulling them up won't stop the bad luck from affecting you. You *can* burn them with regular fire, but Ramble's fire can counter any lingering magical effects."

That was news to me, and I stored that little nugget of information away for later.

"And these?" Preston lifted a brow at the clovers in his rental.

*Take one in your hand, Vânători.*

This earned me another zap that packed a little more

punch but was still just shy of being outright painful. "I'll take care of them," I told Preston, though I had no idea how I was going to do that.

*Now find your focus again...*

I closed my eyes, took a deep breath, blew it out and tried to (mostly) clear my mind. This had been a lot easier to do when Preston wasn't standing so close, analyzing my every move in his lawyerly fashion.

*Focus, Vânători...good. Now call up a very small amount of energy, but keep it focused on your hand.*

Just as I had done in our morning sessions, I pulled a little ball of energy from my core and sent it through my body and out to my hand. I heard a small, surprised inhale from Preston that wasn't quite a gasp and opened my eyes to see my fist glowing. It was too faint even in the waning daylight for a passerby to see it, and since I was mostly shielded by Preston and the car, I wasn't too worried about our little magic show getting noticed.

*Stay focused*, Artemis chided. *Now imagine the energy growing hotter.*

*Um...*

*It will not burn you, Vânători. This energy comes from within you. It will not burn the one from whom it came.*

Keeping my eyes open, I imagined the little ball of light getting hotter and hotter until the glow had grown to be a lot more obvious. There was a weird feeling of resistance from within my fist as the clover fought against incineration. Then I felt it crumble against the energy in my fist with a faint, parting zap.

When I opened my fist, all that was left were ashes.

*Good. Now do the other more quickly this time.*

Preston watched in fascination as I repeated the process with the second clover. I didn't meet Artemis's challenge to be faster, but I didn't need to be coached through the process this time, so that was a win.

"You really are...a little more than human."

I turned to the lawyer and tried for a reassuring smile. I was pretty sure he'd been about to say "not human" but had thought better of it and changed his phrasing at the last second.

"I really am."

Then the lawyer persona was back. "So, I'm having bad luck because someone is leaving multiple four-leaf clovers around me—I don't mean to stereotype anyone in the supernatural community, but does that mean I'm being targeted by a leprechaun? And if so, why?"

I was glad he was taking this in stride. I guess once you learn about hellhounds, gnomes, and gremlins, believing in leprechauns wasn't too much of a leap.

*It is unlikely to be a leprechaun, Vânători. However, the alternative is a matter we shall need to delve into.*

"That's something I'll have to look into more," I told Preston, "But maybe keep an eye out for clovers in and around your house."

"I have cameras around the exterior, but they've never caught anything or anyone."

"You've met Ramble. Not everyone shows up on camera."

"A valid point."

The tow truck arrived not long after that. I offered Preston a lift back to his house, but he said he'd get a ride with the tow truck driver since they'd be taking the SUV back to the rental center, and he would get a different vehicle. Before I left, we made some quick plans for me to visit his house and see if I could help him determine the source of his bad luck.

I got in my sad little loaner car and fished out my phone.

While I'd been talking with Preston, I'd gotten a text from Louis, my blood-donating vampire.

Did Preston's advice also apply to being around people who were *already* dead?

Louis's text read: Do you need a refill, Vânători?

Preston's bad luck problem took a backseat as a surge of need sliced through me. My heartbeat picked up. Louis meant a refill of his own blood so that I could keep the Artemis necklace working. Not only did vampire blood power up the necklace and my abilities as a Vânători, it also allowed Artemis to protect me from Morvalden, the uber-vampire, so he couldn't sneak into my dreams. He made for a truly terrifying Freddy Kruger. Mostly because he could reach into my dreams and pull me into wherever he physically was. Not cool.

It might seem nice that Louis was offering his blood, but the reality was that I'd traded one addiction (alcohol) for another (vampire blood). In return for his blood, Louis got to drink my blood.

*You should meet with the vampire soon.* Artemis's tone was neutral. She wasn't a fan of the vampire since he'd helped me break free of her the one time I'd let the goddess take total control of my body (big mistake on my part). But she knew she needed him and his blood in order to stay connected to me and therefore have access to anything outside the confines of the necklace.

We would need a refill soon since I'd used up some energy by burning the clovers. I reread Louis's text and felt my face flush hot with a need that even the Maine cold couldn't quench. The problem with drinking Louis's blood directly from his veins was that my body wanted a lot more than just his blood.

Have I mentioned that my life is kind of fucked up?

I closed my eyes and took some deep breaths while

thinking of anything else besides Louis. When I'd gotten my blood pressure under control, I texted back: I can't today. Watching a gremlin.

Before I could put my car in reverse, my phone chimed again.

Louis: The gremlin from the church?

I paused.

Me: Yes. Why?

Louis: Why are you watching him? Where's Father Patrick?

My mouth opened involuntarily in confusion. Louis made it sound like Father Patrick should be watching the gremlin. I ignored Louis's question in case he stopped giving me info when he learned Father Patrick had been murdered.

Me: How long has the gremlin been in the church?

It took a few minutes for him to text me back. Maybe he was waiting for me to tell him what happened to the priest. Just when I thought I was about to get radio silence, he texted again.

Louis: I'm unsure. At least a year. Possibly longer.

"A *year*?" I said out loud to myself. "The gremlin lived there for a whole *year*? So why did Father Patrick suddenly want him out of the church so badly? He called him *vermin*." I paused to think about it, then decided to ask one more question.

Me: Did Father Patrick know about the gremlin?

Louis: Of course.

There was a pause while I tried to wrap my mind around the implications of that.

Louis texted again while I chewed over his information.

Louis: Father Patrick is his caretaker.

If the priest knowingly lived with the gremlin for a year and, as Louis said, was acting as his caretaker, why did he suddenly start calling him vermin and demand he be killed or removed from the church? Had the gremlin gone too far in damaging something?

I thought about the church and how it had looked during my short time there. As far as I could tell, nothing had been ripped apart or shredded. So why suddenly trap the gremlin in the belfry and call the sheriff to get rid of him?

Part of me wanted to go meet with Louis to ask him more about why a priest was taking care of a gremlin but another part of me wanted to turn right around and march back into the Sheriff's Department to tell him something was up with this case.

Neither of those seemed like the best option. For starters, as a suspect in the case, any information I gave the sheriff would be scrutinized and possibly not believed at all.

Me: I'm sorry, Louis, but Father Patrick was found dead in his church this morning. He called the sheriff to remove the gremlin. The sheriff asked me to handle it. Then Father Patrick was found not long after I left.

I felt like a total dick for texting this to him instead of just telling him in person. The problem was that I knew myself and my limits. It had been a long, trying day, and I was tired, which meant I was more liable to jump his bones and take way more blood than I needed from him if I saw him in person.

I'd almost killed him the first time I drank his blood. I didn't want that to happen again.

Louis: Please come over and tell me what happened.

Me: I have to keep the gremlin from tearing apart the cabin.

And then I caved.

Me: But if you want to come to the cabin later, I'll explain everything I know.

I waited a few moments for a response. When none came,

I finally left the parking lot and pointed the car toward the cabin.

Hopefully there would still be a cabin left when I got back.

# Chapter Six

Artemis distracted me from my bloodlust on our drive home by speculating about who might be trying to curse Preston with bad luck.

"It seems like whoever is doing this would need to grow or have access to a ton of four-leaf clovers, right? So, who might fit that description?"

*While it could be a leprechaun, it's unlikely they would travel so far from Europe, which is their place of origin. Similar to how a gnome's magic is tied to their land, a leprechaun's magic is directly connected to their gold.*

"Wait, they actually have a pot of gold like in the fairytales?"

*Are you surprised that a fairytale is based on reality?*

"Maybe a little surprised. I mean, stories of vampires and werewolves only had hints of truth to them, so I kind of just assumed most other stories were the same. I'm guessing that they aren't like the stereotypical leprechauns, though, right?"

*What is your idea of a stereotypical leprechaun?*

"I dunno. Small men in green clothes with red hair who are always chipper?"

She didn't laugh, but I felt her amusement all the same. *That is not far off. But I am skeptical that Preston has made enemies with a leprechaun. It's far more likely that someone is illegally growing four-leaf clovers.*

I made a face. "That's not a thing, right? I mean, it's not illegal by modern human laws, at least not to my knowledge. And that seems kind of silly, don't you think? To make growing four-leaf clovers illegal?"

*It was made illegal by the Laws of the Accords, and Denisa Vânători, your ancestor, didn't think it was silly. She was the one who signed off on it.*

There was a beat of silence while I let that sink in. "My ancestors made laws? You've never mentioned this before."

*It has never come up.*

"Oh ho, look at the ancient goddess using a modern turn of phrase." I could tell she was pleased with herself, but I let the moment pass in favor of digging more into this new revelation. "Okay, so what are the accords laws things?"

*The Laws of the Accords are an agreed upon set of laws by...the supernatural community. Your great, great, great grandmother, Denisa Vânători, realized that there would be less bloodshed among those in the supernatural community if she worked with those in the community to create laws that would govern everyone's behavior. She spoke with numerous groups—vampires, werewolves, witches, and others—and asked them all to contribute suggestions on what would be important to their people. Then a meeting was held—The Accords —which was attended by a representative from each group. During the Accords, a final set of laws was decided upon, and those laws have helped maintain peace between groups and humans for the last one hundred years.*

It was a lot to take in. "How many laws are there?"

*Originally, there were 288 laws created during the first Accords. When Gawynna was killed and I was locked away in the necklace, the Laws of the Accords encompassed over 400 statutes, comple-mented by supplementary addendums and sub-laws.*

"Am I...am I supposed to memorize all of them? Even the sub-laws?"

*No. I know them all. I was there when they were created, after all, as a Vânâtori must be present for new laws to be established.*

"Well, that's a relief," I mumbled to myself. Then the implications of what she'd said sank in. "Wait, so that means that no new laws have been made in over a hundred years?"

*Unless the rules for establishing laws have changed, that is correct. If we were not otherwise occupied with your training, we would coordinate an official Accords meeting. However, I do not think it wise at your current skill level to expose you to the powerful individuals who would attend such a meeting. Waiting another year or two will allow us time to improve your skills enough to defend yourself.*

My initial response was a desire to point out that I'd managed just fine with the killer deputy who could turn into a giant monster, but I choked back the words and my pride. I had no desire to coordinate a boring law-making conference with people from the supernatural community who probably wanted nothing more than to see me dead.

"Good point. I'm on board with waiting." Then I quickly changed the subject so she couldn't lock me into promising a specific date or something. "So, what's the four-leaf clover law that the leprechauns wanted on the books?"

*On the books...?*

"Which law did the leprechauns want included in the Laws of the Accords?" I clarified.

*The leprechauns did not request much, save the right to be the only creatures allowed to create four-leaf clovers. It is one of their main weapons. It also serves as one of their only means of livelihood outside of preying on humans.*

I had so many questions, but I settled on the one that was

the most important right now. "Okay, but you're saying they 'create' clovers instead of growing them, right?"

*Yes and no. True four-leaf clovers must be grown much as any other plant. They start out as three-leaf clovers, but when they are imbued with magic at just the right moment, they become lucky four-leaf clovers.*

"I see," I said as I carefully turned onto our road. "But you've said you don't think it was leprechauns that are giving Preston bad luck, which suggests that someone else can create true four-leaf clovers. So, was there anyone who was against the leprechauns cornering the market on clovers?"

There was a long moment of silence until I realized I'd once again used a phrase that Artemis simply didn't know. I tried again.

"Was anyone opposed to the leprechauns' request to be the only ones allowed to create four-leaf clovers?"

*Let me think...* She trailed off, and I gave her a moment. I couldn't imagine trying to remember back hundreds of years like that. *Yes. As I recall, there were a few witches who disagreed with having their powers curtailed, but Gawynna rightly reminded them that they had many other means to create good luck charms without four-leaf clovers.*

"Huh, okay. So, witches might be creating lucky clovers —"

*And of course,* she continued, cutting me off. *The gnome delegation heavily opposed the law.*

"Oh? Why was that?"

*As you know from your interactions, a gnome's entire existence is tied to the earth. Growing plants is sacred to them. They felt that such a law would infringe on their right to exist.*

"I see."

My hands tightened on the wheel. Was Hyssop responsible for Preston's bad luck? I couldn't see the gnome exacting his revenge like this, but did I really know him that well?

"How did the law get passed? Did Gawynna force it through even though the gnomes were against it?"

*Of course not. Gawynna suggested that the law would not stop the gnomes from growing clovers. It would simply make it illegal to transform the clovers into true four-leaf clovers.*

"Clever."

*Indeed.* Pride thrummed in Artemis's voice.

My mind was still stuck on the possibility that Hyssop might be behind Preston's run of bad luck. "So what's the punishment for growing four-leaf clovers illegally?"

*The same punishment one receives for breaking any of the Laws of the Accords, Vânători: Death.*

I winced. "That seems a bit harsh, don't you think?"

I felt Artemis's mental shrug. *It is the best option as a deterrent. Human prisons won't work on creatures who can easily break out. Or worse, who can turn a prison into their own personal feeding ground.*

That was a terrible thought. I shivered and felt the frigid Maine winter press in around me as I finally pulled into the driveway. The darkness of the approaching night sharpened a sense of foreboding that twisted in my gut as I looked at the cabin.

"Nothing's on fire, so that's something," I murmured to Artemis, happily changing the subject. I really hoped the culprit giving Preston bad luck wasn't Hyssop. I didn't think I had it in me to mete out that kind of "justice."

*The gremlin and hellhound are fine. We should have gone to meet with the vampire. You'll need his blood soon as our bond is slowly fading again.*

"It's better if he comes here where we won't be alone. Maybe I'll be less likely to make an ass of myself by throwing myself at him."

Artemis let out a grunt of disbelief.

"What? I said *less* of an ass."

I got out of the car and stood in the stillness of a Maine winter just about to really set in. The sky was just beginning to be edged by the night. Was it just me or did it get dark fast up here?

A sense of foreboding suddenly made my stomach drop.

It was a little too quiet for a cabin that currently housed a hellhound and a gremlin. Worry spiked through me. Had Pamola decided to drop in for another visit? Or maybe whatever had killed Father Patrick had followed us home from the church earlier?

Ramble was the only real friend I had. I knew he would have my back, no matter what. I shouldn't have left him alone with the gremlin.

I stomped up the porch stairs, not caring if whoever was inside heard me. No sense in trying to be stealthy now. If they hadn't heard the car pull in, surely they'd have noticed the sound of me slamming the car door.

I paused outside the cabin door for a second to listen. Still nothing.

With no weapons on hand, I decided the next best thing was to take up the longest piece of firewood on the porch. Someone or something from the woods was still leaving piles of the firewood there every day. Even when I was home. I hadn't gotten any bills for it yet, but it would probably come due at some point.

I'd left the door slightly ajar earlier so that Ramble could let himself out. It was closed now but still unlocked when I tried the handle.

*Be ready, Vânători,* Artemis whispered in my mind.

Taking a quiet breath, I got a better grip on the piece of wood and raised it in my right hand before yanking the door open.

Nothing. The house was still completely quiet.

If I hadn't known better, I might have thought that

maybe Ramble was sleeping, but the hellhound's snoring was as loud as an avalanche most nights. Even when he napped lightly, he snored.

From the foyer, it was a straight shot into the kitchen, which stood dark and empty. Unfortunately, I couldn't see into the living room or the bedroom from here. I'd have to go further into the cabin with only my stick of firewood as protection.

*You must start carrying a real weapon. No self-respecting Vânători would leave her home without at least a sword.*

*We've talked about this. First, I don't own a sword. And second, if I did, I couldn't go traipsing around town with it.*

I left the front door wide open behind me in case we needed to make a quick escape. It would let the cold in, but so what? I'd rather live and deal with heating the house back up than getting grabbed because I had to take an extra three seconds to stop and open the door.

The woodstove creaked with heat in the living room as I slowly made my way down the short hallway. A quick glance to my left told me that my bedroom was dark, but the door was open. In order to investigate the living room, I'd have to put my back to the open bedroom doorway. Not cool. Leaving the light on in the living room could be a ploy just to lure me in that direction to attack me from behind.

But turning to investigate the bedroom meant I'd have to put my back to the open living room entryway.

Who designed this cabin, damnit?

Making a quick decision before Artemis could yell at me, I swiftly moved to the living room entryway—and slammed to a halt.

Ramble and the gremlin were backed into the corner near the wood stove. The hellhound's body curled protectively around the gremlin. His hackles were up, and his lip was raised in a silent growl at someone on the other side of the room.

Before I could look to see who or what he was growling at, a familiar voice dripping with icy amusement broke the silence.

"I'm so glad you could join us, Vânători."

Artemis gasped in my mind as ice slipped down my spine despite the heat.

I slowly turned to find none other than the second most powerful vampire I'd ever met lounging on my ratty second-hand love seat.

It took me a moment to collect my wits. The vampire seemed to enjoy my surprise, fear, and finally resolve that surely showed on my face.

"Hello, Constancia."

I fought to keep my voice even. After the idea of Morvalden finding me, this was my second biggest fear. Constancia, Morvalden's wife or whatever, was batshit crazy. Suddenly, the feelings of paranoia I'd been having all day made sense.

The haughty vampire was impeccably dressed in a white and black satin dress with matching white satin gloves. Her elegance and contempt for her surroundings were starkly apparent in her expression. Her steel-gray hair, pulled back with a jeweled comb, accentuated her pale, almost lumines-cent skin. She was the embodiment of deadly grace, dressed for a ball rather than a confrontation in my humble cabin.

If I hadn't been scared out of my wits, I would have felt vaguely offended at her disdain. I loved my ratty loveseat and my sparsely furnished cabin. As much as I wanted to say something witty, I also didn't want to provoke an attack. Especially since I wasn't the only one in danger here.

"It appears my surprise visit has quite upset your mongrel, Vânători. And his little rat friend, too." She glanced in

Ramble's direction, then back to me with a knowing smile. Though she couldn't see him, she would be able to hear him and see the gremlin.

*Kill her, Vânători. Rip out her throat before she does the same to you.* Artemis's voice held such vitriol that I worried she might try to take me over again if I didn't comply.

*We're not going to make any rash moves here, Artemis,* I reasoned while focusing all my attention on the vampire in the room. *You know I'm not ready for that kind of fight.*

*Of course you are! Let me take over, and I'll take care of her myself!*

*How? Are you going to impale her with this blunt piece of firewood?* I internally asked. She didn't respond. *I'm open to suggestions on how to get through this, but let's be real here: I'm not ready to take her on.*

I refocused on Constancia, who wasn't the slightest perturbed that I'd taken a few extra seconds to respond.

Swallowing my fear, I went for a more nonchalant tone. When facing a much stronger, scarier opponent, bluff. "My guess is that he didn't want to paint the walls with your blood." I forced a slight shrug. "After all, we just cleaned up after beating back a mountain god."

She let out a tittering laugh that would have been better suited to a fancy dinner party.

"No one beats Pamola, Vânători. You either struck a bargain with him or he let you think you beat him." She paused, then looked at me as if for the first time. "But good for you thinking otherwise. You've really come into your own, you know. I'm proud of you and *so* glad I could help make this happen."

I tried not to cringe as Artemis pitched a hissy fit in my mind. The thing was, Constancia was right.

She *had* been the one to steal the necklace from Morvalden and, through various channels, delivered it to me not once, but *twice*. And the second time, she'd literally been the one to give it to me *and* forced me to drink her blood to heal from what were probably fatal wounds.

But Constancia hadn't done it out of some noble act to save me or some convoluted scheme to usurp Morvalden. No. She'd done it because she felt Morvalden was *bored,* and she was bored with his boredom. So she'd brought back the descendant of his arch nemesis to insert a little excitement back into his life.

"Do you know," she said with delight when I didn't respond, "things have been ever so much more interesting at home now that a Vânători is back in the world."

"I'm so glad for you," I deadpanned while ignoring the raging storm in my mind that was Artemis having a meltdown.

"*He* is his bright-eyed and bushy-tailed self again." She paused and cocked her head to the side like a dog hearing a strange sound. "That is the saying, yes?"

That she wasn't saying Morvalden's name told me a lot. The uber vampire could tell when someone was talking about him if they used his name. That meant Constancia was keeping my location a secret from him.

"That's the saying," I said and darted a glance over at Ramble in the corner. He'd lowered his lip and was listening to our conversation, but I could tell that he was still ready to pounce if given the chance.

I'd seen him tear other vampires apart, but I wasn't so sure he could win against Constancia. She wasn't the consort or wife or whatever to the most powerful vampire for nothing. I could always whisk Ramble away using his own magic by imagining him somewhere else, but I didn't think he'd appreciate me doing that. Especially if it meant leaving the gremlin here.

If things got dicey, I'd send him away to safety, whether he liked it or not. Maybe I could send him to Louis's—

Shit. Louis. He hadn't said what time he would come over to discuss Father Patrick's death. Did Constancia know Louis lived here in Ricketts? Surely if she'd been able to find me, then she'd have no trouble tracking him. The thing was, I'd been getting the feeling lately that he was hiding from other vampires. I didn't want to be the reason they found him if he really was in hiding.

Plus, having him and Constancia in the same room might be bad. Really, really bad.

I cut straight to the chase. Maybe I could get her out of here before Louis showed up. Also, there was only so long that I could hold this tense standoff. Especially when Constancia was treating it as more of a simple conversation between old frenemies.

"What are you doing here, Constancia? What do you want?"

"Kids these days," she sighed dramatically. "Always getting right down to business and ignoring formalities." She stood so quickly it was a blur. I let out a little gasp and took an involuntary step back.

A feral look flitted over her features, and her nostrils flared as she took in my fear. Then, just as quickly, she was once again smiling like the belle of the ball.

"If you must know, Vânători, I came to see if you're ready to tussle with Him. I've been keeping your location secret for these past few months—"

She saw the obvious surprise on my face and interrupted herself.

"—Of course I knew you were here, dear girl. What do you take me for? I *am* the first tracker, after all." She said the last while inspecting her pristine nails.

*Is that true?* I asked Artemis. I'd run into one other tracker vampire before. Her name had been Fitha, and Ramble had quickly taken care of her. I didn't think Constancia would be so easily killed.

*Yes.* It sounded like Artemis was gritting her teeth. *She is the first and best tracker. She has always been especially gifted at locating the Vânători, no matter how well they hid.*

I tucked that little nugget of information away for later and stayed quiet, waiting for Constancia to continue her bad-guy monologue. She'd get to the point eventually.

When I didn't comment on her claim of being the first tracker, annoyance wrinkled her perfect features, and she stopped inspecting her nails. "Where was I? Oh yes. I've been keeping you safe from Him all these months, Vânători. I wanted to give you time to come into your power and be worth the fight."

She sized me up again, but this time, with her now standing only a few feet away, it felt a lot more threatening.

*Vânători! What are you doing?! Let me take over so that we can finally kill this vampire filth once and for all!*

*Have you ever fought her before with the other Vânători?*

*Yes!*

*And clearly you lost!* I pointed out. *Those were pure Vânători who didn't even need vampire blood and I'm not even half the fighter they were! We are not fighting her if we can help it!*

When I didn't say anything, Constancia quirked an eyebrow. "Well?"

"Well, what?"

"Have you come into your powers and learned to be a real Vânători?"

"Seriously? If I say no, will you go away and leave me alone for another few months?"

Her brows lifted in surprise and her mouth tipped up ever so slightly, as if she was amused at my bravado. Apparently, she wasn't used to people talking back to her. Then anger flashed in her eyes.

Before I knew what was happening, Constancia grabbed me by the throat and carried us closer to the wood stove. I had zero time to fight her off as she pushed my face toward the scalding stove. The heat from it was immediately unbearable. In the space of a second, discomfort turned into real burning as she tried to push my face against it. Only then did I remember to draw upon the necklace for strength.

Luckily, I had just enough charge left in me to use it. I pushed back enough to keep her from pressing my flesh against the hot cast iron, but I couldn't seem to get more than an inch away from it. It kept her from immediately melting my face off, but I was still too close to the heat. I could smell my eyebrows starting to singe. The heat radiating from the stove became unbearable. It took all my concentration and strength just to keep her from pushing my face any closer to the wood stove, and I had nothing left over to figure out how to escape from the situation. Let alone fight back.

*Let me take over, Vânători! Or she will end us both!*

*We played that game before, and it didn't go so well for me. I'd rather die horribly than be trapped for the rest of my life with no control over my body.*

Artemis fell silent after that. I could still feel her power, but it looked like I'd need to figure out my own plan, or I really would die like this.

Slowly, so damn slowly, I put my weight and Artemis's supernatural strength into pushing myself away from the stove. When I had room to turn my face and look at Constancia, I almost lost my concentration.

She was grinning maniacally, fangs out, as if this was the best time she'd ever had. When I gained another inch of space between my face and the stove, Constancia let out a whoop and then suddenly she let me go and practically flew across the room.

The sudden lack of counterforce completely threw me off.

Without time to pull back, I fell hard to my knees with a grunt.

Constancia clapped her hands in glee like an excited schoolgirl which went entirely against her very sophisticated, adult outfit. It made me think of a sadistic Mary Poppins. Maybe dressing up helped her maintain playing at being human or something.

"You're almost there, Vânători!" She held up a finger. "But you're not quite ready yet. Perhaps another month or two, yes?" Her hand went to her chin as she looked me over again, then gave a final nod. "Yes. I think that will do it. Until then, Vânători." She gave another nod and turned to leave.

I rubbed my throat where she'd grabbed me and managed to choke out, "I don't understand why you want me to win against...him." I hated feeling too afraid to say Morvalden's name, but if his own wife feared it might summon him, then I should be cautious, right?

She twisted to look back and down at me. "Oh, dear girl. I don't expect you to *win*," she tsked and shook her head, "I just want you to put up a decent fight. Otherwise, what's the point of all this?"

And then she freaking blurred into motion I could barely track and zipped out of the cabin.

I was so screwed.

# Chapter Seven

Ramble was at my side the moment Constancia was gone. I was pleasantly surprised when the gremlin followed him and tugged on my shirt with his tiny, clawed paw.

"I'm okay," I tried to reassure them. But was I?

I mean, I would recover from the bruised knees and what felt like a slightly singed face, but for what? If Constancia was just going to come back here with Morvalden in a few months, then what was the point of bothering to build any kind of life? I might as well go back to using fake credit cards and hopping from town to town like Jax, my hunter mentor. Doing so might even buy me a little more time than if I stayed in Ricketts. Here, I was just a sitting target.

*You should have allowed me to take over, Vânători,* Artemis seethed. *We could have exterminated Constancia once and for all! Instead, you let a ridiculous grudge ruin our only chance.*

It suddenly struck me that the people trying to kill me and the people who were supposed to be my allies both tended to call me by my last name only. I wasn't sure what that meant, but it didn't give me a good feeling.

"What?" I pointed at the necklace so Ramble would know I was talking to the dumbass goddess inside. "You already all but admitted that we can't beat her, Artemis! If you couldn't do it with a full-blooded Vânători, you won't be able to kill her using me!"

*If you would just allow me take over—*

"No. You will never again have total control over me. *Ever.* Got it?" I was so angry that my voice shook, but I didn't care. "You blew that chance, and I will never, *ever* trust you like that again."

*Then you will die when Morvalden's huntress returns.*

"His huntress? Whatever, then I guess I'll just die, then."

*This is foolishness, Vânători. Why would you—*

"I don't have to listen to this." I pulled the necklace over my head and stuck it in my pocket. The moment my skin lost contact with it, Artemis disappeared from my mind.

Shit. I'd done it again. I knew it was a mistake, but I needed some space from Artemis.

Ramble and the gremlin stared at me, clearly waiting for what I'd do next. The problem was, I didn't know what that should be.

"What do you think, Ramble? Should we run again? Maybe step Between and see where it takes us? It might buy us more time than staying here."

It suddenly hit me that Constancia never said anything about coming back after Ramble. Just me.

"You know," I looked away and cleared my throat, fighting down a swell of emotion. I was afraid of how Ramble might take this but also needed to ensure he knew he had options. "You know you don't have to stay here, right? Constancia didn't seem to care too much about coming after you. If you leave, you might live a little longer than if you stay here with me."

His head booped my shoulder to get my attention. When

I looked at him, he gave a gruff chuff then shoved his head into me. His message was clear: He was staying with me no matter what.

Tears pricked my eyes. I dashed them away while Ramble pretended not to notice.

"Okay, then." I sniffled. "What do you think? Should we stay?" I held up my left hand. "Or should we make a run for it?" I held up my right hand.

He stared at my hands, clearly thinking through the decision.

"On the one hand," I moved my right hand in the air, "we could make a run for it, steal a car that has actual heat, do the fake credit card thing again, and find warmer places to explore before Constancia finds us."

"On the other hand," I waved my left hand, "we have a place to stay and a sort of job that gives me an opportunity to learn how to fight with Artemis's powers without giving her control of my body..."

I wavered. Constancia had said I had a few more months. That couldn't possibly be enough time to learn how to fight and survive Morvalden.

"Not to mention," said Louis, making us all jump, "you also have a vampire willing to exchange blood with you."

As one, Ramble, the gremlin, and I all spun to look at Louis standing in the living room entryway.

He sniffed the air and froze, eyes slightly widening. "Why does it smell of Constancia?"

"You just missed her," I said. At the same time, the gremlin chittered something and streaked over to climb the vampire's pant leg like a cat. The moment he was high enough, he threw his arms around Louis's neck.

Okay. I guess they did know each other.

Louis patted the gremlin gently on the back. "I'm sorry about Father Patrick," he murmured. "I know he was your friend and like a father to you." He continued to pat and stroke the gremlin's back while it buried its face against his neck, then the vampire turned his attention back to me.

Slowly, I started the process of standing. My knees hurt worse than I thought they would. Ramble pushed his head under my hand, then walked forward a step so I could lean on his broad shoulders to help me stand.

"Is she the reason you're making a pros and cons list about leaving Ricketts?" Louis asked.

"You heard that, huh?" I hobbled over to the loveseat and dropped into it, trying to ignore the light scent of Constancia's perfume wafting up as I sat. It was actually quite lovely and probably cost more than my rent for the cabin would be.

As if to make me feel better, Ramble sniffed the air, then overdramatically sneezed. I gave him an appreciative smile. I guess not everyone liked expensive perfume.

"She didn't kill you. Or drag you back to...him. Why?" His eyes darted around the room as if just now realizing that I was alive and not the recent victim of Morvalden's wife and best tracker. "Did you... did you better her in a fight?"

I laughed—I couldn't help it—and pointed to my face which, judging by how tender the skin was, must have at least been red if not blistered. "Does it look like I beat her?"

"No, but you're still..."

"Breathing?" I helpfully supplied when he trailed off.

He nodded, which was slightly difficult given how the gremlin was directly beneath his chin.

I sat back in the loveseat with a huff. "She's decided to give me a little more time to get better at being a Vânători. Apparently, she wants me to be a worthy opponent for her dear hubby."

The vampire grimaced, which was surprising since Louis didn't usually make a lot of facial expressions. I typically thought of him as Mr. Neutral-Face. When I wasn't lusting after the blood that ran through his veins, that was. Even the thought sent a little spike of interest through me that I had to quickly squash. As ick as it sounded, Louis would be able to tell if I became aroused and that would only set *him* off and then we'd probably wind up doing something we'd both regret.

"I see," he finally said.

"Yup."

There was a moment of quiet as Louis looked around the room for somewhere to sit. I considered giving up my seat—he was a guest, after all—but then I decided my knees were too sore to bother getting up.

In the end, Louis sat cross-legged on the floor near the woodstove. The gremlin still clung to him. Ramble, after a quick glance at his charge to make sure he was okay, gave me a look. I scooted over, making room for the hellhound to take up two-thirds of the loveseat. Hopefully, it would end up smelling more like him than Constancia.

Louis broke the silence. "Can you tell me about what happened to Father Patrick?" His voice was low, and he didn't look me in the eyes when he asked. He'd truly been close to the priest. Which, given my short, mostly negative experience with the man, seemed odd.

I related what had happened earlier in the day while Louis listened quietly, not looking at me as he slowly stroked the gremlin's back. "And then we got back to the cabin, the sheriff called and told us that Father Patrick had been murdered, and I'm apparently their top suspect."

Louis was quiet for a moment, letting the occasional creak from the woodstove fill the room before saying with a surprising note of confusion, "It doesn't make any *sense*. Griffin's been with Father Patrick for years. Why would he suddenly try to get rid of him? And why call the sheriff to do it? Surely he knew that I would take Griffin in if he needed a new home."

"I'm not sure. He called him 'vermin', and the gremlin—"

"Griffin."

"Griffin," I quickly amended, "didn't act like they had any sort of relationship."

Gently, he pulled Griffin away from his chest so he could look the gremlin in the eyes. "Do you know what happened to him?"

"Can you understand him?" I asked.

"I understand him about as well as you understand your hellhound."

Which meant we might be in for a lot of pantomiming. At least Griffin couldn't breathe fire if he got annoyed.

Louis tried to set Griffin down, but the gremlin clung to him, his little claws hooked into the vampire's clothing. "It's okay, Griffin. You're safe here. Vianne is a friend. She won't hurt you."

Griffin glanced at me, then back to Louis before chittering something that clearly was not a positive review of my character. I mean, I *had* chased him around the church with Father Patrick. I couldn't blame the little guy.

Ramble let out a little rumble as if to back the vampire's promise of protection, and the gremlin looked over at the hellhound a little sheepishly.

"Do you know why Father Patrick was cross with you?" Louis asked in his occasionally old-fashioned way. It was things like that which reminded me he was a vampire.

And his fangs.

And his powerful blood.

*Stay focused*, I chastised myself.

Griffin hid his face against Louis's chest, clearly not wanting to relive whatever had happened. Or maybe he didn't want to reveal if he'd done something bad enough that it had warranted Father Patrick calling the sheriff to get rid of him.

Louis rubbed Griffin's back. "I'm sorry that happened, and that you lost Father Patrick. We'll find out who did this, okay?"

"Uh, actually," I said and swallowed as I realized I was about to be a giant dick, "I'm not allowed to officially investigate his death by order of the sheriff."

Louis gave me a more neutral look than usual. "Then officially investigate it for me."

I hesitated, realizing I hadn't communicated very well that I wasn't supposed to go near this *at all* until I could clear my name. In my moment of hesitation, Louis's eyes flashed in anger.

"I can pay you, Vânători."

"It's not the money," I quickly explained. "I'm not supposed to investigate because I'm technically a suspect seeing as how I was the last one to see Father Patrick alive."

Griffin whipped his head around and chittered at me.

"Okay, one of the last two people to see Father Patrick alive," I told Griffin before meeting Louis's eyes again. "The sheriff specifically told me not to poke around at this."

I thought laying things out would help him understand why I couldn't help, but instead Louis radiated cold anger.

"Since when does a Vânători need permission from human law enforcement to do her job?"

I opened my mouth to protest, but Louis cut me off.

"You have an obligation as the Vânători to determine what non-human creature killed Father Patrick and to bring it to heel if need be." He stood and reached into his pocket to draw out a glass vial of thick red liquid. Two strides closed the distance between us. Still cradling Griffin with one hand, he held out the vial to me with the other. "I'm sure you're running low by now. Please use this to find out who killed my friend." Underneath the anger, I saw a flicker of grief.

At the sight of the blood, I had to throttle a sudden surge of need. I wanted to snatch it out of his hand, yank off the stopper, and down it right there. Instead, I forced myself to stay calm as I took the vial.

He stepped back, clearly wanting to put some distance between us again.

"And if you do need monetary incentive—"

"You don't need to pay me, Louis." I quickly said again, catching and holding his eyes. "I'll do what I can to figure out who killed your friend, but I have to make sure I don't end up in jail. I would be easy pickings there."

Amusement flashed across his features then was gone just as quickly. "You're easy pickings here. Was Constancia not just in this very room?"

I sighed. "Yes, but she apparently doesn't want to tell him where I am until I grow into my powers or whatever."

"You can't hide from him forever. Sooner or later, he'll find you."

"I'd rather it be later than sooner if I can help it." I shook my head. "I'll let you know what I find out." I looked at Griffin. "What about him?"

Louis looked down at the gremlin. "Do you want to come and stay with me?"

Griffin nodded and snuggled his head into Louis's chest.

Louis looked pointedly at the vial still in my hand. "Let me know if you need more than that for this job."

My voice was raspy as I asked, "Don't you need some of mine in exchange?"

"Not right now." He let a fang peek out behind a tiny half-smile, his anger from before now gone. "I'll be back to collect soon, though."

My heart beat faster. Blood sang in my veins at the

promise of his fangs sinking into my neck. His mouth would latch onto my skin, then he'd suck, drawing out my blood in what would be ecstasy...

He must have felt my sudden electric need because his normally neutral mouth tipped up into a full, tight smile that put both fangs on display.

If Ramble and Griffin weren't in the room, I might have done a lot to try and convince him to stay. Instead, I nodded, wetting my lips and watching his eyes dilate as I did.

"Okay. Later then." I said in a wobbly voice.

"It's a date."

I'm sorry, what? "Um, okay."

He nodded then left. I heard the door shut behind him on his way out. I'd need to get up at some point to lock it, but at the moment, I was too busy trying to get my lust under control.

Ramble gave me a look and huffed.

"I can't help how my body reacts to him, okay?" I said with some annoyance and a lot of embarrassment.

I levered myself up off the couch and, vial still clutched tightly, gingerly made my way back to the foyer to lock the front door against whatever else was out there tonight. Back in the kitchen, I forced myself to stick the vial in the fridge instead of drinking it. Nothing like a little blood in the kitchen fridge to whet the appetite!

My face still felt tender to the touch, so I ran a clean towel under cold water, rung it out and gently pressed it against my skin. It felt wonderful.

Still holding the towel to my face, I searched the kitchen for something to call dinner and caught a glimpse of the shredded curtains. Ramble ambled into the kitchen behind me.

"It looks like you did a better job gremlin-sitting than I did." I jerked my head at the curtains. "I feel like we got off kind of lucky if that was all the damage he did while he was here."

Ramble looked pointedly away.

"Oh no. What else did he do, Ramble?"

The hellhound crouched down like a normal dog who was in trouble and began to slink out of the room.

"Ramble!" I yelled. "I can still *see* you! What else did he do?"

He turned, tail still tucked and glanced toward the bedroom.

"Nooo," I moaned. "Not the bedroom! I have, like, three nice things in this world, and my bedding is one of them!"

I stomped into the bedroom, Ramble close on my heels, and snapped on the light.

I took a deep breath at the sight of the carnage before me. White feathers and shreds of fabric were strewn everywhere. The comforter, pillow, and sheets were completely shredded. It looked like Griffin had tried to disembowel the bed. I gently lifted the comforter and sheets, holding my breath at what I'd find underneath. It was sheer luck that the mattress seemed to have miraculously survived the gremlin attack.

But nothing else had.

I would not freak out. Everything was fine. It could have been worse, right? I mean, there were no dead bodies at least.

Ramble let out a slight whimper. I opened my eyes to find that he was still hunkered down with guilt.

"Really?" I said, waving at the shredded bedding. "You couldn't have kept him out of the bedroom? Maybe you could have closed the door or something?"

Ramble held up a paw and looked at it, then at me as if to say, "I don't have thumbs."

I blew out a long breath, trying to rid myself of my anger. Everything I owned in this world was here in this cabin, and most of it wasn't even mine. It was borrowed along with the use of the cabin itself. Soon, if I decided to stay, I'd have to pay rent.

But that day wasn't today, and worrying about the future was not something I wanted to waste energy on right now.

"I guess it could have been worse," I said quietly. I retrieved a plastic grocery bag from the kitchen, then cleaned up the mess of feathers. Maybe I could shove the feathers back in the comforter and sew the gashes back together?

I picked up a corner of the comforter and let out another sigh as it literally fell apart in my hands, sending more feathers flying.

Fuck. Was I gonna cry? Over some ripped bedding?

Ramble watched me warily from the doorway.

"Look, I'm not mad at you, but I think I need a few minutes to be alone and deal with this," I told him, not bothering to turn around. "Could you stoke up the fire, please, while I figure out our sleeping situation?"

The sound of retreating claws on the hardwood floor told me I was alone. I started to clean up again and might have shed a few tears in the process. I managed to create a makeshift pillow by stuffing the shredded pillow and some of the feathers into a spare pillowcase I found in the closet. It wasn't a long-term solution, so I'd have to do some shopping tomorrow. It looked like we were gonna be back to ramen for a few meals until I could figure out some other way to bring in some income.

When I'd done what I could in the bedroom, I found Ramble laying on the loveseat with the fire roaring full blast. I sat down in the tiny space he'd left for me.

"I'm sorry. I'm really not mad at you. You're much more important to me than bedding and some curtains. I just got overwhelmed what with Constancia attacking us and then Louis getting mad at me. And I just...I haven't had a lot to call my own in the past few years, and it really upset me at that moment that some of the few things I had were ruined."

Ramble shrugged and nudged me as if to say that it was fine.

That was one good thing about being friends with Ramble. Our conversations weren't terribly long, and we didn't usually stay mad at each other for long because we were pretty much all we had.

"Let's find something for dinner, huh?"

Ramble perked right up at the mention of food, so I knew we were okay.

# Chapter Eight

Ramble and I headed into a larger nearby town the following morning to pick up new bedding and possibly some new curtains. I might have been thumbing my nose at the sheriff for telling me not to leave town. I'd considered checking the secondhand store in Ricketts to see if they had anything, but Rosalyn, the witch who owned the secondhand shop, was also my landlord. It seemed best to avoid telling her I'd had a gremlin guest who shredded the curtains she'd loaned me.

I was also still annoyed with her for putting me in harm's way by not telling me about Pamola. I hadn't really interacted with the witch since we'd come back from Pamola's home in Mount Katahdin. If I ended up staying and officially rented the cabin from her, we'd have to talk eventually. For now, I saw no reason to rush that communication.

After an hour's drive, Ramble and I were both ready to escape the cold car and find somewhere warm. We hit up a discount home goods store and found a cheap duvet and pillow there. I probably would have stayed longer just to window shop, but the burn on my face was drawing a lot of attention. Well, that and Ramble accidentally scared the hell out of a woman when he wasn't paying attention, and she ran into him with her cart.

When she hit him, he let out a surprised, un-hellhound-like yip, and the woman shrieked in response. Seemed like a good time to leave. We quickly made our way to the front of the store while I held in my laughter until we'd finished checking out and were back outside. Ramble rolled his eyes at me and held his nose in the air more like an offended cat than a dog. He sat in the back on the way to our next shopping destination and didn't even ask me to roll the window down. I felt a little guilty for laughing at him, especially since the woman had run into him pretty hard with her cart.

When we stopped, I turned to look at him. "You okay?"

He snorted and wouldn't meet my eyes. I guess the only thing hurt was his pride.

"Alright then. Just be more careful, buddy. I don't want to have to explain that you got taken out by a middle-aged woman with a shopping cart the day after facing down an uber-vampire."

This earned me quite the glare, but I brushed it off with a grin, and we headed into another store for our second round of shopping. Well, mostly window-shopping this time.

Now it was mid-afternoon, and we were sitting outside a fast-food joint eating greasy food and milkshakes. Halfway through our shopping trip, I decided to be a little less frugal with the little money we had left since it was likely I'd be horribly murdered by Morvalden in a few months. I might as well treat myself and Ramble while I could.

"I mean, I'm just saying that if you'd just breathed a little fire at that woman, you would have been justified. Not to mention it would have been hilarious."

Ramble snorted and almost choked on the milkshake he

was lapping up from the cup. I laughed and almost missed the sound of my cell phone ringing.

I didn't recognize the number but answered it anyway just in case the sheriff had given my number out for a non-law enforcement related consult.

"Hello?"

"I can't believe you have the same number, Vânători. Did I not teach you better than that?"

I instantly recognized the gruff, chastising voice that had exactly zero humor in it. Judging by the deep growl that rolled up from the backseat, Ramble recognized it, too.

"Jax?"

"Who the hell else would call you?"

Um. Half the supernatural community of Ricketts maybe? Or the local law enforcement? Since those were both things that would piss off the veteran monster hunter, I ignored his question.

"What do you want, Jax? If I recall correctly, the last time we spoke, you said you couldn't help me and left me stranded in the middle of nowhere."

"Did you make it up to Maine and figure out the necklace with the witch's help?"

That and more, I thought and had to stop myself from reaching in my pocket to touch the necklace. I hadn't worn it since the night before and didn't intend to speak with Artemis until I got back to the cabin. I'd been thinking of today as sort of a day off from the whole Vânători thing, but apparently it didn't just go away.

I kept my voice even as I answered Jax. "Yes. I figured out the necklace..." I almost said more, then decided against it. Though Jax had once saved me from vampires, if he found out I needed vampire blood to power the necklace, he would likely see me as a monster and decide I was on the chopping block alongside all other non-human creatures.

It suddenly struck me as odd that Jax was calling me the day after I'd gotten a visit from Constancia. They'd already worked together once. There was no guarantee that he wasn't still working with her.

"Really?" His tone suggested that he thought I'd still be struggling since I didn't have his help. "I mean, that's really good, Vânâtori. Maybe now we can work together to go after the vampires."

I made a face at the phone though he couldn't see me. "Yeah, I think I'm better off working alone now."

Ramble jerked his head up and glared at me. I made a face back. I wasn't about to tell the monster hunter that I still had my hellhound sidekick. The two hated each other, and Jax had wanted nothing more than to eradicate Ramble. Fortunately for Ramble, Jax couldn't see hellhounds.

"Oh, I see. You're a big bad monster hunter now and don't need anybody's help, is that it?"

"I didn't say that. I said I'd rather work alone. I'm not real keen on putting my trust in someone that kept secrets from me and then left me in the middle of nowhere with no transportation."

Jax let out a grunt of disbelief. "You were fine, Vânâtori. You obviously found your way to where you needed to go in order to figure out the necklace. And you wouldn't have been able to do that if it weren't for me."

I rolled my eyes and poured on a saccharine sweet voice. "Wow. Thank you so much for all your help, Jax. I couldn't have done it without you." I paused then resumed my normal voice. "Is that what you want to hear? Look, you might have pointed me in the right direction, but that's all you did. I'm not hunting with you, Jax. We're not friends like that."

"We don't have to be friends to hunt together. I thought you would have known that by now with the folks you've been working with up there."

"What does that mean?"

"It means," he all but growled, "you need to stay out of the papers and stop being seen with werewolves. It's not good for your reputation."

"Is that why you're really calling? To tell me to stay away from the werewolves? If you saw the news article, you'd know I was never mentioned, and that it was a person responsible for those murders, not werewolves."

"Sure it was."

My temper flared white hot, and I almost hung up on him. Then he broke the silence with, "You need to be more careful, Vânători. You said you don't want to hunt with me, and that's fine, but word is also out among the hunters that the Vânători is back."

"Okay. And...?" I slurped my milkshake, ready for this conversation to be over.

He sighed as if he, once again, had to explain everything to a total idiot. "And it's only a matter of time before another hunter shows up on your doorstep testing to see if you're the real deal."

"Wait, what?" I sat up, milkshake forgotten.

"Most hunters won't believe you're the Vânători until you prove it to them."

I opened my mouth to protest and shut it again. Other hunters were going to challenge me just to see if I was the real Vânători? Didn't I have enough enemies already? The idea that human hunters might not believe me when the actual supernatural community just took my word for it was crazy.

"I guess I'll deal with those kinds of idiots when the time comes," I gritted out. "If that's all, Jax, I have things to do."

"Good luck, then." And just like that, he hung up.

I looked at Ramble. "Did you hear that?" He nodded. "I can't believe other hunters would try and challenge me or whatever just to see if I'm the real deal!" I shook my head. "Absolutely bonkers. Why not just freakin' ask me to show them?"

Ramble gave me a look I couldn't interpret, then went back to finishing his milkshake. Clearly, this news was not that exciting to him.

I started to put my phone away, but it rang again in my hand. Without looking at the screen, I hit the answer button. "Now what, Jax?"

"Uh, hi Vi. I'm not sure who Jax is, but it doesn't sound like he's a friend," the sheriff said.

"Shit. I'm sorry, Sheriff." I thunked my forehead with my palm. "What's up? Everything okay?"

"Well... yes and no. We got the autopsy results back from the coroner."

"That was fast."

"Having a secretary who's related to the coroner in the next town over has its perks."

"Did the autopsy give more clues who might have killed Father Patrick?"

"Not so much the 'who' as the 'when.' Why don't we get a cup of coffee, and I'll share what we know."

"Does that mean I'm officially on the case?" I tried not to let too much hope show.

His voice was muffled as he spoke with someone else, "Oh, just following up on that lead with the parishioner. I'm sure it's nothing, Englewood."

"I guess that's a no," I said. Ramble gave me a pained look.

"Sorry," he said to me, voice full of sincerity, and I honestly believed him. Also, that he wanted to meet with me to talk about what they'd found without involving Englewood meant he trusted me and didn't think I was the killer.

So that was something.

"I've got a few things to wrap up here, but how about meeting me at the Flying Pie later?"

"Later's good." It would take me a little time to drive home, but I didn't want to tell the sheriff I'd gone out of town after he'd specifically told me not to. "I have a meeting with Preston this afternoon," I told him truthfully, "but we could meet in the evening. Maybe around five or six?" At the very least, maybe I could get a meal out of our meeting. I saw Ramble lick his lips, clearly thinking the same thing, though we'd just eaten.

"Sounds good. See you then."

"Well," I said after sucking down the last of my milk-shake, "let's get back home and see if we can solve Preston's bad luck problem."

* * *

The weather was cooperative, and the sky stayed clear of snow clouds on our drive north to Ricketts. That meant I had plenty of time to swing by the cabin and run the new bedding through the wash. While I waited to switch the laundry over, I did a little digging into Father Patrick. It didn't take long. Everything I found seemed pretty normal—some local articles about charitable work he did with the church and information about his recent death. There wasn't much online about where he'd been before being assigned to the small church in Ricketts, though I found mention of his graduation for a master's degree in divinity from Eastern University in Pennsylvania.

The priest had lived a pretty simple life. He'd grown up in rural Pennsylvania and graduated with a bachelor's degree in philosophy before switching to religion and becoming a priest. The parish in Ricketts had been his first and only assignment.

It reminded me of the Witnesses and how their only job was to keep tabs on the supernatural community. Was it possible that the Catholic Church was doing the same thing via Father Patrick? If so, maybe someone in town had decided they weren't a fan of being watched?

I didn't think Louis would appreciate this line of thinking. There was only one other person in town I could think of to ask. I picked up my phone and had to push away feelings of awkwardness before making the call.

"Vi." Donavon purred in my ear over the noisy background of a large crowd. His velvety voice sent a shiver of pleasure through me at the memory of our kiss at this very table. "I wondered when you'd call and beg for my company. Too bad you waited until the one time I'm out of town. One sec."

I rolled my eyes but waited as the background noise grew quieter. I'd been wondering why I hadn't heard anything from him after such a heated kiss. I guess now I knew.

A door closed on the other end of the line, cutting off the background noise.

"To what do I owe the pleasure?"

"Sorry. I didn't realize you were out of town."

"Not a problem. It's our yearly gathering in the mountains. Werewolf stuff."

The non-explanation felt a little like he'd just closed a door in my face. I tried not to let it bother me since it wasn't like we were dating or something. Still, that kiss...

Keep it together, girl.

I kept my tone strictly professional. "I have a work-related question—" Then I hesitated as I realized I was probably about to break some terrible news to him.

But apparently word traveled fast.

"Is this about Father Patrick?"

"Yeah. I guess you've heard, huh?"

"I heard he'd been killed, but not much more than that."

I filled him in on what I knew so far, then, after some mental gymnastics on how to ask delicately, I finally just blurted, "Is there anything about Father Patrick you think I should know?"

There was a moment of silence, then his voice was flat as he stated, "You should know that he'd never allow Griffin to be harmed."

"I gathered that from what Louis has told me so far." I started to hesitate again but reminded myself that this was the job. "My understanding is that he had a pretty good relationship with the supernatural community in town. Did you ever get the feeling that he was part of the community?"

"You mean was he something other than human?"

I didn't love the rephrase of my question, but that was essentially what I was asking. Still, it made me feel like an asshole for separating the town into human and nonhuman like that.

"Yes. That's what I mean."

"Not to my knowledge. I've known—knew—Father Patrick for as long as he's lived in town. It took him a little time to warm up to us, and by 'us' I mean the supernatural community, as you like to say." I could hear the smile in his voice as he took a little jab at my made-up term. "I think his struggle wasn't that we were different but that he needed to figure out how we fit in with his religious beliefs. He didn't ask to switch to a different parish, so I guess he came to terms with our existence."

It would have been interesting to hear how the supernatural community fit into the Catholic Church's doctrines according to Father Patrick, but it looked like I'd never get the chance to ask him about it.

"Do you know of anyone who would want to hurt the priest or was maybe angry with him?"

"Can you imagine someone being mad at Mr. Rogers? Because that's what Father Patrick was like, and he was no different whether you were human or not."

I guess that sort of answered my question in a roundabout way. I started to ask how long Donavon would be gone but stopped myself. That was something that people dating would ask each other, and we definitely weren't a thing. Best to keep it professional.

"Okay, I appreciate the information. Please let me know if you think of anything else."

"Ouch, cold as ice, Vânători. Has the cold weather gotten to you?"

"No, I just—"

"That's okay," he continued, cutting me off and dropping back to that deep purr, "I'll warm you right up when I get back next week. See you then, Vi."

I must have sat there too long with the phone pressed against my ear, thinking about all the ways Donavon could warm me up, because Ramble let out a pained groan. I looked up to find him standing in the kitchen doorway. The moment he noticed he had my attention, he rolled his eyes to let me know what he thought of my phone conversation, then looked pointedly at the front door.

"Alright, alright." I hastily got up and shoved the phone in my pocket, embarrassed at getting caught swooning over Donavon. "We've got some time to kill. Let's go figure out what's going on with Preston."

# Chapter Nine

Preston's house was one of the older homes in town and wasn't too far from the downtown area. It was an expensive-looking two-story Victorian with lavender paint and white trim. Dormant rose bushes waited for Spring out front, while a privacy fence hid the updated backyard which had once been home to Hyssop.

I'd ended up helping Hyssop find a new home but not before getting caught stealing the old dirt from Preston's backyard so Hyssop could use it to start a new life elsewhere. That night I'd ended up staring at the business end of Preston's gun. We hadn't exactly gotten off to a great start and now, here he was helping me stay out of jail. Hopefully helping him out with his bad luck problem would get us back to even footing.

Before Ramble and I left our sad little puke green car next to the much nicer vehicles parked on this street, I took a deep breath in a bid for calm, then put on the necklace.

*Vânători. I see we skipped our morning training.*

I tried not to bristle. "I needed a break after dealing with Constancia."

*That is precisely the reason you should be consistently training. If you refuse to allow me to take control when we are in danger, then you must work harder and learn to keep yourself safe.*

Being told what to do rubbed me the wrong way, but yanking the necklace off wouldn't get me anywhere and only made me feel like a petulant teenager. And...if I was being honest with myself, she wasn't wrong. I fought to swallow my pride. "You're right. Since I won't let you take control, I do need to get better at fending for myself."

See? I could totally handle things like an adult.

"But right now, we're visiting Preston to get rid of the other clovers on his property."

*You have your hellhound for that.*

Oh boy. Who was acting like a teenager now?

"Yes," I said, fighting not to grind my teeth, "but you mentioned before that it's possible there are more inside his house. I'll need your guidance to find them."

She perked up a little at that, and I made a mental note to be a little nicer to her. Ramble ambled along beside us to the front door, ignoring my one-sided conversation. Just as I raised my hand to ring the bell, the door whipped open.

A frazzled-looking Preston stood in the doorway. He held a white dish towel in one hand and ran the other haphazardly through his hair. His lavender button-down shirt was untucked and had a large coffee stain down the front. One pant-leg was rolled up revealing a white bandage wrapped around his calf. The untucked shirt didn't quite hide the fact that his fly was unzipped.

While I took in his un-Preston-like appearance, he'd been doing the same to me. "You don't look so hot yourself." He pointed at my cheek, dish towel dangling from his hand.

I lifted a brow and glanced down. "XYZ."

"What?" He dabbed at the stain on his shirt.

"It means your fly's unzipped."

He froze and glanced down, then blanched. "For the love of—" he cut himself off and waved us in with the dish towel. "Come in, come in before someone else sees me." As he turned from the doorway, I saw him reach down and conspicuously zip up.

I made sure Ramble was inside before shutting the door. We followed Preston down a short hallway, past an old but well-cared for staircase. I stopped when my eyes caught on the first tread which had clearly broken inward underneath Preston's weight.

I caught Ramble looking at the broken stair and murmured, "I guess the bad luck streak is holding strong."

My murmur wasn't quiet enough because Preston, who'd stepped into a room off the hallway, popped his head back out the door. "Yes, Vianne. The curse is still holding strong. Now get in here and have some damn coffee before I manage to spill the rest of the pot."

His head disappeared back into what I could only assume was the kitchen. I don't think I'd ever been offered coffee with such hostility before. I exchanged a look with Ramble. He jerked his head toward the kitchen as if to say, "You go first."

"Chicken," I muttered, then strode down the hall trying not to look like I was waiting for Preston's bad luck to rub off on us.

I'd expected a boring white kitchen and was pleasantly surprised to be wrong. The cupboards were a dark green that went well with the lighter wood of the cutting board counters. Preston stood behind a modest-sized island and poured coffee into two cups on the counter. On my side of the island were tall, brown leather bar chairs. Preston set a coffee down at the edge of the island that was closest to me, so I pulled out a chair to sit.

"Check it first," Preston warned, jerking his head at the stool.

"Wha—oh." I quickly caught his meaning and wiggled the chair a little before pressing my hand into it. Seemed safe enough, so I took a seat just as Preston plopped down a small carton of creamer and a sugar bowl next to my coffee.

"I assume you brought your friend?"

I nodded and went to work doctoring my coffee with cream and sugar.

"Does he want coffee?"

I glanced at Ramble who snorted. "I think that's a no."

"Got it."

Now that he'd finished getting us coffee, he went back to dabbing his shirt with the dish towel. Nothing short of a good soak and wash was going to fix that stain, but I kept my mouth shut.

I took a sip of coffee and grimaced at the salty taste.

"What?" Preston froze as he caught my expression.

"Um," I opened the sugar bowl. "I think you've accidentally filled it with salt."

He chucked the dish towel at the counter then threw his hands in the air before groaning at the ceiling. "Come on! Really? Really?" He turned his attention back to me. I tried not to shrink into my seat. "I filled that this morning, and I would swear under oath that I filled that bowl with sugar. Not salt!"

He turned and leaned over the sink, clearly lost for what to do next.

*This is why true four-leaf clovers are so dangerous. Besides drawing out any possible bad thing that could happen, the magic also plays tricks on the target's mind. If the clovers are not removed, then the target will either meet his end through a stroke of bad luck, or he simply goes mad.*

*We're here to make sure that doesn't happen,* I reminded her.

"I believe you, Preston." I hopped down from the tall chair and walked over to the sink to reassure him, bringing my salt-coffee with me. "Part of how the magic works is to play tricks on your mind until you lose it."

"I think I'm already there."

"Nah, I think you probably have a ways to go yet." I poured the salt-coffee down the drain, rinsed out the mug, then walked over to the coffeemaker and helped myself to another cup. The actions allowed Preston the time he needed to pull himself together.

"Do you want me to find some sugar?"

I shook my head. "Black is fine." I leaned a hip against the sink and held the coffee in both hands. "Alright, why don't we start with the known clovers first—the ones outside. Maybe getting rid of a few will help lessen the bad luck."

*That's not how clovers work.*

*He doesn't need to know that, Artemis. What he needs right now is reassurance and some hope.*

*Even false hope?*

I stifled a sigh, thinking of my vampire problems. *Especially false hope.*

We headed to the backyard which was meticulously landscaped to within an inch of its life. A wooden path wound from the back porch all the way to the back fence. A few rectangular planter boxes and oversized terracotta pots dotted the yard in a pattern I couldn't discern.

"I'm surprised anything is growing since it's been so cold."

"I had the same thought, which was why I noticed them." Preston led us down the path to the first planter.

Sure enough, several perfect four-leaf clovers grew there. Their vibrant green color seemed unnatural among the mostly dormant garden.

"I'd planned to put in some dahlias and maybe some

vegetables in the spring but at this rate, maybe I should just give the backyard back to Hyssop."

There was that feeling in the pit of my stomach again. I really didn't want Hyssop to be behind this. Especially since according to the laws my ancestors had helped create, the punishment was death.

"I'm not sure Hyssop would want to come back, actually. He's got a much cushier life living in the library. Heated house, still has plants, and now he has books to pass the time."

As I spoke, Ramble sniffed around the planter, looking for a scent. Eventually he shook his head at me. No traceable scent, at least, not at this planter box. Next, he put his front paws on the plant and sniffed at the clovers—only to immediately sneeze.

Preston jumped, then looked a little ashamed. "Sorry, I keep forgetting you're here."

At least he was speaking in the right general direction.

Ramble shrugged at me, and I happily translated. "He says he's used to it, but that you can always make it up to him with a burger sometime."

This elicited a grin from Ramble, then he pulled in a deep breath...

"Oh," I tugged Preston away from the planter. "Let's step back a little."

Ramble blew out a gout of orange fire that seemed to go on forever. Preston couldn't see Ramble, but he certainly saw that.

The clovers immediately burst into flames, but Artemis cautioned me to wait.

*Such magic can take a moment or two of powerful fire before breaking.*

She was right, of course. I felt the moment the magic in the clovers finally let go. It was like the twang of a snapping guitar string. I don't think it was something Preston noticed, but Ramble immediately stopped his fire breathing.

"Alright. One down. Next?"

Preston led us around his garden to three more planters, and Ramble burned the rest of the clovers. Preston seemed in better spirits after that, and we returned inside to hunt down any clovers someone might have snuck into the house.

We paused in the living room. A sectional sofa split the large room up into an entertainment area and a professional workspace. The fun side had a wall-mounted TV with fancy built-in shelves and surround sound speakers. The professional side had a neatly organized wooden desk with a closed laptop and two monitors.

"This is gonna be like how I found the clovers in your car," I told Preston. "You can hang out to watch, but it'll probably be super boring. Feel free to do something else if you don't mind us walking around your house by ourselves."

"Help yourselves. Just please take any clovers outside before you burn them." Preston walked over to sit at the desk and open the laptop.

"Let's work our way from the top down," I suggested to Artemis and Ramble.

*That is an acceptable plan.*

Ramble had other plans. He looked at me, gave a clear snort of disagreement, then walked over to the couch before stopping to stare at Preston. Of course, the lawyer couldn't see him, but he'd heard the snort and followed my eyes as they tracked Ramble across the room.

"I don't think Preston wants you on his couch, Ramble." From the look on Preston's face, I thought I guessed correctly. "You probably have dirt on your paws from the garden," I added so as not to hurt Ramble's feelings.

This earned me a dramatic sigh, but he walked over to the door we'd just entered and made a show of wiping first his front paws, then his back paws on the mat there. He stared at me the whole time. When he'd finished, he raised an eyebrow in question.

"What's happening right now?" Preston asked.

"He just wiped all his paws on the mat."

"He wants on the couch that badly?"

I shrugged. "The fire breathing might have made him tired."

Preston looked in Ramble's general direction and, I swear to god, the conniving hellhound let out a plaintive whine. It broke Preston's resolve.

"Oh, all right. But no claws, please. I had the couch shipped in from New York, and it would cost a fortune to fix." Preston stood and headed for the kitchen. "I'll just get him a bowl of water in case he's thirsty."

Wow. It had taken Ramble all of thirty minutes to win over the lawyer.

"Be good, please." I whispered to Ramble as he clambered onto the cushy sofa to stretch out. He closed his eyes and rubbed his head against the fabric, luxuriating in its softness. His claws came out during the stretch, and I quietly reminded him, "He said no claws, Ramble."

His claws quickly retracted, and he opened his eyes a crack. The shit-eating grin on his face said it all: I'd get no help from him in this house search.

"Alright then, your highness. We'll bring you any clovers we find, and you can burn them outside."

He yawned in answer and closed his eyes again.

Artemis and I set about using her magic to search the house. Since we were covering a larger space, and I didn't want to take a million years by having to run my hands a few inches above everything in the room, Artemis showed me how to expand the radius of our magic. It was like imagining a large white cloud of energy expanding like smoke until it filled the room.

The first two searches—one in the guest bedroom and one in a shared bathroom—took longer as I figured out how to expand the cloud.

The other two rooms upstairs were a little faster as I got the hang of it, but our search didn't yield any clovers. We moved downstairs only to find Preston cuddled up on the couch next to Ramble, sharing a bucket of popcorn and watching a movie.

Catching my look at Ramble, Preston quickly covered for the hellhound. "I didn't want to be rude and leave a guest doing nothing while I worked."

"Uh huh." Truth be told, I was a little jealous. I wanted to sit on the couch, eat popcorn, and watch TV, too. But I had a job to do.

"Find any clovers up there?" Preston quickly asked, changing the subject.

"Nothing upstairs. We'll do this floor now, but it's possible whoever is doing this only had access to your cars and your garden."

We started in the kitchen so I could take a few swigs of the cold coffee I'd left in there. We quickly covered the kitchen, the living room and the main bedroom and bath-room. Still nothing.

*It is unlikely that the barrister is experiencing so much bad luck in his home without there being more clovers than those we found outside.*

"Preston," I pulled his attention away from where he'd been hand-feeding buttery popcorn to a hellhound. "Are there any specific spaces where you've experienced bad luck in the house?"

His expression shifted to one of deep thought. I was starting to think of it as his lawyer look. "Well...you saw for yourself that the kitchen can be a hotspot. Oh, and I fell through the stairs early this morning."

*This makes little sense, Vânători. Clover magic has a limited reach.*

*How limited?*

*Perhaps two yards, usually less.*

"Hmm," I looked between the kitchen and the stairwell. "But you haven't experienced any bad luck upstairs?"

He shook his head.

"Do you have a basement?"

"No, but I have a crawlspace."

My stomach sank. "With access from the outside?"

"Yes."

This was gonna suck. I sighed.

"I think that's where we'll find the clovers."

Preston grabbed a flashlight and led me back outside and around the side of the house. This time Ramble deigned to come with us. At the ground level beside a hose spigot was a two by three-foot wooden door on hinges. Preston undid the simple hook that held it closed against animals.

I leaned down and peered inside. It was only two feet tall. The ceiling was all cobwebs. Yup. Definitely gonna suck.

I put my jacket hood up over my head hoping it would protect my hair from most of the spiders there. It was winter, so the spiders should be hiding somewhere warmer, right? Preston handed me his flashlight, and I knelt in front of the opening, putting off the inevitable.

*Can we do the magic-smoke-radar thing from out here?* I asked Artemis.

*Are you afraid of the small, dark space that is filled with spiders, Vânători?*

*A little. And you're not helping by reminding me that it's full of spiders.*

Hard to pretend otherwise when there are cobwebs everywhere. And no, we should go further into the space and let the magic billow from the middle outwards to fill the area, just as we did upstairs.

Fantastic.

Such a helpful magical necklace. I took a breath of fresh, chilly air, then forced myself through the crawl space, flashlight first. I kept my eyes on the ground so as not to keep looking for spiders in the webs above me. It smelled damp and earthy.

I'd probably have dirt stains all over my jeans now. Hopefully, I'd have time to run back to the cabin and change before meeting with the sheriff.

When I felt like I'd crawled far enough, I stopped and tried to call up the same magic I'd been using throughout Preston's house. It was weirdly hard to stay focused while on my hands and knees under a curtain of spider-filled cobwebs. I'd been attacked by a swarm of bugs once, and it wasn't high on my list of things I wanted to do again.

*Concentrate, Vânători. Take a deep breath in...then out. Now imagine the energy rising within you.*

It took longer than it had before, and I had to turn the flashlight off in order to stop myself from looking for creepy-crawlies, but I finally managed to get past the damp smell and the fear of being eaten alive by bugs. I noticed the energy within me was dimmer when I drew it forth this time.

*We have used much energy clearing the barrister's home. You will need more blood from the vampire soon.*

I managed to avoid the now familiar thrill at the idea of drinking Louis's blood but only by throwing my concentration into the little ball of energy as I pushed it from my body. I visualized it inflating, and it obeyed my thoughts, expanding until it looked like a low hanging fog under the house. I definitely was NOT going to notice how it lit up all the spiders hanging out in the webs above me.

*There, Vânători! See them?*

I had a moment where I wondered if she was messing with me about the spiders again, then I remembered why we were here.

As the fog settled to the earth, something lit up on the ground in two spots. It was like those video games that let the players know what to do next by making an object glow white. One glowing spot was about ten feet in front of me and a little off to the right and the other was back and to the left. If I had to hazard a guess, they were probably about where the kitchen and the stairs were located a few feet overhead.

I released the energy I'd been using to keep the fog going, turned the flashlight back on and crawled toward the fading glow in front of me that was furthest away. As I got closer, I could see they were definitely four-leaf clovers. They weren't just lying on the ground though; they were growing there.

"How can they grow here with no sunlight," I quietly asked.

*They're magic, Vânători.*

Well, excuse me.

"Anything?"

I jumped at Preston's voice which was amplified by the small space and carried by remnants of the fog.

"Yup! Found two more patches of clovers growing under here."

"Growing there? How can they grow there if there's no sun?"

Artemis gave a mental eyeroll, and I couldn't help my grin. "They're magic, Preston."

"Oh."

Spirits lifted by giving Preston a hard time, I ripped the clovers up, getting as many of the roots as I could. I stuffed them in my pockets, then turned back and did the same to the other little patch of clovers.

Emerging from the crawlspace, I took a deep breath of fresh air and quickly brushed off my hair to make sure I hadn't picked up any bugs. I felt itchy, paranoid that bugs might have gotten in my jacket. It was a feeling that probably wouldn't go away until I had a proper shower later.

"I think this is the last of them," I pulled handfuls of the clovers from my pockets and threw them all in a pile on the ground.

Preston and I stepped back, and Ramble spent a good while breathing fire on them. It took three, long-lasting gouts of fire to break their magic and burn them. We stared at the blowing pile of ashes when he was done.

"Is that it?" Preston asked with a timid hope. "I can go back to a normal life again?"

"I think so. But let me know if bad luck strikes again. And maybe put a lock on that crawl space. And start locking your car all the time so someone doesn't do this again."

"Oh my god—they could, couldn't they!? They can just keep leaving these damn clovers all over the place around me! Am I going to be cursed forever? I mean, look at me!" He took a step back and gestured to his injured calf and his stained shirt. "I can't run a practice like this!" His voice wobbled a little on his last words, and tears sprang to his eyes.

"Whoa, whoa. It's okay, Preston. We're going to find out who did this and make sure they stop." This soothed him a little, but he still wasn't too far from the edge of losing it. "Why not take the next few days off? At the very least, that will give us a chance to make sure we got all the clovers. And at best, maybe I can figure out who's doing this."

I just really, really hoped it wasn't Hyssop out for revenge. I didn't want to have to uphold the Laws of the Accords or whatever by killing someone I considered a friend. I'd cross that bridge when I got to it, I guess.

Ramble and I left shortly after that, though I had to coax him away from the temptation of popcorn by suggesting that he would likely get a slice of pie in our next meeting with the sheriff.

As we pulled out of our street parking, Artemis surprised me with a rare compliment.

*Well, done, Vânători. We'll find our footing yet.*

It wasn't exactly glowing praise, but I'd take it.

# Chapter Ten

On our way into the Flying Pie restaurant, Ramble rushed ahead of me. He was a big fan of their vast variety of pies. I caught up to him at the door since he couldn't open it himself and no one happened to leave in the few seconds it took me to catch up to him.

"In a rush?"

He huffed at me and looked pointedly at the door until I opened it. "After you," I murmured as he pushed past me.

Mitchell, one of the owners, gave a gruff nod as I entered, then did a double take at my face. He might have seemed like a regular guy, but an impressive bit of magic hid that he was actually a troll. We had initially gotten off to a rough start in our first meeting. They were still repairing the upstairs room he'd trashed when trying to smash me into smithereens.

"You should see the other guy," I quipped. Maybe we could find some common ground in humor?

*The other "guy" was a female vampire who played with you like a cat with a mouse.*

*It's a saying, Artemis.*

*Not a very good one…*

I saw Mitchell trying to decide if he cared enough to ask what happened. Luckily, we were both saved by his wife Delores (also a troll) when she returned to the host podium.

"Vi," she said, all smiles. "How nice to see you!" Her eyes flicked to my burned cheek, then back up to my eyes. "Are you here for dinner or just dessert?"

I smiled back. "Nice to see you, too. Um, I'm not entirely sure yet. I'm actually meeting the sheriff here today."

"Dinner and dessert then," Mitchell grunted. "The sheriff never passes up an opportunity for a full meal here."

"Can you blame him with the pies you have?" I asked in all honesty.

He shrugged and grabbed two sets of menus. "This way."

"See you in a minute when I come to take your orders," Delores said with a half-wave, though she'd already shifted her attention to a paper on the host stand.

The restaurant was broken up into several smaller rooms which helped to dampen the noise of other diners when the place was hopping. I was surprised that it wasn't busier.

"Kinda quiet for dinner time, isn't it?"

Mitchell threw a quick look over his shoulder at me, then waved me toward a table tucked away in a back corner.

"Going into the off season now. Not many tourists come up this time of the year unless they're skiers, but most of the bigger ski resorts are too far away from us to catch many tourists out here."

I decided not to make any jokes about trolls "catching" tourists since Mitchell was actually talking to me. Instead, I nodded at his explanation.

Mitchell continued, "Figured you and the sheriff must be here to talk about Father Patrick's murder. We put ya back here where you won't be bothered."

"You heard about that already?"

"Of course. Whole town knows." He leaned down a little

as I sat at the table. "The whole *community,* if you know what I mean."

I knew what he meant since I was the one who'd coined the whole "supernatural community" phrase. Most of the time when folks said it around me, it was to make fun of the phrase. This was probably the first time I'd heard someone use it without sarcasm.

Then I realized what he was implying.

"Wait, was Father Patrick a part of *that* community?"

Mitchell gave a partial nod. "In a way, yeah, I guess so." At my surprised expression, he quickly explained, "He was human, but he knew about most of us and even took some of us in sometimes when we needed it. If we could be on holy ground, that is."

"Makes sense..." I started then trailed off. "Do you know if anyone would have wanted to hurt him? Or if he argued with anyone recently?"

Mitchell pulled a face and shook his head. "He was hardly the arguing type. He was kinda like our liaison before you got here. Smoothing things over between different folks in the community and keeping things peaceful."

"I see."

*Perhaps there was more to the clergyman than we thought.*

*Maybe,* I agreed.

Mitchell's expression suddenly hardened. For a second, I could almost make out his real troll face hidden under the magic disguise. "I hope you catch whoever did this, Vânători. Father Patrick was a good person. He deserved better than to end up a puddle of mush."

Wow. Word really did get around fast if Mitchell knew how the Father's body had been found.

"Actually, I'm not allowed to be on the case because apparently, other than his murderer, I was the last one to see him alive."

"You were?"

I nodded. "Well, me and a gremlin that was in the church. Father Patrick asked the sheriff to send someone to clear out the gremlin. So that's why I was there."

"He *what?*"

I wasn't sure if I should say anymore or not. Mitchell was clearly getting riled up, and I really didn't need a giant troll trying to crush me under his giant fist. Then again, if I said nothing, I was pretty sure Mitchell could just reach out and squeeze the info out of me.

"The sheriff sent me over and Father Patrick asked me to exterminate the gremlin."

"*What?*" He suddenly looked crestfallen. "Not Griffin. You didn't do it, did you, Vânători?"

*She should have...*

*Artemis. I can't concentrate on two conversations at once like this.*

She grumbled but kept her comments to herself.

"Of course not." I quickly reassured Mitchell. "The gremlin—Griffin—was terrified. I just ended up chasing him around the church until my *friend*," here Ramble let out a small whuff, "decided we would just take him home with us. He's fine."

Mitchell looked relieved for a moment before his face darkened. "I can't believe Father Patrick would ask you to do such a thing. Don't get me wrong, gremlin's can be a tough sort to house, but they'd been getting on so well..." He trailed off and shook his head just as Delores walked up behind him with the sheriff in tow.

"I found your dinner partner, Vi. Had to shoo him out of the kitchen and away from the fresh pies with a broom," Delores said with a wink.

"Sheriff," Mitchell said with a dip of his head, then without further ado, walked away like we hadn't just been discussing the murder of his friend.

The sheriff watched him for a moment as he sat, then turned his attention to me. "Kind of an odd sort, aren't they?" He said with a quirked eyebrow.

Ramble let out a strangled sound of suppressed laughter, and the sheriff jerked a little as if he'd forgotten that we came as a packaged deal.

Oh boy. The sheriff didn't know that Delores and Mitchell weren't run-of-the-mill humans. Well, I sure as hell wasn't going to tell him.

"I guess it takes all kinds to run a town, huh?" I asked with a sardonic smile, then winced when the smile pulled at my sore cheek. Agh, that was gonna take some time to heal... unless I took some vampire blood...

"What happened?" The sheriff's concerned tone brought me back to earth before I could start thinking about Louis.

I looked up to find him staring at my cheek. Apparently, he'd missed it until I'd winced in pain.

"I had an unfriendly visitor yesterday, but they're gone now." I appreciated his concern, but I was starting to feel a little embarrassed by the burn. It sucked to keep getting reminded that I'd gotten my ass handed to me by Constancia.

"Gone because they left or gone because...?" He left the question hanging in the air.

"I didn't kill anyone, Sheriff. Don't worry. They left."

I could almost feel Artemis struggling not to interrupt with a petty comment, but she managed to keep it to herself.

"But not before they did that," the sheriff added.

I stifled a sigh. "Yup. Not before they did this." I waved to my cheek.

He wanted to ask more, but I saw the moment he decided it wasn't his business, and then he switched gears. It seemed that people in small towns tried not to pry too much into each other's business.

"I appreciate you meeting me here, Vi. I'm really sorry

about everything yesterday, but I'm glad you brought your lawyer."

Translation: I had to bring you in and might have interrogated you, but hey, at least I tipped you off that you'd need a lawyer. I grunted since that's all I trusted myself to do, then changed the subject.

"Wanna order something before we get down to business? Or can you put me out of my misery of trying to figure out what you wanted to tell me that couldn't be said over the phone?"

The question was decided for us when Delores returned to the table with two waters and a question. "Vi, what's this about Father Patrick calling to have you remove Griffin yesterday?"

Sheriff Allen jerked his head up. "You're really not supposed to talk about this stuff, Vi. And who's Griffin?"

I gave him a look. "I'm not on the case and not officially the suspect, right?" I didn't wait for him to answer that second question since I didn't really want to know if things had changed since yesterday. "And Griffin is the gremlin." I looked at Delores and nodded. "The sheriff is the one who sent me over after Father Patrick called. The father was pretty keen on getting rid of Griffin."

"You didn't tell us the gremlin had a name, Vi," the sheriff said with a slightly accusatory tone.

"I honestly didn't know he did until last night."

"Is he still with you?" Delores asked. "You can bring him here if he needs a place to stay. Sometimes Father Patrick brought him here with him between rushes. Or we let them eat in the kitchen if it was too busy."

"Wait," the sheriff put his hand up. "Father Patrick brought the gremlin *here* with him?" He shook his head as if trying to clear it. "How long did he have the gremlin, then? When he spoke to me, he made it sound like the thing had just shown up that morning. He demanded I come out to, and I quote, 'take care of it.'"

"*Griffin,*" Delores emphasized, "must have been with Father Patrick for at least two, maybe three years."

"What?" The sheriff was just as shocked as I'd been.

"It's true." I let out a sigh. I hadn't wanted to bring up Louis with the sheriff since I didn't want to inadvertently involve him in the investigation. Unfortunately, I didn't see a way around it if I was going to stay honest with the sheriff. "Louis, the owner of the motel, was also close with Father Patrick and Griffin. When he heard I had Griffin, he came over to the cabin and took the gremlin home with him. He told me the same thing—that the Father had been like a father, I mean, like a parent to Griffin."

Looking confused and more than a little annoyed, the sheriff glanced between Delores and me, clearly unsure what to say.

"Why don't I bring you your regular, Bart," Delores said, breaking the tension in the air. "What about for you, Vi? Soup again and a little something for your four-legged friend?"

Ramble let out a whuff of agreement from where he lay under the table.

"Soup?" The sheriff seemed more annoyed at this than at the Father's seeming duplicity. "You can't have just *soup* at the Flying Pie. Do you like roast beef?"

The question caught me completely off guard. "Um, yes?"

"Good. Can we get two orders of my regular, Delores?"

"Coming right up."

The moment she walked away, the sheriff pinned me with his serious law enforcement face and raised a brow. "They seem to know an awful lot about the supernatural community..."

I raised my hands. "Nope. Not my place to talk about

folks like that." Then I quickly changed the subject. "You said you had something important to tell me from the autopsy?"

He nodded. "I'm not sure what you'll make of this, but the report actually placed Father Patrick's death between midnight and seven in the morning."

"Wait, what? The same day I was there?" He nodded. "That was hours before I got there! That can't be right."

The sheriff nodded and leaned forward. "It also overlaps with when Father Patrick called me about the gremlin." He looked me dead in the eye. "So how did a dead man not only call us but meet you at the church and chase the gremlin around?"

*Oh ho. Now this is interesting,* Artemis mused. *Perhaps the man you met was a ghost.*

I opened my mouth and closed it again. After connecting the first time with the necklace, I'd started seeing ghosts, but I could almost always eventually tell when it was a ghost versus a living person.

*I don't think so. He seemed more alive than any ghost I've seen before. Plus, Ramble and Griffin had both seen him. And he called the sheriff that same morning. I'm pretty sure ghosts can't use phones.*

I returned my attention to the sheriff. "And you're sure the coroner isn't off by a couple of hours or something?" I finally asked.

"He could be off by a little, but they usually figure in that margin of error when they provide their estimates."

We sat in silence for a moment before I had another thought.

"Wait, maybe the person I met with wasn't Father Patrick?" I fished my phone from my pocket and did a quick search online. It only took a few seconds to find the church's website. On the About page, I found a picture of the smiling priest. "This is him, right?"

The sheriff nodded. "And that's who you met at the church?"

"That's definitely the person I met. He didn't smile quite that much though. Honestly, the way everyone has been describing him so far hasn't really matched up with my brief experience with him."

"What do you mean?"

I tucked my phone away as I spoke. "I mean he started out all patient smiles and saying all the right things. He even quoted some scripture I think, but once he realized I didn't plan to kill Griffin, his whole demeanor changed. It was like he was a different person."

"Huh." The sheriff seemed to chew on that thought for a moment.

"What?"

"The coroner estimates that Father Patrick died before either of us spoke to him, and you're describing a version of Father Patrick that no one else experienced. At least, not to my knowledge anyway. Plus–" He cut himself off and looked at me, clearly realizing he was about to say too much.

"Plus, what? You might as well spit it out."

"Well, the thing is, most of the blood on the scene wasn't Father Patrick's."

# Chapter Eleven

❧

"What? Whose blood was it?"

The sheriff shook his head. "It doesn't match anything in our database, so there's no telling." He leaned forward to tell me something important just as Delores whisked in to drop off our drinks, one of which was in a metal dog bowl.

I raised an eyebrow at the bowl. "Won't that draw attention?"

Delores shrugged. "We're not exactly hopping during this time of the season. And if I put his meal and drink between your chair and the wall, people aren't likely to notice." She then addressed an empty space that was relatively close to where Ramble had decided to lie. "That work for you?"

He gave an excited huff and got up to check out his drink.

"But only during the off season," she warned before returning to the kitchen.

Ramble took a few laps of water then gave me a drippy grin as if to say, "See? The troll lady knows what I want." Did I need to carry collapsible bowls with me now?

The sheriff cleared his throat, bringing my attention back

134

to the present. His expression seemed pained, like he needed to tell me something and he really, really didn't want to. That couldn't be good.

"You look like you just bit into a lemon, Sheriff. What is it?"

He opened his mouth, but nothing came out.

"That bad, huh? Might as well spit it out. I already know I'm not gonna like whatever it is."

In a rush, he said, "Englewood wants to get a blood sample from you."

That woman really had it out for me. Then again, I *was* the last person to see Father Patrick alive, and she didn't know me. I couldn't really blame her for viewing me as the prime suspect. I picked up my water and took a sip to give myself time to think. If I voluntarily gave a blood sample, it would show goodwill and, even better, it would clear my name since I wasn't the murderer. I could get back on the case and get paid while also making Louis happy for helping to find his friend's murderer.

However, it would also likely tell Englewood exactly who I was and that I'd skipped out on my parole. That would undoubtedly be a one-way trip to jail. I couldn't risk that.

The sheriff watched me think it over. I saw his face fall when he realized what my answer would be.

"Sorry, Sheriff. If it was just you, I'd say absolutely. But you know your deputy will book me the minute the results come back and say I'm wanted for skipping out on parole."

It was his turn to sigh. "I thought I'd at least try. I could keep Englewood from arresting you, but I can't keep her from informing the police back in your state that you're here. Then I'd *have* to arrest you and extradite you back to Indiana. But you should know that if we end up requesting and getting a warrant, we can force you to comply."

*I would like to see the human try.*

I guess Artemis didn't like us to be threatened.

"I understand and if it comes to that, I'll comply, especially since it would clear my name of murder, but I think it would be smarter for me to hold off on the Deputy finding out who I am."

The sheriff backed off, and I decided it would be good to change the subject. "You mentioned before that the reason you couldn't respond to Father Patrick's request for help with the gremlin was because you and the Deputy were busy with something else. Do you mind if I ask if it has any relation to this case?"

"I don't think it's related. It was a missing person's report. One of the locals, Andy Grant, apparently didn't come home after a construction gig a few days ago. His wife let me know the next morning, not because she thought he was missing but because she thought maybe he'd fallen off the wagon. He's been sober for two years now, but before that, he totaled his car and lost his license. I think the experience woke him right up because afterward he started getting help. Englewood and I went to his house to get more information from his wife on when he was last seen. We're hoping he decided to stay with a friend or something. Otherwise..." he trailed off clearly not wanting to finish that sentence. "Well, it's not good to pass out in a ditch in the middle of winter in Maine."

The concern in his voice reminded me why I liked helping the sheriff. This wasn't just a paycheck to him. He truly seemed to care for the people in Ricketts. My personal experience with law enforcement wasn't so rosy. When I was in jail, they made sure I was well aware that they thought addiction was a choice that made me a deadbeat. They certainly wouldn't work as hard as the sheriff to look for a missing person who happened to be a recovering alcoholic.

"I hope you're able to find him."

Before the sheriff could say anything else about it,

Delores swooped back in with our dinners. She placed Ramble's plate on the floor beside his bowl, then looked at the table for a moment in thought while Ramble wolfed down his roast beef sandwich.

"Maybe we'll get some long tablecloths for these back tables," she mused as she watched Ramble. "No reason you should have to wait until you leave to eat in the busy season. You could eat under the table with no one the wiser."

Ramble paused in devouring his food just long to give a whuff of ascent.

"Excellent." She turned back to the sheriff and me. "Enjoy your meals!"

The fact that Deloris was planning for us to be here when the busy season returned sent a stab of guilt through me. Here I'd been thinking of simply fleeing town to survive a return visit from Constancia, but I hadn't considered that some of the people in Rickets would expect me to stick around.

Deloris returned to the kitchen, and the sheriff and I spent the rest of our meal going around in circles, trying to figure out the mystery around the timing of Father Patrick's death.

"And you're absolutely sure that the coroner isn't off by a couple of hours or something?" I asked again, dragging my last piece of bread from the roast beef sandwich through the juices on the plate. It says a lot that I could talk about something this grisly while still fully enjoying my meal.

The sheriff had already finished his sandwich and was starting on his slice of pie. Delores had brought our favorite types of pies without asking. I was feeling like a real regular in this town. Even Ramble got a slice of his favorite pie (which he'd long ago eaten). If I ever had to fight Mitchell and Delores in their troll form, I was gonna be shit out of luck because Ramble would definitely side with the pie-makers.

"Unlikely," the sheriff said with a shake of his head. "Not off by that many hours, anyway. And the person we use is one of the best in the state." He paused and cleared his throat, clearly uncomfortable about what he was going to ask next. "Do you think Father Patrick coulda been a...you know...?"

I had just dug into my chocolate pie and was about to take my first bite when I hesitated at his question. Was he asking if Father Patrick had been a vampire? How much did he know about vampires? Did he even know they exist? He had to have guessed at their existence by this point, right?

*Better to keep the human out of vampire affairs, Vânători.*

As much as I disliked withholding information, I thought Artemis was right. No reason to tip the sheriff off about what other folks went bump in the night in Ricketts.

"A what, Sheriff?"

"You know," he lowered his voice, though the three of us were still alone in the back room, "a *zombi*e."

Ramble snorted in amusement.

Did zombies even really exist? It didn't seem impossible, but judging by Ramble's response, I guessed that wasn't the situation. "I think Ramble would have smelled if he was a zombie."

"Maybe he was too...fresh."

Clearly, the sheriff had put some thought into this. I wrinkled my nose but didn't let the conversation deter me from my pie and finished my bite before answering. "Even if he was a zombie, we'd still be looking for who murdered him. He didn't have an identical twin or something, did he?"

"Not that I know of. That's some Days of our Lives thinking right there, though."

"I was thinking more along the lines of Nancy Drew."

"You want to be a teenage sleuth?"

"I mean, she always figured out the mystery and got the bad guy, right?"

The sheriff dipped his head in defeat, then sighed. "Unfortunately, life isn't always as cut and dry as that."

"No. It's not." I finished my pie in a long stretch of silence, then finally drummed up the nerve to ask. "So, does this mean I'm still a suspect?"

"Not officially."

I groaned. "You're killing me, Sheriff. You know you're my only means of work right now, right?"

"I know. And I appreciate the information you've shared about the case, though I can't officially say that it came from you. But," he held up a finger, "I think I have another job for you that doesn't involve this case."

I gave him a sidelong look. "You're not gonna ask me to rake your leaves, are you?"

This earned me a small laugh, which was a relief. Given the recent loss of his friend, I figured a bit of levity might help lift his spirits. Also, I really didn't want to rake leaves. Then again, if he paid me my consultant fee for a few hours of labor, I might change my mind.

"No. Nothing like that. There's a small, unincorporated town out in the middle of nowhere that I cover." As he spoke, he reached into his front shirt pocket and pulled out a card. "They've had some strange things happening in their neck of the woods. I thought maybe you could look into it."

I took the plain business card. Ramble perked up at the idea of a job. I showed him the card. "Melt It Down Scrap Metal Yard. Sounds like your kind of place," I told the hellhound. He sniffed the card checking for who knew what.

"Why's that?"

Shit. Did the sheriff know Ramble could breathe fire? Sometimes it was hard to keep track of who knew what.

"Uh, he's pretty tolerant of heat. Likes to practically lay

on top of the woodstove sometimes." We'd just ignore the fact that I had caught him doing literally just that a few days ago.

The sheriff flicked his eyes over to Ramble's general vicinity and grunted before continuing on. He pointed at the card. "Maybe call them first before you visit. They keep pretty much to themselves. I was honestly surprised that they called me at all."

"Huh. Okay..." I drew out the word. "What *did* they call you about?"

Delores appeared with the check and interrupted him before he could explain.

"I hope everything tasted okay." She set down a to-go box. "I thought maybe your friend might want a little something extra. On the house."

Ramble licked his chops.

"He says thank you." I smiled, though internally I knew Ramble would absolutely side with the trolls over me in the future. Damn. They were good.

The sheriff thankfully paid for our food. When Delores left again, the sheriff put on his jacket, patted the pocket, and with a look of surprise, handed me an envelope.

"I almost forgot. Here's what I owe you for going to the church in the first place. I can't pay you for anything else on that specific case right now, but if you're able to find out who murdered Father Patrick, you can send me an invoice for the rest of the time on the job.

"Thanks." I took the envelope. I was honestly thankful I'd be able to afford more food and maybe even put a little away toward rent if we stayed longer. It was a little sliver of happiness that was quickly snuffed out by the memory of Constancia. Her promise to return was a weight hanging over my head. I knew I'd need to make a choice soon of whether to stay and fight or cut and run.

"Be safe out there in this snow. Bit more than we're used to at this time of the year."

"Really?"

He nodded. "Stay safe on the roads." He left as I paused to put on my jacket and gather Ramble's take home food. Before I could head out, Delores came to clear the dishes.

"Everything okay, Vi?"

I guess I wasn't doing a very good job of hiding my mood. "Things are definitely better after dinner and dessert here," I reassured her. Then I had a thought: if other hunters really did come to Ricketts to test whether I was a Vânători or not, wouldn't that put those in the supernatural community in danger?

"Actually, I heard a rumor that other hunters might come to Ricketts to call me out."

"Oh?" The thin thread of violence wound through that single word made me want to find somewhere to hide.

"I'm not sure they know about the community in this town, but I thought it might be good for you all to know. And that you might want to spread the word, just in case."

"We appreciate that, Vânători."

Damn. She was back to using just my last name again. Had I done something wrong? I started to say something about protecting them but stopped. It was unlikely they'd need my protection and saying so might offend her. Still...

"If anyone comes around bothering you, please call me, okay?"

"Sure thing." Her tone was so nonchalant that I thought I'd surely overstepped. Before I could think of anything to say that might fix the situation, she'd disappeared with the dishes.

I wasn't sure what else to do, so we headed for the exit. Just as I was about to pull the front door closed behind me, Mitchell stepped into the foyer.

He locked eyes with me. "Remember that we're your friends, Vânători. And protection goes both ways." Without waiting for me to respond, he turned and walked away.

Well, okay then.

# Chapter Twelve

Night fell before we made it back to the cabin. I was just happy it hadn't snowed any more today since my decision to splurge on bedding meant we couldn't afford a new snow shovel.

I hadn't looked in the envelope from the sheriff, but I could guess that, for an hour of work, there should be about sixty bucks in there. Somehow, I'd stumbled into one of the best-paying jobs I'd ever had. Too bad it came with the risk of violent death. Then again, my life had turned into a constant threat of violent death ever since Constancia had stolen the Artemis necklace from Morvalden and then outed my existence to him. If I wasn't here putting myself in danger as a liaison, I'd still have the vampires to contend with.

Though it hadn't snowed, it was still cold outside, and the unheated drive home had my teeth chattering.

"I'll grab the firewood if you'll start the fire," I bargained with Ramble as we climbed the porch stairs. He whuffed his agreement, then slammed to a stop as we both noticed the open front door.

"What the fuck now?" I grumbled while silently asking

Artemis, *Do you sense anything?* It was likely that Constancia wouldn't be back so soon, but I didn't want to take any chances.

*Someone is inside, but I cannot tell who.*

I pulled my knife from where I kept it in my boot. Artemis had an old-school, wild-west notion that I should open-carry a gun at all times. After my little visit from Constancia, I'd compromised by keeping my knife in my boot. I gestured to Ramble that we'd shove the door open on three. Gripping the knife in one hand, I held up one finger of the other and silently mouthed, "one." Then, "two." Deep breath—

"Stop playing games, Vânători." Louis said from somewhere inside, voice tinged with amusement. "It's only me."

"Are you kidding me?" I slowly lowered the knife and straightened from my attack stance.

The gremlin poked his head through the open door. He and Ramble briefly touched noses. It would have been cute if my heart wasn't beating so fast and I wasn't pissed at Louis.

*Your vampire is overstepping.*

*No shit.*

I opened the front door the rest of the way to let Ramble in. Louis leaned out the living room doorway. "You need to work on your stealth, Vânători."

"This is where I live. I wasn't trying to be stealthy." I scowled and toed off my boots, then stuffed the knife back into one. I'd almost cut the shit out myself several times by leaving the knife just loose in my boot, so I'd finally created a make-shift sheath for each boot. "Maybe you should work on not being such a creeper."

The vampire ignored my jab and waited until I was almost to him before stepping back into the warm living room. At least he'd stoked up the fire. I felt an inkling of gratitude, which immediately disappeared when I followed him into the room and he opened his mouth again.

"I see you haven't partaken of the blood I left you. It doesn't stay good forever, you know."

"Yes. I do know, thank you."

Actually, I *didn't* know that, but I wasn't going to let him know that. "Also," I said, feeling even more annoyed, "maybe stop breaking into my house and going through my refrigerator? It's considered rude in most parts."

"Start leaving the door open, and I wouldn't have to break in."

He stood near the woodstove, leaving me the loveseat. How gentlemanly. I wasn't interested in sitting, though, so I leaned back against the wall near the doorway. Ramble followed me into the room, but I didn't see the gremlin. Not good. I heard the faint jingle of a bell and whipped around just in time to see him heading into my room.

"Nope!" I barked and turned to face him, arms crossed over my chest.

Griffin stopped and turned around, clearly knowing he'd been caught out.

"If I go in that room and find that you ripped apart the bedding that I just bought to replace what you ruined yesterday, we're gonna have words."

He opened his mouth and hissed at me.

"Hiss all you want, just do it in here," I jerked my head at the living room, "where I can see you."

He dropped his head and dragged himself into the room with us. Even his bells sounded dejected as he climbed up on the loveseat beside Ramble.

*Well done, Vânători. One must take such creatures in hand.*

Hmm, I wasn't so sure that was a compliment I wanted.

"You're hard on him, Vânători. He is grieving the loss of

Father Patrick." Louis's sudden somber tone sent a twinge of guilt through me.

"I know, but he can grieve without destroying my property." I felt like a jerk, but was I supposed to let Griffin tear through my house? I bet Louis didn't let him tear up the motel. "And no, I'm not going to leave the door *unlocked*. I already have enough people breaking in here as it is."

"Vânători, the people you don't want in here are going to break in anyway, while those who will benefit you by having unfettered access cannot get in if you lock it."

I rubbed my face, then winced at the painful reminder of Constancia's visit. I was tired. The drive out of town and speaking with the sheriff, paired with the threat of eventual death from Constancia and Morvalden, had taken a toll.

"Listen, I'm not really up for riddles right now. Why don't you just spell out what you mean."

Louis pointed at the small stack of firewood sitting in the metal rack near the stove. The rack had been almost empty when we left. Now it was full again.

"If you leave the door unlocked, then the brownie can leave the firewood inside where it belongs instead of out on the porch. And," he looked around the room pointedly, "they would keep your home clean if you bothered to pay them back for their work."


*More vermin is the last thing you need, Vânători. It would just be another mouth to feed and protect.*

*What?* I silently asked while pushing off the wall and stepping in front Louis. "What are you talking about?"

His mouth tipped up infinitesimally. Did he enjoy pissing me off? The idea only made me angrier, of course.

It felt as if everything happened in slow motion after that.

Louis opened his mouth to say something but was cut off by a high-pitched squeal that came from behind the wood-stove. Louis's eyes flicked up to something outside the window behind me.

"Down!" He shouted just as something shattered the window with a crash.

Louis stumbled backward a step, narrowly avoiding the woodstove. His surprised eyes met mine before he looked down at the wooden stake protruding from his chest. I rushed forward as he fell to his knees, catching him on his way down and softening the fall.

This time when his eyes found mine, I caught a glimmer of fear before he looked away again.

No! I couldn't let Louis die in front of me! A wave of emotions too complicated to sift through hit me, threatening to sweep away all sense of logic.

*Forget the vampire and protect yourself, Vânători! You are under attack!*

I tamped down my emotions.

A vicious growl ripped from Ramble's throat. I threw a quick glance over my shoulder to make sure he was okay. He'd dropped to the floor and turned to secure the window. Griffin huddled behind him, jingling with involuntary trembles.

"Keep an eye out, Ramble!" I shouted as my adrenaline surged.

Louis's head tipped forward and he leaned heavily against me. I had to draw on Artemis to keep him from knocking me over. "Louis? Talk to me. Come on Louis!" Was he already dead? Had the stake hit his heart?

When he lifted his head, I took in a shaky breath.

His eyes were almost fully black. He looked at me, then down at the piece of wood protruding from his chest again. He bared his fangs at me as if he didn't recognize me.

*Careful, Vânători. You remember what happened the last time he lost control.*

I wasn't likely to forget. That time *I'd* been the one bleeding out. The scent of my blood had made him lose control, and he'd almost drained me completely. Only Ramble had saved me that time.

I wasn't sure I'd be able to fight him off without a recharge, and Ramble was too far away to do much good if Louis sank his fangs into me.

"Hey!" I barked at him. He jerked, and I immediately felt bad for yelling at him. I continued in a more soothing voice. "It's okay, Louis. It's just me, Vianne. I'm going to help you."

I shifted my weight a little so I could try to stand with him, but he opened his mouth like an animal giving a warning.

*He's not lucid, Vânători,* said Artemis. Ramble growled again behind us.

A foot crunched in the snow outside.

Son of a bitch. Whoever had done this was still outside. I needed to help Louis, but it wouldn't do us much good if whoever was out there killed us both in the meantime.

*Get his blood, Vânători!* Artemis urged. *Quickly, before the attacker realizes they neutralized the vampire.*

*But, Louis—*

*If he's not dead yet, then the stake did not pierce his heart. If you do nothing, the vampire will drain you to save himself! It is his most basic instinct. Take his blood now! Or you will die, and I will be trapped forever in this necklace!*

For once, I listened to her advice. I stared at where the piece of wood connected with Louis's chest. His shirt was slowly turning crimson around it, soaking up his blood. The sight heightened my senses. I could suddenly smell the coppery tang in the air.

*Vânători!*

I shifted my grip so all his weight was on my left arm. With my free right hand, I swiped my finger into the hole in Louis's shirt and around his wound. He hissed at me, but I'd already scooped up some blood and, quickly, before I could get icked out by it, I stuck that finger in my mouth.

Every time I did this, I expected to be grossed out. And just like every other time I ingested vampire blood, the second the coppery liquid hit my tongue, I only wanted more. Power sang through my veins. It wasn't a lot of blood, but if I used it smartly, it would be enough to fuel the necklace for small bursts of power over a short duration.

I opened my eyes. Time seemed to slow down. I could process my surroundings better and suddenly make more informed decisions. I noticed Ramble backing away from the window while Griffin glanced between Louis and the hellhound, clearly not sure who he should go to.

"Stick with Ramble, Griffin," I told him.

I shifted Louis to lay him on the floor. When he opened his mouth to hiss at me, I gave my voice a small push of power and snapped, "Zip it, Louis! I'm trying to help you!"

A little of the darkness went out of his eyes. Good. I decided it was enough that he wouldn't bite me.

And if he did, I'd bite him back.

The idea was almost enough to make me smile, and I had to hold it in.

I carefully settled him on the floor, then dug my gloves out of my coat pockets. They would have to do for makeshift bandages since it was all I had on hand. I tucked them around the wound, trying to stop the bleeding around the stake. If I removed the piece of wood now without a plan, Louis would bleed out. Better to leave it until I could deal with the more urgent threat outside. Louis winced and let out a groan of pain that sounded more human than animal as I worked. I took that as a good sign he was keeping it together.

Still kneeling, I pivoted toward Ramble. "Stay here with him, Ramble." I pointed at the necklace. "I'm powered up. I'm gonna go after whoever did this."

Ramble glanced at Griffin, then Louis, before turning back to me and dipping his head in agreement. I returned a sharp nod, then stood and dashed toward the doorway.

This might get interesting. Powered up on vampire blood, I sort of hoped it would.

# Chapter Thirteen

Without breaking stride, I leaned down as I approached the front door and grabbed my knife from my right boot which still sat near the door. I let a little of Artemis's knowledge pour into me as I did and immediately shifted my grip to hold the knife at a downward angle. It would be harder to wrestle away like that.

*Prepare yourself, Vânători.* Though Artemis's words were a warning, she vibrated with checked excitement.

Oddly, I felt the same way. I was eager to go out and confront whoever had broken my window and put a stake through my friend. Maybe it was just spillover from Artemis's excitement, but I thought it more likely that I'd just gotten used to the random adrenaline rush. The last few days had been filled with interesting but idle conversations. I might say I didn't want to deal with these life or death situations, but some part of me clearly liked them.

I had to actively work to wipe the smile from my face before yanking the door open. Vampire blood sang in my veins as I stepped out the door and onto the front porch, barely noticing I didn't have any shoes on.

The night was crisp, clear, and, except for Ramble's warning growl coming through the broken window, completely quiet. A waxing moon lit up the night sky, providing just enough light by which to see the figure waiting for me.

He stood on the path between my front porch and my car. No other cars sat in the driveway, which meant he'd come on foot. He held something—probably a weapon—in one hand, but most of it blended into the shadow of his silhouette, so I couldn't tell what it was.

I couldn't make out the details of his facial features, and he wore a black beanie pulled far down over his forehead, further obstructing his identity.

*Easy, Vânători.*

*Of course,* I automatically responded, but my eagerness to spill someone's blood found its way into my voice as I smiled and asked, "Can I help you?"

The figure was silent, still not moving.

I took a step down the stairs. "I said—

"I heard you."

"Fantastic," I said, taking another step down the stairs. "Then maybe you'll explain why you just broke my window and attacked my friend."

"Your *friend?*"

"That's what I said." I tipped my head to the side, fighting the sudden urge to close my eyes and revel in the power running through me. It wasn't enough power to completely slow time down and show me multiple paths. We'd learned through a little trial and error that too much blood usually made me lose too much control and, without consciously giving the reins to Artemis (which I'd never do again), I would literally run straight into a battle with zero plan.

*Stay focused, Vânători.*

The world, which had started to shift into a blur as I gave

into the power singing in my veins, snapped back into focus. With it came a sudden view of shimmering in the sky.

What the hell?

*Can you see that?* I asked Artemis, fully expecting her to again ask what I was referring to.

*…Yes. It's some kind of magic. Be cautious, Vânători.*

"Are you doing that?" I jerked my head toward the sky, where magic shimmered like gossamer netting against the moonlit night.

"Doing what?"

Okay, so he couldn't see the lights in the sky, which meant something or someone else was in play here. I'd just have to deal with that later. I'm not sure if he could see my face or not, but my smile ratcheted up a notch as I took another step down. Just two more steps and I'd be on the ground. Maybe I could rush him. He was larger than me, but with the Artemis necklace charged up, I was pretty sure I could take him. And if I couldn't, I'd call Ramble in for backup.

He tilted his head up a little, shifting his stance and letting the light catch his face. I recognized him as the man I'd noticed in the café the day before. Had he been following me since then? Or maybe even before that?

I forgot the thought when he also revealed the thing in his hand: a crossbow. The only question was, was it loaded or not?

The man drew himself up straight. "Are you the new Vânători?"

Another step down. "I am." Fueled by vampire blood, I could see multiple options for how to attack the man. The clearest and most logical approach would be a straightforward one.

*Caution, Vânători. He appears to be human, but there may be more to him than I can sense yet.*

"Why are you consorting with *filth* like that?"

My eyebrows shot up, and I slammed to a halt as understanding set in. It suddenly made sense why he'd staked Louis. If Ramble hadn't been invisible, he probably would have aimed for him instead. Just what I needed: a closed-minded idiot mucking up my relations with the supernatural community.

"Are you a hunter?"

"Of course I'm a hunter. What the hell do I look like?" He hit his chest with his free hand.

"Honestly? You look like the prick who just broke my fucking window and impaled my friend with a stake."

His mouth dropped open. Before he could say anything else that might further piss me off, I headed him off. Maybe I could reason with him. "You might not realize this, but Vânători aren't just hunters who kill anyone not human. That's not how it works."

"Bullshit," he spat. "Vânători are legendary for protecting humans from monsters like that vampire in there." He offhandedly pointed the crossbow at the broken window.

The idiot hadn't even bothered to reload it yet.

*Be careful, Vânători. You do not know what other weapons he may have. We are not invincible.*

"Noted," I said out loud. At his confused look, I shrugged. "Sorry, that wasn't for you." I took the last step down and off the porch and ignored how my feet immediately went cold as the snow began to melt under them. That odd gossamer shimmer filled the sky. It was hard to ignore. "Listen, I won't hold this attack against you, but I'm gonna need you to leave. Right now. And tell all your hunter friends that *this* Vânători is a liaison for the supernatural community. I'm not interested in murdering someone just because they're a little different than me."

*Are you sure this is wise, Vânători? He could turn the hunters against you.*

*What do you suggest?*

I could feel her mental shrug. *We could take care of the problem here and now. Bury the body in the woods.*

*I think killing him would be a bit much, don't you think?*

*Engaging in combat now means you understand that you or your opponent may die.*

In the back of my mind, I knew that seemed a bit drastic, but another part of me—the part that was high on vampire blood—felt that this hunter's death would be acceptable.

"You're not the Vânători." The hunter's tone turned hard and snapped me back to the present. "You're an imposter." He moved to reload the crossbow.

"Oh, how wrong you are about that." I grinned at the hunter in the darkness.

*A fight then,* Artemis chuckled. She might have been reticent to engage at first, but once her blood was up, anything was fair game.

I readied myself to rush him, but at a growl from Ramble, I slammed to a halt. It was one of those spine-tingling growls and made the hair on the back of my neck stand up.

The hunter took an involuntary step back. "What the fuck was that?"

"You're *ruining* my fun here, Ramble." I said over my shoulder. The hellhound stood at the broken window, visible only to me. He gave a huff of annoyance, then jerked his head at the house as if to say that I should get back inside.

Shit. I'd gotten swept up in the adrenaline rush and had completely forgotten about Louis. I needed to quit screwing around with this idiot and help my friend.

I refocused on the hunter. I desperately wanted to teach him a lesson, but we didn't have time for that. Now I needed him to leave without a fight. His mouth hung open as he stared at the window where Ramble had been. Clearly, he'd heard the hellhound's huff and was even more freaked out that he couldn't see what had made the noise.

"That," I said slowly, ignoring the urge to rush the hunter, "is another friend of mine. Definitely don't call him filth, though." I dropped my voice to a whisper. "He doesn't like it."

Ramble grumbled from inside. The hunter looked between me and the broken window.

"I know. It's a lot to take in."

"You're fucking crazy, lady. Crazy. And you're definitely not the Vânători." He pointed at the window but took a step backwards in the beginnings of a retreat. "That vampire is going to drain you dry. Or worse, turn you."

Unfortunately, the idea of Louis biting me was quite the turn on. There was the added bonus that as a Vânători, I couldn't be turned.

I thought about all the people who the previous deputy had killed and the ghost I'd helped free when I very first started this journey. I shook my head. "There are much worse things in life than being turned into a vampire. But thanks for your concern."

He continued his retreat. "Whatever. Don't come crying to us hunters when your little *supernatural community* turns on you. I can't wait to rub Jax's face in this. He was so wrong about you."

I hesitated. "Did Jax send you here?"

When Jax had called to tell me other hunters might seek me out as a challenge, was that because he was the one revving them up and sending them after me?

The hunter paused in his retreat. "No one sent me here, lady."

"Oh my God! He did, didn't he?" I had to raise my voice a little as the hunter moved further away. "You didn't even realize it, did you?"

"He didn't send me!" He shouted.

"Sure, sure." I didn't bother to raise my voice this time and watched as the hunter walked down the road and disappeared around the corner. A few seconds later, a car started to life then grew fainter as he drove away.

"I need to put cameras around the cabin so we can tell when someone's lurking around out here," I murmured to myself.

*The witches could weave a spell to warn you of intruders,* Artemis suggested, *but it will cost you.*

"We don't exactly have money to spare right now." I didn't bother adding that I still wasn't happy with Rosalyn. My eyes caught on the shimmer overhead again. "What *is* that?"

*Magic of some sort.*

"That's a lot of magic." I craned my neck around. The shimmer filled the entire night sky. The longer I stared at it, the more it started to look less like a shimmer and more like thick threads of woven light. "Hmm. I wonder if this is why I've been feeling paranoid lately?"

*Perhaps...but you may also have sensed Constancia's presence. Or the hunter's. Letting him go was a mistake. He will go on to tell others how weak the Vânători is.*

"So what? I'm not trying to build a reputation with other hunters."

*You should be. Other hunters may decide to try their luck at killing the Vânători. After all, you're not completely human. You would be quite the hunting trophy.*

So much for camaraderie among the hunters. Another huff from inside saved me from thinking too long about that little nugget of happiness. I hustled back to the stairs and left wet footprints across the porch and into the cabin.

I shut and locked the front door, then dropped my knife back into its spot in my boot. I was somewhat surprised to find that I was mildly disappointed I hadn't gotten to use it. Shaking off the feeling, I hurried back to the living room.

Louis was still crouched in the same position as I'd left him. The gremlin made an odd noise as I entered the room and splayed his hands toward the vampire. It was easy to interpret: he wanted me to help his friend.

*You know,* Artemis mused, *this might be beneficial to us, Vânători. In his weakened state, we could coerce the vampire to give us more blood. Or you might consider using this opportunity to bind him to us."*

*What? First off, no to the first suggestion. Did you just completely miss the part where I told the asshat hunter that I'm friends with Louis? And to the second suggestion, I don't even know what that means to bind him to me, but I'm gonna go with a hard no because you sound way too enthusiastic about it.*

She started to protest, and I decided that was about enough of that kind of talk. *We need to conserve some energy. I'll catch you up in the morning.* Before she could pitch too much of a fit, I pulled the necklace over my head and stuffed it in my pocket. I didn't really need her bitching in my ear the entire time while I helped Louis.

The world immediately went back to its normal speed again. While it was fine to wear the necklace a few days after a hit of vampire blood, I'd found that the first few days could be overpowering. Sometimes it really was better not having immediate access to that much power. It could lead me to make poor decisions. Just as I'd experienced tonight when I'd almost fought a human hunter instead of helping my friend.

# Chapter Fourteen

"Alright, Louis." I knelt in front of him. "I'm back. Let's move you somewhere with less glass everywhere." He grunted, but at least he wasn't hissing at me anymore. I took that as a good sign. He was also strong enough to clutch the gloves around the stake to keep from bleeding out more, which was good because I wouldn't be able to move him and hold the makeshift bandages against him.

I looked at Ramble. "Can you stoke the fire back up?" Though it had been warm enough when I'd first entered the cabin, we were now losing most of our heat through the broken window. "I'll get him settled and then figure out some way to cover the window." At his nod, I turned my attention back to Louis.

"Alright, let's get you up." I leaned in and put my arm around his right side. Without the necklace's power behind me, it was a struggle to pull him to his feet.

Now what? Instinct and a lifetime of instruction from Hollywood told me that a vampire needed blood to heal. The close proximity to Louis and his blood were getting to me. I could feel a growing need mixed with desire forming within me. Just the idea of exchanging blood was enough. If I wasn't careful, I would end up giving in and straddling him while I drained him dry.

Unfortunately, the only other room to take him to was the bedroom, and it was devoid of any other furniture but the bed. Not very conducive to avoiding a blood orgy. But hey, it wouldn't be an orgy if it was just two people, right?

*Get it together, Vi,* I chastised myself as we stumbled into the room, then over to the bed. I helped him to sit, then eased him into laying down. Weirdly, I was thankful that I'd bothered to buy new bedding so that it would look nice for him—until I realized that now I'd have a vampire bleeding all over it.

Shit.

"Take care of the broken window," he breathed, clearly still in pain. "I need a moment to get myself under control."

I nodded then paused. When I'd had the necklace on, my sped-up mind had seen one option for covering the window. Without the necklace, it took me a moment to mentally track down the thought again. It was like that tip-of-the-tongue phenomenon where you knew there was a perfect word for what you wanted to say, but it just evaded your memory.

I closed my eyes and stilled my thoughts for a moment, taking a deep breath.

*...There* it was: my shower curtain could cover the broken window.

I finally peeled off my wet socks and went into the bathroom to throw them in the tub for now. Then I took the shower curtain off its rings. With the plain plastic curtain in hand, I retrieved duct tape from the mostly empty kitchen junk drawer and went to shove my now frozen feet into my boots. I almost stabbed myself with the damn knife in there but stopped just in time. I put the knife on the floor of the foyer, stuck my frozen feet in my boots, then headed outside.

I got extremely lucky that the bathroom curtain fit the window. There was even a little bit left over on the edges to tape against the house. Ramble helped by watching my back during the repair process. I didn't think the hunter would come back so soon, but it was nice to have the reassurance of a hellhound beside me.

As I worked, I silently wondered how much a replacement window would cost. Rosalyn had repaired the front door when Pamola ripped it off its hinges, but that was only because it was partially her fault that he'd attacked me in the first place. This, though, seemed like something I'd have to pay for. It wasn't like I had renter's insurance or anything like that either. I'd need to make more money soon or I'd be dealing with a broken window for the rest of the winter.

Or until Constancia came back with Morvalden to murder me.

Dealing with the window was a useful distraction and helped to lower my adrenaline. By the time I retreated indoors, I felt a little more like myself. Still, I had to swallow some nervousness as I entered the bedroom.

I paused in the doorway, watching the vampire still on the bed. "Okay?"

Louis gave a small nod. "I'm able to control myself now, thank you." He let out a shaky breath. "But I need your help to remove the stake, and," he paused and let a small, slightly sardonic smile play on his lips, "I'll have to call in my chips on that blood you owe me."

I nodded and shut the door behind me, then forced myself to ask, "Will you be able to stop if I let you drink from me?"

"Yes." He seemed sure, but I remembered all too clearly how he'd lost control before. At least I wasn't injured and bleeding out this time. Maybe that's what was allowing him to maintain his control. It didn't really feel like I had much choice here. I did owe him for all the blood he'd been giving me.

I knelt on the bed and gently pulled the gloves away. The stake was buried deep in Louis's chest, only narrowly missing his heart.

I shifted on the bed. "What happens once I pull it out?"

"The same thing that would happen if you pulled a wooden stake out of a human—I bleed out," he said between teeth gritted with pain. He shifted slightly in discomfort. "I'll need to drink from you while you remove it."

"Um, okay." I pulled off my jacket and stripped out of my zippered fleece so that I was down to a V-neck t-shirt. "Okay." Leaning over him, I took the stake in both hands. This close to him, I could smell his usual vanilla scent now mixed with blood.

*Stay focused, Vi,* I admonished myself. From this position it became immediately obvious that I wouldn't be able to get the leverage I'd need to pull the stake out. Not without drawing on Artemis for strength.

"Well, this is gonna be awkward," I mumbled and climbed onto the bed to straddle Louis.

"What are you doing?" His voice rose as he stirred beneath me.

"Getting into a better position." I pushed my hair out of the way, got a better grasp on the stake, then leaned down and to the side to give him better access to my neck before taking a deep breath.

"Are you sure you'll be able to control *your* bloodlust?" He asked, real concern laced his voice though he was the one currently bleeding out.

It felt a little like a slap in the face, and he must have realized it because he added, "I've had hundreds of years to gain control of my need. I mean no offense, but I'm not sure you're able to separate your blood lust from normal human sexual need.

If I needed a reminder that the being I was currently straddling wasn't human, that sure helped bring the point home.

"It's fine," I lied and leaned forward to give him access to my neck. "I can handle myself. Just do it."

I don't know why I expected him to take longer. Maybe I thought he'd try to talk me out of it.

I was wrong.

He struck like a cobra, his teeth sinking into my neck before I even realized what happened. Then there was the familiar rush of need that zipped from my neck straight to my groin.

The second he began to pull, drawing my blood into his mouth, I moaned and couldn't help but push myself against him.

He reciprocated the interest, pushing his hips off the bed toward me.

Only then did I remember that I was supposed to be yanking the stake out of his chest.

I let him take one more pull on my neck, luxuriating in the way his wet mouth felt against my skin, then before I could think about it too much, I gripped the stake and yanked up with all my might.

There was a sickening suction sound as the sharp piece of wood came out. Louis gasped in pain against my neck, then bit down harder. I cried out in a mix of pleasure and pain that almost made me pass out as he drew too much blood from me too quickly.

I was dizzy and confused by lust as Louis pulled away from my neck. He pushed my mouth to the spot on his chest that was quickly healing.

"Drink, Vânători," he panted.

He didn't have to tell me twice. I licked at the blood on his chest, then latched on as the coppery sweetness of his vampire blood filled my mouth. Power trickled through me, then poured in as I sucked his blood into me. Was this how full-blooded Vânători's had felt? No wonder the supernatural world was scared of them. Scared of me. If only I could have this power all the time without needing vampire blood to fuel it.

Louis's hands found the hem of my t-shirt and slipped underneath both it and my bra to squeeze my breast almost painfully. I took another pull of his blood, and he let out a grunt of pain before yanking me off his wound. Sitting up now as I straddled him, I realized I wanted more than this. I rocked hard against him and watched with a small smile as his eyes completely dilated.

In a blur, he yanked the neck of my t-shirt and my bra to the side, exposing my breast while, in the same move, he managed to sit up and wrap his mouth around my exposed nipple. Sweet electricity turned painful as he took me into his mouth. His fangs nipped at my skin.

I ground against him, wanting to both give and take more, while at the back of my mind, a little voice asked if this was really what I wanted or if I just was giving in to an addiction again.

*Am I not allowed to enjoy myself a little?* I thought at that voice.

Suddenly Louis stopped moving, almost as if sensing my own inner turmoil.

"It's fine," I mumbled. It wasn't, though. I couldn't help but wonder if I would want him as much if vampire blood weren't involved. After all, I'd made plenty of bad choices in the bedroom when shit-faced drunk, and I'd hated myself in the morning for most of them.

But the coppery taste of his blood and the *rush* of drinking from him mixed with the pain and pleasure of him drawing my own life's blood out of my veins until I was dizzy with it...

I fumbled at the button on my jeans, ready to get rid of the pesky material separating us. At the same time, I lowered my head to nuzzle Louis's neck. His wound had healed into a pink welt that stood out against his pale skin. Were my teeth sharp enough to break the skin and draw more blood?

I licked his neck and bared my teeth to bite him—

Like magic, he jerked himself out from underneath me so fast it almost made my head spin. I was barely able to track his movement and keep myself from toppling to the floor.

I shook my head to clear it. When I looked up, Louis stood near the bathroom doorway, watching me. His neutral mask was back in place, making it difficult to tell if he was angry at me or not.

"You cannot control yourself, Vânători." His crisp tone was almost as harsh as his words.

It was a sentence I'd heard several times before. I took a breath, automatically starting to argue. It was a call and response really:

Them: You have a drinking problem, Vi.

Me: I don't have a problem! I can handle myself. It's not my fault you can't keep up!

Deny. Lie. Reassign blame. It was a classic alcoholic response. Anything for another drink.

I dropped my eyes, took a shaky breath, and forced myself to face reality.

"You're right." I yanked my bra and t-shirt back into place. "I'm sorry."

We stood there for a moment before Louis broke the silence, his words slow and halting as if he wasn't sure of his own words. "Perhaps you should wear the necklace. Or we should only exchange blood in a controlled environment."

I looked up in surprise. He wasn't shouting at me which I took as a good sign. "What does that mean?"

He tilted his head slightly. Only then did I notice his eyes were still black with blood lust. Maybe I should just change the conversation entirely?

"When a vampire is made, they require a controlled environment during feeding for a time or they lose control and harm their blood donor."

I decided to ignore the term blood donor. "Could I learn to control it?" I asked, forcing myself to unclench my fists and rebutton my jeans while trying to hide my embarrassment.

"Honestly? I do not know. You are not a vampire though you seem driven by blood lust very similar to a young vampire. If *he* discovers this weakness though, Vânători, things will be very, very bad for you."

He meant Morvalden. Super. My ick factor went through the roof.

"I don't think I'm likely to be seduced by *him*," I said as I walked to the bedroom door, ready to flee what had almost been an awful mistake.

Okay, maybe not *awful*. After all, vampire or not, Louis was pretty hot. But it definitely would have made our relationship awkward.

His vampire speed never failed to surprise me. He was across the room with my hand in his, turning me to face him before I even realized it. I took a step back and found myself pressed against the door. His body followed me until his hips met mine. My free hand automatically went to his hip. A hard bulge pressed into me in just the right spot making me gasp as he leaned in to kiss me.

In an automatic response, I closed my eyes and parted my

lips, only to have nothing happen. When I opened my eyes, his face was still the same distance from mine.

"Are you sure you don't want this?" He asked, rotating his hips ever so slightly to rub himself against me in a very, very *good* way. He lifted my hand above my head and pressed it against the door, trapping me in place before he leaned his full weight into me. I let out a soft moan.

He leaned in slowly to lightly blow air across the spot on my neck where he'd bitten me.

Tingles started at my neck and lit through my body until they found where he pressed against my sweet spot. He moved his hips again, and I couldn't help it when my own hips rocked forward into him. My free hand slipped down to his firm ass and pulled him into me. I wanted nothing else in that moment than to open myself to him. He could do whatever he wanted as long as I could have him, body and blood.

"I could take you now, and you would want it." He whispered in my ear, breath tickling my neck and sending more tingles through me. He captured my free hand, putting it above my head and trapping both my wrists in his one hand. It left his hand free to rove over my body, starting at my neck, then running down until he cupped my breast in his hand.

He squeezed and my hips rocked forward.

"Do you see how easy it is, Vânători?" His fingers found their way inside my bra and pinched my nipple. Hard.

This time I let out a gasp of pain followed by a real moan. I wanted him and his blood more than anything right now, and what scared me was that I was willing to do whatever it took to get what I wanted. I closed my eyes, trying to block out the reality of what I'd do for just a small lick of his blood.

Suddenly, all his weight disappeared and my hands were free. When my brain finally registered that he was no longer leaning into me, I opened my eyes.

Louis stood across the room, glaring at me, almost angrily.

"Now you see how easy it would be for *him* to control you through your blood-lust, Vânători."

My brain was still foggy with lust as I mumbled, "But you're not *him*, Louis."

"You're not drawn to me, Vânători." Louis raised his hand and tapped his neck with a long, delicate finger that I knew had more strength than most men's arms. "You're drawn to what's inside me. And *he* has the same blood running through his veins." Louis leaned forward, and whispered, "Morvalden is my maker, Vânători." Louis shook his head once, almost sadly. "You would be like putty in his hands."

"But the necklace—

"The necklace is only useful if you wear it all the time and if you learn to use Artemis's full powers. If *he* returns before you're ready, the only way you'll survive is if you give full control to the goddess."

"That's not going to happen."

His tone shifted, and he seemed more annoyed at this than the fact that I'd almost taken advantage of him while he was injured. "Then you will perish if you cannot master the powers of the necklace."

We stared at each other for another moment before he dropped his head and briefly closed his eyes. When he opened them again, they were more back to normal, the lust almost entirely gone.

"Thank you for helping me to heal, Vânători. I will take my leave."

It took me a second to jumpstart my brain and step away from the closed door. He opened it then paused and turned to me before he left. "Please let me know if you learn anything else about Father Patrick's murder."

Without waiting for a response, he strode to the living room, called to Griffin, and they left together.

I stayed rooted to the spot, overwhelmed by the last few

minutes. I wasn't sure if it was just sensory overload from the blood, an unfulfilled sexual need, or the revelation that Morvalden had made Louis a vampire.

I knew that Morvalden was called the father of all vampires, but I'd just assumed there were several levels of other vampires separating Louis from Morvalden.

Ramble ambled into the living room doorway, looked me up and down, and gave me a snort of disappointment.

"That makes two of us, buddy."

# Chapter Fifteen

I nursed a hot coffee at the dining room table while morning light peeked through the shredded curtains I hadn't yet taken down.

"I really need to get new curtains," I mumbled.

Ramble grunted at me. We were both irritable from a long night of tossing and turning. While the shower curtain had done a decent enough job keeping the wind and snow out of the cabin, it had zero insulation capabilities, allowing the warmth from the woodstove to escape too quickly to heat any other parts of the cabin. I'd ended up dragging my new bedding into the living room and sleeping on the floor near the wood stove while Ramble dozed on the loveseat.

It wasn't just the cold that kept us awake though. It was the thought that the hunter might come back and have easy access to the cabin through the flimsy shower curtain.

Though I'd told the sheriff I'd check into the strange happenings in that little unincorporated township, I really needed to spend the day figuring out how to get the window fixed or, at the very least, buy some plywood or something to make it a little more insulated and secure.

Not that I had any money for either of those things.

I'd also spent the night dealing with the lingering high of drinking too much of Louis's blood. When I'd had vampire blood like that before, I'd been able to take the edge off by using Artemis's powers in a fight. Doing so drained away some of the energy from the vampire blood. Without some way to release it, I'd spent the night feeling like I'd just pounded a pack of Red Bulls followed by a few lines of cocaine.

Since I didn't have any bad guys to fight or vampires to seduce (or be seduced by), I put that energy into cleaning the cabin. Of course, that didn't last very long since I had limited cleaning supplies.

Like any good high, once the initial few hours of euphoria wore off, I was left exhausted and deflated. I still had power from Louis's blood, but I was nowhere near as powerful as I had been last night. The worst part was that a little whisper of a voice inside kept reminding me that there was a vial of unused blood in the refrigerator. I could take the edge off just by heating it up and taking a hit.

I knew the voice of addiction all too intimately, though. It didn't matter that it was trying to convince me to drink vampire blood instead of alcohol. I wasn't going to let it win... but man, it was an uphill battle.

My one year of sobriety had been hard-won through complete abstinence with the support of AA meetings. I couldn't do that with vampire blood, though. Not if I wanted to live. Without it, I'd lose my connection to Artemis's powers. If it was just a matter of not being able to go all superwoman and fight monsters, I could give it up and maybe just stay on the run from Morvalden and his vampire cronies. But without Artemis's protection, Morvalden could reach through my dreams and drag my physical body back into reality wherever he was.

So, rather than being able to embrace the life of a teeto-taler, I had to battle my addiction and take just enough vampire blood to power the necklace but not get lost in the euphoria it brought. I'd definitely lost that battle last night.

"One day at a time," I murmured into my cup of coffee. It felt like I'd just come off a three-day bender. "I really need to get control of this thing."

Ramble grunted again from where he lay sprawled in the kitchen doorway, clearly agreeing.

I blew out a sigh and let my eyes fall on the phone in front of me. I took a swig of coffee. I needed my only accept-able form of liquid courage to do what I needed to do next.

"Alright. Time to call Rosalyn. Wish me luck."

This time Ramble let out a fake snore. I wasn't sure if that was to let me know that I was interrupting his sleep or boring him to sleep. Either way, I'm sure he meant it as some kind of insult.

"Whatever," I told him before finally taking up the phone and calling the local coven leader.

It rang once. Twice. I crossed my fingers hoping it would go to voicemail.

No such luck.

"Good morning, Vianne. What can I do for you?"

Ever since she'd set me up for a showdown with Pamola then gone and gotten herself kidnapped by him, we'd been on eggshells around each other.

"Had a visitor last night." At her sharp intake of breath, I quickly added, "Not the horned one."

"Oh? Someone I know?"

"Probably not. It was a hunter coming to see for himself if I was the real deal or not."

I let out a sigh. "He, uh, broke the living room window."

There was a long silence, and I had to force myself not to play with the coffee cup out of nervousness. I wasn't sure whether Rosalyn could see or sense me fidgeting but I didn't want her to think I was scared of her. Though I'd be dumb not to be. I'd seen her wield some pretty heavy power. I might be able to take her on but only with a fully charged necklace.

"And did this hunter have a name?" She finally asked when I wasn't forthcoming with more details.

Huh. "I didn't think to ask," I honestly admitted.

Ramble snorted from the floor.

"I see. Well...we don't currently have an official rental agreement. While I was happy to fix the broken front door due to the nature of its destruction—

(translation: due to her setting me up to get attacked by an uber powerful being)

—as a landlord, I cannot be expected to fix everything in the cabin that your line of work destroys."

*Shit.* I couldn't blame her for not fixing the window without me paying something for it. After all, if someone else had been living here instead of me, then the place likely would still be in its original state.

This might be a bad time to mention Griffin shredding her curtains. I decided to keep it to myself.

"However," she continued before I could respond, "seeing as how I feel that I owe you for putting you in such a predicament with Pamola, I'm willing to pay for half of the window repair cost."

"Sounds fair," I quickly agreed. It was more than I'd hoped for, and I didn't want to give her the chance to change her mind.

We hammered out the details of her sending someone over to get measurements and have a new window installed. As I was about to end our awkward conversation, she suddenly added, "Not that it's any of my business, but have you been using magic around town? My sisters and I have felt several large and small uses of magic."

"No," I said, thinking of Father Patrick's odd death. "But did you hear that the Father was murdered?"

"Yes...was it someone from our community?"

Her hesitation suggested she wasn't sure she wanted to know the answer to her own question.

"I'm not sure yet. Actually, I'm not officially on the case since I'm technically a suspect." I quickly explained helping Father Patrick roust Griffin from his church then followed that with the suspicion that the man had been dead during the entire interaction.

"That's...odd," she finally said. "There are some magics that can reanimate the dead..."

"Like a zombie?"

"Yes and no. While the corpse's body might function, none to my knowledge have ever held a conversation."

I nodded to myself and filed away the information. Who knew when it might come in useful? I also had a slight ping of hope that—zombie discussion aside—since this seemed like a normal conversation, maybe Rosalyn and I were finding a smooth footing again. I thought about what she'd said earlier and shifted topics. "You mentioned you felt someone using magic—I didn't know you could do that."

"After losing Cassandra and Sadie, we decided to be more active in monitoring the use of magic in town. We cast a spell that allows us to sense any active uses of magic. Two other witches and I can now feel when someone uses magic."

"Oh?" I peeked out the window and squinted at the mostly clear blue sky. It was faint, but I could still see a shimmer here and there. I also still had that paranoid feeling of being watched. "Does your spell look like a woven net of shimmery threads?"

"You can see it?" Her voice rose a little in surprise.

"Oh, I can see it," I said, but didn't add, *and feel it.* I wasn't sure how much information I should continue giving her about my abilities. Though Rosalyn already knew my darkest secret: that I required vampire blood to power the necklace, I wasn't sure I should trust her with anything more until she could show me that she was trustworthy again.

"So, it's like a type of magic radar then?" I asked.

"It's slightly more complicated than that, and we can only sense what's happening within the town proper, but I suppose that's a sort of explanation. We can tell a general location when magic is used in town, and someone was definitely doing something with magic near the church."

"That same day that Father Patrick died?"

"The night before, actually."

"Huh. You mentioned that there were other pings on the radar-net-thing around town as well."

"I did. There have been several uses of magic near the old town well and one larger one used behind the motel."

"Can you tell who it was?"

"No, not unless it's someone within the coven."

"Oh." I chewed my lip in thought. "What about what kind of magic it was? Like can you tell what they were doing?"

"No." This time her tone held a note of defense. "Only that magic was used. We would have investigated ourselves, but I thought it best to make sure it wasn't something you were working on."

Hmm. Except that she hadn't bothered to call me. I'd had to call her first about something unrelated. I didn't love that. So much for building back trust.

"Alright. I appreciate the heads up. I'll check into it." I got the location of the town well. I already knew where the motel was. It was where Louis lived, and I'd stayed there when I'd first come to town.

"On a side note," I said, wondering how to approach this delicately, "do you know Preston Powers?"

"Of course. He's the lawyer that forced Hyssop from his home. Willomena has a few nicknames for him that I won't repeat. She's really taken to Hyssop and is quite protective of her new tenant."

That probably meant that Rosalyn wouldn't be too keen on providing information that might help Preston, but I needed to ask anyway.

"Do you know anyone who might have a vendetta against the lawyer? I mean, other than Hyssop?"

"Now *there*'s a question..."

I puffed out a sigh and quickly relayed everything about the four-leaf clovers and Preston's spate of bad luck. When I finished, Rosalyn was quiet for a moment before finally asking, "Do you think that someone in my coven might be creating four-leaf clovers illegally?"

I guess I'd failed at being diplomatic.

"I'm not saying someone in your coven is doing this," I quickly backpedaled. "I'm just wondering if you know anyone around town who can create four-leaf clovers and might have beef with Preston."

"Any witch worth her salt can create a four-leaf clover. But, with the exception of perhaps Willomena, I don't think anyone in my coven has issues with the lawyer. And, quite frankly, I don't think Willomena would risk breaking one of the Accords to get revenge for someone else."

"I see."

Before we hung up, I decided it would be best to pass along the warning I'd already given to Delores. "Just a heads up, you might want to keep an eye out for other hunters. Apparently, they're bored and want to come test the new Vânători for a certificate of authenticity."

"I'm not sure it's us who need to be careful, Vianne. Let us know if you need any magical assistance."

"Sure thing." I hung up and looked at Ramble. "Well, the hard part is done. I'm not sure we're back to being besties with the witches, but at least we're talking to her again."

Ramble shrugged, clearly unbothered that we weren't gonna have a sleepover with the witches anytime soon.

"Looks like our to-do list has changed. First, let's swing by the library and chat with Willomena and Hyssop." I sighed. "I really hope he's not the one leaving clovers around Preston, but he's the most likely suspect. After that, we'll check out the town that the Sheriff asked us to follow up on, then we'll pay a visit to the town well." I paused, and when Ramble looked up at me, I forced myself to say, "Then I'll call Louis this evening and see if he knows anything about some magic going on outside his motel."

Ramble rolled his eyes at me.

"What? He's a vampire! We should be polite and wait until after dark to call."

This earned me a snort. Whatever. He didn't have to deal with being embarrassed at throwing himself at a vampire.

As a little treat for doing one hard thing, I took a long hot shower. Of course, the shower curtain was still being used to seal the broken window, so I had to strategically direct the shower head toward the inside wall and avoid any large movements that would spray water everywhere. I let my brain turn off while the hot water pounded my skin. On the plus side, because I'd had *quite* a bit of vampire blood, the burn on my face was completely healed, so the hot water didn't bother me. I only dragged myself out when the water started to lose its heat. I opened the bathroom door to let the steam escape and get dressed. The ready-made bed looked super tempting. Maybe I could just take a quick nap before we left?

A huff from Ramble standing in the bedroom doorway kept me moving.

I needed to make the most of our time today. Though I'd told the sheriff I would stay out of the official investigation, I'd also promised Louis I'd do my best to find Father Patrick's murderer. So, we were gonna do a little bit of both today.

At the last minute, I put on the Artemis necklace. As much as I dreaded getting an earful from her about removing the necklace, I had to admit that the little wave of magic that rolled through me when I put it back on felt almost comforting now. It was like pulling on a warm, cozy blanket.

I gave Artemis a quick rundown of our plans for the day and was met with stony silence. Uh oh. The silent treatment. I'd been through this with her before, so I ignored it and got on with our plans. "Alright, to the library we go."

A short time later, I breathed deeply as we stepped inside the quiet library. There was something almost reverent about visiting libraries. Even in this smaller one, the moment I stepped through the doors, I felt a little more relaxed.

Ramble moseyed off to do who knows what. "Don't light anything on fire," I murmured to him before he disappeared. He ensured that I heard his snort of annoyance even from the other room.

Willomena wasn't at the front desk, so I wandered around a bit, perusing the science fiction shelves, then the fantasy section. I probably could have checked something out, but honestly, now that my life had become like something I'd previously read about, books were no longer really a viable option for escape.

*Unless I checked out the romance section?*

*Yes, I'm sure that would go well,* Artemis said, breaking her stony silence. *You'd just end up in the arms of the vampire when your blood was up from reading that tripe.*

"Whatever," I murmured. "And we don't say tripe

anymore. We say smut. And you only think it's tripe because you never had a love life."

*You know nothing about me, Vânători.* Her voice was cold. Clearly, I'd touched a nerve.

"You could, I dunno, try telling me about yourself. That might help."

Before she could respond, a haughty voice behind me made me jump. "Talking to yourself now, Vânători?"

I turned to find Willomena standing in the doorway to the small room where the sci-fi and fantasy books were shelved. With her jet black hair and a penchant for wearing long black dresses, she definitely fit the classic description of a witch. She might also sound like a bitch and stand like a bitch, but really at heart…okay, yeah, she was a bitch.

But we'd settled into a sort of truce in our mutual friendship with Hyssop, so that was something.

"I've gotta talk to someone," I quipped. "Might as well be someone with intelligence."

A small man with a white beard stepped up beside her. His brightly colored clothes made him look exactly like a garden gnome statue. If I hadn't already met him, I would have jumped when he appeared and started talking.

"Vânători!" He walked over and held out his hand. "Well met!" He grinned as we shook.

"You're going to be seen wandering around the main area like this," Willomena glowered.

"Oh, take a calming potion, Willa. You know there's naught else in the library but her four-legged companion."

"You brought the hellhound in here?" The witch's voice cracked with disbelief. "What if he decides to burn the place down?"

I threw her an annoyed look, totally ignoring the fact that I'd made the same joke to Ramble myself. Maybe Willomena and I didn't get along because we were too much alike?

Nah.

"Actually, I'm here on business. I'm sure you've heard about Father Patrick's murder?" They both nodded solemnly.

I haltingly explained the state in which his body had been found and also the odd part about how the coroner had estimated his time of death as occurring well before I'd met with him. For their part, both Hyssop and Willomena seemed horrified by all of it.

"Do either of you have any ideas on what kind of creature could leave a person's remains like that?"

*The witch won't know more than I do, Vânători.*

*Maybe not, but if there's a small possibility that they know of something we don't, then it can't hurt to ask.* I kept my attention on Hyssop and Willomena while I silently answered the goddess. *Plus, you were locked away in your necklace for like a hundred years. Maybe some new creatures have sprung up since then.*

She grumbled in disagreement.

"Not me," Hyssop quickly said. "We gnomes usually keep to ourselves. I'm already going against traditions by making my home in such a public place."

Willomena seemed lost in thought before finally answering. "I can't think of anything local to this area that might leave a body like that."

"Does that mean you have an idea about something that can do that, but it's not local?"

She hesitated. "I mean, the blood draining part leans toward the vampire, but I've never heard of a vampire leaving a body in that kind of state. What would be the point? It's extra work and sounds... *messy.* Plus, the only vampire in town is Louis. He wouldn't do something like that. Especially not to Father Patrick since they were friends. And you'd think he'd notice another vampire in a town this small."

"True."

*He didn't notice Constancia,* Artemis quipped.

*Also true,* I mentally responded.

*Maybe your vampire is losing his touch.*

*Maybe...*

It seemed I'd hit another dead end about who or what had murdered the priest. Now time for the crappy part of this visit.

"Actually," I cleared my throat, "I do need to ask a more sensitive question." I turned to Hyssop. I'd decided on the drive over that I wouldn't beat around the bush when asking the gnome about the four-leaf clovers, but now that it was time to do it, I really didn't want to know if he was guilty.

*This is your duty, Vânători.*

"You look like the cat got your tongue, Vânători." Hyssop said with a small but worried smile.

I sighed and forced myself to be blunt. "Hyssop, I have to ask you, do you know anything about Preston Powers having bunches of four-leaf clovers left around his house and in his car?"

"What?" If she were a cat, Willomena's hackles would have been up. "The lawyer who almost killed him?"

"Yes." I kept my attention on Hyssop. "Preston has suddenly had a streak of bad luck, and it was caused by dozens of four-leaf clovers we found growing in his backyard and some scattered around his house and his car."

"Someone grew true four-leaf clovers in *my* fucking garden?" Hyssop's surprised anger seemed genuine.

"Well, what's left of your garden. And right now, you're the only person I know of who might hold a grudge against Preston."

"He's a lawyer," Willomena offered. "I'm sure there are hundreds of people out there who might wish him harm."

"Maybe, but how many people can create true four-leaf clovers?"

Willomena's face fell.

*Well-played, Vânători.*

I felt sick to my stomach. I *really* didn't want it to be Hyssop, but things weren't looking good for him.

Hyssop caressed his long white beard in thought before answering. "I'm not interested in offing the lawyer, Vânători."

"See? He's innocent." Willomena beamed.

*Don't be too hasty to believe the gnome. I have witnessed many creatures lying to protect themselves. He may be no different.*

"I mean, you did once try to kill Preston by pouring garden chemicals in his coffee."

Willomena's mouth opened in a little "O" of surprise, and her eyes shone with newly found respect for the gnome.

Hyssop started to argue, then paused to reflect before speaking. "That is true, Vânători. I might once have wished the lawyer harm in the heat of the moment. And you can't really blame me for it—he was slowly killing me by killing my garden. It was truly an act of self-defense. Now, though, I've found a way to live a different life than any other gnome has ever experienced. I can *travel* now, Vânători." Excitement showed in his eyes as he spoke. "I could go live in an entirely new city. Or even a different country if I wanted!" He'd been winding his beard around his fingers in a nervous gesture as he spoke. When he realized it, he unwound his beard and smoothed it back down, continuing more seriously. "Honestly, if that idiot lawyer hadn't come along and upended my world, we gnomes would never have known it was possible to outlive our gardens." His eyes met and held mine. "I can't imagine wanting to do him harm now, but there may be others of my kind who feel differently for what he's done to me."

"Do you know of anyone in particular who might do this?"

He frowned and looked down at the carpeted library floor in thought. Or maybe to avoid my eyes. "No one in particular." He glanced back up. "There's a group of local gnomes who aren't too keen on the idea of change. They're stuck in their old ways and feel like I'm breaking tradition."

"Do you think that would be enough to go after Preston? Seems more likely that they'd go after you instead for being the one to break with tradition."

Hyssop scoffed. "A gnome attack another gnome? Not hardly! That hasn't happened since Tulip Jersey and Snowdrop York fought their legendary battle over their garden borders."

That sounded like an interesting story.

*Do not be distracted by the gnome, Vânători.*

*Right.*

I cleared my throat and tried to get us back on track. "So, it's not likely but still possible that one of the folks in this unhappy, traditionalist group might have gone after Preston?"

"It's possible." Suddenly Hyssop's expression shut down. "But before you ask, I won't give you their names or where they live. I'm enough of an outsider as it is. I don't want the whole community thinking I'm a snitch."

Super. Well, at least I didn't think it was Hyssop anymore.

I changed the subject after that and chatted with Hyssop about his new garden, though I knew very little about flowers and growing things. Mostly I just nodded and smiled at the right spots.

Thankfully, Willomena didn't try to make small talk. That never seemed to go well between us. Instead, she just shot me glowering looks throughout the rest of the conversation.

Ramble eventually saved me by padding up and letting out a giant sigh that was audible to everyone. I said something about not wanting to bore the hellhound while in a building full of flammable objects, and we got out of there.

I liked Hyssop, but there was only so much one could hear about the challenges of gardening in potted plants while being glared at by a potentially wicked witch.

Artemis waited until we left the building to give me her feedback. *You should have pressed the gnome to give you the names of those who might be doing Preston harm.*

"Going around and forcing people to snitch on their neighbors isn't a great look, Artemis. And it definitely won't earn us any allies."

*And not forcing the names from the gnome hasn't earned us any leads.*

I sighed. "You're not wrong. We seem to have hit a dead end on both our cases. I guess it's time to move on to door number three and follow up on the sheriff's request to check out Fielderstown." I glanced at Ramble. "At least with this one we might make a little money."

He grunted at me in agreement. I could already see the wheels turning behind his eyes on how much cheeseburger money we might earn from this new case.

# Chapter Sixteen

Only when we were halfway out to the tiny town did I remember that the sheriff had recommended I call first. I glanced at my phone. No signal.

"Shit."

Ramble looked at me.

"I was supposed to call first, remember?" The hellhound shrugged, and I rolled my eyes at him. "Sure, it's all fine and dandy for the invisible hellhound. They're not gonna shoot at *you* for trespassing because they won't be able to see you."

This earned me a grin before he stuck his head back out the partially open window.

*I'm sure we'll be fine, Vânători,* Artemis said with wry amusement. *It's unlikely the people in this town will be able to take us this close to full strength.*

I'd decided it would be best to continue wearing the necklace just in case I needed to draw upon Artemis's powers. After all, what if this place was into human sacrifice or something? It just made sense to go into an unknown situation with the best weapon I had available. Wearing it would also let me bleed off some of the excess energy I still had.

Plus...I hated to admit it, but Louis had made a good point about asking Artemis to help me deal with my vampire blood addiction. I'm not sure I'd ever actually ask her for her help outright, but just having her in the back of my mind helped me be a little more cautious and quell the need to go beg Louis for his blood.

It only took five minutes stuck in the car with the goddess to regret my decision. She'd spent that time reaming me out for taking off the necklace and almost "succumbing to the vampire's wiles." Her words, not mine.

Telling me not to worry about this mysterious town was the first time she'd actually said anything helpful since we'd left the cabin.

It didn't take long for us to get to Fielderstown. It was just a blip along an old state highway. The road itself was so rutted and pitted from years of rough winters and even rougher snowplows tearing it up that I feared for my poor car would pop a tire. The only thing to really mark the town was an old gas station with pumps where you had to pay inside first because they didn't have credit card readers.

I pulled into the gas station, thinking that I'd call the contact I'd gotten from the sheriff, but I still didn't have a signal. Maybe they'd have a phone inside that I could use? Or maybe I should just take my chances and drive over to the scrap yard. I could always just apologize for not calling beforehand.

The gas station looked a little sketchy even for a vampire hunter with a super-charged necklace. I pulled through its empty parking lot and turned onto the only other main street in the tiny town. There was a run-down town hall and a "Grange"—whatever that was—on the main road. Besides the gas station, that was pretty much it for Fielderstown infrastructure. All the other buildings were residential homes. Most of them were old clapboard or had that distinctly New

England cedar shaker siding. Each one looked like an old farmhouse with an attached barn or one nearby.

The town felt eerily empty and quiet. All was completely quiet. Not even dogs barked. How was there not a single other person around? Had everyone run and hidden the moment I turned down the street? Maybe I should have followed the sheriff's advice and called ahead.

"This is weird, right?" I asked Ramble, pitching my voice low.

*Why are you whispering, Vânători?*

"Because this town is creeping me out."

I went a bit further down the road. Eventually a tall chain link fence popped up on the right side of the road protecting a field full of cars and piles of junk and scrap metal.

"Looks like we're in the right place."

A second later, I pulled through the open front gate and into the scrap yard's parking lot. It seemed quiet here, too, but at least there were a few cars outside. They didn't look that much better than the scrap cars in the field though, so who knew if that meant there would be actual people inside.

I got out and held the door open to let Ramble out. Still tired from the night before, he seemed annoyed to be coming along.

"You can stay in the car, but don't get mad when you miss all the action."

He snorted but came along, sniffing the air as he went. We made it to the glass front door when he stepped purposely in front of me to cut me off.

I dropped my voice to a whisper. "What's up?"

One ear flicked back in answer while he continued to sniff the air. Unfortunately, I wasn't fluent in hellhound ear twitches, so I was left waiting for him to give me a little more to go on than that.

He closed the distance between us and the door, then put

his ear up to the glass like an eavesdropper. Though the door was glass, it led into a small foyer with an adjoining hallway branching to the left. Which meant all we could see was a wall with a bulletin board that had random For Sale notes and flyers tacked to it.

Ramble's ears twitched a few times as he listened, clearly hearing something I couldn't detect. I jumped when he suddenly jerked back and let out a growl.

He threw me a look then put his paw on the door as if urging me to open it.

I didn't waste time. I jerked the door open, and he rushed inside and through the short foyer with me trailing after. When he slammed to a sudden stop, I almost ran right into him.

The front room was set up with a long counter to separate customers from employees. Beside the counter was a longer hall with closed doors that must have led to private offices. On the other side of the counter was a unisex bathroom.

Papers were strewn about the counter like a whirlwind had come through. A laptop that had been broken in two lay half off the counter. Blood spatters covered everything.

I pulled my phone out, thinking to call the sheriff but found I still didn't have a signal. Not good. I tucked the phone back in my back pocket and instead pulled the knife from my boot. I was just about to tiptoe forward and chance a look behind the counter when I heard a muffled sound from the hallway. Ramble whipped his head toward the sound.

Cautiously, we followed the noise and discovered we were also following a trail of smeared blood. Someone had obviously been dragged down this hallway.

As we rounded the counter, I looked behind it and was relieved to find there weren't any bodies back there. A purse lay overturned on the floor where it had fallen in a large pool of blood. It looked like someone must have laid there where the blood was before they were dragged out from behind the counter and down the hallway.

We followed the bloody drag marks down the hallway but stopped at the first door on the right. The trail didn't end there. It went the length of the hallway and out through a backdoor. I didn't want to walk down the hall and let someone pop out of the doors behind me, though. Better to make sure there wasn't anyone inside the building before we went out that backdoor. Plus, I wasn't sure I was ready to discover what had left that blood trail.

Ramble stopped at the first door in the hallway and sniffed at it. It wasn't completely shut like I'd initially thought and creaked open at Ramble's touch. I put out my free hand and swung it fully open. Just as I'd guessed, the room was a small office with a desk and an overturned chair. It had been ransacked with more papers and office supplies tossed about.

Ramble snorted and backed out into the hall, ready to move on.

I really hoped we weren't following the bloody trail on the floor again.

*Careful, Vânători,* the necklace cautioned. *I don't like this.*

*Me neither,* I thought back, *but if someone is hurt and we can help, then we should do what we can.*

The sound came again. This time it sounded like muffled crying. Thankfully, it didn't seem to be coming from the backdoor where the blood trail went. Instead, it came from the next office.

As one, Ramble and I approached the door. This one was shut and had marks around the handle and door frame like someone had been trying to get in. I tried the knob. Locked.

At the sound of me touching the handle, someone inside let out a choked cry filled with fear. "Please go away! Please!"

I jerked back and had to still my own racing heart.

"It's okay," I tried to project my voice through the door

without outright shouting. "I'm here to help. Are you alright?"

The woman let out a sob. I heard movement on the other side of the door, then louder, the woman said, "How do I know this isn't just a trick to get me to open the door?"

Good point. How do I argue with that?

*We don't have time for this. Break the door down, Vânători.*

*Uh, no. That would just reinforce her not trusting us. And what are you talking about? We have plenty of time.*

*Oh? Do you think whatever did this is gone?*

*Good point.* "Listen, you don't have to open the door, but can you tell me what happened here?" I asked.

"Who are you?"

"My name is Vi. The sheriff in Ricketts asked me to come here and look into some odd incidents around town." I looked around the hall as I spoke, but my eyes kept getting drawn back to the trail of blood. "There's a lot of blood out here. Are you hurt, or did someone else get hurt? Are they in there with you?"

Judging by the blood trail, whoever had been bleeding out was probably dead by now from blood loss, but I felt like I should ask.

"Oh god!" She sobbed. "He took Wayne. He attacked him and *took* him!"

She'd said "he" took him. Not "the monster" or "it." Then again, there were certain kinds of magic that could make a person into a monster and what I might once have considered a monster into a person.

"Listen, you stay here, I'm going to go look around and make sure no one else needs help."

She didn't say anything so I jerked my head at Ramble for us to go. We followed the trail of blood while avoiding stepping in it. The last door led to a make-shift storage room. Rows of heavy duty metal shelves held an assortment of scrap metals that must have been worth more than the stuff outside.

Only when we got closer did I notice that the door handle had been crushed by something and the door no longer latched.

*I do not believe a mere mortal did that. You should gather power, Vânători. Do not go out there unprepared.*

I knew she was right. I took a brief moment to collect my wits. Switching the knife to my left hand, I shoved down my fear and looked for that core of energy within. It wasn't hard after so much vampire blood last night. It was as if the energy had been waiting for me to call it up. It practically leapt down my arm and into my right hand until I had a small, ping-pong-sized ball of light in my palm.

I glanced at Ramble, lifting a brow. "Ready?"

He nodded. I yanked the door open, ready to try and throw Artemis's power at whoever might be outside. Instead, the blood trail continued on for another twenty feet through a thin layer of snow, then ended in a grisly pile of what I could only guess must once have been a human.

Keeping my head on a swivel to make sure we weren't blindsided by an attack, I walked beside the trail and up to the pile of ripped clothing and bones. I didn't want to look but felt like I needed to make sure the person was actually dead.

*This must be Wayne,* I thought. My stomach roiled at the idea that the pile before me had recently been a person. I had to cover my mouth and look away for a few seconds while I got myself under control.

*You must learn to have a stronger stomach, Vânători, or you will not live long.*

"What could have done this?" I asked her. Ramble tentatively sniffed the body, then snorted and looked at me with surprise.

"What is it?" I asked him, realizing how dumb it was to ask since he had no way to actually tell me. I quickly changed my question. "Do you know who did this?"

Ramble tilted his head to the side but nodded.

What the hell did that mean? "So...you might know but you're not sure."

He blew out a breath of annoyance.

"Okay, can you tell if they're still here or not? Like, should we be prepared for a fight?"

He let out a huff and stared at me. At the same time, Artemis said, *Look at the blood, Vânători. It's congealed and where the trail is thin, the blood has dried. Whoever or whatever did this is long gone by now.*

She was right. I only noticed those details when she pointed them out, though. Good thing I wasn't doing this shit alone.

"Um, what do I do with this?" I waved my knife at the ball of energy still blazing in my right hand.

*You should try to reabsorb it. It would be a good lesson to learn.*

"Nothing like learning a lesson while standing in the middle of a bloody murder scene, but okay."

She pointedly ignored my complaint. *Imagine the reverse of drawing out the energy. In your mind's eye, see the ball of energy shrinking into your palm and retreating back to your core.*

I took a deep, calming breath, trying to slow my racing heartbeat, and followed her instructions. Drawing the ball of energy back in felt like reeling in a really long fishing line. I could almost feel it spooling back into my core.

I was sweating a little with effort by the time I finished.

"Alright. We should go back in and talk to the lady in the office to make sure she's not hurt, but first, let's see if they have a landline we can use to call the sheriff."

Ramble let out a huff and looked around the yard pointedly.

"Okay, if you want to look around, go for it. Just be

careful."

I put my knife away and retreated inside, all too ready to get away from the mangled body and the smell that still clung to it even in the cold.

The thought of the cold and recent snow we'd had made me look more closely at the trail of blood on the ground outside. I'd assumed that the attack had happened that day maybe even only a few hours ago, but the trail suggested otherwise. Snow had fallen on *top* of the blood trail, covering some of it up.

It was possible that it had snowed here today and not in Ricketts. Maybe I was just trying too hard to Nancy Drew this, but it hadn't really snowed hard since yesterday.

"I've got a bad feeling about this," I murmured as I went inside.

The phone at the front counter had been smashed to pieces, but there was one in the first office that was still intact. I picked up the receiver.

"Shit."

It was dead.

"Please go away! Please!"

I jumped before realizing it was just the woman in the office next door. She sounded a lot louder through the thin office walls.

"It's okay!" I shouted back. "It's just me again. I'm trying to find a working phone to call the police."

"How do I know this isn't just a trick to get me to open the door?"

"What?" I asked. Then my heart sank. I knew this song and dance.

This time I heard the fear in the woman's voice as she asked, "Who are you?"

I waited another heartbeat, hoping I wouldn't know the exact lines she'd say next.

"Oh god. He took Wayne. He attacked him and *took* him!"

"She's a repeater ghost, isn't she?" I asked, though I didn't need to hear the answer. I'd encountered a ghost like this before. Doomed to continually repeat their last few moments of life until their bodies were laid to rest.

*Yes. I'm sorry, Vânători.*

I briefly considered breaking down the door just to make sure, but the more I considered it, the dumber it seemed. I was already a suspect in one murder. No reason to make myself more suspicious by messing up a crime scene. After all, it was unlikely anyone else would be able to hear the woman's ghost.

I left the office just as Ramble came back inside. "We need to go and find a phone to call the sheriff. None of the ones here are working." Ramble looked pointedly at the locked door of the middle office.

I shook my head and let out a sigh. "She's a repeater ghost."

As if to back up my statement, the woman's ghost started her loop again.

"Please go away! Please!"

Ramble's ears drooped.

"Sorry, buddy. I thought we could help her, too."

*You cannot save everyone.*

"Maybe, but we can at least try," I said out loud for Ramble's benefit. He knew Artemis enough to know what I'd be responding to.

He bumped his head into my thigh as we left the building and escaped the terror that the repeater ghost would re-experience over and over. I was glad to have a companion who understood the importance of at least trying to save someone. Part of me wondered what I might become if I only had Artemis to turn to.

How ironic that it was a hellhound and not a goddess who

was helping me maintain my humanity.

# Chapter Seventeen

I drove us back to the gas station to find a phone. The drive was silent, which only punctuated the complete stillness of this tiny town. I parked and turned the car off but hesitated to get out. Ramble and I both stared at the small building. Everything still seemed a little too quiet. And the same truck that had been in the parking lot earlier still sat in the same spot. Maybe it was the employee's vehicle? That made sense.

Still...

"Does something feel off here to you?" I asked quietly.

Ramble sat back from the open window and raised his lip at me to bare one sharp tooth.

I took that as a yes and also that I should keep my guard up.

"Maybe you should stay out here to keep an eye on the car. After all, we don't have a cell signal, and I really don't want whoever killed the people at the scrap yard to sabotage or hijack our car. It would be a long walk back to Ricketts."

He quietly whuffed his agreement. I made sure to leave the window down so he could make an easy escape if needed.

*Something is not right in this town.*

"No shit," I muttered under my breath. I pulled the glass gas station door open. A little bell at the top let out a jingle. It reminded me of the gremlin. Hopefully he and Louis were having a much better day than we were.

The gas station was small enough that I could easily see the whole thing with only a few minor blind spots at the end of the shelves. It was also totally empty.

I walked up to the counter. "Hello? Anyone here?"

Silence.

Just in case, I did a brief round of the store only to find another pool of blood and a familiar trail leading to the bathroom.

"Shit."

Should I just assume that whoever was in there was dead?

My shoulders drooped. I needed to check. I would have trouble sleeping at night if I learned that whoever was in there had still been alive and there'd been some chance I could have helped them.

I sucked in a breath, stepped to the side of the blood smeared trail on the white linoleum, and pulled the door open—only to find another pile of a person who looked like they'd been chewed up and spit out.

My brain would have an awful lot of material to fuel my nightmares tonight.

*This town is cursed, Vânători. You must leave at once.*

I pushed the door closed. No reason to continue burning that sight into my brain. "Cursed? Are you serious?"

*Yes. You know it to be true. Go outside and listen. There is no one left alive in this town. And if you and the hellhound don't leave now, it's likely you'll join them.*

I shook my head. "We have to call the sheriff and show him what we've found." I paused as I thought through the implications of not one but three murder scenes all clearly linked by the state of the bodies. "He'll probably have to bring other law enforcement agencies in for this." More was not merrier in this situation since it just made it more likely that someone would eventually figure out that I'd skipped out on my probation.

*Then they will also be cursed,* Artemis spat. *It may even be too late for us.*

I started to roll my eyes, but I honestly couldn't ignore that she had more knowledge about this stuff than I did. Was she really being over the top, or did places carry legit curses in her time?

Before we left, I checked out the front counter to see if there was a working phone. The cordless phone had no dial tone.

Had whoever killed these people cut the phone lines to the entire town?

I went back outside and escaped to the relative safety of the car.

"There's another dead body inside," I told Ramble and locked the car door. Ramble lifted a brow in question. "She thinks this town is cursed and that we should get the hell out of here."

He tilted his head a little as if to say that she might have a point.

"Agh, not you, too." I threw the car in reverse and got us the hell out of there. I didn't think the place was cursed, but I couldn't shake the creepy feeling running down my spine while we were there.

Artemis was right. The place was too damn quiet.

We drove back the way we'd come. After a few minutes of tense driving, I finally got a cell signal. I immediately pulled over and called the sheriff.

"Hey Sheriff, you're gonna want to come out here to Fielderstown. I don't know when you last talked to these people, but the only thing I found were bodies."

"What?"

I swallowed and explained what we'd encountered at the scrapyard and the gas station. We hung up with the agreement that I'd wait right where I was so I could head back into Fielderstown with him.

*This is a poor plan, Vânători. Can you not feel the difference between that town and where we now sit? Something is wrong in that town.*

She wasn't wrong. It did feel like there was a pall over the town. It was like that drop in my stomach I got when I worried that something bad was about to happen. I'd had it the entire time we'd been in Fielderstown. Only now that we were clear of it did I notice the lack of that feeling.

I squinted up at the sky but couldn't see the shimmering witch-net that Rosalyn and her coven had created. It seemed that we'd driven beyond its reach. The feeling that came from Fielderstown was different than the witch's magic net though. I made a mental note to try and notice the witch radar on our drive home.

"There's definitely something off about the town," I admitted to Artemis. "I mean, besides all the bodies that are nothing more than meat sacks now. How is it that we've never heard of something that could do that to a person's body? The way it leaves people's remains is...pretty memorable. You would think if something like this had happened before, there'd be stories about it.

Ramble gave a negative snort, but Artemis hesitated. *Only once, and it wasn't just a few bodies. It was an entire town—men, women, children, animals—it didn't seem to matter, it killed everything in its path.*

I repeated her words to Ramble as she spoke so he wouldn't be left out of the loop.

"And? What did it?"

*I've no idea, Vânători. By the time we heard about the town, it had been almost a week. We had no way to identify who or what had done it. The survivors—that is, those who happened to be away from the town when it happened—salvaged what they could from their homes, then burned the whole thing to the ground including the bodies.*

"Seriously?

*They believed it to be cursed...as do I. If you can avoid returning to the town, Vânători, then I recommend doing so.*

"We've already been there once," I grumbled. "If we're cursed, we're cursed." We sat in silence for a few moments before my patience wore thin. "There isn't even a folk tale or something that might tell us what did this? Or what happened in that town so long ago?"

*No, Vânători. Not all things can be explained.*

"I have to disagree with you there. Clearly there's an explanation here, and it's not some random curse. Those bodies didn't mangle and drag themselves around. And that woman at the scrapyard locked herself in that room to get away from someone or something that was trying really hard to open that door. A curse doesn't leave marks on a door like that."

*Unless it is a person or creature who has been cursed.*

Damn. That was a good point. I relayed what she'd said to Ramble, who thought it over.

"It could be a curse that makes someone kill others I guess," I said slowly, feeling out the idea as I gave it voice. "It doesn't explain Father Patrick's ability to interact with us like normal after, according to the coroner, he'd been dead for a few hours."

Neither Ramble nor Artemis had a response to that, so we sat in awkward silence until the sheriff arrived. Rather than stopping, he drove up beside us with his cruiser lights going and slowed down just enough so I could see him wave for us to follow. Behind him was an ambulance and another sheriff's department car with Englewood behind the wheel.

Great. This would be fun.

I didn't experience that feeling of dread until we passed the gas station on the way to the scrapyard. I couldn't tell if it was just psychological as I thought about the bodies in this town, or if it was something else causing me to feel an utter sense of dread. The feeling stayed the same all the way to the scrapyard, so if it *was* something causing this, it didn't seem to be more powerful in any specific spot in town.

"You have had some really bad luck lately, Vi," the sheriff said when we both got out in the scrapyard's parking lot.

The sheriff's words caught me off guard. *Should I check my car and house for four-leaf clovers?*

Artemis quickly reassured me, *I would have detected their presence.*

*Good point*, I thought back at her.

To the sheriff, I said, "You're telling me." I shook my head then caught his eyes with mine. "It's pretty bad in there." I blew out a breath and quietly added, "I think there's another body in the locked office. I...I think I heard her as a ghost."

The sheriff's bushy eyebrows went up at that. Though he had a vague idea about what went bump in the night, he'd never really asked me about the details other than what was needed for an investigation.

He watched me for a moment, as if gauging whether or not I was messing with him, then almost imperceptibly, he nodded.

"Do I need to go back inside?" I asked. The front room wouldn't be bad, but I'd have to hear that woman's ghost plea for whoever had been outside to go away again.

"No, just walk me through what happened and tell me anything you might have touched while you were in there."

He hesitated before adding, "It'd be better if you stay outside."

Translation: I might be a suspect here. Again.

I thought he might change his mind about that once he saw the bodies, but I gave him the blow by blow anyway of what had happened since we'd arrived. I finished with, "I touched the front door handle and the door handles on the offices and back door."

Ramble, standing at attention in the back seat of the car and listening through the open driver's side window, gave a quiet whuff. The sound made the sheriff jerk in the hellhound's direction.

"Oh, and the phone on the front counter. I touched that too because I didn't have a cell signal and tried to call you from their landline."

He let out a resigned sigh. "Stay out here, please."

"Gladly."

I opened my car door and settled into the seat, watching as the sheriff rounded up his small team of EMTs and Englewood. They disappeared inside. I tried not to hold my breath. Five minutes later, one of the EMTs came stumbling back out to throw up in the parking lot.

Well hey, at least I'd done better than that.

He wiped his mouth, gathered himself, then forced himself back inside. Poor guy. It sucked that he had to witness all that carnage even though there weren't any people inside who needed his life-saving services anymore.

It seemed to be a day of waiting for us. Ramble and I sat in the cold car which was much more preferable than going back inside anyways. I'd rather huddle in a chilly car any day than deal with the bodies inside. When Ramble's stomach started rumbling, I rummaged around in the glove compartment and found him a granola bar. We didn't need to add a hangry hellhound to the mix today. Bad things happened when Ramble got too hungry for too long.

Finally, the sheriff came back outside, his deputy trailing behind him with a pinched look on her face. Super. Looked like we were gonna have to deal with her again.

*Try not to get arrested, Vânători. It would be all too easy for Morvalden to come for you then.*

*Thanks. That's really helpful.*

Beside me, Ramble grumbled at the idea of having to deal with the deputy.

"Let's just keep it together and civil until we can get out of here, okay?" I told him.

He let out a sigh but then went quiet when I opened the door and got out. No reason for the deputy to suspect that I had an invisible hellhound for a partner.

"Vi, can you walk me through what happened again?" The sheriff asked.

"Sure. You asked me to come here since folks said they had some strange things going on in town—"

"What kind of strange things?" Deputy Englewood interrupted.

I shrugged. "I don't actually know. The sheriff never said. I figured I'd just come here and ask."

"You didn't call them beforehand like I suggested?" The sheriff asked.

I made a face. "I might have forgotten to do that. Things have been...a little busy."

This earned me an odd look from the sheriff, but he didn't pursue it. Instead he explained, "Wayne Fielder, the owner of the scrapyard, called to let me know that his dog and a couple of the other pets and livestock had gone missing recently."

Englewood gave a dismissive shrug. "They live in the middle of nowhere Maine. Probably just wandered off and got eaten by something bigger than them."

"Could be," the sheriff said while giving me a look that suggested he thought otherwise, "but Wayne's dog was highly trained and never wandered further than Wayne's backyard. Apparently, Wayne was working late one night and let Copper outside before they headed home. He left the dog out back, within the scrapyard fence, then a few minutes later, he heard a yip." The sheriff took a breath, clearly thinking the same thing I was. "When he went out to investigate, Copper was gone."

"You think whatever did this to the people here started with the animals in town?" I asked since it was what *I* thought.

Englewood shot me a look of annoyance. "Or, if the dog was so highly trained, maybe someone who knew Mr. Fielder's routine came at night and nabbed the dog when they knew it'd be alone."

"Cool story," I said, "Except that now there are at least three people who have been killed in a pretty gruesome way."

"Three?" The deputy said.

"Yeah," I jerked my head toward the building, "the two in there," then I hooked a thumb backwards, "and the one at the gas station"

"We only found one body," the sheriff said with a warning look.

"Oh."

Shit. It sounded like they hadn't opened the door to the office yet and discovered the other body. The Deputy was unlikely to believe I'd heard the woman's repeater ghost. "From the state of the place and that woman's purse on the floor behind the counter, I assumed that there must have been another person in there when whatever happened, happened. And since the one office is locked, I just assumed that's where the other person was."

"What would make you think they're dead?"

"I mean, I knocked and asked if anyone was in there," I lied. "I guess they could still be alive in there and just not be able to open the door or respond?"

As if summoned by magic, one of the EMTs came outside. "We got the door open, sheriff, though we might have broken it beyond repair."

"That's fine. It's not great for the crime scene, but I'd rather make sure no one is hurt or dying in there."

The EMT suddenly sobered. "There was another body inside. A woman. It looks like something stabbed her once in the stomach and once in the chest. She bled out some time ago, sir, but that's not really my area of expertise."

"No, we'll have to get the bodies down to the coroner. Don't move them before we can take photos, though, Ethan."

The EMT, Ethan, shot me a quick glance of curiosity, then headed back inside.

"So, three bodies then," the sheriff sighed.

"And all *discovered* by someone who is already a suspect for another murder where the victim's body was found in the same state as one of the bodies here," Englewood said while staring daggers at me.

"You think *I* did this? When? I was with you two the other day. And then I went south of Ricketts yesterday to go shopping—which I have receipts for if you want to check the timestamp on them."

"Oh? And where were you last night? You could have come here, killed these people and gone home to clean up before coming back today."

I stood there with my mouth open. "You really think I did that to the body outside? How? Like, honestly, I'd love to know because I have no idea how someone mangles a body so badly that it comes out looking like that."

Englewood's mouth creased in anger but before she could respond, the sheriff cut her off. "Enough, Deputy. Vi didn't do this, and you damn well know it. Just like you know that she didn't murder Father Patrick. Someone did, though, and we'd better find out who sooner, rather than later." He took a breath and turned to me. "You're back on the job, Vi, so you need to know that it's going to be difficult for the coroner to pinpoint an exact time of death for the body—which we think was Wayne Fielder—outside the scrap shop."

"What about the other bodies?" I asked.

"It's possible, but it'll take time and by then, we may have more murders on our hands."

I nodded. Something was nagging at me in the back of my mind. Something I was forgetting...

Then it clicked.

"What about the security cameras inside?"

The sheriff shook his head. "They were tied into the broken laptop. It'll be some time before we can get access to the footage if at all. I'll probably have to send the hard drive to someone at another station that does that kind of thing."

"How about the ones at the gas station?"

Both the deputy and the sheriff's eyebrows went up.

Thirty minutes later we stood outside the gas station. The sheriff had made us wait while he'd gotten the photographic evidence he needed from the scrapyard. Since it was obvious the EMTs wouldn't be needed yet, they hung out in their ambulance, sticking around in case we got called to help someone who might still be alive. I didn't think that would happen, but I couldn't blame the sheriff for being prepared just in case.

I pointed toward the bathroom in the back. "That's where the body is." As if they couldn't figure it out from the bloody trail on the floor.

Englewood went to verify that I wasn't making shit up, I guess, while the sheriff and I looked around behind the counter for the security camera equipment.

"Just don't touch anything," the sheriff said under his breath. "Is your friend here?" He all but whispered.

"No, he stayed in the car."

The sheriff nodded, then pointed at an old-school security set up, complete with box TV and VCR.

Super.

"Englewood," the sheriff barked, making me jump.

The deputy hurried over while the sheriff stopped the live footage and rewound the tape.

On screen, we watched ourselves walk backwards out of the store. Then there was nothing for quite some time before I appeared, walking backwards into the store, going up to the counter to check the phone, then back to the bathroom, around the gas station, and back outside.

After that there was another streak of nothing happening.

"With these old systems, it's possible that it might have erased over the incident—"

He cut himself off as something changed on the screen. The clear picture turned to snow for a few seconds, then cleared back up to reveal a different scene. On the floor where the bloodstain now was, knelt a man who was clearly looking up at the camera.

"Is that...?" Englewood trailed off.

"Yup. That's Wayne Fielder."

# Chapter Eighteen

I looked back and forth between the sheriff and deputy. "The other body at the scrapyard wasn't Wayne's?"

The sheriff shook his head slowly, "Apparently." He was still rewinding the tape, trying to get to the beginning of Wayne's visit to the gas station. We watched in horror as the gas station attendant came back to life before our eyes with the magic of the rewind button. When the sheriff got to the beginning of the murderer's visit, he hit play.

Wayne Fielder, a middle-aged wiry man who looked like he regularly put in a hard day's work, walked in and immediately focused on the cashier, who was an older woman, sitting behind the counter. It was hard to tell since the security camera was directly behind the cashier, but it looked like she said something to him when he came in. Probably greeting him or something. In a town like this, everyone knew each other.

Without hesitation, Wayne strode up to the cashier, grabbed her by the throat, and unceremoniously dragged her over the counter then slammed her to the floor. The back of her head hit the linoleum with a silent but almost audible thwack.

"That's really the moment I was done in."

I yelped and couldn't help but jerk back.

A translucent head had appeared between me and the sheriff. It was the cashier, watching an instant replay of her own murder. She looked at me and jerked her head at the screen. "I babysat that little shit. Did you know that? And what does he do? Decides to get drunk off his ass and kill me." She shook her head and looked back at the screen.

Both the sheriff and the deputy were staring at me. Clearly, they couldn't see the cashier's ghost and were wondering what the hell was wrong with me.

"Uh, sorry. I...I thought I saw a mouse on my foot." I scuffed my shoe against the floor. "Just my imagination."

This earned me a disgusted look from the deputy. The sheriff though knew there was more to it than that. His was a look of concern and curiosity. When the deputy turned away, I tilted my head a little to indicate that I'd tell him later.

*Ask her what happened, Vânători.*

*We're watching what happened. I don't need to ask her. And besides, if I do ask, then the deputy will think I'm bonkers.*

Artemis sighed. *It is possible that the ghost will move on once she sees her death. I have seen it before. If you want any information from her, now is the time.*

*Shit.*

"So..." I started, not exactly sure where I was going with this. "Wayne killed her? Do you know any reason he might have done something like that?" I directed my question toward the sheriff, but flicked my eyes at the cashier's ghost when she looked over at me.

"Wayne Fielder had exactly *zero* reason to do me in." The cashier said it like this was a 1940's detective novel. "That man came in here every day for a pack of cigarettes and never said one cross word to me. Even that one time I was all out of his favorite smokes, he just got the lights instead." She shook her head, watching the tape play out as Wayne bent over the woman and reached for her throat again.

On screen, the woman scrambled away, trying to run but clearly struggling to make her body coordinate with her brain. The smack to the back of her head was clearly more damaging than it looked. She stumbled, catching herself on a shelf and trying again in a bid at reaching the relative safety of the bathroom. Maybe she thought she could get in there and lock the door.

She wasn't fast enough, though.

Wayne caught up to her just outside the bathroom. We couldn't see his face as he grabbed a handful of her hair, then yanked her backwards and slammed her into the floor again. He knelt between the cashier and the camera, essentially blocking our view of what he was doing.

"Is he choking her?" Englewood asked.

"No," the ghost answered, though the deputy couldn't hear her. "I only sort of remember..." She screwed up her face, trying to tease out the memory. "He put his hand on my face, and it felt like part of me was being pulled upwards, from my toes all the way through my body and out my head —"

Her words cut off in a gasp that myself, the deputy, and the sheriff all echoed. Wayne's head had whipped up as he looked over his shoulder straight at the camera.

Straight at us.

"Fucking creepy," I murmured.

It felt like he was looking *through* the camera at us. We all jumped as the TV turned to snow.

I tried to make my next words sound more like I was just musing to myself. "So then what happened in the bathroom?"

The ghost turned toward me, and I knew that Artemis

had been right. The cashier was already beginning to fade away. "The same thing that happened outside the bathroom. He put his hand on my face, and I had that weird feeling that turned into tingles, and then it was like my skin was on fire...I don't know what happened after that..."

She trailed off as she disappeared altogether.

"We've seen the results of what happened in the bath-room," Englewood said in answer to my question.

The sheriff looked at me, then flicked his eyes to where the cashier's ghost had just been standing. He'd caught that I'd been watching something that he couldn't see.

"The question is," he said slowly, "if Wayne Fielder is going around murdering people, whose body was that outside his scrapyard?"

* * *

There wasn't much else I could do to help their investigation after that. Not in front of the deputy, anyways. So, with the sheriff's permission, I started to leave for home.

Before I got in my car though, the sheriff pulled me aside. "Don't leave town, Vi. You're not a suspect," he quickly added as I opened my mouth to protest, "but these murders are just too weird to be perpetrated by a human. I'm going to need your help figuring this out."

"But not where Englewood can hear," I said, filling in what he wasn't willing to say.

He seemed annoyed at himself but nodded. "She's new to town. It's gonna take her some time to acclimate to the idea of hellhounds and witches."

"She's gonna need to acclimate quickly, then, if you want any hope of finding out who or what is responsible for leaving piles of meat where regular people were." My own words stopped me in my tracks. "Wait...you said that the folks out here liked to keep to themselves. Is there any chance that they weren't just *regular* people?"

This earned me some side eye from the sheriff. "What do you mean?"

"I mean, is there any chance that the cashier, and Father Patrick, and whoever died at the scrapyard were something more than human? It could be an explanation for why they aren't leaving behind a regular body."

There was an edge to the sheriff's voice as he said, "I find it hard to believe that Father Patrick was anything other than a human devoted to this faith."

I raised my hands in surrender. "I'm not trying to say anything *bad* about him. I'm just saying that's an angle we haven't really looked at. After all, he didn't just have Griffin for a day. He'd been living with him for over a year. And I know for a fact that he was friends with some of the folks in town from the supernatural community, and he *knew* what they are."

"Aren't you friends with some of those same people? That doesn't make you less human, does it? Or a monster?"

Technically speaking, I was more like three-fourths human and one-fourth Vânători, but it seemed like I should keep that to myself.

"I wasn't calling Father Patrick a monster, Sheriff. Just trying to look at this from a different angle so we can figure it out." I paused. "I'm sorry if I offended you."

He stopped and wiped a hand across his face. "I'm sorry, Vi. I just...I almost don't even know where to start with this case."

"I'll ask around and see if anyone knows what could leave a body like that." I got in my car but didn't shut the door right away. "I'll let you know what I learn."

He nodded, and I shut the door, cranked the engine, and

got the hell out of that creepy ass town. With any luck, we'd never have to go to Fielderstown again. The moment we were clear of the town, I finally felt my hackles go down a little. Maybe there really was some kind of magical thing happening in Fielderstown that either caused the murders, or was a result of the murders. I wondered if I should go pay a visit to Father Patrick's church to see if it exuded that same feeling.

I also needed to follow up on the idea I'd had when speaking with the sheriff. "We've been looking at this as the work of someone leaving bodies behind," I said to Artemis and Ramble. "Are there any kind of creatures who leave behind remains like that when they die?"

*If so, I am not aware of them. Shifters will sometimes leave the skin of their victims behind when they shift to someone new, but when the shifter dies, they simply leave behind a body that permanently looks like whoever they'd shifted to when they died.*

"Shifters? Like Donavon?"

Ramble snorted as Artemis let out a silent chuckle. Yup. I'm an idiot. Haha. Everybody laugh at the new Vânători who doesn't know anything because she missed the class on super-natural creatures.

*No, Vânători. He is a werewolf, and while he may* shift *between human and canine, he is not what is considered a shifter.*

"So, what's a shifter, then? How are they different?"

*A shifter is someone who can take on any form as long as they touch that person first. Once they give up that false form, they cannot retake it again unless they touch that person again.*

"Would they leave behind a mess of a body like that when they shifted to another person?"

*Not like that. When a shifter switches bodies, they shed the first body, not unlike a snake skin. But they aren't shedding the original person's skin. It's merely a false front made from the shifter's own cells.*

"That's super gross but makes sense. So this wasn't a shifter then."

*Not one that I'm familiar with.*

"Well, let's go talk to someone who hasn't been trapped in a necklace for a hundred years then."

* * *

I knocked on Hester's door a second time and waited. The cryptozoologist's front stoop and walkway hadn't been shoveled yet, and I didn't see any car tracks in the unmarred snow covering her driveway. It didn't look like she was home, but I'd figured I might as well give it a try just in case.

No one answered.

"Shit."

*Did you really think a Witness would know more than I?* Artemis testily asked.

"About this, yes," I murmured while trying to nonchalantly glance in the window. It was no use though. She clearly wasn't home. "Before I woke you up, you'd been sleeping for over a hundred years. Who knows what new supernatural creatures exist that you don't know about?"

She started to give me an earful as I walked back to the car. *New supernatural creatures? New things don't just appear from nowhere, Vânători! They've existed for thousands of years! They don't just* change *suddenly.*

I rolled my eyes as I started the car. I'd planned to go home, but I wondered if I should stop by Louis's place to see how the gremlin was doing and to see what he might know about Wayne Fielder. Also, I needed to ask him about the use of magic near his motel that Rosalyn had mentioned. It was definitely not so I could test myself against Louis's ability as a vampire to seduce me with his blood.

"Perhaps you're not familiar with the theory of evolution, but my guess is that supernatural beings evolve just as human beings do. Who knows, maybe they can evolve even faster than human beings."

*That is unlikely, Vânători.*

"Okay, except that *something* is killing people and leaving their bodies as bloody meat piles. I'm pretty sure it's not a human doing that. And," I added, thinking of the security video from the gas station, "you saw the way that Wayne Fielder looked at the camera and it suddenly went snowy. If that's not some sort of magic, then I don't know what is."

Rather than tempt myself by driving to Louis's, I decided to be a responsible adult and called him instead.

No answer. I left a voicemail summing up what Ramble and I had found in Fielderstown and asked if he knew who and what Wayne Fielder was. When I hung up, I gave it a few minutes just in case he listened to his message and got right back to me.

When my phone stayed silent, I dropped it in the cup holder and drove us home just in time to catch the handyman pulling out of the driveway.

"Shit. I totally forgot the window guy was coming."

I pulled into the driveway beside him and rolled down my window. "I'm so sorry to be late meeting with you. I had a consult out of town and didn't have any service where I was."

"Not to worry." He said and didn't seem annoyed which calmed my nerves a little. "I was able to take measurements from outside. I put up some plywood to keep the elements out for now. I have to special order the window, though, so it'll be a few days before I can get it delivered and installed."

"I completely understand. And thank you for putting the plywood up. That'll definitely help keep it warmer." I smiled and started to roll my window up, but he stopped me.

"Ah, I did want to let you know that an odd fella stopped by asking a lot of questions."

"Oh?" That couldn't be good. Was that hunter still creeping around?

The man nodded. "He was very curious about what I was doing, and..." he paused as if only now realizing how odd the situation had been, "he asked if I was there with you or Rosalyn's permission, and...this is gonna sound weird, but he wanted to know if you and I were allies...?"

"That's...different." I said, feeling just as puzzled as the poor repairman. "Did he say who he was?"

"He said he owned the land here and that you were very lucky to be allowed to live in his domain." The handyman gave me a funny look. "That's how he said it, his 'domain.' That's odd, right?"

Shit. I knew exactly who'd been bothering my poor repairman: Pamola.

"Ohhhh. I think I know who that was. He does technically own the land here and allowed Rosalyn to build the cabin." I got a prickling sensation at the back of my neck and saw Ramble lift his lip out of the corner of my eye. Was Pamola still here, watching our exchange?

*If he is,* Artemis said, *you'd better show him that you're grateful to him for letting you stay here and that you know this man and that he is welcome back.*

How was I supposed to do all that in this brief interaction?

Damnit.

I almost rolled my eyes as I forced myself to say, "I'm very lucky and grateful to be allowed to live here. It's a great spot." I stuck my hand out the window and, not wanting to leave me hanging awkwardly, the handyman took it, and we shook. "I appreciate you coming out so quickly and look forward to when the window arrives and you have the place back in normal condition."

"Uh huh." The guy pulled his hand back slowly. "I'll send

Rosalyn the invoice. Uh, you have a great day now." He rolled his window up then left as fast as he could.

Nothing like weirding out the locals by making sure they don't get murdered by the local mountain god.

I parked and looked at the cabin. True to his word, there was a piece of plywood covering the broken window. Hopefully it would keep most of the heat from escaping and we could sleep in the bedroom on a soft bed tonight.

When we got out, I still couldn't shake the feeling of being watched. Like me, Ramble had his head on a swivel, clearly experiencing the same feeling that someone watched from the woods.

I hoped it was Pamola and not that damn hunter back to break another window.

The moment I made it to the stairs, a pair of legs suddenly appeared, dangling from the porch roof. Startled, I jumped back. "Hey!"

"Relax, Vânători. It's just me, your friendly neighborhood mountain god."

Had Pamola just made a Spiderman reference? Surely not....

*I do not like this,* Artemis grumbled.

*And what would you like me to do about it exactly?*

The goddess said nothing. She knew that we'd barely held our own against the Power before. No reason to pick a fight just because he'd come for a visit.

"Pamola," I said, tilting my head a little then craning my neck to look up at him. I took a couple of steps back so I could see him a little better and to put a little distance between us. Ramble followed suit; his side practically glued to my thigh. And who could blame him? The last time we'd gotten a house visit from the mountain god, he'd been in an indestructible part-man, part-moose, part-bird form that was limited to animalistic thinking. He'd also kidnapped Ramble. "To what do we owe this pleasure?"

To my relief, he'd decided to stay fully human for this conversation and was even wearing relatively normal, modern clothes. Actually, he looked like he'd just walked out of an outdoor hiking magazine. I wondered briefly if he'd seen some hikers wearing something similar and just decided to copy their style. Hopefully he hadn't kidnapped them and locked them away in his mountain home since that was kind of his thing.

He was playing with a stick and waved it around to emphasize his words. "You have a lot of visitors, Vânători."

This was a surprisingly cordial conversation so far. Last time we'd interacted, there had been a lot more bellowing. Well, if he could play nice, so could I. "I didn't know I had a limit on who was allowed to come and visit me."

He gave me a tight but polite smile. "So far, I count two human males, two vampires, one gremlin—who I would appreciate that you do not release into my woods—and one creature that I do not know." He looked down at me and tossed me the stick he'd been playing with.

Only it wasn't a stick. When I caught it, I recognized it as the wooden stake that the hunter had impaled Louis with. "How...?" I didn't need to finish the sentence. Clearly everyone could get into my cabin without my knowledge. I might as well accept it. Maybe I really should just start leaving the door unlocked so the brownie could bring the firewood inside.

Pamola pointed at the stake. "I do not understand why you let the human who harmed your vampire live."

"He's not *my* vampire. And I had a choice to make: pursue the hunter or save my vampire *friend.*" I emphasized the word just so he'd know we weren't an item. "I'm sure I'll run into that hunter again. When I do, he'll regret attacking my friend in my home."

Pamola gave me a mischievous smile.

Uh oh.

"No need. He's been taken care of."

Oh boy. Did that mean Pamola now had a new guest in his mountain home? Or did he mean that he'd killed the young hunter and left him in the woods? I wasn't sure I wanted to know. If it was the latter, I'd feel an obligation to go searching for his body and notify the sheriff. I really didn't want to associate myself with another body in this town.

"Wait," I said, playing back what he'd said about visitors. "You said there was a creature that you didn't know? Do you mean the brownie?"

In one smooth motion, the Power leapt down from the roof to land gracefully in front of the porch stairs. He stepped to the side and back in order to lean against the porch, looking every bit like a middle-aged man having a perfectly normal conversation rather than a powerful mountain god protecting his territory.

He waved away my question. "No, she's one of mine and served the witch who lived here before you."

I wasn't sure about the word served. Seemed a little too close to servant for my taste, but it would be in poor taste to argue with him right now. Plus, I needed more information. "So, who's the other creature then?"

"As I said, I'm not familiar with it. It looked like a human, but it most certainly didn't *smell* like one. In fact, it didn't smell like anything I've ever encountered before. And it moved like a predator." He gave me a pointed look. "Vampires and gremlins I accept, some humans I'll allow, but dangerous new creatures in my woods? That is not acceptable, Vânători."

His eyes flashed, and I had to fight an instinct to back up a step.

"Now hold on just a second. You can't blame me for something that I have no control over. And do you really think I'd be okay with something creeping around the cabin?"

He gave a very human shrug. Had he been watching people lately to pick up on their modern mannerisms? Even his speech was more modern. I put the thought away for later and focused on not getting fried by the Power before me.

"Look, I don't know who or what has been lurking around my cabin, but there have been some odd deaths here in town and in another town that's nearby called Fielderstown."

His eyes flashed again, and his mouth drew down with a sudden anger that made me want to duck and cover. "I know that town, but not by that *colonizer*'s name."

*Easy, Vânători.*

Okay, clearly a touchy subject. Moving right along then.

I cleared my throat. "There were three deaths there, and two of them were odd."

He gestured for me to go on and when I did, he seemed pleased with himself that he'd done the movement correctly and that it garnered the result he wanted. Okay then.

"Two of the bodies in Fielderstown and the body here in Ricketts all looked like they'd been chewed up and spit out. They were less a body and more like a pile of meat but with way less blood than a body should leave behind." I grimaced as I said it since it sounded so cold toward the lives lost. I didn't know how else to describe it though.

"And was there magic on those bodies?" The Power asked.

*Uh, was there?* I mentally asked Artemis.

*Not on the ones we encountered.*

"No," I said, then decided to add another detail just in case it made a difference. "In Fielderstown, the deaths left a feeling of dread for everyone who entered the town."

"I see." He rubbed his chin, looking very much like Louis when he was deep in thought. Had Pamola been watching the vampire and picking up his mannerisms?

"We think we know who did it since one of his attacks was partially caught on camera, but we don't know what he is—if he even is anything other than human."

"I would need to see these piles of meat if you want my help."

"I think the sheriff would already have taken the bodies away by now. Sorry." Bringing Pamola into the Sheriff's Department would probably be a really bad idea anyways. Not knowing what else to say, I asked, "Could you let me know if you see the odd-smelling predator around my cabin again?"

The power grinned at me. "Does the Vânători need my protection?"

*Not hardly,* Artemis harrumphed. *Tell antler-head to go back to his mountain where he belongs.*

I was definitely not going to say that.

"There's no reason we can't help each other out occasionally. Especially when it comes to some unknown creature running around your woods."

"You just don't want to end up as a meat pile, Vânători."

"No. I really don't."

He let out a booming laugh, turned on his heel, and disappeared into the night.

"Alright then. I guess our conversation's over," I grumped, then, still holding the wooden stake, went inside. Once Ramble did his business outside and had joined me in the cabin, I double-checked my locks. If something was sneaking around outside the cabin, and it was the same something that had murdered all those people, I didn't want to take any chances.

I'd be sleeping with my gun on one side and a hellhound on the other tonight.

*And me, Vânători. I think it would be wise to sleep with the necklace in case we must act fast.*

For once I didn't argue.

Hopefully that would be enough protection to get us through the night.

# Chapter Nineteen

No one broke in overnight to drain our blood and leave us a pile of mush, so the next day I swung back by Hester's house. Before we left, I decided it couldn't hurt to at least try and make friends with the brownie who was leaving me firewood. I put out a small bowl of milk on the front porch as we went to the car.

"I'm leaving the door unlocked," I told the open air. Ramble jerked and looked at me like I was crazy. "I'm just telling the brownie so they know they're welcome here," I explained before addressing the open air again, "Um, and there's a bowl of milk here for you. I hope that's what you like." I hesitated for another moment, then decided that would have to be enough since I didn't know what else to say. We piled into the car and headed to Hester's.

It was a bust though. Her driveway was still empty, and there were no tracks in the melting snow. As a last resort, I tried calling her, but it went straight to voicemail.

Super.

I almost hung up but then decided that it couldn't hurt to try.

"Hey Hester, it's Vi. We've had some strange deaths in town. I just wanted to see if you might have some info that could help. We think the killer is a guy named Wayne Fielder, but from the way he left the victim's bodies, I'm pretty sure he's a little more than human. Give me a call if you happen to know anything that could help."

That done, I looked over at Ramble. He had his head out the passenger window, taking in whatever scents were on the cold mid-morning air.

"Well? What now, fearless sidekick?"

He turned and gave me some serious side-eye.

"No? Don't wanna be the sidekick? But they get to swoop in and save the hero all the time with zero thanks." His expression didn't change. "Okay, fine. You be the hero, and I'll be the sidekick. I have to warn you though, I'm not very great at swooping in for the save."

He snorted in agreement, making me smile.

"Alright hero, so what's next? We've got two potential leads on this thing from Rosalyn's magic radar." I held up my left hand, palm out. "We can either check out the town well since we didn't get to that yesterday..." I held up my right hand, "or we can pay Louis a visit." I wrinkled my nose at the idea of visiting the vampire.

Ramble agreed with the sentiment because he booped my left hand with his nose.

"Alright, town well it is."

I pulled up the location on my phone and headed that direction. It was near an older section of the downtown, a street over from the main drag where most of the shops were. I definitely would have missed the historical marker for the well if I hadn't had the map app guiding me.

I found some street parking that was only a short distance away, then Ramble, Artemis, and I backtracked to the marker. The area wasn't very well maintained. If it hadn't been winter with all the leaves on the ground, the low hanging branches of nearby trees would have completely covered the modern metal sign. The old dirt path was flanked on both sides by mostly younger trees at the mouth of the trail. Patches of ice and a few small branches had fallen over the path. I couldn't see the well from here as the trail took a sharp left turn, blocking our view.

I turned my attention back to the sign.

"Fortune Spring, first drawn from in 1733," I read out loud for Ramble's benefit in case he couldn't see the sign from his vantagepoint. "Huh, the original date is scratched out and someone wrote something else in." I stepped closer, squinting to make it out. "It looks like they changed it to 1616."

Ramble let out an impressed noise.

Artemis scoffed. *My people had a thriving civilization long before that.*

Alright then. I rolled my eyes and pointed to the necklace so Ramble would know I was talking to Artemis. "That's pretty old for this country's standards."

*Only if you completely ignore the existence of indigenous people as the colonial settlers did.*

Dang. She was totally right. *Good point,* I mentally replied and relayed her response to Ramble. He dipped his head slightly to acknowledge her point.

"Still, if the well was around in 1616, it's probably the oldest thing in town." I peered down the path, glad we were doing this in the daylight. I bet this place was super creepy at night. "Well, let's go see who's setting off the witch's magic radar net thing."

We made our way down the path and after slipping twice, I did my best to avoid the icy patches. Ramble purposely sought them out so he could look at me while digging his claws into the ice with a satisfying crunch.

"Yeah, yeah," I muttered. "You're awesome because you

have natural grip on ice. All hail the hellhound, conqueror of ice."

He snorted, and I couldn't help but smile.

*You need to pay attention, Vânători. If the creature that killed those people is here, you don't want it to hear you coming.*

It was a little late for that, but she was right. We weren't out here for a casual stroll to see the historic forgotten well. We were following a tip that might lead to a creature that had already left several mangled bodies behind. The problem was, I was having trouble picturing Wayne Fielders jumping out from the woods to turn us into mush. Maybe it was because it was broad daylight, but I just had the feeling that I wouldn't find our murderer out here. Still, I sobered and tried to pay more attention to our surroundings.

Ramble sensed my mood change and stopped making so much noise as we followed the path around a long curve. When it straightened out again, we finally caught a glimpse of the well. It looked exactly like I'd expected with a wooden housing around the well shaft and a crank where someone could send down a bucket. Except, as we got closer, I realized there wasn't actually a bucket or a rope attached to the crank.

Next to the well was a relatively new hand pump set in a concrete block. At the bottom of the block was another little historic placard that read, Fortune Spring, 1996. A closer inspection of the old well proved that it was just a non-functioning replica.

I walked all around the well and even tried to peer down inside, but it was capped with a cover about a foot below the lip of the wood housing. Ramble sniffed the old well, then around the outskirts of the path that surrounded it. When he got to the hand pump, his ears perked up.

"Find something?"

He glanced up at me, then back at the pump as if to say, "Hold on a second," then followed a scent that led away from the handpump and into the woods. There was a faint desire path there, suggesting someone had walked through that section to visit the well enough times that it had created a faint trail. I stayed on the official trail while Ramble soundlessly slinked ahead, tracking a scent.

*How about you, Artemis? Sense anything?*

She was quiet, feeling for some form of residual magic.

I suddenly realized that, so far, I wasn't much more than a glorified driver in this mission, bringing Ramble and Artemis out here so they could use their respective gifts to do some detective work.

*It appears that the well itself is magic.*

"The well is magic?" I asked out loud for Ramble's benefit. "Is that what set off the witch's radar?"

*I do not believe so. Someone must have used the magic water from the well in a spell. I can sense the spell they cast, but only very faintly. It feels a little like your gnome friend...*

*Oh?*

Maybe I shouldn't have been so hasty in believing that Hyssop was innocent.

Ramble let out a quiet whuff to get our attention. He'd gone far enough that I could no longer see him. I followed the faint path, but it was only slightly less overgrown than the wild woods around it, which meant a lot of noisy rustling and twig snapping as I made my way to Ramble.

I really hoped I wasn't about to find a body out here in the woods. I didn't think that would go over too well with the sheriff.

Thankfully, instead of a body, Ramble had discovered a small, sunny clearing that was a little greener than the area around it. In the middle were three clear plastic tunnels about two feet tall that were used to grow plants in the cold. Condensation on the inside of the plastic blurred whatever greenery they were keeping warm. My first thought was that someone was growing marijuana out here, but that didn't make much sense since that was legal in this state. Plus, I was pretty sure marijuana was a taller plant than what was under the short tunnels.

Ramble looked up at me and jerked his head at the plastic tunnels. Someone had used the well to water whatever was under the grow tunnels.

"Can you sense anything magic here?" I asked Artemis out loud for Ramble's benefit.

*Yes…a lot of magic, Vânători. Be cautious.*

I guess it was finally my turn to make myself useful. I approached the nearest grow tunnel and knelt in front of it, trying to see what was inside. The ends of the tunnels were covered in a thick plastic sheet weighed down on the ends by rocks. I lifted the plastic, displacing the rocks. Magic tingled through my hand, and I heard a faint hum in the back of my mind when the stones hit the ground.

*Carefully, Vânători. I was wrong about the magic. It might feel like a gnome, but it's too intricate for their level of magic. It appears a witch cast a spell on these.*

I paused, waiting. It felt like I'd disturbed some kind of spell, but now it was gone.

"Maybe it was a spell to keep animals from getting to whatever's inside?"

*Or it was a ward spell to let someone know that we are disturbing their things. We should be on our guard.*

When nothing else happened, I lifted the plastic higher and peered inside.

"Four-leaf clovers."

The grow tunnel was filled with the shiny, green clovers. They were a bright contrast to all the dead brown grass outside their little pocket of warmth.

"I guess we found our culprit's growing space. Now we just need to find out who they are."

*Only a witch could cast a spell to ward the clovers. It appears your friend Rosalyn has been hiding things from you again.*

"I wouldn't go so far as to call Rosalyn my friend. And we don't know that it's a witch from her coven. She said she didn't recognize the magic being used at the well."

*And she is always so honest with you…*

"Wow, look at you using sarcasm."

Ramble suddenly perked up. His attention laser-focused on something in the woods in the opposite direction we had come from. I let the plastic fall back to cover the clovers and quieted as Ramble shifted into a cat-like mode, stalking something I couldn't hear or see yet. He melted soundlessly into the woods.

A second later, I heard a rustle—

Like a shot, Ramble zipped off. There was an exclamation, then a growl followed by a muffled cry of surprise. I rushed to follow Ramble, but he'd already turned around and was proudly carrying something—no, some*one*—gently in his mouth.

"You drop me this instant, beast, or you'll regret the day you escaped the fires of hell! You hear me?" The squeaky female voice sounded a little too dainty and cute to have her threat taken seriously.

Ramble was certainly unfazed.

He passed me and dropped his prisoner on the ground. At least he'd chosen a spot in the clearing that was clear of snow and ice. It did look a bit muddy though.

"How *dare* you, hellhound?" She demanded, immediately jumping up and tugging her skewed blue dress straight again. She was a few inches shorter than Hyssop's three feet with long blond hair and blue eyes that matched her dress. Her red pointy hat had tumbled into the mud, and she'd dropped a small watering can when Ramble dropped her.

She completely ignored me and twisted to look at her

backside. Her mouth dropped open. "You got *mud* on my brand-new dress!"

I had the brief misogynistic thought that a face that cute shouldn't be able to contort with such anger, then I had to step forward and get between her and Ramble when she put her hands up as if to cast a spell.

"Whoa, hold on now." I moved to put myself between the gnome and Ramble. Only then did she pay any attention to me.

*Do not be wary of the gnome, Vânători. Their magic is limited.*

*You keep writing off what you consider 'lesser' creatures, and they keep surprising you. Maybe, just this one time, we assume she might be a danger.*

I followed my own advice and held up my hands. "We just want to talk."

The gnome peered around me at Ramble who was trying and failing to look meek. "Tell that to sulfur-breath over there," she said, keeping her hands at the ready and jerking her head at Ramble. "He just knocked me down, kidnapped me, then *ruined* my new dress. And *you*," She waggled a finger at me, "are trying to steal my four-leaf clovers."

*We don't have time for this. Let us smite the gnome as punishment for growing four-leaf clovers, then destroy the rest.*

*What? No! We're not going to smite her!*

*That is your role as a Vânători. She already admitted that these are her four-leaf clovers. Merely growing them is a violation of the Laws of the Accords, and the punishment is death. In addition to that, she is also using these four-leaf clovers as a weapon against the barrister which is another violation—*

*—punishable by death. I get it. Breaking the Accords Laws is bad. But don't you want to know why she's going after Preston? What if she also has something to do with the murders?*

*Unlikely.*

*But we don't know for sure.*

This earned me a thoughtful silence which was good because the gnome and Ramble were both staring at me, clearly waiting for me to finish my internal conversation. Funny, Hyssop had always seemed to know that I was mentally speaking to someone when conversing with Artemis around him. Perhaps it was a gnome ability or something.

I cleared my throat. "Listen, there's been a murder in town and Ramble over there—"

"You *named* the hellhound?" She squeaked. "I mean, I'd heard that you were new, but *no one* names a hellhound and lives."

"Then I guess my name is No One," I mused. I mean, yes, I'd broken some unwritten rule about giving Ramble a name which thereby freed him from a deal I'd made with him (which I also hadn't intended to make), but was it really that big of a deal? "And he hasn't killed me yet, so I think I'm good as long as I keep him happy."

Ramble cocked his head to the side as if reconsidering that decision. Wise ass.

"As I was saying, we're investigating some murders in town and also looking into who might be leaving large amounts of four-leaf clovers around people's homes and causing them bad luck."

"I didn't leave clovers around multiple homes," the gnome said, then blatantly admitted, "I left them around Preston Powers' house so he'd get what he deserves."

*And there you have it,* Artemis gloated. *A clear confession.*

Before I could respond to either of them, the gnome suddenly grew solemn. "And I didn't have anything to do with Father Patrick's murder. I liked him, regardless that he was a human. Most of us did."

I nodded. "Did you know him well?"

Her arms slowly drifted down to her sides. "Donavon

introduced us. He said I grow the best roses, and Father Patrick's roses at the church were struggling."

"Wait," I said as a memory stirred. Something about roses and a gnome that lived in Donavon's garden. Then it came to me. "Are you Blush?"

She dipped her head in acknowledgement, but a little anger returned to her eyes. "Aye, I'm Blush, and I know you, too, Vânători. How you *helped* Hyssop. It's downright unnatural, you know, a gnome living indoors and growing plants *inside*." She tsked twice.

"I mean, better alive and living inside the library than dead, I guess."

She harrumphed and crossed her arms over her chest.

I stifled a sigh. It looked like Blush was part of that traditionalist crew who didn't like the changes Hyssop had introduced to the gnome community.

"So...you're growing illegal four-leaf clovers all the way out here? Seems kind of out the way—"

*She's using the magic well's water to grow the clovers, Vânători. It's part of what turns them into true clovers.*

*Oh.* I guess that made more sense now. I switched gears. "But then you're leaving the clovers around Preston's house to give him bad luck?"

"What of it?"

*Impertinent creature.* Artemis scoffed though she knew only I could hear her. *We are the judge, jury, and enforcer. Vânători, find out who the witch is that put the ward spell on the clovers. Then we'll punish the gnome, find the witch and punish her, then return to hunting down the real monster.*

That all seemed a bit over the top for me, and I tried not to roll my eyes. We did need to learn who the witch was though.

"I'm surprised one of the witches would be willing to help

you hide or ward the clovers. Was it Willomena? I know she's not too happy with Preston after what he did to Hyssop."

"What are you even talking about, Vânători? I don't need help from those spell-slingers! We gnomes have our own magic."

*Their magic is used for growing things. Not for complex spells like warding.*

I said this to Blush who somehow managed to look even more indignant.

"I don't know how Hyssop can sing your praises when you're really this dumb, Vânători. It's the witches who can't do complex spells. The magic they weave leaves great big traces even an infant could see. I mean, just look up there!" She pointed at the shimmering net in the sky. "Look at the giant monstrosity that they stuck in the sky over our town! Not only did they not *ask* anyone else in town if it was okay for them to cast a spell that affects all of us, but they have zero finesse. They aren't even trying to be subtle. It's like slapping a giant billboard in the sky that says, 'We're watching you.'" She shook her head in disgust. "It's downright sloppy."

*I guess gnomes have more magic than we thought.* I told Artemis who stayed silent during Blush's tirade.

"Wait," I said to Blush as I realized she'd done more than just complex magic to create the clovers, "did you use magic to get around being seen on Preston's cameras?"

This earned me some serious side-eye. "And if I did?"

"I mean, I don't really care about magicking the cameras —it's honestly a pretty cool skill—but we both know that it's illegal for anyone other than leprechauns to use four-leaf clovers as a weapon, so why chance it and give Preston bad luck?"

Blush threw her hands in the air. "Because he drove Hyssop from his home! The lawyer would have killed him had

Hyssop not fled. And now he's in an unnatural living situation with a *witch*." She shivered. "It's just wrong, Vânători. Even I know that! And what happens to the human who caused this? Absolutely nothing. How is that justice?" She straightened up to stand taller and jutted out her chin. "So, *I'm* giving Hyssop justice by getting even with the lawyer."

"Oh!" Sudden understanding hit me as I recognized the protective tone in Blush's voice. "You *like* Hyssop, don't you?"

"Of course I like him, Vânători? What kind of stupid question is that?"

"No, I mean, you *like-like* him."

"What? N...no, of course not," she sputteringly denied, but she couldn't hide the obvious blush that rose in her cheeks.

"Uh huh. Sure. So you're willing to break the law for someone you just kind of like. Sure. Sure."

"You don't understand, Vânători. I can't say that I *like-like* someone who is breaking so much with tradition. I can't even be friends with him right now! But if the lawyer leaves—"

"—or dies?" I interrupted.

"Or dies," she bit out, glaring at me, "then maybe Hyssop can move back home and be normal, and I can court him again."

Courting? Wow, they really were into some old-school traditional stuff.

"Except that using four-leaf clovers is against the law."

*The Law of the Accords, Vânători*, Artemis corrected.

"I didn't agree to those laws! They're antiquated and no one's enforced them in years."

Artemis choked back indignation.

I held my hand out, palm up. "Why do you think *I'm* here?"

With a quickness I didn't expect, Blush dashed around me on the opposite side from Ramble and dove for one of the grow tunnels. She shoved her hand through plastic at the end of the tunnel and yanked it back out to brandish a four-leaf clover at me.

Okay...

"You think I'll just roll over and let you take away my clovers?" Her breathing was heavy from her efforts as she moved first to her knees, then to a standing position. She didn't seem to notice the mud now smearing the front of her dress.

"You're in for a surprise, Vânători!" She held the clover out between us as if warding me off with it.

We stood awkwardly for a moment.

"What's happening right now?" I finally asked.

Ramble snorted in amusement. I had a feeling if I got into a physical altercation with Blush that he wouldn't be much help. He'd done his part by finding her stash then capturing Blush and bringing her to me.

*She is using the luck of the clover against us,* Artemis explained unhelpfully.

I frowned. *Am I supposed to feel something?*

*No, Vânători. But if you attack the gnome, the clover's luck will prevent you from doing so. You might step wrong and break a leg, or accidentally fall and impale yourself on a tree limb, or slip on a patch of ice, or—*

"Okay, I get it,' I said out loud. "She's using her good luck against me."

Blush jerked the clover at me. "That's right! You'll have to overcome the luck of the clover to kill me, Vânători!"

"Whoa. Okay. Nope." I put out a hand and took a step back. "No one is killing anyone today, so let's just all calm down." Ramble and Blush both looked at me, waiting for me to continue. Blush still held the clover up in front of her. I took a beat to think.

*You cannot just ignore this breach of the Laws of the Accords!*

*The gnome made her choice in growing four-leaf clovers. You are duty bound to uphold the law,* Artemis argued.

"It kind of sounds like a stupid law." I looked at Blush, "I mean, *I* didn't make the law. My ancestors did."

Artemis roared with outrage in my mind. *How dare you mock the Laws of the Accords! They've held together the fabric of nonhuman civilization for decades.*

"Just because a law is old, doesn't make it right. I mean, it's kind of dumb to make growing four-leaf clovers illegal."

Something clicked behind Blush's eyes. "You don't believe in them, do you?"

"The laws?" I asked, unsure at her sudden intensity.

"No, Vânători. The luck of the clovers. You think they're hogwash, don't you?" She vibrated with an intensity that made me want to take a step back.

"I mean..." I stammered, wondering what corner I'd backed myself into here. "I can feel the magic from them, and I've seen first-hand how a bunch of them can cause bad luck. But..." I hesitated then decided to be honest since she was actually listening to me. "I mean...how much luck could they really bring someone? You haven't exactly been terribly lucky if we were able to find you, and Ramble captured you."

A new emotion glittered in Blush's eyes. She took a few steps forward and thrust the clover at me. "You should take it then."

I held up my hands and retreated a step. "Oh, erm, that's okay. I'm good."

"Come on, Vânători. What's the problem? It's just *one*, so it will bring you luck. But you don't *believe* in it, so it won't do anything, right?"

I wasn't so sure about that. In the last few months, I'd learned that a lot of things existed which could hurt me whether I believed in them or not.

Ramble leaned around me and craned his neck forward to sniff the clover. I put out a hand to block him.

"Hey, we don't need a clover, Ramble."

"Oh, I think you do," Blush's grin was slightly maniacal. "I think you might need *alllll* the luck you can get, Vânători." She took another step forward, arm extended, pinching the clover between her thumb and index finger. "Take it. It's a gift. No strings attached. Maybe it will even help you find Father Patrick's murderer."

I didn't move and didn't know what else to say. She just stood there, holding out the clover, clearly not giving up on this.

"Fine." I held out my hand and she dropped the clover into it.

That now-familiar tiny zap of magic hit my palm like static-electricity and was gone just as quickly.

Blush smirked with satisfaction. Artemis was ominously silent.

The clover seemed almost unnaturally green, especially when everything else had gone brown with dormancy in the winter. I waited for something lucky to happen. When nothing stirred but a cold gust of winter wind that rattled the remaining leaves in the trees, I frowned and looked back at Blush.

"I don't get your logic here. If you prove four-leaf clovers are magic, then wouldn't that mean I should be more concerned about you breaking the law by making all these four-leaf clovers and using them against Preston?"

Her smirk only ratcheted up a notch. "Maybe, but it will be worth it when your clover-luck wears off."

"What does that even mean?"

"You'll see." She picked up her hat and watering can like she was preparing to leave.

*You must uphold the laws!* Artemis' voice was like steel. *If you allow the gnome to break the law without any consequences, you signal to the rest of the nonhuman creatures that the new Vânători is too weak to do her job.*

*And if I go around murdering members of the supernatural community for laws that haven't been enforced in years, then I run the risk of making myself their enemy.*

*You are their enemy, Vânători. You won't change that by coddling them.*

*I'm not sure that not killing them is the same as coddling them. Plus, I thought I was supposed to be building up allies who can help me stand against Morvalden? Going around killing people isn't going to win me any friends here.*

Artemis didn't respond. Apparently, she'd said her piece and wouldn't be advising me any further on this. I'd have to decide what to do now. Awesome.

Our silent exchange only took seconds, so Blush hadn't left yet.

I added steel to my voice as I called her name, "Blush." Ramble stiffened beside me, all business now, waiting for whatever judgment I decided to make.

Blush stopped and looked back at me. I got the feeling that if Ramble's demeanor hadn't changed, she would have left. When her eyes fell on him, I saw the fear there. She swallowed and turned fully around to face us again.

"You know I can't let you keep growing all these clovers."

"What—" her voice squeaked, and she swallowed before trying again, clearly afraid now, her eyes darting between Ramble and me. "What are you going to do?"

"*I'm* not going to do anything. This is your mess, so you get to take care of it. You can keep one of the clovers, but you're going to destroy the rest of them."

"What? You can't make me destroy them!"

"Fine, if you don't want to keep one, then you'll keep

none." I looked at Ramble. "Would you kindly do the honors of carrying out this sentence?"

Ramble gave me a confused look and darted a glance at Blush. I quickly realized my error.

"Not her. The clovers. They're dangerous and need to be destroyed."

He jerked his head in a nod, then stepped toward the grow tunnels and took a deep breath.

"Wait!" Blush ran forward, dropping her watering can and putting herself between Ramble and clovers. "We can work this out! Do you want more clovers, Vânători? Is that it?"

"This isn't a shake down, Blush. The clovers are illegal and dangerous. You can take the grow tunnels, but I can't let you break laws that you fully know about."

"That's not fair, Vânători! I didn't make those laws!"

"I understand that, and maybe we can change them someday, but right now, the law says no four-leaf clovers. Consider this a warning. If I hear of you growing another patch of clovers, I'll have to follow the full letter of the law. No more warnings." When she didn't move, I added, "I'm sorry, Blush. Please take your grow tunnels, or Ramble will burn those as well."

Mouth screwed up in anger, Blush stomped over to the tunnels and yanked them out of the ground. Her angry silence was deafening.

I wanted to apologize again but managed to keep it to myself. It would only make me look weak. "You can take one clover with you."

"I already have one on me," She bit out and stomped a good distance away from the clovers.

I realized that meant she'd been bluffing about using the luck of the clover against me since she technically had two clovers at the time. Ah well.

I nodded to Ramble. He took a deep breath, then let out

a WHOOSH of orange and red fire. The clovers immediately blackened and withered to a crisp, but it took several more fiery breaths for the magic to snap out of existence.

When it was done, Blush piled her watering can onto the upside-down grow tunnels, then picked them all up, spun on her heel, and marched off in the direction she'd come. Over her shoulder she shouted, "I hope that clover gets you exactly what you deserve, Vânători!"

"And I hope you learn to see past Hyssop's non-traditional way of living and tell him how you really feel," I hollered after her retreating figure. As retorts, it was kind of lacking, but whatever.

I waited until she'd disappeared before murmuring, "I guess we didn't make any friends today."

Ramble huffed in agreement.

*She's lucky you didn't have your hellhound rend her limb from limb.* I opened my mouth to tell her I wouldn't ask Ramble to do that, but then she added, *And you should not have taken the clover.*

I rolled my eyes. "I wouldn't ask Ramble to do something like that. And with the clover, she practically *forced* me to take it." We found our way back to the sidewalk and started toward the car. "And what's wrong with a little luck?"

*It's not what's wrong with luck, Vânători. It's what happens when the luck runs out. When a person has unnatural luck for too long, they grow accustomed to it. Their behavior begins to change: gambling more because they're lucky or taking unnecessary risks because they had been somewhat protected by the luck of the clover. Then the luck is suddenly gone, but it's not so easy to change their behavior back to be less...reckless.*

As we crossed the street to the car, I saw a piece of paper fluttering on the ground. "Sweet! Five bucks!" I snatched it up.

*And so it begins.*

"What? It's just a five! It's not even a hundred dollar bill. I

promise I won't start expecting money to rain from the sky."
Ramble and I paused in unison and looked up at the sky.

*Neither of you are amusing. Do not say I did not warn you to burn that clover.*

We piled back in the car, and I debated whether I should bother calling Rosalyn to tell her who had been using magic at the well. Was it really her business? I decided against it for now. Maybe I'd call her after we investigated the magic out at Louis's motel.

Instead, I pulled out my phone to text Preston and realized I had a missed call from Hester. I must not have had a signal near the well, but luckily, she'd left a voicemail. I put it on speaker and hit play so I wouldn't have to repeat any information to Ramble.

"Vi, I'm not actually supposed to be speaking to you right now," Hester whispered in the message, "but I felt I should tell you that I've been called away *specifically* because of what might be in town. They're keeping quiet about what it is, but the fact that they *pulled* me when I could have been documenting a Vânători in action..." She sounded more annoyed that she was missing out on the show than that I might be in imminent danger. As if remembering her train of thought, she went on, "I don't think it bodes well. Be careful, Vianne."

*A Witness warning a Vânători?* Artemis said with some surprise. *That's practically unheard of.*

"See? Making friends and having allies can be a useful thing."

She grumbled something to herself but I couldn't tell what she was saying. I looked at Ramble. "Why make her leave, though? I thought the whole point of the Witnesses was to *witness* what was happening within the supernatural community."

Ramble tilted his head slightly and lifted a brow. I could almost feel his silent thought,

"You think they pulled her because they knew this creature would wreak havoc on the town?"

This earned me a shrug.

"Well, shit." This thing was definitely bad news if that was the case. After all, Hester had excitedly accompanied me into Pamola's cave and hadn't seemed at all afraid of him. Then again, maybe the Witnesses viewed her actions as reckless. Making her leave town might simply be their method of separating her from the dangerous temptation to investigate this new creature.

Either way, it didn't sound like she'd be much help.

Remembering why I'd pulled out my phone in the first place, I texted Preston and let him know we'd found the culprit behind his bad luck. Hopefully the warning would be enough to stop Blush from targeting him with clovers again. Maybe I'd swing by his house in a couple of days and do another sweep. Just in case.

I was lost in thought trying to decide our next best course of action when the phone rang in my hand at full volume. My soul almost left my body at the unexpected noise.

It was the sheriff.

"Vi. We've got access to the security footage from the scrapyard. You're gonna want to see this."

# Chapter Twenty

I was back in the sheriff's little office, standing in the corner. The sheriff and Deputy Englewood leaned over a laptop sitting precariously on a stack of folders and papers on the sheriff's desk.

"It didn't take long for the tech guy we use out of Portland to crack the security and access the video. Wayne literally used the word 'password' for his password." The sheriff threw a tight smile back at me. Under other circumstances, it would have been a full grin, but there were too many people turning up dead on his watch. His typically crisp uniform was creased with more than one day's wear, and the coffee waiting on his desk was doing nothing to get rid of the bags under his eyes.

His movements were a little jerky as he turned back to the laptop. Whatever was on the video had shaken him up.

"Okay, start it from there," he told Englewood. She hit play and backed up to give me a clear view of the screen.

We were looking at the inside of the scrap yard's front room. The camera was in the corner behind the counter, angled to catch anyone who walked through the door. Occasionally, you could see someone's head bob along at the very bottom of the picture when they walked behind the counter.

Movement at the top right of the screen drew my attention to the front door as a man walked in. It was Father Patrick.

"What the hell?"

"Keep watching," the sheriff grimly directed.

The priest smiled as he approached the counter, then clasped hands with someone behind it. From the person's build, it looked like Wayne Fielder.

"When was this?" I asked.

"Two days ago."

My mouth dropped open, and the sheriff reached out and paused the video.

"Exactly. Father Patrick's body had already been discovered by the time this video was taken. So either the body discovered in the church somehow *wasn't* Father Patrick, or the person in this video isn't Father Patrick."

"Maybe he has a twin brother," Englewood dryly quipped, though she looked just as shaken up as I felt. And she'd presumably already seen the video at least once.

It took me a moment to gather my wits. "How sure are we that the DNA from the person found in the church was a match for Father Patrick?" I paused as another possibility came to me. "Could someone trick a DNA test somehow? Like could they leave enough of their own body fluids so that it got tested instead of the actual remains?"

The sheriff shook his head. "It was a definite match, and it's unlikely Father Patrick somehow faked his death like that. There was too much..." he hesitated, clearly unsure what word to use without sounding cold. "...*matter* left over that the coroner double-checked just in case there was more than one victim in that, uh, pile."

Englewood leaned against the edge of the sheriff's desk.

"So, let's look at this whole story because there are obviously a *lot* of holes in it. According to the coroner, the priest may have died *before* he called the sheriff and met with you in person, Vi." She shook her head in disbelief at her own words but continued on, "Then, *after* we've found his verified remains, he somehow pops up again in security camera footage from a murder scene?" She paused and looked at us before asking in a tone dripping with disbelief, "Is that about right?"

I realized she thought we were all in on some kind of joke. Which...okay, yes. We *did* have information we hadn't shared with her about the people who populated this town. I wasn't sure how she would take the existence of citizens who were a little more than human. It didn't feel like it was my call to make though, since I wasn't the one in charge here. I was merely a consultant.

But why would the sheriff call me in if he didn't want me to provide some paranormal insights into the murders? Maybe he wanted to use this as an opportunity to break the news about the town to Englewood. If so, it was time I started earning my consultant fees.

If I was being honest, I kind of relished the idea of shaking up the deputy's neat little black and white world.

"There may be a third option," I finally answered, then hedged, "I mean, besides this guy on camera being a long-lost evil twin or the zombie version of Father Patrick," I started, but stopped at the sheriff's look.

"You might want to see the rest of the footage before you give any suggestions, Vi," he cautioned.

Okay. Maybe I was wrong and he didn't want to reveal the truth about Ricketts yet. I nodded and he hit the play button again.

On screen, Father Patrick and the man I presumed to be Wayne, were still clasping hands when Father Patrick said something and let his smile slip into something more sinister. Whatever he said caused an instant change in Wayne. The man tried to jerk his hand back, but the priest had it in a death grip. His grin grew until it was grotesquely comical. Without warning, the priest leapt over the counter to land behind the other man, but he was still gripping Wayne's hand as he did so. The move pulled Wayne's arm behind his back at a decidedly wrong angle.

Wayne's knees buckled, but the priest kept him standing by forcing his hand up behind his back. Wayne let out a silent scream. It must have gotten the attention of the woman we'd found in the office because the priest suddenly looked off camera to the left. Wayne twisted, opening his mouth to shout something at the woman.

The next thing happened so quickly that the sheriff had to go back and play it again, several times, in slow motion before I believed it. Even Artemis let out a surprised note at what unfolded on screen.

Father Patrick raised his free left hand, which shifted to a flesh-colored liquid state before elongating until it was several feet long with something sharp and serrated on the end.

In the next split second, he took one lunging step to his left and swiped his new appendage at the woman off screen twice in quick succession.

Wayne, with tears of pain in his eyes, shouted something else and tried to use his other arm to stop the priest. The priest turned back to Wayne and shortened his arm back to normal length but kept the bladed form which now dripped with blood. He raised the knife-arm and in a flash, shoved it through Wayne's skull.

I might have let out an involuntary noise of surprise when I saw that. The second time the sheriff played it in slow-motion, though, I wondered how much strength a person needed to shove a knife through someone's skull.

*You should know that, Vânători. After all, you shoved a knife into the previous deputy's head.*

*That was entirely different, Artemis. He was a giant monster-beast on a murdering spree.* Then I realized that I was clearly focused on the wrong detail here. I looked at the time stamp in the video.

"Wait, this security footage is from *before* the security video at the gas station?"

The sheriff nodded soberly, clearly already having thought through the implications of that. It was Englewood who echoed my own thoughts. "So, if Wayne Fielders was just murdered by this terminator wanna-be, then how the hell did he walk into the gas station and murder the cashier there three hours later?"

My attention snapped back to the screen, and I all but forgot my question. The priest was looking up at the security camera. It felt like his eyes bore right into mine. A chill went down my spine. He then very clearly mouthed one word: Vânători.

Then, just like at the gas station, the footage turned to snow.

*Did he just...?* I asked Artemis.

She sounded just as spooked as I was. *That monster just said your name, Vânători. I think he's calling you to duel.*

I glanced at the sheriff who knew exactly what my last name was. Had he told Englewood yet that it wasn't actually Mason? Or was he keeping her in the dark for now to protect me?

He cleared his throat and looked away from me briefly before turning back.

Okay, so he hadn't told her yet.

"Now that you've seen the footage, we wondered if you might have some ideas of what's going on here."

What was going on here was that I was thinking about

cutting my losses and getting the hell out of Ricketts. Not only would Morvalden find me soon, but now a zombie-priest was calling me out *after murdering a guy with a sword arm?*

That was a hard no for me.

I suddenly wished that Ramble was here with me. It had seemed like a bad idea to bring him into the Sheriff's Department where it would be difficult to hide his presence. Now I wish I'd thrown caution to the wind.

*Pull yourself together, Vânători. We've faced worse.*

*No, we haven't! You might have, but I have not faced worse than that. This is an entirely new supernatural being, Artemis!*

*You're right that it's something new, but it's not so much different than a shifter, taking on the likeness of its victims and using their visage to earn the trust of its next target.*

*Um, except that it can turn its body parts into weapons!*

*Morvalden is quite a bit more terrifying than that creature, yet you faced him.*

*I faced him in my* dreams, I said. *There's clearly a difference.*

"Vi?" The sheriff said, snapping me out of my internal dialogue with the goddess.

I looked over at him. He was watching me carefully. Did he think I had something to do with the murders again since the bad guy had said my name? Or did he realize that the guy was calling me out?

Englewood, still leaning on the desk beside him, waited for my response with a neutral expression. She *definitely* didn't trust me.

"I think," I started, brain whirring as I tried to piece together what I'd seen, "that there might be an explanation, but it's not one that science will back up." I cleared my throat. "One quick question though: Do we know whose body was outside the scrapyard?"

"Not yet," the sheriff said. "We had to send the remains away to the same place as before but if there's a match in the system, then we should know in the next day or so. If not, then we might never know."

I took a breath. What I was about to say next would shake up Englewood's world. I had a feeling she was someone who liked to stick to the facts though, so I was going to lean into that with everything I had.

"If I had to hazard a guess, I'd say that the remains outside the scrapyard belong to Wayne Fielders, and I don't think it was the real Father Patrick that killed him."

"Oh?" Englewood intoned, crossing her arms over her chest, "and if Father Patrick didn't kill Wayne, as we just saw on camera, and Wayne didn't kill that cashier, as we saw in the other security footage, then what, exactly, do you think happened? Because we already know that the footage isn't doctored in any way other than getting cut off for some reason."

"I think there's someone or some*thing* in town right now that doesn't care how many people it kills so long as it gets what it wants."

"And what does it want?" Englewood shifted back to neutral again.

*Me, apparently,* I thought but said, "I'm not sure, but I think I'm getting a better picture of what kind of creature it might be." I looked Englewood dead in the eyes and decided to be somewhat straight with her. "You're not going to believe what I'm about to say, Deputy, but I think the thing that's murdering people is a new type of shifter that can turn into the person it kills. It's different from other shifters, though, in that, when it takes on the identity of a new person, it leaves that person's body as a steaming pile of meat."

"You're right about one thing, Miss Mason. Or should I say, Vianne Vanator?" She paused dramatically to catch my look of surprise. "I don't believe you."

Even the sheriff was surprised. Well, shit. I guess the cat was out of the bag. Maybe I'd end up back in jail after all.

"Don't worry," she said in a condescending tone that made me want to do the exact opposite of what she'd ordered. "I'm not going to turn you in just yet, but only if you cooperate with our investigation. So, do please share why you think the murderer is some magical creature? Also, it would be great to know why he seems to be specifically calling you out."

I'm not gonna lie, I had a moment where I almost called Ramble to the station. I could do it, too. With just a thought, I could pop Ramble into the room, and he could help me avoid getting arrested by yet another Ricketts deputy.

But adding a fire-breathing hellhound to the situation probably wouldn't help. Especially since Ramble didn't give a rat's ass if he burned the building down.

Instead of popping Ramble in and making a run for it, I decided to go for total honesty.

"Well," I said, mostly thinking out loud and trying not to sound like an idiot as I stumbled over my words, "I'm glad you know who I am now. I don't like lying to you." (That might have been a lie.) "And though you sort of know what I do, there's a bit more to it than you think. But one reason I think that there's a new type of shifter in town is because the other beings in this town have said that even they don't know what it is."

"So, a shifter and, what was the other thing? Oh yes, a gremlin. Anything else? Vampires? Maybe a werewolf or two?" She gave a bark of forced laughter. "You're really something, you know that? Was it you who burned down that house in the suburbs that day you missed your parole check-in?"

I froze, and she nodded.

"I thought so. You know," she turned to the sheriff, "they found two bodies in that wreckage. Well, what was left of two bodies. The fire wiped out everything but two partially full sets of teeth."

Yup. That sounded about right. The two people they'd found were actually vampires who'd kidnapped me and the hunter Jax. They were also keeping Ramble hostage, which was how I first met the hellhound and unknowingly made a deal with him. It wouldn't matter to the deputy that Ramble had been the one to kill the vampires and technically set their house on fire. Of course, I'd been the one to pour gasoline all through the house. I'd also taken the vampire's fangs after Jax insisted that it was what hunters did.

I still had the teeth in a backpack at the cabin. Talk about damning evidence.

But none of that would matter to the deputy because she didn't believe in hellhounds or gremlins or vampires or shifters.

*Be cautious, Vânători. I'm sure she'll give you an opening to attack.*

*I'd rather not attack her if I can help it. Besides, it's not her fault she's ignorant about the supernatural community. Let's see where this goes and if we have to defend ourselves, we will.*

In response, I felt a slight tingling sensation as Artemis allowed some of her pent-up energy to spill into my core. I guess she wanted me to be ready.

Englewood was still talking. "And now you're murdering people and leaving behind mutilated bodies?" She finally pushed off the desk to take a step toward me. "How do you even manage it, let alone live with yourself? I mean, it's obvious you have some sort of mental illness since you clearly believe in imaginary things, but how do you sleep at night with all that blood on your hands?"

"Now hold on a second." The sheriff stood up, putting himself between us a moment before Englewood would have gotten too close for comfort. "Vi might not be squeaky clean." He held up his hands in a placating gesture. "But I can tell you that she is most certainly not a murderer." He glanced back at me and raised a brow. "I'm sure there's an explanation for the house that burned down—if she was even involved with it."

"Well..." I started and my slightly guilty tone made the sheriff turn to get a better look at me. "I did help burn down that house, but only because of what was in there." I looked at the deputy. "You'll just say I was delusional, but the remains inside weren't humans, they were vampires."

She scoffed and rolled her eyes, but the sheriff watched me, clearly taking in the existence of vampires and applying that fact to his little town.

"I know, it sounds crazy, right?" I said, almost tripping over my own words. "Hell, *I* thought I was losing my mind when I first learned about this world of the supernatural, but now I have a hellhound partner and live in a town full of supernatural creatures where I'm getting paid to consult with local law enforcement to track down what might be a totally new creature."

Whew. I had to take a breath after all that.

"Really? A hellhound?" She shifted her attention to the sheriff. "Are you just going to stand there and listen to this?"

He dropped his head for a moment, focusing on the floor while he clearly struggled for what to say next. "Englewood, when I hired you, I told you that this town was *different* from where you worked before."

"Not you, too." Englewood groaned, then straightened up, all serious suddenly. "Sheriff, I can't in good conscience allow this to continue without notifying the proper authorities."

The sheriff surprised us both with a grin. "Good luck with that. Most of the folks who would be the 'proper authorities' are wise to the real ways of the world. You sort of have to be when you keep stumbling across unreal scenarios that can't be explained by modern science." He shrugged but made sure to continue standing between us.

"So what, you just want me to believe in hellhounds and vampires now?" She asked.

"I mean," I hedged, "I could prove it to you if you'd like, but you've gotta promise not to draw your gun and start shooting."

Her attention fell on me. "And just how exactly are you going to prove it? Is your widdle imaginary hellhound in the room with us?"

Her babytalk wasn't going to phase me. Wait until she found out I'd killed her predecessor when he turned into a giant monster-dog.

"Well, he *is* invisible—"

"Of course he is," she cut me off, rolling her eyes.

"—but he isn't in the room right now," I finished.

"Do it then," she challenged. "Prove to me that this supernatural world exists, and I won't arrest you right now and have the sheriff arrested for aiding a wanted person."

Yikes. I hadn't thought about the repercussions the sheriff might face by hiring me as a consultant.

"Alright," I replied, striving to maintain my composure and not match her growing agitation, "I'm going to call him here, but you have to promise that you won't shoot him."

"That's not gonna be a problem because he doesn't exist." At my pointed look, she threw up her hands. "Fine. I promise that I will not shoot the imaginary, invisible hellhound."

The sheriff murmured, "I'm not so sure this is a good idea..." just as I pictured Ramble standing on the floor beside me in the only other open space in the office.

POP!

# Chapter Twenty-One

❧

The sheriff and deputy both jumped at the sound as Ramble appeared in the empty space. Of course, neither of them could see the predator whose eyes glowed red. He'd popped into place in a crouched position, ready to pounce on whomever had threatened me.

"It's okay, Ramble," I quickly told him. "Sorry to spring this on you, buddy, but this is just an introduction between you and Deputy Englewood, here." He relaxed a little, though I could still tell that he was ready to respond should the deputy try anything.

I glanced over at her but saw that the surprise was already gone from her face. She'd heard him pop in but wasn't convinced he was actually there or existed at all. I stifled a sigh. But I mean, who could blame her for not believing? My introduction to the supernatural world had been to be attacked by a vampire who almost killed me, and I'd still been skeptical. I tried to see the situation from her point of view. I could have played that popping sound from my phone. Or maybe made the noise some other way. A simple sound wasn't going to be enough. We'd need to do a bit more to convince her.

I turned back to Ramble and tried to catch him up to speed. "We just watched the scrapyard security footage, and it showed Father Patrick killing Wayne Fielders by turning his arm into a sword."

Ramble's brows rose in surprise.

"Yeah, and the footage was timestamped for after Father Patrick died but also before the gas station security camera where Wayne Fielders killed the clerk there. So, I'm thinking some kind of new shifter."

He turned his head to the side when I was done talking, taking in all this new information then jerked his head at the computer. He wanted to see the scrapyard security footage for himself.

"We can play it again in a second, but first, the Deputy still thinks I'm somehow involved with the murders because she knows about the house we burned down in Indiana that had the vampires in it... but she doesn't believe they were vampires."

He snorted his amusement. Unlike me, Ramble had no qualms about ridding the world of a few vampires and committing arson. Maybe I should try to be more like him. Then he realized that I'd let the cat out of the bag on vampires. He looked from me to the sheriff in question.

I shrugged. Surely the sheriff would have figured out the existence of vampires eventually. I mean, we'd kind of tiptoed around it in a few of our conversations. The question was, would he put two and two together with Louis? That wouldn't be so great. It hadn't really been my place to say what Louis was.

Not much I could do about it now, though. I refocused on the situation at hand.

"So, I called you here to show the deputy that there's

more to this world than just humans. I was hoping maybe you could do something to show the deputy that you exist?"

This earned me a downright annoyed look and a raised eyebrow.

I held up my hands. The thing with Ramble was that we could joke, and I knew we'd have each other's backs, but I wouldn't put it past him to singe my eyebrows a bit if I crossed a line. "I know, I know. You're not a dog that I can ask to do tricks on command, but if there's something you wouldn't *mind* doing to show her you exist, that would be really helpful right now." As a last resort, I added, "And it would mean I don't get arrested which also means you get a burger for dinner tonight."

Ramble let out an over dramatic sigh and my spirits rose. That meant he'd do it.

"But, uh, maybe don't burn my office down, huh?" The sheriff asked a little sheepishly.

This time Ramble actually grumbled to himself and slowly looked around the office, clearly sizing it up and deciding what he could do to prove he existed.

I could see the deputy growing a little uncomfortable as she clearly heard Ramble grumbling. Too bad. She'd brought this on herself.

I watched as Ramble continued thinking over how to prove his existence to a disbeliever. I'd always considered invisibility to be a pretty cool ability, but now that I thought about it, it must kind of suck. Ramble didn't get to pick and choose who actually saw him. Sure, he could *make* someone aware that he was there as he was about to do, but they still wouldn't be able to see him. I'd never really thought about how annoying that must be to have to make a conscious effort to be noticed.

No wonder he put up with me.

The sheriff stayed where he was, letting things play out

without interference. I couldn't blame him. His life would be a lot easier if his deputy knew what was up in her new town.

Having come to a decision, Ramble started toward the deputy. I wasn't sure what his goal was, but I didn't want him to startle her too much. "Remember that you said you wouldn't shoot him, Deputy."

"We both know there's nothing here to sh—oh!"

She jerked and jumped backwards to land against the sheriff's desk as Ramble lifted his head and let out a small gout of fire. He was careful to direct the flames toward the ceiling and only let the flames burn for a second or two since there was a fire-sprinkler system overhead.

Apparently, he wasn't done there. He walked forward, ensuring his claws clicked extra loudly on the tile floor, and then gently brushed against the deputy's thighs.

I was glad I'd made her promise not to shoot him because her immediate response was to jump backwards and reach for her service weapon.

"You said you wouldn't shoot," I reminded her.

Eyes bulging, the deputy scanned the space in front of her before glancing up at me.

"It's not... it's not real," she said though she was clearly talking more to herself than to us. "It's some kind of trick."

As if to send the point home, Ramble sat next to the deputy and leaned his not inconsiderate weight against her legs. It reminded me of the way a dog will lean against you when it wants to be petted. I'd never make that comparison out loud, though. I didn't need my skin burned to a crisp, thank you very much.

She started to reach for her gun again and stopped herself. Closing her eyes, she took a deep breath then looked down where her brain was telling her that something big and warm was leaning against her even if her eyes couldn't see it. After a second's hesitation, she reached down with one trembling hand and touched the top of Ramble's head.

He wasn't a fan of being petted and let out a long-suffering sigh.

The deputy immediately jerked her hand back and looked at me with wide eyes.

"He's very, very real, Englewood," the sheriff said. "I can't begin to tell you how many odd creatures I've encountered in these parts." He looked over at me. "Heck, I recently went tumbling down an embankment wrestling with a guy who had a damn moose head where a normal human head should have been."

I had half a mind to tell him I'd just had another run-in with the Power but decided we had more important things to focus on right now.

The sheriff continued, "It's better if you know that there are beings out there which don't fit our definition of normal, nor do they abide by the laws of science most of the time. "But," he added, "they do try to abide by our human laws if they want to live in this town."

Ramble decided he'd been nice enough to the deputy and stepped away from her. He took a seat to the side where he could see the three of us at once and let out a light whuff. The deputy flinched at the sound but seemed to be maintaining her control better now that Ramble was no longer leaning on her, though she scanned the room for some sign of where he'd gone.

I brought the attention back to our discussion. "You have a lot of folks from the supernatural community living in your town. Most of them just want to live their lives quietly and fit into normal human society. On occasion, I help out as a sort of liaison to make sure everything stays peaceful."

The deputy looked over at me, then went back to scanning the room as she spoke, "What makes you so special?"

Her tone was more curious than angry, so I decided to answer her.

"I come from a long line of vampire hunters who have… abilities." I waved at Ramble, "Like being able to see hellhounds."

The sheriff nodded. "She's the real deal, Englewood. She's the one who figured out and stopped those murders last month."

"I did have some help," I admitted then got back to the point. "Look, I know this is super weird, and you'll probably go home and convince yourself that you imagined this whole thing or that we somehow tricked you, but what I need you to know is that I didn't kill Father Patrick or any of those other people." I caught her eyes and held them. "You saw that yourself from the security camera footage. But I'm trying to get a better idea of what *did* kill them, and all my sources are saying that it's a new type of shifter that no one's familiar with."

*Am I one of your sources, Vânători?*

*The less people who know about you, Artemis, the better. I don't want anyone getting the idea that they can just steal you and be the next Vânători.*

*Hmm.* She seemed disappointed that I hadn't mentioned her but at least she wasn't going to keep griping. Not right now anyways. I was sure I'd hear about it later.

"So," the sheriff broke in, "what *do* we know about this thing?"

"Not much, but I think one thing about it is pretty obvious."

"And what's that?" The deputy said as she slowly gained more confidence and stopped leaning so hard on the desk (though her eyes still occasionally scanned the room for evidence of Ramble).

As we spoke, I'd been thinking about the shifter's moves

so far. It might have said my name in the security footage from the scrapyard, but I wasn't the one it kept trying to get to come out to meet it somewhere alone. In fact, so far it seemed that I'd been foiling all its plans by showing up where I wasn't wanted.

"I hate to say it, Sheriff, but I think this new shifter is after *you*."

"What?" The sheriff's voice was full of disbelief. "How do you figure that? It was your name the thing said at the scrapyard."

"You're right, but it wasn't Father Patrick who called you to take care of the gremlin—it was the shifter." I watched their faces as they processed this. The deputy still wasn't sure she wanted to buy into the supernatural thing, but at least she was listening. "The shifter had already killed Father Patrick to take on his likeness. Then he took on Father Patrick's likeness and Griffin, er, the gremlin, knew that it wasn't really Father Patrick." I paused as realization and guilt hit me. "That's why the gremlin tried so hard to open the door to that little room while I was there. He was trying to show me Father Patrick's remains."

*If you had taken me with you that day, we could have stopped him there and then,* the necklace chided. *I would have been able to see the magic on him.*

Super. Thanks for the guilt trip, Artemis. She was right though. If I'd brought her with me that day, maybe she could have warned me that the priest wasn't a normal human. Had I missed an opportunity to save those people in Fielderstown simply because I'd childishly avoided wearing the necklace?

No, that didn't quite track. *You might have been able to tell me he wasn't human, but then what? We might still not have discovered that he'd killed the real Father Patrick. Plus, would you have believed Griffin? You called him vermin and wanted me to exterminate him the moment you met him.*

Her silence proved my point.

Guilt trip avoided.

Ramble cleared his throat, making both the sheriff and the deputy jump. Apparently, I'd paused for too long to have the side conversation with Artemis. I needed to work on that.

"Sorry, just mentally working some things out." I focused on the sheriff. "When Father Patrick, who was really the shifter that just *looked* like Father Patrick, called you to ask for help with Griffin—that's the gremlin—did he ask for me specifically or was he looking for your help?"

The sheriff narrowed his eyes as he thought back to the conversation. "He asked if I could come out, but when I got a better idea of what he wanted, I told him I'd send you."

I nodded. "Then he tried a different tactic. He went all the way out to Fielderstown—maybe to get away from so many people or maybe he was targeting Wayne Fielder for a specific reason—but he killed Wayne and took on his likeness. When did Wayne Fielder call you to say that strange things were happening around his town?"

"The day after Father Patrick called, actually. He asked me to meet him at the scrapyard to talk with him about some strange occurrences out there. But I told him it would have to wait until I could get a handle on the Father Patrick investigation."

I nodded, waiting for things to click for the sheriff and the deputy. They gave each other a blank look, then Englewood stuck her hand out in a 'come on' gesture. "Are you gonna share, or are you gonna make us guess what you're thinking?"

"It was the shifter calling you as Wayne, Sheriff. The shifter is trying to get you alone so that he can become *you*. First, he became the Priest with the bogus story about Griffin. When that didn't work, he tried to lure you out to Field-erstown where he'd already killed several people."

"If he wants the sheriff so badly, why not just come here and be done with it?"

"Because here, the sheriff has backup, and his backup has weapons."

The sheriff didn't look convinced. "Even if you're right, why would he want to be *me?*"

The deputy, who'd been leaning on the sheriff's desk, suddenly stood up straight. "You're one of the most trusted people in town, Sheriff. Even more trusted than Father Patrick." She stopped and thought it through another step. "And we're the only law enforcement within an hour's drive. If this guy took us out, then he could wreak havoc in town for quite some time before help would come."

"You believe me then?" I asked her.

She gave me a look that said we'd never be besties. That was fine with me.

"I'm not sure *what* I believe, but it's hard to question the security footage we saw. This is the only motive that makes any sense."

I'd take my wins where I could get them.

"Alright, so if this guy is after me, what do we do?" The sheriff asked. "If he's some sort of shifter like you said, then he can take on anyone's likeness, right?"

I started to nod, then stopped. "We know that he can look like *humans,* but I'm not sure he can do the same thing with other creatures from the supernatural community."

"Okay..." the sheriff said slowly.

"So maybe we partner you up with someone non-human for a bit."

"I don't really think that's necessary, Vi. And with Donavon out of town, I'm not sure who I'd even go to for that. I don't think anyone from that community would appreciate me tagging along with them all day."

"You don't think the pack would give you their protection?"

He shook his head. "Not without Donavon there. He warned me away from connecting with them while he's gone. Said it would be best to let any issues wait until he got back."

I shrugged. "I guess that leaves me."

His eyebrows climbed his forehead. "You seem pretty human, Vi." His eyes narrowed. "Unless this is just a ploy to get more consulting hours?"

"It's really not," I said and held up my hands.

At the same time, the deputy said, "I think we'll be just fine."

When I raised a brow in question, she coolly explained. "We just have to be on the lookout for the last body he took, right? So, Wayne Fielders."

"No, it's the lady from the gas station, remember?" I reminded her. "He looked like Wayne Fielders when he killed her, and he left another body behind. If you could run tests or something to see who that body was, I bet it would be her. That means he's walking around looking like the cashier from the gas station." I turned my attention back to the sheriff. "Do we know who she was or at least have a name yet?"

"Arielle Cape. She lived in Fielderstown her whole life and doesn't seem to have many people who know her outside that small community other than the church."

"Father Patrick's church?" I asked.

The sheriff shook his head. "No, a smaller Baptist church between here and Fielderstown."

An image back from my pre-vampire hunter days flashed in my mind of the mostly filled parking lot of the Baptist church next door to the Pawn Shop where I worked back in Indiana. It was always full on Sundays, of course, but they had some sort of service on Wednesday nights, too. Sometimes their services were so well-attended that people from there parked in the Pawn Shop's lot when the church lot was full. I remembered because my asshole boss, Garth, had frequently asked me to call a tow truck when that happened.

"Uh, today's Wednesday, right?" I asked, earning an odd look from the sheriff and a small 'no duh' nod from the deputy. "I think I know the shifter's next move, then."

Chapter Twenty-Two

After laying out a plan with the sheriff and deputy, Ramble and I headed to the motel to investigate the magic that the witch's radar had caught and also speak with Louis.

*Why are we still looking into this use of magic, Vânători? We know what the creature is and where it will be next. We should instead be preparing for battle.*

"We know next to nothing about this new creature, Artemis," I countered. "I want to speak with Louis and see if he might know something. And we still don't know who used magic near the motel. What if it's this new creature?"

*Shifters don't use magic other than their innate ability to become someone else.*

I shook my head as I pulled into the motel lot and parked near the small front office. I didn't see Louis's car, but that didn't mean he wasn't here. "You keep speaking in these absolutes that might have been true during your time with the last Vânători, but we've already learned that things have changed. Just look at Blush. She can work more magic than you thought possible. And we know this shifter works differently than any you've encountered. What if this creature can also do magic? I'd rather learn everything we can about it before I go up against it."

Ramble whuffed in the backseat, though the noise was somewhat garbled by the last bites of hamburger I'd stopped to get him on the way to the motel.

"Sorry," I said, turning in my seat to look at him. "Before *we* go up against it."

He nodded his approval.

Artemis still grumbled as I exited the car and opened the back door for Ramble. I tried the front office, but it was locked. A note on the door said, "Back in a few minutes," but it didn't specify when that would be.

I didn't want to go snooping around the motel without letting Louis know what I was doing, so I sent him a long text to catch him up on the shifter and also to let him know about the use of magic behind his hotel. I waited a few minutes to see if he'd text back and when nothing came through, I sighed.

"Maybe he's sleeping? It is still daytime."

*Vampires do not have to sleep during the day, Vânători. That is a myth. You know this.*

"Just because he doesn't have to sleep, doesn't mean he isn't. Then again, his car isn't here, so maybe he's out running an errand."

*Let us get this over with then. I'm sure it will be nothing more than gnome magic or something of that nature.*

I didn't bother to reply, just headed toward the rear of the motel. The building was a typical motel set up: long, single-story building with an office on one end and an amenities building on the other end. From my brief stay here, I knew that the amenities consisted of an ice maker, a crappy washing machine, and a dryer. I walked in that direction just to make sure Louis wasn't doing something in that section of the building.

Nope. Empty.

There was only one other car in the lot, parked in front of a motel. As we passed the room in front of the car, I heard the sounds of a tv from inside.

So far, everything seemed pretty normal.

We walked around the side of the motel to find that the building was backed by a short, flat section of overgrown weeds before rising into a steep hill that was topped by trees. It looked like the motel's building site had been cut right out of the hill. I was pretty sure if we climbed up it and walked a short distance through the trees that we'd run into a more residential area of town.

I wandered along the flat strip of grass, glad that the back of the motel didn't have windows. Still, I kept my voice low as I asked, "Alright…feel anything, Artemis?"

The goddess was silent for a moment, then tentatively said, *There is some lingering magic here, but you'll need to wander around until we step into it or stop and use some energy to find it. The process would be much like we used under the barrister's house to locate the clovers.*

I scrunched up my nose, not really thrilled by the need to waste our energy on this side quest. Especially if we'd need that energy later when we might confront the shifter.

Luckily, I didn't end up needing to use any energy. Ramble wandered around for a moment, then honed in on something that was closer to the backside of where the motel's office was. He stopped, looked back at me, and gave a pointed whuff.

I jogged over to him. Ramble looked from me to something in front of him that I couldn't see. I certainly *felt* something though. It was an odd feeling of *wrongness,* similar but smaller in scale to what we'd experienced in Fielderstown.

I raised a hand to investigate what it was, but Artemis's words stopped me.

*It is a tear in the world to Between...* The awe in her voice was tinged with fear.

A shiver rolled down my spine. There wasn't much that scared the goddess. "What else can open a doorway to Between?" I asked as I tried to see the tear. Only by stepping past it and using my peripheral vision could I see it. Even then, it was merely a faint line in the air. Almost like a suspended spiderweb except that instead of a perfect line, it was raggedy. It really did look like it had been torn into reality.

*Not a doorway—a tear. I...I do not know of any living creature who can do such a thing.*

"It's got to be the shifter, right? And maybe he opened a tear like this—or maybe multiple tears—in Fielderstown and that's why we had that feeling of dread while we were there." I paused in thought, still trying to see the tear in my peripheral vision. "I wonder if that's why the cameras in the scrapyard and the gas station acted up. Maybe it was a reaction to the shifter's magic?"

*Perhaps, but your hellhound did not find a tear in the scrapyard.*

"True." I relayed her words to Ramble, then added, "Maybe you just didn't notice because we were focused on the bodies there."

He cocked his head to the side then shrugged.

Only then did it hit me that we were standing behind Louis's motel. Had the shifter been watching Louis? Or had it already gotten to him? Maybe that was why he wasn't answering his phone.

"We need to make sure Louis is okay."

*We must close this hole first, Vânători.*

I started to argue, but she cut me off.

*Leaving an opening to Between could allow creatures from the world on the other side of the tear to enter your world.*

Shit. I was reluctant to use energy before a possible fight with this clearly powerful shifter, but I didn't want to face something even worse that might crawl through the tear.

"Okay, tell me what I need to do, then we need to see if we can find Louis."

*I have never corrected a tear in the world before, Vânători.* She paused, considering how best to tackle this problem. Finally, she said, *We will only be able to stitch it back up and hope that, from there, it will heal on its own.*

"Like a wound."

*Yes, an astute observation.* Her words might have sounded sarcastic, but she was actually praising me for once. *That is exactly how we will approach this: as if healing a wound.*

Artemis walked me through the process. I drew on her energy to create a sliver of power to act like a needle. As I "stitched" the tear closed, I focused on letting the energy continue flowing from my core, up through my arm and into the needle, essentially acting as the thread that I was stitching the hole up with. I worked like that for twenty minutes before I reached the top of the tear. Luckily, the tear wasn't higher than I could reach, or we might have been in trouble.

I was sweating a little from the effort when I finished. It had been difficult to keep the thin silk of energy flowing to the needle without sending too much or too little of it at a time. I could barely see the tear now even in my peripheral vision.

*Excellent work, Vânători,* Artemis practically beamed.

Wow. Two compliments in one day. We'd hit a new record.

"Now, we need to look for Louis."

We trod back around to the front office. I checked the front door: locked. Peering inside didn't give me much information other than there weren't any bodies or meat piles that were once bodies. I took that as a good sign.

*"I'm sure your vampire is fine, Vânători."*

Just in case, I texted him one more time to ask him to let me know he was okay.

Then we headed back out of the town. It was time to get to our shifter sting.

* * *

Ramble and I walked toward the small Baptist church. Their evening service had just started, and the parking lot was a little less than half-full, which was good, but it still meant that the shifter would have its pick of people to murder and shift into.

"I don't hear any screams coming from inside, so that's good," I murmured to Ramble.

*Perhaps the creature has already completed his goal and massacred the people inside,* Artemis helpfully offered.

I started to tell her not to be so negative, but she wasn't wrong to think about the possibility. The shifter *could* have already killed everyone here, leaving a bunch of meat piles that once were members of the church. Not only would all those people be dead, but we'd also have no way of knowing which person the shifter had turned into.

"Let's hope not," I whispered as we approached the door.

We could have come earlier, before the service, but that would likely have tipped off the shifter. It was also possible that the shifter might have killed again and taken on a different skin, but I didn't think it would do that since it was trying to gain the likeness of someone the community trusted. In this case, my guess was on the preacher.

We'd opted to wait for the service to start so that everyone would be inside and wouldn't see us arrive. The sheriff had already taken up a position behind the church while the deputy sat in her cruiser watching me. The plan was for her to stay at the front door in case the shifter got past me. Though the sheriff had argued that he should be the one entering the building, not a civilian, the deputy had convinced him to let me go in to flush it out.

"Law enforcement walking into a church during the middle of a service is bound to be disruptive. It might set this thing off and we want to avoid that, so no one gets hurt," she'd said. "If we send *her* inside," the deputy had jerked her head at me, "then best-case scenario, she scopes out the church to see if this thing is in there. Worst case scenario, this thing makes a run for it, and we catch it and arrest it at one of the exits. This might be our only shot at nailing it while we know what it looks like." She'd looked at me then, her mouth tipping up in a slight smile, "And if she wants to be so special, and is supposed to *liaise* with things like this, then let's let her take the first stab at it."

I still wasn't sure that the deputy truly believed anything I'd told her about the supernatural community, even after her little meet and greet with Ramble. Clearly, she didn't regard me as her law enforcement equal, which honestly didn't bother me. I didn't see myself in that light either. I was less concerned with that and more concerned that she had written off her experience with Ramble as some kind of trick that the sheriff and I were playing on her. And if she didn't believe in Ramble and the threat that he posed, then she'd likely underestimate a shifter she didn't believe in.

I mean, hell, she thought she'd be able to *arrest* the shifter. And since the sheriff hadn't corrected her on that point, I decided I wouldn't either. I ended up agreeing with Englewood's plan though, because I thought I had a better chance against the shifter than she or the sheriff would.

So that was how I'd been nominated to be the idiot

walking into a church in the middle of its mid-week service when there was definitely a murderous shifter inside.

Super, right?

At the church's front door, Ramble peeled off from me to stand just to the side of it, clearly indicating that he'd wait there.

"Seriously?" I whispered. "You're not gonna come in with me?"

He gave me a slight huff, but that was his only answer. Maybe he couldn't go inside the church because he was a hell-hound? I still didn't know all the rules for stuff like that, but this was the second time he'd chosen to wait outside a church instead of coming in with me. It was starting to look like he really couldn't enter churches. Which kind of made sense.

"Fine. Here goes nothing."

*Courage, Vânători. I am here.*

While Artemis meant that to be encouraging, it was diffi-cult to forget that, given the chance, she'd try to take over my body again in a heartbeat. Still...her presence and the powers she provided were better than nothing.

I mostly ignored her comment and opened the door to the church. Behind me, I heard the deputy get out of her car. She sure was taking her sweet time getting in place as back up.

Though it wasn't a large building, the church was just large enough to have a small anteroom where a few people had left their coats and hats. To the right were restrooms and straight ahead was a set of red double doors that must lead to the larger room where services took place. A man's voice rose and fell almost melodically from behind the red doors. It didn't sound like fire and brimstone. More like a professor giving a passionate lecture.

Church and religion had never really been my thing, even before the whole monster-fighting thing. Going into the

Catholic church to help Father Patrick had been different since there hadn't been a sermon going on.

*Are you afraid of the Christian God, Vânători?* Artemis asked with a note of curiosity and some amusement.

*No,* I silently shot back. *I'm afraid of what people do in the name of being Christian.*

This wasn't really the time for a theology debate. I told myself to get over it and pushed one of the red doors open just enough to slip through, hopefully unnoticed.

Fat chance.

"Please, please, come in," the preacher said from the front of the church. He stood on a slightly raised dais. "It's always good to have a guest with us."

I forced a sheepish smile as every single person turned to lay eyes on the newcomer.

Oh boy.

I found an empty pew toward the back and sat, but not before I briefly locked eyes with the shifter. They were still wearing the guise of the woman from the gas station and sat only a few pews from the front of the church next to another woman who looked to be about the same age. Sweat beaded the shifter's forehead, and she looked pale like she had the flu or something. Was she just nervous about being in the church like this?

The shifter was a little slower than the others to turn back around to face the preacher. I held my breath and braced myself in case she made a dash for the back exit. If she did, she'd run right into the sheriff waiting outside the back exit. Finally, the shifter flashed me a tight smile before turning to face the front with the others.

The preacher slipped right back into his sermon as if I'd never interrupted him.

I let out a quiet breath. I'd really expected the shifter to run for it in that moment. I didn't know what to do next. I'd honestly expected a fight right off the bat. Or at the very least, that the shifter would flee the church once they saw me.

Now what?

The space didn't really look all that much different from the Catholic church except that it was a little more sparing with the crosses and decorations. No stained-glass windows here. Maybe that was just because it was a smaller church with less funding or something.

The shifter turned to the woman beside her and whispered something in her ear. The woman immediately whipped her head around to glare at me.

Uh oh. That couldn't be good. What lies was the shifter spreading about me up there?

These people clearly knew and trusted the poor woman whose identity had been stolen by the shifter. It wouldn't be that difficult for the shifter to use them as a weapon against me while she slipped out the back door and disappeared.

I began to feel uncomfortably warm as I waited, but I didn't want to take my jacket off in case the shifter bolted for one of the doors. Mild discomfort slowly turned into what felt like full on heat stroke. My body dripped with sweat. I started to feel like I couldn't breathe.

"Are you alright?"

I looked up to find that the preacher had stopped his sermon yet again and was looking at me with worry.

"I'm fine," I said and tried to wave away his concern as sweat dripped down my forehead into my eyes.

*What's wrong with me?* I silently asked the necklace as the preacher continued to stare at me.

*Perhaps imbibing vampire blood has made you susceptible to their weaknesses?*

*What the hell does that mean?*

I could feel the necklace's mental shrug. *Vampires can't*

*enter places of worship and can be fended off by those with a strong enough faith.*

Shit. *Am I turning into a vampire?*

Artemis scoffed, *Not hardly, Vânători, but it seems you've imbibed too much vampire blood recently to stay here.*

Super.

A burning sensation began to take over, and, though I could see the preacher's mouth move, the haze of pain slowly enveloping me made it difficult for me to understand him.

I couldn't take it anymore. I tried not to rush as I stood and gave what I hoped was a reassuring wave to the preacher and fled the service. I burst out through the double doors, then sprinted outside, unzipping my jacket and gasping for air.

The moment I was free of the building, the burning sensation disappeared.

Ramble was immediately by my side, his concerned eyes clearly asking what was wrong. A half second later, the deputy rounded the building, gun drawn and ready for action. She clearly had expected the shifter.

"What happened?" Her tone was sharp, edged with irritation. She seemed less concerned about my well-being as I took gulps of sweet, cold air. "Did she run? Was she not there?" Her words were clipped and impatient, her frustration with the situation directed pointedly at me.

I held up a hand as I tried to catch my breath. "She's still...in there." I finally choked out. I took another long breath. "Sorry. I had a weird...allergic reaction to something in there." My pause that time was less about trying to catch my breath and more that I didn't want to tell the deputy that I was apparently too unholy to enter a church.

*But I went into the Catholic church without a problem,* I whined to Artemis.

*Perhaps the difference is that these people are actively worshiping their God. In the other church, there was no one else there but the shifter and the gremlin.* She paused. *Or it could be that what the shifter did in that church—murdering the Priest—desecrated the space and made it unholy? That would have allowed you to enter.*

While Artemis spoke in my head, the deputy returned her gun to the holster on her hip but kept her hand on its butt as she watched the church door. "Shit," she said. Then, "Shit, shit, shit." She paced before the doors, looking from them to me before finally pausing and pulling the little radio off her shoulder.

"Sheriff, we have a problem. Your *liaison* just fled her post, and now we don't have eyes inside."

I tried not to roll my eyes. Did she think this was a sting operation? I'd finally caught my breath and my body temperature had mostly returned to normal. I straightened up and glared at the deputy as I zipped up my jacket. "I did not *flee* my post. I had an allergic reaction and had to remove myself from the irritant."

In this case, the irritant being people who were worshiping the Christian God.

How come a murdering shifter could sit there smiling while they worshiped and I, the good guy, couldn't? This was some absolute bullshit. I guess I now knew how Ramble felt.

The deputy stared at me and kept her finger off the radio button, thereby keeping our conversation private. "You left your post, and now we need a new plan."

Her radio crackled as the sheriff's voice came through. "Sit tight. We'll wait this thing out where we are. There are only two entryways to the church. Stay out front and cover that one. If it comes out your way, tell it you just have some questions about an incident at the gas station. Then hold it there until the others leave."

The deputy finally broke eye contact with me as she answered the sheriff. "Got it." She walked to the side of the front door and took up a post leaning against the building.

Great. Now I had to awkwardly stand out here with her in the cold, made even colder by the fact that the clothes under my jacket were soaked in sweat.

*I could warm you with a small bit of power,* Artemis offered.

I considered protesting. After all, using that power would drain my metaphorical magic battery which meant I'd end up having to drink more vampire blood soon. What would happen if we couldn't find Louis?

*I dunno, Artemis. I can't even sit in a church now because I have unholy blood or something. I'd rather not have to drink more vampire blood right away if I can help it.*

*Don't be foolish, Vânători. That is a poor reason not to use my powers to keep from freezing to death.*

*Fine.* I turned away from the deputy and went to lean on the wall on the other side of the door. At least over here, I was somewhat out of the wind. Ramble followed me and instead of leaning against the building, he let the bulk of his wait rest against my hip. Though he couldn't hear my conversion with Artemis, he clearly guessed that I was in some internal distress.

Folding my arms over my middle, I leaned against the building. I could tell when Artemis started working her magic. My fingers and toes got a slight tingling sensation, just shy of feeling like pins and needles. I squinted my eyes, stealing myself for things to become painful, but instead the magic shifted to feel like a warm wind on a hot day. It was like standing under one of those bathroom hand dryers.

Tendrils of my hair floated up in the magical wind. To any onlookers, like the deputy who was side-eyeing me, it would just seem like a stray bit of wind. I glanced down and saw that Ramble, too, had his eyes closed, clearly benefiting from this warming magic.

Wait, was he just leaning against me so he could get some

residual warmth? So much for sensing my distress and wanting to comfort me.

When the magic receded, I couldn't help but release a small sigh of relief. I was dry and warm once again. Was it worth not being able to go into a church? I wasn't sure on that front yet. I'd never been a churchgoer before, but that was before I needed a place to potentially hide from legendary vampires.

*See? Much better*.

I could almost feel Artemis's smirk but ignored it.

# Chapter Twenty-Three

*o you really think the vampire blood is tainting me so much that I can't go into a church anymore?*

The goddess paused. *I do not believe that it is the building that poses a problem but more that the people inside were actively worshipping while you were in there. Their specific worship might also have been the reason your body reacted.*

*What does that mean?*

*Were you not listening to the man speaking?* At my obvious silence she sighed. *He spoke of casting out the evil within humans. And the people listening believed his words which gave those words power.* That *is most likely the reason why your body reacted the way it did.*

I thought back to a conversation I'd had with the hunter, Jax, when all this had started. When I'd asked him if crosses worked against vampires, he'd explained that you had to believe in that religion to make it work against vampires. It wasn't so much the physical cross itself or the physical church I'd been sitting in, but more that the faith of the people in the church that had caused my body's reaction.

Before I could ask, Artemis guessed the direction of my

"

thoughts. *Magic and belief or faith are wrapped tightly together. And faith does not have to be belief in the Christian God. There are many religions and gods or goddesses that humans can gain a kind of protective magic from by simply having faith in that deity.*

I started to nod, then remembered that the deputy would probably notice and stilled my movement before I had another thought.

*But* you're *a goddess, so does that mean*—

My question was abruptly cut short as Ramble suddenly came to attention, looking at the church door. A second later, I heard the murmur of conversation getting louder as people began to leave the larger part of the church and gather their coats and other belongings.

I pushed off the wall and caught the deputy's attention before jerking my head at the door and walking over to stand with her. She also pushed off the wall and quickly whispered something into her radio.

The door opened, and an older couple who'd been sitting not far from me in the back of the church walked out. Though I pasted a sheepish smile on my face, I didn't get one in return. Seeing the deputy, the man jerked his head in a nod, curiosity lighting his eyes, but it wasn't enough to make them stop and ask why the deputy was there.

Most of the other members who left the church had a similar reaction: respect for the deputy mixed with curiosity for why she was there with the crazy woman who had so abruptly left in the middle of their service.

I couldn't blame them. I'd probably feel the same way.

None of them stopped to ask questions, though. Instead, they made a beeline to their cars. Eventually the parking lot was almost empty save for a few stray vehicles. I wondered which one was the shifter's car.

My attention was on the parking lot when suddenly someone opened the door. "You!"

I whirled around and found a finger in my face. It was the woman who'd been unknowingly sitting next to the shifter. "You stop harassing my friend."

"What?" I was caught off guard.

"Don't play stupid, young lady. You go around harassing an old lady at work and then follow her all the way into the church?" Her tsking was cut short by the sight of the deputy. "Are you just gonna stand there and let her stalk an old woman?"

Now it was the deputy's turn to be caught off guard. "Uh, n-no." She stammered, then seemed to pull herself together. "I appreciate you informing me of the situation, ma'am, but trust me when I say we have it fully under control." The deputy's eyes slid to mine as she added, "Don't you worry, ma'am. This one isn't likely to be in town much longer."

What a bitch.

The older woman gave me one final glare. "Good thing Arielle is good friends with the preacher." A sneaky smile slipped across her face. "He's letting her out the back. Good luck catching up to her now." She let out a little note of triumph then marched off to her car.

I started to watch her leave, but the deputy grabbed my shoulder and turned me to face her. "Hey, we have a job to do here. I'm going inside to do a walk through in case it's still in there or in case it made another kill and nobody's noticed. *You* stay here and watch the front in case the old lady is lying."

"Okay," I agreed, but she'd already turned away from me, clearly not needing a response. Before I knew it, she was inside. I looked at Ramble. "What do you think? Do we follow her orders and stay here to watch the front or do we go around the back to help the sheriff?

He looked at the church, clearly thinking through the situation. Finally, he jerked his nose at me, then at the ground, clearly saying I should stay here, before he trotted off around the side of the building. I guess he was going to go act as backup for the sheriff. Not a bad idea considering the carnage we'd seen this shifter cause so far.

I stood there waiting and feeling stupid.

*This is ridiculous, Vânători. You should be the one inside! That law woman is going to get herself killed.*

*I told the deputy I'd stay outside. Charging in now without a reason would be abandoning my post.*

This apparently wasn't a good enough answer, and she continued grumbling about how Vânători had lost all respect in this world. I'd heard it before and pulled out my phone to keep myself busy by texting the sheriff.

Me: Just a heads up, you have some invisible help on your end.

I'd rather let him know Ramble was there than for him to get spooked by something Ramble did and start shooting at my sidekick.

Just as I was thinking about testing my luck and going inside, the sound of small wings beating right next to my ear made me jump.

"Whatcha doing, Vânători?"

"Jesus, Summerstorm!" I jerked off the wall and flinched back from the tiny person flying a foot from my face. "Don't sneak up on me like that!"

And hey, look at that, I could still say the lord's name in vain, and my partial vampire blood didn't start boiling. That was something.

"I wasn't sneaking, Vânători." The pixy rolled her eyes. Her previously brown hair was now a bubblegum pink that clashed loudly with her bright yellow one-piece outfit. At least her hair matched her hot pink fingernails. "You just weren't paying attention." She zipped over to look at the church door then turned to get a better view of me. "What are you doing here, anyways? You're not going all pious on me and getting religious, are you?" She paused, one hand on her chin in mock-thought. "Then again, maybe religion might save you from your vampire problems?"

"I don't have vampire problems," I tried not to snap. "I'm helping the human law enforcement not get horribly murdered by a new creature that's like a shifter. The better question is, what are *you* doing out here? I thought your agreement of marriage to Pamola meant you had to live in his mountain?"

She let out a burst of laughter I wouldn't have thought could come from such a small body. "Marrying Pamola doesn't mean he *owns* me, Vânători. Jeeze, what is human marriage like that you thought that?" Her eyes sparkled as I tried and failed to come up with an answer. "I'm here because Pamola said you *do* have some vampire problems and also that you might need some assistance with a new creature lurking around his territory."

She looked at the closed door to the church and back at me, her wings fluttering faster and lifting her up a little higher as she grinned, "And how is it that you're helping the human law enforcement by standing out here in the cold with your thumb up your ass while the deputy gets attacked inside?"

"What?"

Adrenaline shot through my system. I yanked the church door open and ran inside. Summerstorm zipped in with me at shoulder height. We paused outside the doors to the larger room just long enough to hear the muffled, frightened notes of a man's voice from inside. I felt a small thread of fear that I might not be able to stay in the church again, but forced myself to ignore it. Throwing open both doors like an action hero, I rushed inside—and slammed to a screeching halt at the scene before me.

Arielle—the shifter, I reminded myself—stood at the

front of the church just before the raised dais. She was holding the preacher hostage, her hands on either side of his head as if she was going to snap his neck at any second. Or maybe shift her hands into knives and stab him. The deputy stood in the aisle facing them, gun drawn and pointed at the pair.

"I thought you said it was attacking the deputy," I murmured to the pixy.

"Close enough."

I didn't dare take my eyes off the scene to see her, but I could hear the smile in her voice.

"Stay back, Vianne," the deputy said without breaking her staring contest. "I can handle this."

The shifter smiled. "Can you, Deputy? Because, I'm not so sure you can."

I was impressed by the deputy's calm demeanor as she responded, "We know who and what you are now. There's no reason to run. Why not just come with us, and we'll figure all this out?"

"Figure it out?" The shifter said at the same time that Artemis silently laughed.

*What does the law woman think she will do with this creature? Talk it into being a better person? She cannot hold it in the human jail.*

I mentally shushed her so I could focus on the shifter's response...which was not that different from Artemis's.

"You're dealing with things above your pay grade, Deputy." She cocked her head to the side. "Isn't that the phrase?" A grin split her face. "Now, why don't you run along and let the preacher and me—" She moved her hands to his shoulders and jerked him backwards a step, "—have a little chat."

"No," I said, taking a step forward.

The shifter flicked her eyes to me and did a double-take

when she noticed Summerstorm. "You have strange allies, Vânători."

I shrugged. "I'm a different kind of Vânători."

"P-please," the preacher stammered, eyes wide in fear, "let us help you, Arielle. I'm sure whatever this is can be sorted out, right Deputy?"

The shifter laughed. "So pathetic."

I caught the preacher's eyes and slowly shook my head. "I'm sorry, but that's not Arielle. The creature behind you murdered the real Arielle and took on her likeness."

My attempt to explain to the preacher was only met by an expression of confused disbelief, which only intensified when he spotted Summerstorm hovering beside me.

Clearly annoyed that she wasn't the center of attention, the shifter let out a hiss as her mouth elongated in an unnatural way. "I am not a *creature*, Vânători. I deserve to be here just as much as you do! You think that anything that doesn't conform to human norms doesn't deserve to live—"

"—Actually," I interjected feeling more annoyed than scared of this monologuing murderer, "I think that anyone running around murdering people just so that they can pretend to be those people in order to murder *more* people, should be stopped."

"This is my nature, Vânători."

"Bullshit. I mean, you don't see the werewolves running around every full moon ripping people apart, do you?"

"Werewolves?" The preacher squeaked, his voice fading out to a whisper at the end. It seemed to be sinking in that he was in real trouble here.

"You are not helping things, Vianne," the deputy barked. She didn't turn around, but I was pretty impressed by the authority in her voice. It almost made me want to listen.

Almost. I was feeling a little more confident since I hadn't spontaneously exploded from reentering the church.

"Look, if you let the preacher go, maybe we can figure out some kind of solution," I said as nonchalantly as I could.

"What?" Summerstorm squawked in indignation. "You can't just let this monster go! It murdered Father Patrick!"

The preacher gasped and suddenly looked a lot more scared. Clearly, he'd still thought that the person holding him was just a troubled church member.

The deputy finally glanced back at us to see who the other female voice was. A look of surprise lifted her brow, but to her credit, she went right back to keeping her attention on the shifter and her hostage.

I flicked a look at the pixy. "You knew Father Patrick?"

"Of course I knew him! Almost everyone did. He was a frequent visitor and guest in our woods." Here she stopped and pointed an accusatory finger at the shifter. "And *this one* killed him just because!"

"Okay, let's all just take a moment," the deputy said, voice straining with tension. "How about you just let him go, and we'll—"

Not listening, the shifter jerked the preacher by his shoulders to emphasize her words and more effectively cut the deputy off. "I didn't kill him *just because,* pixy. His death served a greater purpose: to get me closer to the sheriff. But now I see that I don't need the sheriff to wipe out this town. I could just use his new deputy..."

*Get ready,* Artemis silently cautioned. At the same moment, a sliver of her power trickled through me. It felt like static electricity and made the hair on the back of my neck stand up.

In one smooth move, the shifter shoved the preacher forward into the deputy. She had just enough time to lower her gun before the preacher hit her, knocking them both down..

As they hit the floor in a jumble of limbs, the shifter zipped past them and leapt at me so fast it was almost a blur.

I got my hands up just in time but only because Artemis had warned me to be ready. The moment the shifter hit me, I felt the power from Artemis zap down through my hands and straight into its body. The power bounced the shifter backwards at an angle, throwing her into one of the wooden pews. Whatever Artemis had done was more like a forcefield than a concentrated attack.

I stumbled backwards from the impact but managed to keep my feet as Summerstorm zipped forward in the air, drew her tiny sword, and began stabbing the shifter in the face and neck.

The shifter threw its arms up to fend off the pixy's attacks, but Summerstorm was too fast and continued to open small gashes in its skin.

*Prepare to attack. Just like we practiced, Vânători!* Artemis barked, not unlike the deputy.

Shit. All the energy balls I'd been able to summon always fizzled out before they amounted to much.

Regardless, I followed her orders and raised my right hand, palm up. I imagined magic building up in my core and, unlike in our practice sessions, I felt an immediate flow of energy that became a glowing ball inside my chest. It was like suddenly turning on a tap and getting full pressure where before there had only been a trickle.

*Have you been holding back on me?*

*Now is not the time, Vânători! Send the energy to your hand and throw it at the creature!*

I filed the complaint away for later and did as I was told. The result was immediate. The ball of energy flowed down my arm and straight to my hand where I could see it pulsing a red-orange color like a ball of flames.

"Um..." I started to caution Artemis about throwing

flames around a church filled with flammable furniture, but the creature had landed a blow to Summerstorm, knocking her from the air and onto the seat of one of the pews. The second the shifter was free of the pixy's frenzied attack, she came at me.

I barely had time to notice that the hand she swiped at me had morphed into long, sharp claws. I managed to dodge them, then chucked the fireball of energy at her—

—and totally missed as she ducked.

The fireball hit a pew and burst into unnaturally hot flames, incinerating the wood like kindling.

Shit.

*Again,* Artemis calmly ordered.

I jerked back from another swipe of her claws and quickly channeled energy back down through my arm to my hand, but this time I held onto it.

*Throw it, Vânători!*

*In case you hadn't noticed, I don't have the best aim!*

*Then throw two at her and don't miss!*

*Great. Let's start more fires in the church. Fantastic plan.*

I didn't see another option though, so I followed her suggestion and sent another ball of energy zooming into my left palm.

The creature squared up with me, its unnaturally clawed hands raised in a defensive stance.

"Don't worry, Vânători. I'm not going to kill you."

"No?" I asked, buying time to get the best possible shot. "And why's that?"

She grinned at me, contorting her borrowed face into an ugly expression I was quite sure the real Arielle had never worn in life.

Fear dropped into my stomach as I saw gleaming fangs in its mouth.

*What the actual fuck?*

"Because I'm going to take you back to my father and watch as he sinks his fangs into you and makes you his."

Before I could respond, it whipped around, slashed a clawed hand in the air, and opened a doorway out of thin air. It flashed me an absolutely insane grin before leaping through the open doorway, but not before I chucked the energy balls at it. The first one exploded against the church's wall, setting it on fire. The other disappeared into Between with the shifter.

I stood there, mouth hanging open with a totally silent Artemis, staring at the ragged tear that the shifter had so easily torn to Between.

"Did...did the shifter just *make* a door to Betwee*n with just its claws?*" I squeaked. "I didn't feel it use any magic—did you?"

It took a full minute for the goddess to respond, her voice quiet with shock. *That creature is an abomination...*

I felt a familiar wave of dread emanating from the new tear now hanging a few feet from raised dais. I'd have to fix it or something worse might come through to attack members of this church. It would have to wait though. I stayed on my guard in case the shifter decided to pop back through the tear for the deputy.

"Where did it go?" She asked, finally freeing herself from the tangle with the preacher.

# Chapter Twenty-Four

I turned to find the deputy holding up the poor, shaking preacher while she scanned the room, gun still drawn. Did she think the shifter had become invisible? Which, now that I thought about it, was a fair point. After all, I'd already introduced her to an invisible hellhound.

"It's gone. It...went to another place," I said, trying to put her mind at ease. Probably best not to mention that I thought the Between was a different dimension. That might be a bit too much to swallow right now. One shock at a time here.

The preacher finally found his bearings and snapped to attention. "Fire!" He shouted and sprinted for the flames that had engulfed the pew.

Oops.

I pulled my jacket off and ran to help put out the fire while asking Artemis, *Can we put these out magically?*

*I could pull all the oxygen from the room...*

*But then we'd all die.*

*That is true, Vânători.*

Looked like we were doing this the old-fashioned way.

Trying to smother the flames with my jacket only singed the coat with zero effect on the fire. "Is there a fire extinguisher in here?" I asked the preacher.

He paused in thought, then ran for the back of the church where there was a small storage closet. Seconds later he ran back with a dusty red fire extinguisher. I held my breath, hoping it would still work. They required those things to be annually inspected for a reason.

Lucky for us, white powder shot from the nozzle and was enough to put the flames out on both the pew and the wall.

"Summerstorm?" I called, looking for the pixy as the preacher continued to douse the flames. She was still out cold, sprawled in the corner of a pew. The only sign she was still alive was the faint glow on her skin. I watched for another second just to make sure she was breathing.

Frantic barking and growling from out back made me whip my head around.

"The sheriff," I said, locking eyes with the deputy before we both dashed for the back door. "Yell if something comes back into the church!" I said to the preacher before we hit the door.

The deputy got to the door first, almost running headlong into the sheriff's back. He was being pushed backwards toward the church exit by Ramble who stood between the human sheriff and the snarling shifter.

The shifter had gotten its ass handed to it by Ramble. A gash across its face yawned open, revealing a red, glistening layer beneath. Three parallel slashes marred its chest, hanging open like tattered clothing. They oozed blood, and it was only then that I understood the creature's method: it didn't literally *shift* into the people it killed—it wore their skin like a grotesque costume.

If I'd had a moment more to process that, I might have felt nauseous, but the moment it saw the deputy and me, it lunged for the sheriff again. Ramble immediately responded by slashing a clawed paw at its outstretched leg.

The shifter screeched in pain as Ramble's claws connected, leaving another ragged opening in the skin and clothes it had stolen from Arielle. The hellhound must have connected with the actual creature's body that time because blood began to soak into the pant leg around the gash and it jerked backwards, almost falling over itself in retreat.

Realizing it was outnumbered and outgunned with Ramble around, it turned and ran for the woodline so quickly it was almost a blur. Its quick movement reminded me of Louis the few times I'd seen him vamp out.

*This is very bad,* I thought at Artemis.

She didn't answer. I wondered if she was still in shock at this weird vampire-hybrid creature or if she just didn't know what to say.

"We should go after it," the deputy said and took a few steps in the direction the shifter had taken. She whipped back around to us with urgency. "Come on! Before it takes someone else!"

She was right, but I'd need another hit of vampire blood to be that fast, especially since I'd drained some of Artemis's power by closing the tear behind the motel then throwing fireballs around the church. But, more important than the fact that I wouldn't be able to catch it, I needed more information on it before approaching it again. I needed to regroup with Artemis and talk to Louis. See what he might know about this new vampire-shifter.

I shook my head at the deputy but addressed the sheriff more than her. "I don't think we'd be able to catch up with it. Not in the woods anyways and definitely not at night." *Especially if it's part vampire,* I thought and suppressed a shiver.

Only then did I remember Constancia's foreboding promise that they had sent me a present. Jesus. Was the shifter what she had meant? Dread made my stomach knot. The shifter had said it planned to take me back to its father so he could sink his vampire fangs into me. Surely, it hadn't meant Morvalden?

Shit.

I needed to go get some blood from Louis ASAP.

The deputy's face clouded with anger as she strode back to me. "That *thing* is going to kill someone else tonight! You saw how messed up it was. It can't pass for human like that, so it seems to me that its next move is to shift into another person! And that means it'll kill that person to take on their body. We can't let that happen!"

Ramble stepped forward as if he agreed and was ready to go with her. If they went off by themselves, there was a big chance the deputy would die and Ramble might too while trying to protect her.

I couldn't let that happen.

"I'm sorry, but this shifter is something different than we initially thought." I was mostly talking to Ramble, but I shifted my focus back to the deputy. "It is *way* more powerful with a lot more tricks up its sleeve—which means going after it right now would be suicide for *all* of us." I looked between the deputy and Ramble, trying to make them understand. "We need to get more information on it before we face it again. So that we can beat it," I finished, looking pointedly at Ramble's glowing eyes.

The sheriff let out a shaky breath and wiped his face. "We should listen to her, Harriet. Her four-legged friend just saved my life." He started across the parking lot, still talking. "That thing came out of nowhere, literally. One second we were out here by ourselves and the next there was this, *tearing* sound behind us." He paused and leaned down to retrieve his gun from a pile of snow before walking back to us. "By the time I turned around to see what the noise was, the shifter knocked my gun from my hand and shoved me backwards hard enough to make me fly through the air."

His words made me realize that there was another tear to Between that I'd need to take care of. I guess that explained some of the dread or *wrongness* I was feeling.

The sheriff's eyes fell on me. "That thing is strong, Vi. We definitely can't overpower it." He looked down at his gun. "And it's too damn fast to shoot."

He shook his head and scanned the ground around us. "I'm lucky you sent me back-up. Ramble opened a gash in that thing's face, then stayed between me and it the whole time." He settled on looking somewhere that was about a foot off from where Ramble actually stood. "I very much appreciate it, sir."

Ramble snorted and the glow in his eyes lost some intensity. Good. Maybe that meant he wouldn't try to go after the vampire-shifter himself. I wondered if he'd noticed the shifter's vampire fangs or not.

"What can we do to stop it from attacking and shifting into someone else?" The deputy asked. "All it has to do is pretend to be a hurt old lady and BAM!" She clapped her hands together. "Suddenly, it's got a new face to wear."

"Literally," I muttered.

The deputy whirled on me. "What?"

"You saw how those gashes looked. It doesn't shift to become like the person it kills," I paused and swallowed so as not to gag, "It *wears their skin*. Like clothes."

It seemed to take her a moment longer than the sheriff to process this new information, but when she did, her mouth dropped open in horror. It still didn't deter her, though. She closed her mouth, swallowed once, twice, then seemed to rally.

"It doesn't change the fact that it will kill again. It could look like someone else by tomorrow."

She wasn't wrong, but now that I'd seen it in action, I knew there was no way she or the sheriff would be able to fight it and win. It was vampire-fast which made their guns all but useless. I wasn't so sure I could keep up with its speed even if at full power. There was no way I'd be able to fight it while also trying to keep her and the sheriff alive.

No, I needed to get them to leave and go somewhere safe.

"You're right." I looked at the tracks it had left in the snow, then back up at the sheriff. "But I don't think we should risk going after this thing in the dark. It outmaneuvered us in a closed environment in the church. How do you think a fight with it in the middle of the woods at night would go?" I shook my head. "We're better off going after it at first light tomorrow." I looked at the sheriff. "I think it would be best if you find a safe place to be tonight." I glanced at the deputy. "Both of you. I might be its overall target, but I think it still really wants you, Sheriff. And it will take you as a consolation prize, Deputy."

"I can handle myself," the deputy shot back with some heat. Apparently calling her a consolation prize hadn't gained me any brownie points.

But I wasn't here to make friends.

"Yeah? You think you're fast enough to shoot it? And what happens if you manage to hit it? You think a bullet's gonna stop it?"

She faltered. "You don't think it will?"

Now it was my turn to waver. Just because it had vampire-like fangs didn't make it a vampire, right? I cleared my throat. "Look, there's more to this shifter than I first thought. For starters, it can apparently open a doorway to Between—"

"What's that?" The deputy interrupted.

*That is more information than they need,* Artemis declared.

I ignored the goddess. I might not need friends, but I certainly needed allies. And keeping information to myself might condemn those allies to death at the worst and make them less helpful at best. If sharing some information kept them alive, it was worth it to spill some secrets.

"It's complicated, but basically Between is like another dimension. It's a little unpredictable, but it can be used to travel long distances quickly. That thing easily opened two doorways which is pretty much impossible. It's...impressive to say the least. If *I* wanted to go into Between, I'd have to find a special doorway into it. I don't have the power to just *make one* out of thin air." I paused, then shook my head. "I can't really explain it any better than that."

"Okay..." The sheriff started, looking between me and his deputy. "So if it can open this magic door thing, why not do it just now instead of running off into the woods?"

"Maybe it got spooked and ran off before it could make one," the deputy offered.

"Maybe." I thought about how haggard the creature had looked before running off. How it moved more slowly when attacking us the second time. It had seemed fatigued. It hadn't even tried to monologue.

"I think going Between took a lot out of it. Or being Between did. Either way, I think the shifter ran into the woods because it wasn't strong enough to open another door.

I remembered the first time I'd visited Between and the being I'd met there. It had been helpful, leading me, Ramble, and Jax to another door out of its realm. But what if there were other creatures in Between who weren't so friendly? I'd been under the impression that it was rare to travel Between, not just because you had to know how to open a door to it, but also because the creatures there didn't allow just anyone to pass through.

If the story I'd been told was true, one of my ancestors had earned herself and any future Vânători safe passage through Between by defeating a dragon. So why had the shifter been allowed to pass safely Between?

*Perhaps it has struck a deal of its own. Or its master has,* Artemis suggested.

My stomach twisted. So Artemis also thought the shifter was a product of Morvalden. I thought I'd have more time after Contancia's little visit before I'd have to face him. It didn't seem like that was the case if this vampire-shifter was set on dragging me to him.

"Well, Vianne?" The sheriff asked.

I shook my head to clear Morvalden's image from it and looked at the sheriff. "Sorry, what did you say?"

"I said maybe we should come back in the morning and see where this thing's tracks go. We're not supposed to get more snow until the weekend, so the tracks will still be there in the morning."

I nodded. "Sounds like a plan." Anything that would get the human law enforcement off the case for a bit. I'd talk to Louis and see if he'd help me track this thing. Maybe even help me kill it, though I wasn't sure if that might be asking too much from the vampire or not.

"Um, Sheriff?" A voice squeaked.

As one, we turned to find the preacher in the doorway of his church. Though he still seemed shaken, he looked like he'd had a moment to gather his wits.

"Um, there's a fairy...creature...woman...on one of the pews of my church."

Shit. I'd forgotten about Summerstorm. If she was still alive, I'd need to take her somewhere safe before Ramble and I went after the shifter.

I walked back to the church. "She's a pixy, actually," I told the preacher as I stepped past him and back inside. Thankfully he stayed outside to speak with the sheriff. I heard him ask just what was going on, then decided to stop listening in.

Summerstorm was still out cold, lying in the same position I'd left her in before we'd heard the shifter attacking the sheriff. I hoped she didn't have a concussion or something worse. How do you provide medical care for a pixy? I'd have to take her back to the woods where her clan lived and see if they could help.

I gently scooped her up.

*We do not have time to play healer to a pixy, Vânători.*

"She's our ally, and we aren't going to leave her here. In case you forgot, Summerstorm is the only reason I'm not currently married to a mountain Power."

*We could have staved off Pamola if you had allowed me to fully fight him.*

"By taking over my body again? Fat chance. I'd rather be married to him than lose all my autonomy to you." I looked around the church for something to carry Summerstorm in. "The bottom line is that we owe her. And not just for marrying Pamola. She also held off the shifter today and gave us time to attack him. And you know what? Even if we didn't owe her, she's an ally and maybe a friend and we don't just leave our friends behind when they're hurt."

*You're not here to make friends. Your goal is to make allies who can help you stand against Morvalden. Friends are a weakness that Morvalden can exploit.*

Maybe I could put Summerstorm in my jacket pocket? I turned to find the burned remains of my only jacket on the floor of the church. Damn. I'd forgotten that I'd tried to use it to put out the fire Artemis and I had started.

I sighed as I retrieved the charred jacket and draped it over my arm. "In case you haven't noticed, we aren't exactly batting a thousand here by ourselves."

*I do not understand.*

I dropped my voice so those outside wouldn't hear. "I mean, even with help from friends like Ramble or Summerstorm, I'm still struggling to control your powers. And before you say it, no, I'm not going to let you take over."

The goddess was quiet as I pulled off my winter beanie and placed Summerstorm gently inside. I wanted to keep her warm but not smother her in the knit fabric, so I put the hat on my open palm and shaped it around her like a sleeping bag, leaving her head exposed.

"And losing control of my body to you is not the only reason I won't do it," I continued. "I mean, do you really think that you can take on Morvalden and win just because you're in control? You've worked with stronger Vânători and still weren't able to kill him. I highly doubt you'd be able to do it now with a weaker Vânători. I'd rather take my chances without becoming your puppet, thanks."

*I never assumed control of your ancestors. Perhaps if I had, we might have triumphed over Morvalden.*

"Well, you didn't, and you're not going to get another chance with me." I wished I could walk away from this conversation, but unless I took the necklace off, I couldn't flee the goddess. Lucky for me, she seemed to understand that I was done with that subject.

*We must close the tears to Between, Vânători.*

Which meant using more energy that would drain our power. It couldn't be helped though. I gently set the beanie with Summerstorm in it back on the bench and set to work closing the tear. At least this time around I was faster at stitching it up. We were lucky that the preacher stayed outside with the sheriff and deputy while I worked.

When the tear was stitched up and almost invisible again, I carefully retrieved Summerstorm and headed out the back-door. I grimaced walking past the charred remnants of a wooden pew I'd hit with an energy ball. It had burned right down the center, breaking it in half. Whoops. Time to get the hell out of there before the preacher decided I was responsible for the damage. I mean, I *was* responsible, but it's not like I had the money laying around to pay for it.

"You're saying that was some sort of creature that only *looked* like Arielle?" The preacher was asking the sheriff as I emerged from the church carrying the beanie with Summerstorm in it. "So where's the real Arielle, then?" He demanded.

The sheriff cleared his throat and shifted to a slightly softer tone. "I'm sorry, David, but we believe the real Arielle was murdered recently."

"You *believe*? What does that mean?"

"It means," the deputy said in her usual no-nonsense tone, "that the remains we believe to be Arielle Cape are unable to be verified by traditional means and must be sent away to a specialist for an official identification to be made."

The preacher's mouth dropped open, and he looked to the sheriff for an explanation.

The sheriff sighed and patted the preacher's shoulder. "You don't want to know the details, David. Trust me. " He grimaced. "Just know that we're doing everything we can to catch the creature who did this."

"I knew the devil existed," the preacher said, shaking his head in a mix of disbelief and horror, "but I thought he was only metaphorical, in the hearts and minds of men. I would never have guessed that creatures could climb out of the pits of hell to attack us here on Earth."

I caught a half-open grin from Ramble the preacher's words. Good thing the man couldn't see the hellhound.

"Well, it's not the literal devil," I piped up, drawing their attention, "but the good news is that your faith may help defend against it if it comes back."

This only earned me an annoyed look from the sheriff and a confused one from the preacher.

"When you were holding your service," I explained, "did you notice that the shifter—the creature who looked like

Alice—was struggling to stay in the church? Some supernatural creatures are affected by strong faith. So if the creature comes back, that's at least one weapon you can use against it."

"Like vampires in a movie?" The preacher asked.

Kudo points to him. "Exactly like a vampire." As I said it, I caught the deputy eyeing me. Clearly she was remembering that I'd also been unable to stay in the church. Whatever. She could think what she wanted about me. At least the preacher seemed to have forgotten my abrupt exit. For now, anyways. There was always the chance he'd remember later, put two and two together, then muster up a mob to come after me with pitchforks and torches.

I didn't love the way the deputy was watching me now, so when she opened her mouth to say something, I quickly cut her off.

"We should meet back here at first light to follow the tracks. I'll let others within the community know to be wary of this thing."

"The *community?*" The deputy asked with a skeptical tone.

"Yes." I said with no further explanation. I didn't want to reveal anything more around the preacher. Though the actual Father Patrick might have created a positive relationship with the supernatural community of Ricketts, that didn't mean other religious leaders would. I looked at the sheriff. "I need to go and get more info on this thing. I'll let you know when I know more."

He nodded and jerked his head at the deputy. "We'll hunker down at the jailhouse tonight. I'd rather not have that thing coming to our houses. We're both lucky that we don't have anybody else to worry about at home.

"Well..." The deputy started then stopped.

We all looked at her, waiting.

"I do have a dog. What if that thing tries to mimic him?"

I decided not to correct her on how the creature worked.

It wouldn't mimic her dog, it would kill it and take its skin to wear. Then again, I had no idea if it could do that with animals, but it was better to be safe than sorry. Apparently, the sheriff felt the same way.

"Go get him and bring him to our little pajama party." The sheriff turned to the preacher. "David, you're welcome to a safe space to stay tonight as well."

I let David, the sheriff, and the deputy hash out details of how they'd stay safe. I saw the moment that the sheriff glanced over at me and realized he'd left me out.

"You're welcome to the safety we can offer at the Sheriff's Department, too, Vi.

I smiled. "Thanks, Sheriff." I glanced over at Ramble "I think we're gonna be busy digging up information on this creature. The more we know about it, the better we can fight it."

He nodded in understanding but before he and the deputy disappeared inside with the preacher, I added, "We do need to establish some questions or passwords to ask each other in case the shifter tries to take one of our identities. That way we'll know whether the person we're with is themselves or if they've been taken over by the shifter."

We stepped back inside the church and shut the door briefly while Ramble watched from outside. That way if the shifter had stayed nearby, it wouldn't overhear our conversation. It took less than ten minutes for everyone to pick a password that was unique enough to not be easily guessed by the shifter.

I chose "pickle" as my password. I could feel Artemis mentally roll her eyes, but whatever. She probably would have picked Olympus or chariot or some other weird word that I'd never remember. I'd definitely remember pickle, so she could just suck it.

Once the others settled on their passwords, I wished

everyone a safe night, then met back up with Ramble outside. I put Summerstorm in his care for a few moments while I found and stitched up the tear that was still emanating that feeling of dread. Once that was done, we retreated to the car and headed for town.

For his part, Ramble seemed just as interested in getting away from the church and the preacher as I was. After having my blood literally boiling beneath my skin as a reaction to worshippers' faith, I wasn't sure I'd ever set foot in another church.

# Chapter Twenty-Five

❧

"Where the FUCK am I?" Summerstorm demanded. I jumped at her sudden outburst and jerked the wheel of the car a little. With nowhere else safe to put her, I'd cleared out the center console and carefully tucked her into the space with her beanie sleeping bag, leaving the lid open in case she woke up.

Apparently she wasn't too happy about the situation.

"Hey, it's okay. You're with Ramble and me in our car." I glanced down to make eye contact with her and watched as she rubbed her head before I had to look back at the road. "We're about halfway to where your clan lives." I glanced down again at her grunt of indignation. "When you didn't wake up, I wasn't sure what to do. I thought maybe your family would know how to help you." I quickly explained.

"My family think I'm trapped in Pamola's mountain, remember?" She sat up and rubbed her head. "You can't let the cat out of the bag, or I'll have to go back and take up duties as my mother's daughter, Vânători."

Her mother was the queen of the pixies. I hadn't realized that Summerstorm had some kind of official duties for her clan, though I guess if the pixies followed the same rules as human royalty bloodlines, then that meant…

"Wait, are you technically a pixy princess?" I said with a grin. I glanced down and caught a look of severe disdain and annoyance from the pixy. Of course, this just made my grin ratchet up even more. "Are you Princess Summerstorm? Is that what I should be calling you?"

Ramble huffed in laughter from the backseat where he'd been moping because I wouldn't let him open the window for fear of freezing Summerstorm to death.

The pixy buzzed her wings a little, as if testing them, then flew up to perch on the edge of the console. "If you call me that, I'll call the whole thing off with Pamola, and he'll be back to harassing and stalking you until you marry him."

I dropped my teasing tone and lowered the wattage of my smile. "I'm just kidding. How's your head? You got whacked pretty hard."

She gingerly rubbed first the front of her head where the shifter had connected with her, then the back of her head where she'd slammed into the pew. She winced when she found a sore spot, then shrugged. "I'll live." Suddenly her demeanor changed, and her wings buzzed in excitement as if of their own volition. "What about the shifter? Did you smash him into the ground? Or did Ramble rip him to pieces?"

Why was I not surprised by her penchant for violence? I shook my head. "He got away."

"What?" She zipped up into the air, hovering only a foot from my face. "How could you let him get away, Vânători!"

"Uh, he opened a door to Between and disappeared from the church."

"Holy shit!"

"Yeah, then he opened another door from Between and

jumped through to attack the sheriff before Ramble chased him off. Now he's running around the woods somewhere."

Ramble grumbled something from the back where he lay full length across the seat. I couldn't tell if he was mad about the shifter having access to Between or if he was still pissed that I hadn't let him go after the shifter.

The pixy's buzzing calmed down a little. "I can't even open a door to Between. That's nuts."

"Yup. I don't think the shifter can do it very often, but that's just a guess." I sighed. "You should also know that I think it's half vampire. Or part vampire. It had fangs and struggled to sit through the church service."

"Seriously?"

I glanced down to meet her eyes and nodded.

"Shit," she said a little breathily.

"My thoughts exactly."

She flew over to perch on the shoulder of the passenger seat, leaning against the headrest. "So, if this thing is a clear menace to both human and nonhuman society, why the hell are you babysitting me instead of chasing it through the woods?"

"You wanted me to leave you in the hands of a guy who thought the shifter was an incarnation of the devil?" I let out a snort. "I think you might be better off with a Vânători and a hellhound." I glanced in the rearview mirror and caught Ramble baring his teeth a little. Was that a grin of agreement or a silent snarl to leave him out of it? Sometimes it was hard to tell. "Anyways, we're heading back to town. I need to talk to Louis and let other folks in the community know that this thing might be a danger to them."

"You think it is?" I couldn't see her expression but she sounded genuinely interested—intrigued, really—about the idea of a threat to the supernatural community.

"I honestly don't know. If it can skin people and wear

them like a suit, what's to stop it from doing the same thing to witches or werewolves?"

"For starters, our local witches are pretty powerful." She pointed out, "And you'd think one of the werewolves would notice if one of their own was acting peculiar."

"Maybe..." I shook my head. "We also found a tear to Between behind Louis's motel. It could be that this thing is planning on trying its hand against a vampire. And who knows, because it's part vampire, it might be able to take on another vampire's likeness. I'd rather be safe and warn others about the shifter than to take the risk that it might sneak up on them. Did you want to come with me to speak with Louis?"

She waved away the suggestion. "Hard pass. That one is pretty boring."

*The pixy is right, Vânători. The vampire is rather boring.*

I tried to keep a neutral expression. Louis? Boring? Every time I was around the vampire, crazy shit happened. Sometimes my clothes came off.

Rather than disagree and put myself in the awkward position of admitting I had the hots for Louis, I ignored them both.

"Okay. Do you want me to drive you somewhere else?"

"Nah, just roll the window down, and I'll head home to talk with the old man."

At my questioning look, she laughed. "Pamola hates it when I call him that. I mean, I might be older than I look but he's olllld." She drew the word out then laughed. "I love yanking his chain."

"So... you're really okay with him? I mean, being married to him?"

"It's got its perks. For example," her eyes glittered, and her wings buzzed slightly as she spoke, "I bet he'll be mighty interested to hear about me being attacked by a vampire-shifter. Might even want to help nab this thing."

"Good luck with that. Your old man showed up at my house the other day and made it clear that I needed to take care of it. He called the shifter unnatural...I wonder if he knew then that it was part vampire and could step into Between?"

Summerstorm tapped her teeth with her long, hot pink nails. "Maybe. He does know a lot. Still, this sounds like something entirely new."

I nodded.

"Do you know why this thing is so hellbent on getting you?" She asked.

"It wasn't after me at first. It wanted the sheriff, mostly so it could wreak as much havoc as possible in town. I think I was its eventual target though. And...I think it was sent—maybe even created—by Morvalden."

Summerstorm let out a choked noise. I could feel her just staring at me now. "*The* Morvalden? Like the uber-vampire guy?"

I found myself nodding again.

"Wow. That's not good. What did you do to piss him off?"

"Exist?" I shrugged.

"Hmm."

"What?"

She looked away when I glanced over. "That's a really, really bad enemy to have, Vianne."

I briefly threw a hand up before putting it back on the steering wheel. "I'm not sure what exactly it is that you'd like me to do about it. It's not like I chose to be on his hit list."

"Okay, okay. Don't get upset about it." We rode in silence for a moment while I wondered if I could manage to not be upset that the uber-vampire wanted to kill me.

Summerstorm finally broke the awkward silence. "I mean,

if it were me on his shit list, I woulda picked somewhere a lot further away from him than here. I would have flown to the other side of the globe. Or at least to the other coast."

"What? Why?"

"You know, because he's in New York somewhere."

"What?" I sounded like a broken record, but how could I not?

"Yeah. You...you didn't know that?"

"No! I thought he was in Indianapolis or something! That's where all his little minions found me. And then he showed up!"

"Holy fuck, Vi! You've met him? Like for real?"

I couldn't have this conversation and continue driving. Luckily, we were just passing a snow plow turnaround area so I pulled off and turned to the pixy. "I've sort of met him. I mean, he was chasing me, and I was doing my best to run away. And he used to haunt me in my dreams sometimes."

"Meeting Morvalden would give me nightmares, too!"

"No, I mean he'd haunt my dreams, like Freddy Krueger style." I hesitated to say more but also wasn't sure if she knew the pop culture reference. I also didn't really want to reveal to too many people that I wasn't a full Vânători and that I had to drink vampire blood to gain access to Artemis's powers.

The look of horror on her face made me think maybe I should have kept the dream thing to myself.

"That's fucked up. He can follow you into your dreams?"

"It's complicated but Artemis makes sure it doesn't happen anymore." I was quiet for a moment, then said, "So you actually know where he lives?"

She shook her head. "Only vaguely. Ramble could probably do a better job of pinpointing his location if you went out there...but you're not trying to find him, right? Because only a lunatic would go after him."

"No, no, of course not." I paused and decided not to tell

her that he might be coming after me. No reason to chase away my only allies yet.

*You may have to tell them if you want to keep them alive, Vână- tori. Friends are a weakness in more than one way. You wouldn't want them to die trying to protect you when Morvalden finally comes for you.*

I didn't want to admit it, but Artemis was right. It was one of the reasons I'd be tracking the vampire-shifter tonight instead of waiting until the morning when the sheriff and the deputy came to help. I didn't want them to get hurt going after something that was beyond their ability to fight. Hell, this thing might be beyond *my* ability to fight.

Summerstorm sensed my mood and shifted the conversation. "Did Pamola ask you if you liked the early winter storms he created for you?"

"He did. Thanks so much for that," I sounded annoyed, but I couldn't keep the grin from my face. "Did you really tell him I'd never seen snow before?"

She grinned as an answer, then sobered. "So what's your plan, Vânători?" The pixy asked, head cocked to one side and one hand planted on her hip. "You gonna go get the vampire then track this thing down?"

"Maybe. It depends on what Louis knows about it."

"Might be too late for somebody else by then if you know what I mean."

I shrugged in defeat. "I'm not sure what else to do."

She cocked an eyebrow. "You could try using your human technology and call the vampire and have him meet you out there."

Ramble let out a snort while I opened and closed my mouth. I'd let my desire for fresh vampire blood cloud my judgment. I had the vial of vampire blood Louis had left me. Technically, I didn't really need to visit the vampire. Finally, I said, "Yeah. I guess I could do that."

"Good." Suddenly the pixy leapt into the air, wings almost buzzing. "I'll go talk to Pamola and see how he feels about an interloper who's attacked people on his land. If we can help, we'll see you out there."

She zipped past my face to hover expectantly next to the driver's side window.

It took me a split second to realize I needed to crank the window down for her. As I turned the finicky window handle and let cold air inside the car, I asked, "How will you find us?"

This earned me another look.

"You think Pamola can't find someone on his own land?" She flicked her pink hair behind one shoulder in a smooth move and shrugged. "Being married to a Power has its perks, Vânători. You might even be sorry you turned him down."

Before I could disagree, she flitted out the opening and disappeared into the night. Rather than get back on the road, I took Summerstorm's advice. By some miracle, I actually had service out here.

"What is it, Vânători?" Louis's voice was edged with annoyance.

Relief flooded me at hearing his voice. It wasn't that I had feelings for Louis, I was just happy that he was okay. Then annoyance set in.

"Thanks a lot for texting me back." My voice dripped with sarcasm. "It's not like there's a shifter running around killing people and wearing them as a meatsuit or anything."

"What are you talking about?" His voice grew distant as he pulled the phone away from his face and checked it. "I never received any texts from you..." He trailed off. Clearly just now seeing my text from earlier. "Oh. My apologies. I left it on vibrate and did not see that you had messaged me. I'm reading it now."

I gave him a few seconds to catch up on the outdated

information, then said, "The shifter I talked about in my text definitely killed Father Patrick."

He sucked in a small breath that he didn't actually need. I guess I had his attention now.

"You're sure?"

"Had a little run in with her," I continued. "She admitted to killing Father Patrick and basically told us her next target is the sheriff or the deputy. And you can update her resume to part-shifter, part-vampire who can turn her hands into weapons and tear a doorway to Between with her claws."

"What?"

Well, hey look at that. It turns out I could shock a vampire.

"Yup. I don't know exactly how it works, but it looks like she finds a victim, drains them of their lifeforce and also drains them of blood. At some point, she turns the victim into nothing more than a bloodless pile of meat and takes their skin and wears it so she can look like them." I thought maybe if I said it quickly, it wouldn't sound so terrifying and gross.

Nope. Still awful.

"That's not possible."

"Well, I've met her, and I've seen her handiwork, so clearly, it is possible. And right now, that impossible shifter-vampire is running around the woods out here near the Baptist church." I gave him a brief rundown of what had occurred in the past few hours, including my guess that the creature was sent by Morvalden and finishing with, "I thought I should call you and see if you might know anything about a creature like this or have ideas for how I might fight her."

He was quiet for a moment as he took all that in. Then slowly said, "I cannot say that I have ever heard of something that can do that. If she truly is a vampire, a stake through the heart would work. Or beheading. Ramble's fire might also make a difference."

"Maybe... but this thing is faster than anything I've ever seen before. I'll be hard-pressed to keep up with it. And the sheriff and deputy definitely won't be a match for it. I sent them back to the Sheriff's Department to stay safe through the night with the agreement to track it in the morning."

"But you're going to track it tonight by yourself to keep them safe." It wasn't a question.

"Exactly. Listen, if that thing gets to me before you do, my password is pickle."

"Your safe word is pickle? Really, Vânători? Of all the words you could choose, that's your safe word?"

"It's a password, not a safe word," I said through gritted teeth, "and I'm telling you this so that if this thing murders me and starts wearing my skin around, that you'll be able to tell the diff—" I stopped as realization and horror washed over me. My next words came out as a whisper. "Oh shit."

"What?" demanded, hearing the fear in my voice.

"Louis, it's a vampire that could drink my blood and then wear my skin. What if...what if Morvalden is trying to create a Vânători that can use the Artemis necklace?"

Artemis made a sharp noise. *That...that cannot possibly work. I would know who the real Vânători is. I would be able to stop them from using my powers.*

It sounded like she was trying to convince herself.

At the same time, Louis said, "Surely that can't be possible. Wouldn't the goddess be able to tell who the real Vânători is?"

"Yes, but what if it doesn't matter?" I asked both of them. "The power lies in the Vânători blood, right?"

*The powers lie with me, and the Vânători blood just awakens them,* Artemis explained. *Just as I have held back my powers from you so that you would not be overwhelmed during our training sessions, I could keep this imposter from tapping into my power. You have nothing to fear, Vânători. I would not let a monster disgrace the Vânători powers.*

*I don't know, Artemis. I don't think we should underestimate this thing. It can open a way into Between.* I pushed back silently. *And if it can do that, it might be able to overpower you.*

Louis, not hearing our internal conversation, was still half a step behind. "By that logic, Vânători, I could drink your blood and gain access to your powers. If that were true, Morvalden would have tried this route long ago. I do not think that is this creature's goal. And if it were, it would not succeed in accessing the power within the Artemis necklace."

*As much as I dislike saying it, listen to the vampire, Vânători. His logic is sound. Even if this creature were to drain your blood and wear your skin, be assured that I would never let it use my powers.*

"Easy for you to say." I told both of them. "It might not be able to access Artemis's powers, but I'd still be dead."

Both were silent as they chewed that over. I decided to take the break in conversation as an opportunity to change topics and get this show on the road. I wasn't enthusiastic about facing the shifter again, especially now that I thought she wanted to wear me like a wetsuit, but I didn't want her to kill someone else just because I was scared to go after her.

"I'm going back over to track her now," I told Louis, then tried not to hold my breath as I added, "I'm not sure I can take her on my own though. I could really use your help, Louis."

The vampire hesitated. Shit. Maybe I'd asked too much of him? He was, after all, acting as my blood donor already. When the silence grew to an awkward length, I quickly backtracked.

"Nevermind, I can handle it. It's not your problem."

I started to hang up, but Louis suddenly found his voice.

"It's not that, Vi..."

The sound of my name on his lips sent a tiny lick of desire through me. I quickly squashed it. I didn't have time for that, and it wasn't even real anyways, right? It was just my addiction intertwining sex and vampire blood.

"So what is it then?" I asked, forcing my voice to stay even. "This creature killed your friend. I thought you wanted to stop it from killing anyone else."

He sighed, which, for him, was practically an emotional outburst. "This is a creature of Morvalden. If I help you kill it, I will be making an official stand against him and siding with a Vânători."

"Okay...?" I prompted, not really seeing his point.

"You don't understand."

"Uh, I understand that you've already been providing your blood to a Vânători. Is that not also taking a stand against Morvalden?"

"It's not the same."

Silence hung in the air punctuated by my hurt disbelief at his stubborn refusal based on some ancient loyalty to the father of all vampires. Why did I continue to trust and believe in people who ended up breaking that trust? Tears pricked my eyes, but I refused to let Louis hear the hurt in my voice.

"Alright then," I said, and hung up.

*You will hunt the shifter without the vampire's help?* I could hear the poorly masked disbelief in her silent voice.

"I have you and Ramble, Artemis. If I drink the vial of blood I brought along, then I'll have enough power to take this thing on. And, if there aren't civilians in the way, maybe we can win against this vampire-shifter.

Ramble gave a huff of agreement.

I just hoped I didn't get him killed.

❧

# Chapter Twenty-Six

It took only a few minutes to drive back to the church. I'd expected that the preacher might still be there cleaning up the fire damage, but the parking lot was empty save for one vehicle: a Sheriff's Department cruiser.

Shit. Had the sheriff decided to track the shifter tonight after all? I sincerely hoped not.

I parked next to the cruiser and peered inside. Empty.

"Looks like we might have company after all."

Ramble snorted and rolled his eyes.

"Yup. That's pretty much how I feel, too. Hopefully the Sheriff is smart enough to stay back when the fighting starts."

*We cannot stay our hand again if a human gets in the way, Vânători.*

Now it was my turn to do an over-dramatic eye roll. "If we can keep him from getting into the crossfire, that would be good. But we aren't going to outright blast the sheriff if he's in the way, Artemis."

She grumbled something in the back of my mind, but I ignored her and started getting ready. One of the only things that actually worked in this car was the old school cigarette lighter. I pushed it in to heat up, then put on my hat and dug through the glove compartment for the pair of men's gloves the late owner of the car had left there. Pretty sure this was the first time I'd ever used a glove compartment for what it was named for.

The gloves would be a little big, but they were better than nothing against a Maine winter night.

When the cigarette lighter popped out, indicating it was ready, I pulled the glass vial of Louis's blood from my purse and balanced it on the hot part of the cigarette lighter. If you've had a jar of real honey and let a little at the bottom get too cold, you know what it's like to try and get a congealed substance out of a jar. Now imagine trying to drink congealed blood from a small vial. Heating it up was the best way to get at it.

Plus it made drinking the substance a little more palatable.

Unfortunately, this task was only made more complicated because the vial had a rounded bottom, so I had to hold the lighter in one hand and the vial in the other while I waited for the blood to heat up. The gloves kept my hands from getting burned on the vial as it heated up.

While I waited, I started planning out loud with Ramble.

"I think it would be best if we tried to stay together as we track this thing. I know you're a great tracker and can move more quickly if you don't have to wait for me, but I don't want you to end up taking this thing on by yourself. So let's stay close and keep an eye out for the Sheriff."

The hellhound gave a small nod, then looked at me with such intensity that I knew he wanted to tell me something. This was the downside of working with someone you couldn't fully communicate with.

"What is it?" I asked, internally cringing that I sounded a little too close to Timmy asking Lassie what was wrong.

He tilted his head a little and narrowed his eyes to indicate that he knew I was close to Lassie territory but let it go instead of frying me to a crisp. Instead, he looked out the window at the sheriff's car parked next to us, then back at me, bared his fangs with a menacing growl, then stopped and lifted an eyebrow.

It took me a minute to work it out, but when I did, I closed my eyes and thunked my head back against the headrest. "Crap. You're right. If we run into the Sheriff, we'll have to assume he's been compromised and ask him for his password."

*He will also need to ask you for your password, Vânători.*

I opened my eyes and answered the necklace out loud for Ramble's benefit. "True, and if the Sheriff doesn't ask me for my password, it might be an indicator that he's the shifter."

Ramble dipped his head in a nod.

I checked the blood in the vial by swirling it around. It was definitely a little more liquidy. Good enough. I sighed. I hated this part. I wasn't sure what was worse—being grossed out by the idea of drinking blood or the fact that once it touched my tongue, I craved it and wanted more.

Truth be told, I was still disgusted with myself that I was addicted to vampire blood. There wasn't much I could do at this point though.

Artemis read the direction of my thought. *You cannot help what you are, Vânători.*

I didn't love that her attempt at reassurance sounded a heck of a lot like what the shifter had said.

"Bottom's up," I said, then held my breath and closed my eyes again before throwing back the vial of blood like that first shot of tequila on a Friday night.

Revulsion immediately flipped to an unsatiated need the moment the coppery liquid hit my tongue. At the same time, I felt power flow through my body, re-energizing me and creating a brief moment of clarity that I only got from the first hit of vampire blood. In that moment, it seemed so obvious that I was on the right track, but that I needed to work harder on learning how to use Artemis's powers in order to survive Morvalden.

My skin warmed from the inside out until I was almost, but not quite, sweating. I opened my eyes and thought how useful it was that I felt warm since my jacket still had burn holes in it. The moment I thought about the coat, I got a whiff of smoke and burned plastic. The shifter would be able to smell me from a mile away, but it wasn't like I had a choice. This was the only jacket I had. Though I might feel warm now from the hit of vampire blood, that would wear off and, unless I wanted to needlessly waste Artemis's powers just to keep warm, I would need the jacket if I didn't want to freeze my butt off.

I checked that my knife was still in my boot, then put on my hat. I was as ready as I was gonna be. I looked at Ramble.

"Ready?"

He whuffed an affirmative.

Less than a minute later, we found the shifter's tracks. There was another set of footprints where the sheriff had followed the shifter. We began to follow the two sets of tracks into the woods. I hoped we weren't too far behind him. I had to ignore a little voice in the back of my head telling me that this was a bad idea, but it felt like the only option to ensure the shifter didn't kill anyone else.

The night was cold, but I felt lucky that there was no wind and it wasn't snowing. Maybe Pamola had decided he'd shown me enough of a Maine winter already. Though there was only a fingernail's worth of a moon in the sky, its light reflected on the snow and provided just enough illumination through the trees that I didn't need a flashlight.

*That is a crescent moon, Vânători. It is a good omen. It is my sign from long ago.*

*Um, that's good, I guess. I'll take all the luck I can get.*

We followed the footprints down a hill into a ravine where the light from the moon couldn't quite penetrate. A bad feeling worked its way into my stomach, but we'd already come too far to turn back simply because I didn't want to go into the darker woods. Besides, Ramble had already disappeared into them. I wouldn't leave him to deal with whatever might lay waiting in the dark.

I trudged in after him, feeling like the crunch of snow under my feet was abnormally loud. It took a few minutes for my eyes to adjust to the darker area of the woods, and I didn't realize Ramble had stopped in front of me until my thigh touched his shoulder.

At first I thought he'd stopped to wait for me to join him, but then as my eyes adjusted, I saw him sniffing the air. His head snapped up to look at me, but since I couldn't read his mind, I didn't know what he wanted to tell me other than that someone else was here.

I nodded and thought quickly. It could be the sheriff, or it could be the shifter. Or it could be the shifter wearing the sheriff.

I hadn't exactly been quiet while slogging through the snow, so if there was someone else out here with us, they would definitely have heard us.

A foot crunched in the snow. Adrenaline shot through me, and I whirled to face the sound as the person took another crunching step.

*Be ready, Vânători.*

Ramble looked at me to convey the same message as the goddess, then refocused on whoever was still steadily coming toward us.

Crunch. Crunch. Crunch.

Now I could see the dark silhouette of a person walking toward us.

"Hello?" I said, forcing my voice not to waver. "Is that you, Sheriff?"

A low laugh broke the night. "You had a fifty-fifty chance to guess the right person," the deputy said from the dark, then stepped into a more sparsely wooded section which let more moonlight through the treetops and lit her features, "and you failed that test, Vianne."

I blew out a breath, trying to bleed off some of the adrenaline spike. "I thought you were heading back to the station?"

"And I thought you were waiting until the morning to go tracking this thing?"

I ducked my head. "Touché."

As she approached, I saw she had her gun out in a ready position but pointed toward the ground. Apparently she wasn't taking any chances. "What's your password, Vianne?"

"Pickle." I paused, realizing that if I asked what her password was and she couldn't answer, she could just shoot me. If I didn't ask though, it would be obvious that I thought she was the shifter. "What's yours?" I finally asked before it could get awkward.

"Glock."

I tried not to sigh in relief at hearing the correct password.

"How's the tracking been going so far?" I asked to hide my obvious discomfort at being in the middle of nowhere working with a woman I really didn't like.

She didn't put her gun away but turned a little to face out, keeping an eye on the woods beyond us. "Meh. Seems like a dead end. I followed the tracks about a mile that way," she jerked her head toward where the tracks disappeared into the dark, "but then they just dead ended."

I raised a brow. "Dead ended? What do you mean?"

She shrugged. "The tracks just stop in the middle of the woods. They aren't even near a tree or anything, so it's not like she climbed up and traveled through a few trees to throw us off his tracks. I looked around just to make sure its tracks didn't pick up again somewhere else, but there's just nothing."

"Shit." I thought about it. "Maybe she was able to open a doorway after all. I thought she was too tired to do that again but maybe I was wrong."

"Looks like it." She turned and, was that a smile on her face? It was hard to tell with all the shifting shadows. "Might as well call it a night." She nodded at my jacket. "At least this means you can go home and get a different coat."

I looked down at my poor singed and holey jacket. "Unfortunately, this is the only one I have." I shrugged. "Might have to hit up the secondhand store to see what they've got." I turned around, all too ready to go back to the cabin, but the deputy's next words stopped me in my tracks.

"Maybe I have something in my closet you could have."

What the fuck? I tried not to let my surprise show. Since when was the deputy all sisterly toward me?

Dread dropped into my stomach.

*I do not believe your deputy friend made it, Vânători.*

Dammit. I closed my eyes briefly since the deputy couldn't see me with my back to her. Somewhere out there in the thick Maine woods was what was left of the real deputy's body. I hadn't liked the woman very much, but that didn't mean she deserved to be drained and worn like a Halloween costume.

I opened my eyes and glanced over at Ramble. He hadn't moved, but his hackles were up, and his whole being was focused on the deputy who I now knew was the shifter. Slowly, the hellhound lifted his lip, showing sharp teeth in a silent growl that was visible only to me.

I realized I'd let the silence play out a little too long. "Uh, yeah. That would be nice," I stumbled to say. "I'm not sure I could take charity like that though, you know?" I added, hoping it would explain my hesitation.

"How about you buy me a coffee on the way back into town, and we'll call it even?"

Her tone was way too chipper to ever pass for the deputy. I hadn't even known her a whole week and even I could tell that she was a fake. If the shifter was this shitty at mimicking people, how had it passed for Father Patrick so well? Then again, I'd never met the priest before, so I wouldn't have noticed if his behavior was off.

For some reason, the fact that the shifter was doing a terrible job pretending to be the deputy really pissed me off. I could only imagine that the deputy's ghost would be livid that the shifter was using her body to be *chipper* of all things.

This vampire-shifter was a real dick.

I forced my mind back to the moment as the shifter began to follow me. "Sounds like a plan," I said and turned around to smile at her. She still had the gun out. I looked at it then at her. "If it's gone, you probably don't need that out anymore, huh?"

She made a show of looking around the woods as she answered. "Better safe than sorry."

I nodded and started forward again.

"Didn't you bring your four-legged friend with you tonight?" She suddenly asked before I took another step.

Crap. Would the shifter believe me if I said no? If I said, yes, Ramble might move to follow us, giving away his location and she would then be able to shoot him. Would she believe it if I said he was in the car? Probably not.

I turned again, this time all the way around to face this fake deputy. "He's out here, but he got ahead of me." I tried not to make too much of a show looking around. "I don't see him anywhere nearby. Do you think it's safe to yell for him? I don't want to tip-off the shifter that we're out here, ya know?"

The shifter stared at me for too long.

*Here we go, Vânători. Get ready!*

Invisible energy spooled in my chest, ready to use.

"I think," the deputy-shifter said as a smile slowly crossed her face, "that you won't have time to call for anyone." Without further warning, she raised the gun and unloaded the clip into me.

The moment she lifted the gun, I threw my hands up and sent energy streaming into them. The first deafening shot rang out just as I imagined a barrier that snapped into place. It lit up in front of my face like a golden-orange force field directly in front of me. The vampire blood made me fast, but not faster than a close-range speeding bullet. The first two rounds hit me before I got the shield up. The rest of her bullets slammed into my shield.

Pain lanced through my shoulder and torso. I dropped to my knees, but somehow managed to keep my hands up, warding against the rest of her bullets. I felt each one hit the shield and ricochet off into the woods. I hoped Ramble was safe. I couldn't spare any attention to look for him. All my concentration was focused on keeping the shield up.

Only when her clip was almost spent did I realize that my shield's power was being drained every time it had to repel a bullet. It was getting smaller and smaller with each strike.

The shifter paused, sudden realization dawning on her as well. As if to experiment, she shot at the shield again. It withstood the hit, but flickered as if threatening to fade out.

Shit! Why was the power from Louis's blood fading so fast this time?

*Fight back, Vânători!* Artemis shouted in my mind.

I'm a little busy not dying, here!

The shifter shot again, and this time when my shield flickered, it died and didn't come back up.

Uh oh.

A look of triumph lit the deputy-shifter's face in a grin I didn't think the real deputy would ever have worn. She stuck her gun loosely in its holster and stepped forward, batting away my raised hands. Reaching around, she grabbed the hair at the base of my neck and dragged me to stand. The gunshot wounds in my shoulder and torso flared with white hot pain. A cry tore from my throat.

While the shifter pulled me up to stand with one hand, she used her other hand to open a door to Between in mid-air.

I had a brief moment of clarity when I saw Ramble charging to attack her, and then she dragged both me and Ramble into Between, and the world disappeared.

# Chapter Twenty-Seven

M y first sensation was that of falling.

When I'd previously opened a door to Between, there had been a literal door that I'd opened and the ground on both sides of the door had mostly lined up.

Unfortunately, things in the Between weren't always parallel to the real world. Rather than merely falling a foot, we seemed to drop at least ten feet. I hit an oddly rubbery ground with a smack and bounced twice before coming to a stop. It was like I'd fallen on a weird trampoline, but it didn't do much to cushion the fall. Pain lanced through my torso and shoulder at each impact.

I lay there for a moment, stunned and breathing hard. Was the oxygen less rich here? Or was I just in shock and dying of blood loss? It was a toss up. It took me a moment to pull myself into a sort of sitting position. The pain in my torso was so much worse than my shoulder. I clutched the wound with one hand, hoping I could at least staunch the blood flow.

I looked around the strange world we'd landed in. The last

time I'd gone into Between, I'd been in more of a cave-like setting. This was totally different. We were on a rolling plain, devoid of any structures. It made me think a little of the Midwest, but instead of rolling hills covered with tall grass, here there were strange, undulating mounds of large, earth-toned elastic-like bands. They stretched out in all directions as far as my eyes could see. On the horizon were what looked like strange trees that seemed to float above the ground.

*Stay focused, Vânători,* Artemis warned.

Right. The murderous vampire-shifter.

Though our fall into Between had been pretty brutal, it had served to separate me from the shifter. Still wearing the deputy's body, she'd landed a few feet away. By the time I'd fought to a sitting position, she'd already gotten to her feet and was heading my direction.

I closed my eyes for a brief moment, blocking out the shifter and this strange world of Between to reach out with my mind and call Ramble. I waited for the telltale popping noise that would indicate his arrival.

Nothing happened. Shit. Maybe he couldn't pop into Between or something?

*Any ideas, Artemis?* I asked in desperation.

*We have a small amount of power left,* the goddess said, her voice slowly fading as she spoke. *Channel it into your hands like before, but don't use it unless we have a definite chance of success.*

So, wait until she's in close range?

*Yes.* The goddess was getting fainter and fainter. How had we used up that much power already? Usually I was good for at least a few days on the amount of blood that had been in the vial. Then again, I'd never created a shield like I just had, either.

If I lived through this, I really needed to do more training with vampire blood to test the limits of my abilities in relation to the amount of blood I ingested. Maybe the lack of power was because the blood was old?

*Focus, Vânători!* The goddess snapped, clearly sensing that my mind was all over the place.

Easy for her to say. She'd lived for hundreds of years inside the necklace and who knew how long before that. Here I was, bleeding out, each heartbeat, loud in my ears, acting like a countdown. I tried to ignore the pain and the fact that I was definitely going to die if I didn't get some vampire blood. Even a human hospital was unlikely to save me at this point.

The shifter took her time stomping over to me. It took me a second to realize that she wasn't stomping but was instead having trouble walking. There was something off about the gravity in this part of Between. That and the bouncy rubber ground seemed to be working against her.

As we watched her struggle, Artemis directed me. *Wait until the opportune moment, Vânători, then zap her and find a doorway back to your world.*

I managed to nod, though it made me dizzy with all the blood loss.

By the time the shifter made it over to me, I'd pushed the last of Artemis's power into my hands and held it there while focusing on keeping it from glowing like it had in the church earlier. Just a little closer, and I could zap her.

She stared down at me, hands on her hips, looking a lot more like the actual deputy than I cared for. Then her eyes kind of went faraway, like she was having a private conversation. It was probably what I looked like when I spoke mentally with Artemis.

*There is only one being who can create a mind-link like that with his children.*

Morvalden. The vampire-shifter was speaking with Morvalden.

...or at least, she was trying to. Her face scrunched in

concentration, brow furrowed and a frown creasing her mouth. Either her conversation wasn't going the way she wanted it to, or she was having trouble connecting with the uber-vampire.

Maybe it was for the same reason that I couldn't call Ramble. Something about Between seemed to be throwing our mojo off.

"Performance problems?" I clutched the wound in my side, hoping it would stop bleeding. I suddenly didn't want to be on the ground anymore. There was a very high likelihood that I wasn't going to walk away from this. I didn't want to die cowering like every woman in a scary movie.

I slowly dragged myself up to a hunched over standing position. It was better than nothing. It also gave me a view of the knife hilt just below the top of my boot. Huh. How come I kept forgetting that was there? And why did I never have my gun handy when I needed it?

Not that a gun would do much good against this vampire-shifter. Probably the knife wouldn't make much of a dent either.

*Vânători! You must focus, or you are going to die!*

"Yeah, yeah," I muttered as the shifter closed the short distance between us.

That feral grin was back on the deputy's borrowed face. "As soon as I drag you out of here, I'll call on my Master, and he will come to collect you, Vânători."

"Super." I tried and failed to suppress a shudder, but honestly, I couldn't tell if it was from a fear of Morvalden or merely sheer blood loss. It was a toss-up. "You know, "master" is a pretty outdated term rooted in quite a bit of racism, right?" I babbled. "Maybe you should rethink working for someone who expects you to call them that."

"You know nothing about me and my father's rela-tionship."

"Father?" I cringed. "That's still as gross as it was the first time you mentioned it." I noticed I was swaying and took a breath to steady myself. "Let me guess. Maybe if you capture the great Vânători, your father will finally see how great you are."

She jerked to a stop. Oh-ho. Looks like I'd hit a nerve.

"So why go after the other people in town? Why target the sheriff? Why not just come straight for me?"

She stared at me for a moment then amusement lit in her borrowed eyes. (Oh my god? Had she stolen the deputy's eyes, too? How did that even work?)

"You're smart but also so ignorant, Vânători, it's like talking to a human. My father wants this town to pay for harboring his enemy. He wanted to raze it to the ground, but I convinced him to give me the power to teach the people of Rickett a lesson myself." She gently touched her pointy fangs as she spoke, then caught her action and stopped. "What better way to terrorize the town than to use the most trusted citizens to kill everyone?"

Morvalden had made a shapeshifter into a vampire.

*It must have warped her powers.* Artemis's voice was a mere whisper I could barely hear.

"Seems like you went out of your way to kill the people in Fielderstown, too."

"All a ploy to get to the Sheriff. But then you kept interfering."

"Ah yes. If it weren't for us meddling kids." I sighed. "You're kind of a pathetic villain, you know that? Mono-loguing about daddy issues. Awe," I continued, "maybe daddy will be vewy pwoud of you." I baby-talked. "Cuz that's all you've ever really wanted, right? For daddy to love you?"

Her face contorted in rage. "You have no idea what you're talking about, filth. All he ever talks about is the Vânători and all the different ways he'll end you."

"So...your plan is to...what? Kill me yourself?" I looked down at my shoulder and side, then quickly looked away at the site of all that blood that should really be on the inside of my body. "I bet...I bet he'll be thrilled to hear you killed me rather than bringing me to him."

*Stop antagonizing the stupid creature, Vânători!*

I'm just buying us time.

*For what? No one's coming to save us. You'll have to save us yourself.*

Shit. Artemis was right.

I watched as the vampire-shifter considered her options, then shook her head. "You're too far gone to take back to him now. But at least I'll be able to tell him that *I* was the one to kill you. I'm sure he'll thank me eventually. Maybe I'll take him your head as a consolation prize." The vampire-shifter closed the distance between us and reached out as if to grab me by my injured shoulder. Before she could, I pushed past the pain and pushed my hands against her, letting the power that was left inside me hit her full force.

Two orangish-gold balls of energy left my hands and slammed into the shifter's chest. Her mouth dropped open, first in surprise, then pain as the energy tore a hole right through the deputy's uniform and her borrowed skin. A scream ripped from her throat. She fell, landing with a bounce on her back while frantically trying to tear off the borrowed skin. The energy from Artemis slowly died out as it tore into the shifter's real body.

Bummer. I'd really hoped it would do more than just give her 3rd degree burns, but it looked like that was all it was going to do.

Very faintly, I could hear Artemis say something in the back of my mind, but I couldn't decipher it.

Plan B! I mentally shouted then dipped down to pull the knife from my boot. It was awkward as I couldn't get my injured shoulder to cooperate, so I used my other hand, reaching over to grab the handle.

Using the last ounce of my strength, I lunged at the shifter, but it turned into a calculated fall, knife leading the way. I let gravity pull me down, driving the knife into her neck while at the same time, channeling some of the last of Artemis's energy into the knife's tip.

The shifter let out a garbled cry and frantically tried to dislodge me, but I wouldn't let go. I couldn't. This was it. If she succeeded in shoving me off her before I did enough damage, it would be the end for me.

I focused everything on repeatedly stabbing at her face, neck, and upper chest while dodging her flailing hands. I was honestly surprised that she didn't use her vampire speed or strength. Maybe she was out of gas, like me.

I managed to score a few more hits—one on her chest and another on her neck—before she was able to push me off her and to the side.

My movements were starting to get sluggish as I grew more and more tired. It felt like I was trying to move against an impossible force, but really I was losing the battle against blood loss. My hands and clothes were slippery with a mix of my blood and the shifter's. I wondered what a sight I must be. My vision began to tunnel.

Through my fading consciousness, I caught the shifter rolling onto her side. Almost lazily, I slowly turned my head and looked over at her. Eyes wide in fear, her mouth opened and closed like a fish out of water while blood poured from the gashes in her neck. Her hand hit the rubbery ground of Between, opening and closing as she reached for me. Her fingers shifted into sharp claws, then back to regular human hands as they hit the ground. A gurgling sound came from her open mouth. Then...nothing.

I stared at her, waiting for her to move again. Her eyes

remained fixed on me, frozen forever in those last moments of fear. It took my brain a moment to realize that she was dead.

Holy shit. I'd somehow managed to kill the vampire-shifter.

I closed my eyes and let out a sigh. It was blissfully silent in my mind. That feeling of floating began to creep at the edges of my awareness. I'd felt it before when Louis had almost completely drained me. Only Ramble's interference had saved me then.

This time, I was completely on my own. No hellhound leaping in to save the day. No goddess barking orders. No vampire to gift me with his blood to heal my wounds and save my life.

Garbled, stray thoughts clamored in the back of my mind, trying to catch the last of my attention before I lost consciousness for good. Was this how the Vânători line died? What would Ramble do if I was no longer there? Maybe he'd find a more meaningful life than getting dragged around by me. Would someone find the deputy's body out in the woods? Would someone find my body here, in the Between? What would happen to the Artemis necklace?

The thought that made me open my eyes was: If I died here, did that mean that Morvalden had won after all?

A slow surge of emotion rolled up from somewhere deep within me. It took me a moment to recognize it for what it was: anger. Anger that after I'd fought to stay alive, had found a place where I sort of belonged, and was finally building a life—albeit a weird life, but a life all the same— and I was going to end up dying alone.

*And what are you going to do about it?*

The voice was quiet but indignant. It wasn't Artemis. It was me, but a part of me that I hadn't heard from in so long that I hardly recognized it. A voice that had once been carefree, full of wild abandon, telling me to go after whatever I wanted because I was young and the world was mine to explore.

That inner voice, silent since my parents' death, now roared back to life, defiant as we circled around the edge of death's drain.

*Are you just going to lie here and die? You're going to let that fuck, Morvalden, win? Because that's what giving up and dying means: that Morvalden wins and that you LET him win.*

*I'm not letting him win,* I whined. *I'm literally dying here! What do you want me to do? Magically heal myself? I don't have any vampire blood to do that!*

There was a long internal silence, then a coy whisper, *Don't you?*

My brain slammed to halt.

I forced my eyes open though they really, really wanted to just stay closed.

The shifter was still staring at me. The *vampire*-shifter.

*It might not work,* I thought in panic.

*But it also might. You won't know unless you make the decision to try.*

What kind of fucked-up after-school special was this? And how was it possible to actually be annoyed with another part of myself? It—or I—was right, though. I could do nothing and thereby make the decision to let myself die. Or I could take the chance that the shifter's blood was vampire enough to heal me.

Was I really going to go over there and lap up blood from someone I'd just violently killed?

*You have a choice: You can choose to keep pretending you're human and let yourself die...or you can accept that you are something else and finally live.*

It felt like a choice I could never come back from which made no sense. After all, I'd already been drinking Louis's blood…but somehow this felt different. Louis's blood had been freely (if not grudgingly) given. This was something else entirely.

Was it because I didn't feel that addictive pull to drink from the vampire-shifter?

I didn't think so.

*Well?* The inner voice prompted. There was a thread of something thrillingly wild in it. It was that feeling of sneaking out at night in high school to hang out with friends after curfew. Or when I'd decided to take a leap and ask out my first boyfriend. Then later, pushing myself to surprise him with our first French kiss.

*I have always been here,* it whispered. *Take this leap, and we'll see where it leads together.*

I trusted this old part of myself more than I'd ever trust Artemis.

*Okay.*

I took a long, steadying breath, wincing as pain lit up my torso at the movement. Then, drawing on the last dregs of my strength, I rolled over onto my stomach. White hot pain like fire lanced through me. I still couldn't use my right arm and instead pushed myself up to my knees with only my left arm. My head spun, and the Between spun with it.

Apparently this was as far up as I was going to get.

Okay. Crawling it is. I slowly half-crawled, half-dragged myself the short but agonizing distance to the shifter's body. I ran out of strength once there and landed on the top half of her. It wasn't heroic or impressive, but it put me in a prime position to do what I needed to do to survive.

I tried not to think about the next step. Instead, I closed my eyes, lowered my head, and put my mouth on a large gash in the shifter's throat. When her blood touched my lips, I immediately noticed the difference of how warm it was compared to Louis's cold, coppery blood. The taste was different, too. The shifter's blood tasted salty, almost gamey. There was also a hint of decomposition there.

I tried not to retch as I realized I was probably tasting the deputy's stolen, decomposing skin.

It took longer than usual for the addictive need to keep drinking kicked in. Even when it did, it wasn't the mind-numbing, blissful experience that I got when drinking from Louis. It was more like feeling thirsty and settling on the opened plastic water bottle that had been sitting in your car for a few days. It wasn't my first choice, but it would do in a pinch.

Rather than the familiar zing of almost immediate power, this blood was a little slower, as if there was a little less energy in it. It took longer than I care to admit to drink enough of the shifter's blood to heal my gunshot wounds. Then even longer to build up enough power to speak with Artemis again.

*You have...prevailed, Vânători.* Artemis sounded more than a little surprised.

The moment she spoke in my mind, I pushed away from the shifter's body, wiping my mouth to hide any lingering evidence of what I'd just done. I might be willing to do what it took to live, but that didn't mean I was proud of it. Merely resigned.

A little wobbly, I stood and picked up my knife, then carefully leaned down and wiped it on the shifter's clothes before tucking it back into my boot. I looked up at the tear in the sky that would lead back to my world. It was too far off the ground for me to reach by myself.

*Now what?* I asked the goddess. *I can't reach the door from here.*

Artemis silently mulled it over. *It's possible that the shifter's blood gave you its powers to open another door. It cannot hurt to try, Vânători. Otherwise we may need to see if we can get one of those tree-like things over here and climb it to escape. Or we may have to travel through Between until we find another open doorway.*

I let out a huff but agreed that less walking would be better.

*Try to remember the shifter's movements when it opened the door in the church,* She suggested.

I nodded, then planting my feet shoulder-width apart, I swiped my hand diagonally through the air.

Nothing.

I tried it again and thought, *Open.*

Still nothing.

I spent another five minutes gesturing in the air and willing a door into existence but nothing worked.

*It appears you did not inherit the shifter's unique power with its blood.*

"That would have just been too convenient, wouldn't it?"

I finally sat down on the surprisingly comfortable ground. I wasn't dying anymore, but man, I was tired. I needed a quick break if I was going to have to walk all the way out to where those trees were. I looked around this strange world again, only now noticing that even the sky here was different. It swirled with vibrant blues, purples, pinks, and hints of orange and pulsated with an otherworldly energy.

I laid down on my back, watching the sky continue its mad swirl. This wasn't so bad. Maybe I'd just rest here awhile. In a little bit, I would get up and start walking toward those strange trees. Seemed like as good a plan as any. I let my eyes drift shut but could somehow still see the colors swirling behind my closed lids. That was weird.

I started to ask Artemis if she thought that was weird but realized her presence in my mind felt oddly quiet and peaceful. Was she sleeping?

The colors swirled.

Maybe I'd just take a little nap, too...

# Chapter Twenty-Eight

❧❧❧

A booming voice jerked me from my nap. My eyes snapped open. A disembodied head floated four feet above me. I quickly sat up and scooted backwards. If something was coming through to Between, I didn't want it to land on top of me.

Once I was out of the way, I was able to make out who the owner of the floating head was. My mouth dropped open.

"There you are, Vânători," Pamola boomed with a grin. His eyes shifted to the figure on the ground. "I see the battle is already won. Pity I missed it."

Hmm. Was he really sad that he'd missed it? I didn't think so from the way he'd basically ordered me to take care of the shifter a few days ago.

His head disappeared, and now I could see a small hole into our world.

*Wake up, Artemis,* I mentally nudged the goddess. Her response was sluggish.

*Don't look…at the sky, Vânători,* She warned, her voice groggy. *It will mesmerize you into sleep.*

Dang. Had we almost died again? Or would we have just stayed here and slept forever?

I had a horrible thought and whipped around to check on the shifter. Her eyes still stared lifelessly at nothing. That was a relief. I'd thought maybe I hadn't killed her after all and that she'd just been put to sleep by the swirling sky.

A tinkling voice came through the opening in the sky and suddenly Summerstorm darted through. She looked all around, finally looked down, then zipped down to me.

"Holy shit, Vianne! You killed the vampire-shifter!" She whipped her small but focused attention to me. "Tell me everything!"

*Perhaps we should have stayed alone*, the goddess muttered in my mind.

As the pixy bombarded me with questions, I almost agreed with her.

It was the work of only a few minutes for Pamola to enlarge the tear the shifter had made. He simply pushed downwards and ripped the hole into a longer oval.

Before leaving, I forced myself to return to the shifter's body and retrieve the deputy's badge. I wasn't sure what would happen to the shifter and the deputy's remains in this section of Between, but for some reason, I really didn't want to bring the shifter's body back into our world. I was pretty sure it wouldn't magically reanimate but better safe than sorry.

After some grumbling on Summerstorm's part, Pamola agreed to help pull me out through the tear. Which was good. I wasn't sure I'd have the strength to climb out and probably the tear would just rip even more if I tried to use its almost invisible edges to haul myself out.

I landed on my feet, back in our world, and was immediately accosted by a flying ball of teeth, claws, and spiky fur that knocked me onto my ass into the snow. Ramble stood over me, his eyes glowing a concerned yellow. He shoved his head against my chest, and I immediately hugged him back.

"I'm sorry, buddy." I told him fighting back tears that pricked my eyes. "I didn't mean to leave you."

He sniffed at the two bloody holes in my clothes where the shifter had shot me, then met my eyes in question.

"I know. I got really lucky."

The hellhound blew out a snort like he didn't believe my luck. I put my head against his briefly, then we broke apart again. It was nice to know I'd been missed by someone.

Just then, I felt a soft, somewhat familiar *snick* as some faint magic disappeared. It took me a moment to realize what it was. I felt in my jacket pocket and pulled out the wilted remains of the four-leaf clover Blush had forced on me.

Artemis, Ramble, and I were silent as we stared at it, quietly recognizing that my luck had been anything but random.

The next thing I knew, a pale hand was thrust down toward me. I looked up to find Louis standing there, wearing his typical neutral expression.

"Glad to see you made it back, Vânători."

I thought about ignoring his hand, but I couldn't really hold a grudge against him. He might have said he wouldn't come, yet here he was, standing in the middle of the woods next to a pixy, a hellhound, and a Power. Apparently, he'd chosen to take a more official stand on the side of a Vânători after all. It would be rude to refuse his help now.

That and I was really tired. Though vampire blood usually left me feeling amped up and ready to take on the world, the shifter's blood had merely done the job of healing me and reconnecting me to Artemis.

I took Louis's hand. He easily pulled me to my feet and, a little over-balanced, I steadied myself against him for a brief second.

"Thanks." I wasn't sure what else to say so I just left it at that.

Before Pamola closed the rip in space, he slipped through it to investigate the shifter's body. With a snap of his fingers, the body ignited in greenish white flames.

So much for worrying about that, I guess.

"He couldn't have done that before?" I muttered mostly to myself.

Ramble heard me though and quietly grunted in annoyed agreement.

"Tell me everything, Vânători!" Summerstorm said again. At the same time, my phone connected with cell service and began chiming with missed texts and a voicemail. They were all from the sheriff.

"Just a second, Summerstorm." I scrolled through them quickly. The deputy hadn't met him back at the station as they'd agreed, and she wasn't answering her phone, so he'd reached out to me to see if I knew anything. His texts became more frantic and demanding when I didn't answer either.

I quickly shot him a text to meet me at the church parking lot and gave him my password so he'd know I wasn't the shifter. Not that the passwords had actually made a difference since the shifter had somehow known the deputy's. Maybe the shifter had overheard us somehow. Or maybe it had tortured it out of the deputy. I'd probably never know.

Once Pamola returned to our world, he closed the rip to Between by smudging his thumb over the edges of it. It was a much faster process than my stitching method. I was jealous.

Ramble stayed practically glued to my side as we walked through the woods and back to the parking lot. At Summerstorm's continued insistence, I related what happened. How Ramble and I had run into the deputy out in the woods, then how it had turned out it was really the shifter. I explained how she'd attacked us, then pulled me Between and how I'd blasted her with the last of my power before stabbing her with my knife.

"You expect us to believe you extinguished that creature with a knife and the luck of a clover?" Pamola asked in an offended tone. "Vânători, I am not stupid. Or gullible. That creature could not have been killed by a human weapon."

I stifled a sigh. The shifter blood hadn't really done much to make me feel more awake or motivated to deal with the mountain Power's holier-than-thou bullshit. What I wouldn't give for just a drop of Louis's energy-filled blood...

"I mean," I shrugged, "I put Artemis's energy into the knife to make it pierce the shifter's skin better."

"I'm not sure even that would have been enough to extinguish that creature. It could heal itself, Vânători. Why did the wound you made with the knife not heal?"

Well healing itself was news to me, but then again, I should have put two and two together. After all, Ramble had wounded it at the Baptist church, but the deputy-shifter hadn't been limping.

"Listen, I don't know what to tell you."

"Maybe something about using Artemis's power kept the wounds from closing this time?" Summerstorm hazarded.

This earned her a harrumph of disbelief from the Power.

"Do you have the knife still, Vânători?"

*It is nothing more than a piece of sharpened metal, Vânători. It is a good blade, but nothing more.*

*Should be safe to let him take a closer look at it then, right?*

Without waiting for her to answer, I bent down, pulled the knife from my boot, and held it out to Pamola. "Knock yourself out," I told him before resuming my slow trudge through the snow back to the parking lot. The faster we got there, the faster I could go back to the cabin and collapse into bed.

The Power stopped walking briefly as he examined the knife, making him fall behind while my little group continued on. Then he was suddenly walking beside me again. He must have magicked himself to catch up.

"Vânători, this is not just any knife."

*What? Take the knife back, Vânători!*

"Of course it's not," I responded to Pamola, ignoring Artemis. Was my voice dripping with sarcasm? Maybe. Pamola gave me a look.

"She's being sarcastic, old man," Summerstorm explained.

He pulled a face that could have been directed at her for her use of "old man" or at me for being sarcastic. "Where did you get it?" He asked, gingerly balancing the weapon in his open palm. His attitude toward it was almost...cautious.

Holy shit—was Pamola afraid of my throwing knife? Since when? I was pretty sure I'd used it around him before. "I... acquired it from some vampires. It was part of a set, but I lost the other ones."

Pamola choked, his steps hesitating, then he quickly stepped ahead of me and stopped, blocking our path. I felt Louis stiffen beside me and saw Ramble lift his lip in a silent growl.

The Power ignored them, his eyes boring into mine. He closed his hand around the knife and turned his hand over before holding it out to me. Instinctually, I held my hand out, palm up. When he placed the knife in my hand, he loosely closed his hand around mine and added his other hand around it.

His eyes flicked from our hands up to my eyes.

"Vânători, I think this knife may be...very special."

"Okay..." I waited a beat, and when it didn't seem like he was going to say anything more, I finally asked, "So, are you going to tell me what makes it special?"

He stared at me for another frustrating second, then

released my hand. "I must go," he boomed a little overdramatically then he snapped out of existence.

Summerstorm let out an outraged squawk and hovered in the air with her hands on her hips. "You have to stop leaving your wife behind! It is not very husbandly!" She turned and tossed her pink hair over her shoulder. "Magical knife, huh, Vânători? You been holding out on us?"

"No! If I'd have known, I would have been more careful with it." As it was, I wasn't sure what to do with it now. It seemed somehow wrong to tuck it back into my boot. But I couldn't just walk around openly carrying a knife, right?

Ramble gave me a shrug as if he'd read my mind and wasn't sure what I should do either.

Can you feel any magic in it? I asked Artemis.

There was a quiet pause, then, *Now that I'm looking for it, yes.*

But you couldn't feel it before?

I got the equivalent of a mental shrug. *Even now, its magic is almost too faint to notice.*

I harrumphed and stuck the knife back in my boot. Maybe the Power was wrong and the shifter just wasn't as difficult to kill as he'd thought it was. When I straightened again, Summerstorm zipped up to hover a few feet from my face.

"I've got to go, Vânători. Next time, wait for us to help you kill the bad guy. It's no fun otherwise." With a grin, she flew off into the dark woods. I could only assume she was heading back to her mountain home with Pamola.

They definitely made an interesting couple.

That left just Louis, Ramble, and me trekking the rest of the way back to the church parking lot. My pace slowed with every step until I felt like I was dragging myself to the car. I really didn't look forward to driving back to the cabin. Maybe

I could just stay here for a bit and sleep in the car? It wasn't that cold out tonight. I didn't think I'd freeze to death.

Artemis sighed, *I will not let you fall asleep on the drive back to your home, Vânători.*

All I could picture was Patrick Swayze's character singing "Ninety-Nine Bottles of Beer on the Wall" to drive Whoopie Goldberg's character crazy in Ghost. I'd probably get some medieval version of that song from Artemis.

We came out of the woods in a completely different spot than where I'd followed the deputy's tracks behind the church. As we broke free of the trees, I saw that we were closer to the actual parking lot in front of the church. The whole time I thought I'd been following our original tracks. Looking down, I saw it was just one set of tracks that originated from Louis's car.

"How did you know where to find us in the woods if you didn't follow our tracks?" I asked the vampire.

"I could hear Pamola and Summerstorm...mostly Summerstorm."

Was that a tiny smile on his face or a trick of the light? Maybe he showed more emotions than I realized, and I just hadn't been around him enough to learn to recognize them? I mentally shook my head. That was a lot of thinking when I was this tired.

I don't know why, but I was surprised to see Louis's car in the lot. I still had way too many vampire stereotypes in my mind from movies. I guess it wouldn't make sense for him to run all the way out here. I also had kind of hoped he was harboring some cool superpowers like flying or teleportation or something.

"You can go if you want," I told the vampire. "I'm not sure it's a great idea if you're here when the sheriff arrives. No reason to get you more involved and have to make a statement or something."

There was a moment of awkward silence while he decided what to do, then he stiffened. A moment later, I heard a car speeding our way.

"Too late now," he murmured as the sheriff's car swung into the lot. Then he did some sort of vampiric trick where his face lost all expression, and he almost seemed to fade into the background. The overall effect was that he seemed like a boring person and made me want to look elsewhere.

Ooh. So he did have a secret superpower. Interesting.

The sheriff didn't bother with an actual parking spot, opting instead to stop behind my car. Maybe it was a tactic to block me in or something. He hopped out almost before it had stopped moving. "Well?" He demanded. "Did she go haring off into the woods without you? Why didn't you try to catch up?" He turned toward the church, maybe to follow the tracks there to go looking for her.

"Sheriff." My tone was sharp enough to get his attention. When he turned, I opened my mouth to explain, then stopped. Apparently, the look on my face was all he needed. His head and shoulders dropped.

"Goddammit," he said mostly to himself as we closed the distance between us.

I dug the badge out of my jacket pocket and held it out to him. "I'm really sorry."

He stood quietly for a moment before finally saying, "It was like she thought she was immune to anything out here because she was a big city cop." He shook his head slowly as he spoke, then met my eyes briefly before finally noticing Louis. "What's he doing here?" His voice had a surprising edge to it as his gaze shifted back to me. "What actually happened?" He held up a hand. "And I want the real story, Vianne. This is the second deputy I've lost to this town."

I couldn't blame him for being angry, but I didn't want him to take his anger out on Louis. He was right that he deserved an explanation, though, even if I still needed to leave out a few details. I did the best I could, backing up to when I'd left the church and how I'd called Louis.

The sheriff held up a hand to pause my story. "So, after telling us you were going to wait until morning, you decided you could just handle this thing on your own?"

"It was more than just a shifter, Sheriff. It was also part vampire." I did my best not to look at Louis when I said that. He was being quiet, doing that I'm-not-here thing so he could stay out of the conversation. "I didn't want you or the Deputy to get hurt, so I called in Louis for backup."

I didn't mention that Louis had initially decided to sit this one out.

"We headed back here, and that's when I saw that the Deputy's car was still in the parking lot." I managed to explain the rest without bringing the mountain Power or pixy into the mix. When I finished, the sheriff glared at both of us.

"So, my Deputy is dead out there in the woods some-where and somehow you two—"

Ramble whuffed quietly.

"—three," the sheriff quickly amended, glancing in Ramble's general direction, "are still standing without even a scratch?"

I'd left out getting shot and having to drink the shifter's blood to heal. I mean, I was still covered in my own now mostly dry or frozen blood, but the sheriff hadn't seemed to notice. Or maybe he thought it was someone else's.

Louis finally decided to pipe up to defend our actions.

"We're very sorry about the deputy, Sheriff." Louis's voice was soft but still somehow lacked emotion. "She was long gone by the time the Vânători arrived. Searching for the shifter creature alone sealed the Deputy's fate. It is not the Vânători's fault."

The sheriff sighed. "No, of course not. It's just," he met

my eyes, "it's hard to keep losing people to things I don't completely understand." By the time he finished his sentence, he was looking back at Louis again, making it clear that he knew Louis was someone who fit into that category of something that he didn't understand.

There was a beat of silence, then Louis offered, "Perhaps it's time for more transparency." The vampire turned to me. "If you are well enough to take yourself home, Vânători, then I will assist the sheriff in retrieving the deputy's body." He shifted so as to catch the sheriff's eyes. "I should have spoken to you about this sooner, Sheriff, but one can never tell how humans will respond to someone like me."

"And what, exactly, are you?"

"I can explain more about myself as we work."

I felt like I should stay to help, and honestly, I kind of wanted to hear what he told the sheriff about himself, but another part of me was ready to take him up on his offer if it meant I got to go home and sleep. The sheriff, however, didn't look too keen about running around in the dark with Louis.

"He's one of the good guys, Sheriff." I told him. I glanced at Louis briefly. "I've trusted him with my life on more than one occasion, and he hasn't let me down."

*Until tonight,* Artemis helpfully reminded me.

The sheriff seemed to chew this over then nodded. "Go home, Vi. I'll call you tomorrow for an official statement."

I nodded. His emphasis on the word meant I'd be leaving out even more of what had happened. I'd need to come up with quite the story. How many lies would I have to spin?

No reason to worry about it now. Tomorrow would come soon enough.

With a quick dip of the head as a goodbye, Ramble and I piled into my car and headed home.

## Chapter Twenty-Nine

True to her word, Artemis kept me awake on what felt like the longest drive ever back to the cabin. I rolled the front windows down for Ramble, and the chill air helped almost as much as the sharp-tongued goddess in my head.

Almost.

*Vânători!* She shouted a few seconds before the turn to the cabin.

My head jerked back up, and I had to force my eyes open. Luckily the roads were clear, or we probably would have ended up in the ditch when I slammed on the brakes to slow down enough and make the turn.

Lucky too, that it was so late (or maybe so early, depending on how you looked at it), that no one was driving behind me either. Otherwise, we would have been rear-ended. Maybe my luck hadn't disappeared with the four-leaf clover after all? Better not to push it, though.

I managed to get myself out of the car and up the steps to the cabin. The window still had a plywood covering but at least it kept the cold out. On the way inside, I forced myself to grab an armful of wood from the newly restocked pile next to the door.

Just a little bit further, I told myself and opened the unlocked door.

*You're just inviting someone to be waiting in your home by leaving your door unlocked.* Artemis warned again, just as she had when I'd left the cabin earlier.

"I mean, it's not like people weren't already doing that when I locked it. So, what's the difference?" I leaned against the wall and toed off my boots, careful not to cut the shit out of myself with the knife in the one boot, while precariously still balancing the armful of wood.

The short walk to the living room felt like a slog through quicksand. I turned the corner to find Ramble sniffing at a pile of firewood that hadn't been in here earlier. It was a safe distance from the wood stove but not so far that it would be a pain to refill.

The wood stove itself was stoked up, which meant the room was nice and warm. Huh.

*Are you going to stand here all night, Vânători?* Artemis asked testily.

Was she mad that Louis had been right about the brownie just needing to have the door unlocked and something left out for it in trade for its services?

I finally set down my armload of firewood next to the neatly stacked pile. I wouldn't have to go outside to get wood anymore. That was pretty great. I looked around the room and only then noticed that the shower curtain was gone from where I'd left it tacked to the window.

Also, was the floor cleaner? The wood ash from the stove tended to leave a thin layer of dust on everything no matter how careful I was when cleaning it out. Now the dust was completely gone. The room was spotless.

Ramble looked at me and gave a shrug.

I could definitely spare some food or trinkets for the brownie if it earned me a clean house, a stoked fire, and an unlimited supply of firewood. I made a mental note that I needed to put out something else for the brownie before bed.

I finally peeled out of my bloody, burned jacket. There was no way I'd be able to wear it again without someone calling the cops. The sheriff might not have noticed all the blood on it, but he'd been a little busy processing the death of Deputy Englewood. Plus, it had been dark out.

I pulled everything out of the jacket pockets before wadding it up and making my way to the kitchen to throw it away. Ramble padded after me. When I flipped the kitchen light on, we both stopped to stare. The kitchen was spotless. And not only that, all the dishes in the sink had been done.

Ramble's head suddenly jerked up at something above the cupboards, but I couldn't see anything there.

I cleared my throat as I threw away my sad jacket. "Thank you for doing all this. I'm sorry I didn't realize what to do before." Rather than wait until later and possibly forget, I went to the fridge. I didn't have much in there, but Ramble pointedly looked at the hotdogs, so I pulled those out as well as some milk.

I wasn't hungry, but I washed my hands and threw a few raw hotdogs to Ramble and heated one up in the microwave. When it was done, I sliced it up and put those in a bowl. I poured milk into a second bowl and left both out on the counter.

"I'm not sure if you'll like hotdogs or not. Other than milk, I'm not really sure what else you like, so unless you're able to let me know, we'll just do some trial and error here." I tried not to look up at the cupboards as I spoke. I didn't want to spook it. "If you don't like something, just leave it in the bowl so I know."

I wasn't sure what else to do after that, so I put every-thing else away and turned the light off. "Good night."

Would the brownie sleep inside? Did I need to give it permission to do so? Maybe I'd ask Louis tomorrow. That was a problem for another day though, because I was out of gas and was about to fall down if I didn't go to bed.

I had planned to skip a shower because I didn't want to deal with getting water everywhere, but the brownie had apparently put the shower curtain back up. I decided I had just enough energy left to clean myself up so I wouldn't get my new bedding dirty. I got in the shower and stripped out of my blood-soaked clothes, leaving them in the bathtub. Might as well kill two birds with one stone.

I paused for a moment when my finger slid through one of the bullet holes in my shirt. It was a jarring reminder that I'd almost died. Again. I expected to feel some sort of emotion, but all I felt was numb. I got myself moving again until I finally stood under hot shower water.

It took forever to get all the blood out of my hair. I had a moment where I thought I might have to just cut it all out, but I forced myself to have patience and go through another round of rinse and repeat.

Ramble was waiting for me on one side of the bed by the time I finished. I crawled in beside him, thankful I'd been able to get new bedding before this. Honestly, I was so tired I would have just slept on the mattress. Or the floor.

I'd kept the necklace on the entire time and was thankful Artemis had stayed silent throughout my shower. I decided it would be best to keep it on while I slept, too. It was time I started leaning into this whole preparedness thing. Especially if Morvalden was going to send his lackeys to drag me back to him or if Jax was going to keep egging on other hunters to test themselves against the Vânători.

No more thinking about that, though. Or about my

throwing knife which was apparently magical enough to scare a Power. Or about the fact that I'd need to figure out how to pay rent soon—but only if I decided to stay here instead of running from the uber vampire trying to kill me.

Why couldn't killing the shifter-vampire just solve all my problems? Maybe I needed to get another four-leaf clover from Blush...

I made a mental note to backtrack along the shifter's trail of murder in the morning and close any tears left to Between. I'd have to get more blood from Louis in order to do that. I'd also promised the sheriff an "official" statement. I'd probably need to check in on Preston to make sure his bad luck problem was actually gone and that Blush had given up her clover-growing ways.

Well, hey, look at that. It looked like I'd already made the decision to stay in Ricketts instead of running away.

With that settled, I told my brain to shut up and snuggled into the sheets.

"Good night, Ramble."

He huffed in response, blowing hotdog-tainted breath in my direction. Lovely.

"Good night, Artemis."

*Good night, Vânători.* I felt her hesitate and just before I was about to drift off to sleep, heard her add, *You did well today. There is hope for you yet.*

Yippee for me.

# About the Author

J.J. Russell lives on a small farm in Downeast Maine with her husband and two adventurous dogs. When she's not writing, you can find her growing veggies or out on a trail running (very slowly).

Visit her author page at www.JJRussellWrites.com and sign up for the newsletter to hear when new books are released and get free short stories for characters in the Artemis Necklace Universe!

www.ingramcontent.com/pod-product-compliance
Lightning Source LLC
Chambersburg PA
CBHW071938210726
48293CB00001BA/230